# HOMEFRONT

*Also by Winston M. Estes*

WINSTON IN WONDERLAND
ANOTHER PART OF THE HOUSE
A STREETFUL OF PEOPLE
A SIMPLE ACT OF KINDNESS
ANDY JESSUP

# HOMEFRONT

by

## Winston M. Estes

*A NOVEL*

J. B. LIPPINCOTT COMPANY
Philadelphia and New York

105012

Printed in the United States of America

U.S. Library of Congress Cataloging in Publication Data

Estes, Winston M        birth date
    Homefront

    I. Title.
PZ4.E794Ho  [PS3555.S8]    813'.5'4    76-17579
    ISBN–0–397–01147–4

FOR RIZZIE

# HOMEFRONT

# 1

WHEN DR. JESSE RANDOLPH married Miss Mattie Cofield, he was seventy-six years old and she was sixty-nine. It was a first marriage for both, and the town turned out en masse for their wedding. That was understandable.

During the preceding fifty years Dr. Jesse Randolph had delivered at least three-fourths of the babies born in Bentley and had doctored most of them all their lives. It was said that he had been inside every house and knew every family in the southern part of Walton County, most of whom felt that they had a special claim on his affections. For the same fifty years Miss Mattie Cofield had taught every white child in town who had attended public school and many of the colored ones over on 'Struction Street and Tin Can Alley, where from time to time she assisted with county or state vocational education projects. When her pupils grew into adults, she taught their children and, at the time of her marriage to Dr. Jesse, a few of their grandchildren. It would have been difficult to find a family, white or colored, who did not regard Dr. Jesse and Miss Mattie with esteem and consider their relationship with them to be more personal than professional.

They were married after the regular Sunday morning service on a hot day in August at the First Baptist Church.

Every pew was filled and friends stood at the rear and around the walls. Outside, the churchyard swarmed with people milling about under the massive, wide-stretched arms of the oaks, seeking shelter from the heat and waiting for the wedding service to end so they could eat dinner, which had been brought by the ladies of the town and spread over a long table that was almost the length of the churchyard.

Mamie Holly could not remember a time when she had felt so sticky and steamy. She longed for a strong breeze to sweep past and dry the perspiration that tickled her upper lip and oozed down from her hairline across her forehead. If she could only mop her face as men did without regard to appearances and decorum, she would have liked nothing better than to take the dish towel from the table before her and do it. She cut a peach cobbler into rectangles with small movements, hoping that if she remained as still as possible, her dress might dry under the arms, where she knew without looking that the embarrassing circles were darker and more visible than she cared to confirm. She moved the cobbler aside, slid a molasses pie in front of her and cut into it.

Reeves Buckley, banker, sauntered up to the table, fanning himself with his hat.

"Mornin', Mamie," he said. "I'll bet those pies are still baking."

"I wouldn't be surprised," she replied. "I know I am. Isn't this heat just terrible? I declare, I don't know how those people inside the church can stand it!"

"How come you didn't go to the wedding?" he asked.

"There was too much to do out here. Just look at all this food!" She waved her knife toward the other end of the table. "Have you ever seen anything like it in your whole life?"

Reeves shook his head and smiled. "I'll bet you won't have any leftovers," he said, studying the molasses pie. "Save me a slice of that one, will you, Mamie?"

"Take it now if you want it," she said. "In fact, you can take the whole pie and nobody will miss it."

He looked at the pie wistfully, shook his head again and started to move on.

"Oh—Reeves? If you see Alex, send him over here, will you? I ran off this morning before he came back from the depot, and I need to talk to him."

"I saw him over— Hey! They're coming out of the church!"

Reeves Buckley disappeared into the crowd.

Alexander Holly stood on the sidewalk outside the stone wall, his coat over his arm and his necktie loosened, and watched the crowd close in. He let himself through the lace iron grilled gate. Something about the excitement and jubilance of the people was contagious, and he gave himself up to it. He made his way across the yard, dodging people, nodding to some and stopping to talk with others. As he walked past the long table, he surveyed the food, impressed by its variety and abundance. He did not look up until he heard Mamie call his name.

"Did you go to the wedding?" she asked.

"I just got here," he said. "Anyway, it was too hot. I wish I hadn't brought this coat. Nobody else is wearing them."

"I got a glimpse of Miss Mattie going into the church. She looked so sweet with that little blue hat perched on top of her head. Is Perry coming?"

"No. I left him on the back porch working a jigsaw puzzle. He didn't want to come."

"Bless his heart. If I fix him a plate, will you take it to him?"

A shadow crossed Alexander's face. "Why can't he come get it himself?"

"You know why he won't come, Alex." She glanced about her and lowered her voice. "Please be nice about it."

"I'm being nice," he said. "Perry's not going to starve. He can fix something to eat at home, or he can come over here like everybody else."

She bent her head and pretended to be occupied with one of the cakes. "Alex, please," she said, without looking up. "It would be a shame for him not to have some of this food. Look at that mountain of fried chicken down there!"

"But Mamie, it's not right to wait on a full-grown twenty-one-year-old boy like that. He's not exactly an invalid, you know. Just because he's—"

"It'll only take a minute for you to run home," she broke in hurriedly. "You can cut through back of Mollie Satterfield's and across the school yard."

He took his watch from his pocket and studied it. "Well—but you spoil him, Mamie," he said with a sigh. "You don't think you do, but you do." He returned his watch to his pocket. "You'll have to step on it, though. Number 12 just might surprise us and get in on time today."

"That would be a surprise, wouldn't it? I wish you would let just one train go through Bentley without your being at the depot to cheer it on."

"I did," he said pleasantly. "An eastbound freight with a shipment of Army trucks and jeeps went through at three fifty-six this morning while I was in bed sound asleep."

"It's a wonder it got through," she said. "Now stand right here, and I won't be a minute. You're going to have to hurry back and eat, because everybody's hungry and they'll eat up everything."

"Well, fix me a plate while you're at it," he called after her.

Later, he walked uptown on Chiles Street. Chiles Street was Bentley's main street, and uptown was its business district. It was one block long from Madison Road to Depot Street. A few random businesses that changed from time to time spilled over on each end and around the corners. He turned the corner onto Depot Street by Holder's Five and Ten Cent Store. The ground fell off sharply to the east. The concrete pavement gave way to asphalt with ragged edges and no curbs. It narrowed and curved between the tiny doll-like frame house that was the telephone office on the right and the messy, cluttered, ramshackle tin building that was Cy Darby's garage on the left. The ground leveled off under a deep, dark and cool overhang of hickory, sycamore and elm. The Georgia Railroad lay beyond. Alex cut across the open graveled expanse past Selman's old red brick cotton warehouse to the depot.

The hearse from Williams's, the colored undertaker in Monroe, was backed up to the station platform with its rear doors open. He stopped and tried to remember a colored death in the area. Then he crossed the platform and let himself into the depot through a side door.

Emory Haynes, telegraph operator, was receiving a message and transcribing it on his L. C. Smith typewriter. Suddenly he exploded into a boisterous laugh and turned off the key. He looked around at Alex.

"Hey, Alex! I got a good one this time!" he shouted. He tore a scrap of paper from the carriage of his typewriter and held it out to him. "Take a look. It's *good!*"

Alex ignored the paper. "Now look here, Emory, I keep telling you that if you and that operator in Union Point don't stop sending dirty jokes over the wires—"

"This one's not dirty! You can tell it in Sunday school."

"Well, any kind of joke. You're going to get all of us in trouble. The company monitors that traffic, and they don't like all that horseplay. Those wires are for business."

"Aw, whatta you talking about? I used to know an operator over in Decatur that got recipes for his wife over the keys."

"I don't care what somebody did in Decatur—just stop doing it here in Bentley."

13

"How can I help it if that guy in Union Point keeps sending me jokes?"

"You can turn off the key," Alex snapped. "Anything going on?"

"Not much," Emory replied absently, his mind apparently still on the funny story from Union Point. "Number 12 is on time out of Buckhead, but that doesn't mean anything on our board. You know, I think Goochie McDaniel stops that engine just around the bend and takes a nap just so he won't be on time. It must be some kind of religion with him."

"I noticed Williams's hearse outside. Have we got a shipment going out?"

"One's coming in from Augusta," Emory said. "It's a colored family up on the Jersey Road across the river. They're all down on the freight end of the platform. One of their sons, I think. The bill of lading is on the file there with the other stuff."

The telegraph key began to click, and he turned back to it.

Alex took a sheaf of papers from the stick file on the dispatcher's desk and hurried through them without much curiosity, then went outside. He stood on the platform and looked to the east, listening for the hum on the rails that few people but experienced trainmen could hear until the train was almost in sight. He heard nothing. Emory Haynes claimed that on a still day he could hear that hum when the train cleared the last switch coming out of Madison, and if he put his mind to it he could tell how far out of Bentley it was as it approached. He had never been proved wrong, primarily because no one had ever called his hand.

Bentley was situated on the highest point along the Georgia Railroad and in times past had boasted of an unusually healthful climate—so healthful, in fact, that enterprising citizens turned the boast into a business. One such citizen established the Bentley Dinner House on the

14

site where Selman's Cotton Warehouse now stood. It was a hotel that served dinner at noon to passengers and crews when the train stopped for water from a tank that was spring fed through hollow poplar poles. Within a few years its reputation had become so widespread that many travelers built their schedules around a noon stop at the Bentley Dinner House.

Inspired, no doubt, by the hotel's success, another forward-looking citizen began to pity the evening travelers on the same railroad who had nowhere to eat supper, for the Dinner House served meals only at noon. Whereupon he erected a hotel of his own on the opposite side of the tracks and served supper to passengers when the train stopped for water in the evenings. He named it the Bentley Supper House.

The two hotel owners thrived happily across the railroad tracks from one another. A comradeship, rather than a rivalry, grew up between them. The Dinner House sent its overnight guests across the tracks to eat supper, and the Supper House sent its overnight guests across the same tracks to eat dinner. So friendly and profitable was their association that they advertised on the same handbills, one of which, yellowed by the years, still hung in its original frame in the white waiting room of the depot:

> Bentley is noted for pure air and water, good health and refined society, and as a resort for invalids or seekers of pleasure equal to any place in the Southern Country. In connection with our hotels are Livery Stables with fine stock and careful drivers always on hand, and the roads to any point in the interior are among the best in Georgia, board as good as can be had anywhere for $20 per month.

Strangers in Bentley were usually surprised to find mementos of that era in greater abundance than reminders of the Civil War, which were there for the asking, listening and looking. The left flank of General Sherman's army camped on the west bank of the Alcovy River three miles from town, burned its bridges, destroyed the Georgia Railroad all the way to Madison and cut off supplies from the Confederates in Atlanta while plundering and burning at least one-third of Bentley itself. The town and the gentle rolling land for miles around bore the scars for years. A few of the old plantation houses escaped damage and still remained, gracious and lovely, not far from town. Most of the big plantations, however, had been broken up by the Civil War and the Reconstruction that followed.

Around town the storerooms and garages in several back yards were former slave quarters or detached kitchens that had outlasted the big houses they had been built to serve. A number of surprisingly modest homes were genuine antebellum, their original structure unchanged from the days when cotton wagons creaked along the dirt roads to the markets. Others retained fragments of themselves: a brick chimney and fireplace, a room with exposed ceiling beams and wood wainscot, a suggestion of a formal garden with a few rectangles of boxwood hedge and patches of a walk.

Bentley, like its giant neighbor, Atlanta, refused to be tied down by nostalgic memories of an old romantic way of life which had vanished, if it ever existed so romantically in the first place. It bounced back to become an active farming, commercial and railroad center where sawmills, banks, retail stores, doctors, dentists, lawyers, produce markets, grain mills and cotton exchanges thrived; where colorful drummers got off the train with their trunks overflowing with glorious samples of wondrous merchandise; where comfortably fixed families came out from the city to take the air and shop in the stores.

It was the post-Civil War era that clung to Bentley like a fog. It was evident in the folklore and visible in the architecture of some of the proudest homes and the original parts of some of the buildings uptown. Newcomers and tourists looked at the ornate cornices over Pet Wilkerson's windows on Calhoun Street, or the elaborately carved balustrades around Reeves Buckley's front porch on North Chiles Street, or the fluted columns that supported the deep veranda of the old Lassiter house on West Madison Road and thought they were looking at fine examples of antebellum architecture. They were often disillusioned to learn that the houses were built in the seventies and the eighties.

All of that was before Alex Holly's day. He had come to Bentley as a young brakeman on the Gainesville Railroad that connected the Georgia Railroad with the Southern Railroad in the northeast part of the state. He had started as a flagman on the Southern Railroad, but when he saw an opening for a brakeman on the north-south connecting line, he asked for, and got, the job. It was during a layover in Bentley that he met the lovely Margaret Meade Harrison from Madison, who was visiting a distant cousin. She returned later for a second visit and a third, then still another, each visit coinciding with Alex's layover. When he told her good-bye at the end of her fifth visit, he asked her to marry him.

"You *know* I will," she said without hesitation. "But you've got to come home to Madison with me and meet Mama and Daddy and my whole family first."

He agreed, and several weeks later he went. Then for the three months following, he dropped out of sight. She wrote to him regularly, but he did not answer her letters. During his layovers in Bentley he kept to himself, sleeping in the caboose, fearing to venture away from the tracks and the depot lest he run into her or someone they both knew.

Then one night while the town was asleep, he swung down from the caboose and walked across the tracks and onto the station platform to stretch his legs and get a breath of air. A single light was burning inside the waiting room of the depot. Through the window he saw her sitting alone in the dimness. He hurried past, then turned

17

back and went inside. He stopped with his back to the door and stared at her unbelievingly.

"Can't you at least tell me why?" she asked simply.

He continued to stare at her. In the dimness and shadows and separated from her by the width of the cheerless waiting room, he could see in sharp detail every feature that made her beautiful. Her wide brown eyes were questioning, but they glowed with warmth and a yearning to understand. Her face was round and full, and its silky white skin formed a startling contrast with the gloomy grayness of the plastered wall behind her. A few vagrant strands of her soft brown hair had escaped the puff and ribbon atop her head. She sat straight. Her white hands, almost plump, lay in her lap, one on top of the other.

"It's right, Mamie, but it's not right," he said from across the room. "When the hack stopped in front of your house in Madison, I was afraid to get out. I never had been in a house like that in all my life. I've seen pictures of them in magazines and on postcards, and I've passed by them on the streets, but I never thought about you living in one of them. You should have told me."

"We never talked about what kind of house I live in," she said. She tried to smile.

"I'm not blaming you, and I don't have any hard feelings toward you, but I just didn't know what to do or how to act," he went on. "And to make it worse, your brothers and all the Harrison kinfolks were so good to me about it. Your daddy showed me all that farmland that's been in the Harrison and Meade families for generations, and I couldn't even think of a decent question to ask. When your mama was telling me about your ancestors in all those paintings in the hall and up and down the stairs, and when she was showing me that silver and those dishes that came from back before the Civil War, I was tongue-tied. I couldn't talk about the same things your brothers talked about. All I can talk about is the railroad, and I don't really know a lot about that—not yet."

"They liked you, Alex," she said.

"But they haven't seen me like this," he said, looking down at his clothes. "You haven't either until now. You've never seen me in overalls and a gray work shirt and thick-soled work shoes and leather gloves hanging out my hip pocket and a striped trainman's cap like I've got on now. I dressed up for them, just like I dressed up for you every time I thought I would see you. This is how I look most of the time. It's how I look every morning when I go to work and when I come home at night. I'd be an embarrassment to you, Mamie, and I wouldn't want to embarrass you for anything in the world."

"They gave their permission for me to marry you," she said.

"They did?" he asked blankly.

"They were upset, though, because you didn't ask them yourself."

"I was afraid to."

"They kept waiting for you to ask. I had already told them it was the reason you were coming."

After Margaret Meade Harrison became Mrs. Alexander James Holly in the largest and most lavish wedding within Madison's memory, they went to live in Gainesville, and Alex continued to work on the Gainesville-Midland line, sometimes taking the passenger run to Bentley, but more often the freight, which he liked better. Most of all, however, he liked to work in the yards with the switch engine, shunting cars onto and off sidings to make up a train or to take one apart. He observed and he learned about the work of other men who helped keep the trains on their tracks: the conductor, engineer, fireman, dispatcher, freight agent, telegraph operator, yard superintendent, station-master and even the maintenance gangs out on the tracks and the mechanics who worked in the roundhouse.

As he gained experience, knowledge and seniority, he advanced in position. Before their first child was a year old, Alex was offered the dispatcher's job in Bentley and took it.

They named her after his grandmother Ferraby Holly. Mamie loved the sound but not the appearance of the name, so they modified its spelling to Ferebe. When Susie was two years old and the twins were still in their cradles, he became the Georgia Railroad's Stationmaster in Bentley.

He was a proud and happy man. Sometimes, however, he wondered how he was regarded by Mamie's brothers, all of whom had married within their own circles and kept to their own world of wealth, position, background, education and graciousness. The boll weevil of the twenties had wiped out their wealth, but they retained the rest. He grew to be fond of them personally, and their regard for him was genuine, but he was an outsider among them. Mamie told him repeatedly that it was his own assessment, not theirs. She felt that he was unfair to them. But as the years went by, they moved from Madison, got caught up in new businesses and raising families, and Alex lost his self-consciousness when around them. By then, however, they saw one another only occasionally.

After the elder Harrisons died, the children did not realize much from the sale of the family mansion, especially after taxes and when divided four ways. Mamie's share was enough to buy their house in Bentley. She also inherited some lovely old pieces of furniture, her Grandmother Meade's wedding china, silver and crystal, and some ancestral portraits that had been stored in the attic since the day they were delivered to the house. They were far too large and on too grand a scale for the Hollys' small living room or hall. Several of Georgia's historical associations and fine arts societies had approached her about the possibility of making them parts of public collections, but she had never found the right time to invite their representatives to come and talk seriously about it.

Alex stood on the station platform and looked down the double tracks. They lay at the foot of a curved embankment that rose steeply on the opposite side and was blanketed with kudzu vine. Across the top he could see a clump of tall, feathery cedars that partially hid one corner of the cotton mill. He turned and studied the little knot of colored people huddled together saying nothing at the far end of the platform. He approached them.

"The baggage car will stop along about there," he said, pointing down the platform. "You can wait in the shade there or, if you'd like to go inside, someone will notify you when the train is coming. It's not any cooler inside, but you can sit down. And there's a water fountain."

They wore their Sunday best, dark and serious, but touched with enough color to make them suitable either for a wedding or a funeral. The man touched the brim of his hat and nodded gratefully. His black face was without wrinkles, but his eyes were old, his brows were white, and the posture of his body testified beyond question that the years had worn him down and had tired him beyond the reaches of rest. The lean old woman standing beside him was tall and straight with a pink flowered hat crowning her gray hair. She fingered a white handkerchief nervously and watched Alex with anxiety. She spread a corner of the handkerchief tightly across her fingertips and dabbed at her mouth. Suddenly she began to sob. The four or five young men and women clustering around her made no move; they only stared at her, wide-eyed and frightened.

"If I can do anything for you—" Alex went on.

"I guess they ain't nothin'," said the old man. His voice was soft and it cracked. "We jes' haf' to wait, I reckon. He's our oldest son. Died of TB in the hospital down in Savannah. We jes' waitin' for him to come back home."

"I'm awfully sorry to hear about that," Alex said. He waited for a moment. "Well—let me know if you need anything. My name's Holly, and I'm the Stationmaster. I've got to get back."

21

He tipped his hat to the old lady, nodded to the others and walked away.

While the train waited and hissed in the station, he stood and watched as the long wooden box was off-loaded onto a baggage wagon and transferred into the hearse. The young colored man from Williams's spoke to the old man, who pointed to a dilapidated Ford parked in the shade behind the depot. With the young people following, they made their way to it, looking back at the hearse with anxiety and uncertainty.

Two bedraggled soldiers were coming alongside the train toward Alex. Their khaki uniforms, wrinkled and splotched with sweat, hung on them in disarray. They swung their tightly filled barracks bags off their shoulders onto the brick platform and looked about at their surroundings.

"This doesn't strike me as a very racy place to spend two hours of my hard-earned furlough," said one.

"It's not," said the other. "I used to change trains here when I was a little kid and went to Lamkin to see my grandma and grandpa."

"Maybe they've at least got a juke joint where we can get a bottle of beer."

"You kidding? Beer on Sunday? In Georgia? How long have you been away from that little town where you're going?"

"Seven months, two weeks and three days. My daddy says I'll be back home to stay in a year from the day I was drafted. He still believes that song everybody used to sing —'I'll Be Back in a Year, Little Darling.' "

"Didn't he hear about the Emergency Plus Six Months?"

"Yeah, but he says it's illegal for President Roosevelt to go back on his word and extend the draft like he did. I'm on his side, but I told him he ought to tell that to Roosevelt. He might not know he's breaking the law."

22

He picked up his barracks bag and heaved it onto his shoulder again. "Well, I'd better go find the bus station," he said. "There ought to be a bus heading south before this time next week. Don't forget to send your first sergeant a postcard saying 'Wish you were here.'"

"Wheeee! You don't know my first sergeant. He'd give me two weeks KP for taking up his time. Besides, I don't think he's learned to read yet."

Alex looked on with amusement as the two soldiers parted. He went back inside the depot. With no difficulty he could see his own son, Paul, in uniform, and he could hear him trading wisecracks with a fellow soldier under similar conditions. With a kind of projected pride, he decided Paul would make a good soldier. He had a wild streak in him just wide enough to lead him into the risks good soldiers must be prepared to take. He was brash and swaggering enough to have total confidence in his own abilities. Alex smiled at the prospects. Paul's draft number would be coming up soon. Then he could find out for himself.

# 2

THE HOLLYS' HOUSE was on West Madison Road. It was a friendly street lined with walnut trees, broad oak and elm that reached out over the sidewalks and past the curbs. The west end of it was only three blocks long before it gave way to a hard-topped farm road that curved around the Macedonia Baptist Church and out of sight beyond the Clegg Line of four old slave quarters that had been defying time for more than a hundred years. On a clear day Stone Mountain was visible from there. The Alcovy River was at the other end of the road three miles from town.

The Hollys' was the last house on the street. It was small and ordinary, the kind that had been popular with moderate- and low-income Georgia farmers and planters before the Civil War—plantation style with an upstairs one room deep, a one-story shed porch across the front and brick chimneys on both ends. They had been copied and adapted throughout middle Georgia in the years since. Mamie knew of several in Walton County that were identical, but she suspected their own was genuine antebellum.

The lacy, exquisite scrolls of the rose fanlight over the front door were a clue. She knew similar and larger ones in the great houses of Madison whose antebellum origins could be fixed to the exact year they had been built. The sturdy old pine flooring was another, for it was fully an

24

inch thick in places and worn down to a bare quarter inch in others. Two outside doors, also of pine, looked as though they had been weathered by at least a hundred years of sun and rain. Long ago when she and Alex had been repainting the living room, they scraped the paper and plaster from a difficult patch on the walls. The boards were hand planed. She wanted to strip the entire wall, but Alex did not have the time to spare. Besides, Ferebe came down with the measles before they had finished their job, so they repaired the patch and repainted it. Two layers of wallpaper had been pasted on top of it since then.

Mamie paused for a moment on the front porch to catch her breath. She shifted her load of sticky pans and plates from one arm to the other, inhaled deeply and pushed her damp hair back from her forehead. The Macedonia Baptist Church had let out. Only two cars remained out front, and the few people at the entrance were scattering.

She opened the screen door, stepped inside and stood in the doorway in the cool darkness of the hall, imagining that the faint breeze sweeping across the screened porch at the rear and through the door to the front was cooler than it actually was.

"Whew!" she breathed. "I'm not going to set foot outside this house again until I see Pet Wilkerson go by next winter in her old Army overcoat and that lavender shawl tied over her head."

Perry came in from the back porch, a big, well-formed silhouette against the light. He raised a hand in greeting and came to meet her, smiling. She pinched his cheek.

He followed her into the kitchen, where she deposited the pans and dishes in the sink. With her hands empty she turned about and faced him.

"You should have come to the church for dinner," she said. "Even poor old Smiley Finch was there, giggling and winking at everybody and pushing that old wheelbarrow in and out all that mob. I don't know what kept him from running over somebody. This time he had it loaded with old inner tubes and empty fruit jars! Where do you suppose he gets all those things? And what on earth does he do with them?"

She made the signs with her hands while she spoke the words with her mouth. She faltered more often than she liked, but she did well, although she was never certain exactly how much Perry understood. "Somebody found Josh Bullock stretched out on the ground, and people thought he had a heat stroke, but it turned out that he had simply crawled under a bush to sleep off a full stomach." She stopped and smiled fondly. "You would have enjoyed seeing everybody," she added.

He shrugged. "But they wouldn't enjoy seeing me," he replied. "They work too hard trying to talk to me—or not hard enough." His signs were more fluid and more natural than hers, made without self-consciousness and with the grace and eloquence of a ballet dancer. "I can't understand what they're saying most of the time. And the only thing they can think of is to ask me how I like my job at the cotton mill."

Studiously she watched his hands and the expression in his eyes, trying to connect the two of them into one meaning. He was going too fast. She motioned for him to slow down.

He laughed. "I'm paying you back for all the times you talk to me without signing."

She laughed, too. "I get carried away," she said. "They ask about you because they're interested in you. They do the best they can, but you don't give them a chance. You even disappear when Flora Etheridge runs in and out of the house, and you've been living next door to the Etheridges all your life! It's the same way with the Robinsons. Vernon Robinson told your daddy it doesn't seem like you live across the street at all, because they never see you. They're bound to think it's strange, don't you think?"

Perry waved a finger at her playfully. "You're nagging at me again. I told you I'd make you stand in the corner if you didn't stop it."

"I know, darling, but I can't help but be concerned over the way you stay cooped up here by yourself. You could have gone to Atlanta with Paul this weekend and had a marvelous time."

"He didn't invite me."

"Didn't invite you? My goodness! When did that ever stop either one of you from doing what the other did? Maybe you can go down to the train and meet him tonight. He's coming back on the seven twenty."

"That's what he said last time, and he didn't come home until the next morning."

"He missed the train."

"That was because he didn't go down to Union Station to get on it until Monday morning." He made a face at her. "I'm going to order me a new mother from Sears Roebuck's. One that won't fuss at me."

She started for the door. "When you do, be sure and order one who's not as hot as I am. Every garment I've got on is stuck to my skin."

He wandered out onto the back porch and stared for a moment at the jigsaw puzzle scattered in tiny look-alike fragments across the card table. He picked up a piece at random and made a halfhearted attempt to fit it; then he went out into the yard.

The leaves of the old walnut tree by the garage were stirring. An occasional leaf shook itself loose and drifted down onto the roof. A blue jay swept out of a branch and across the rear fence into Mr. Spencer's garden. As he watched it disappear from sight, he wondered if it made a greater sound than the leaves of a tree. The bird moved more swiftly and traveled greater distances, but he could not be certain that the sound it made in flight could equal that of

27

hundreds and thousands of leaves in motion at the same time. Paul told him that airplanes made more noise than any other moving thing, but that hardly seemed reasonable. The big passenger planes from Atlanta scarcely seemed to be moving when they plodded across the sky; and on the ground at the Atlanta airport they could not possibly make a great noise as they lumbered across the concrete strips, trembling and unsteady like feeble, tottering old giants. It was strange that such slow-moving objects could create more noise than a swift-flying bird. But then he was by no means certain that his own concept of sound was the concept he had been taught.

To him, motion was sound. Stillness was silence. While his mother and father were at the church and he was in the house alone, the stillness had begun to weigh down upon him. Nothing moved but his own body. Even the white curtains sagged without life at the open windows. The heat was oppressive, but the stillness was worse. To escape it, he had moved his jigsaw puzzle out onto the back porch, where he could watch the graceful sounds of clouds moving across the sky and the gentle, whispering noise of smoke spiraling in the distance.

He walked to the rear of the yard and leaned on the fence, waiting for Mr. Spencer to see him. So familiar was the rear view of Mr. Spencer's house and garage that when he saw them from the front he scarcely associated them with the customary sight from his own back porch. He noticed he was standing too close to the beehives and moved to the other end. It was a reflex. Mr. Spencer's bees had been his enemy ever since he could remember. The three hives were backed up to the fence near the Hollys' garage. When he was little and played in the yard by the garage, they buzzed across the fence and stung him with no warning of their approach. If Paul was nearby, he could hear their buzz and fight them away. He was almost old enough to go off to school at Cave Springs before he learned not to play alone in that corner of the yard.

Mr. Spencer was a middle-aged widower who lived alone and operated a feed store down back of Chiles Street on Design Street when he was not at home working in his garden, tending his bees, tinkering with an old automobile kept in his garage for that specific purpose or pursuing whatever hobby might be absorbing him at the moment. His regular customers had long considered it routine to stop by his house for the key to his store and serve themselves rather than stand around hoping he might interrupt himself long enough to go down to the store and make the sale in person.

Perry watched Mr. Spencer moving in and out of his crop of vegetables, inspecting and studying. He bent over to steady a wood frame that was leaning under the weight of a tomato plant heavy with fruit, then moved on to uproot a handful of weeds. He reached the end of a row no farther than three feet from the fence and looked up to find Perry staring at him.

He waved a forefinger in greeting, smiled broadly and began to move his lips. He looked at the ground, pointed to a tangle of vines at his feet, then stooped over. He came up with a cucumber in his hand, still talking, and came toward Perry. Holding up the cucumber, he traced its spiny ridges, explaining as he demonstrated. Perry looked on in bewilderment. Apparently something was unusual about that cucumber, although it seemed to be identical with the dozens of others still on their vines. Mr. Spencer's enthusiasm mounted as he talked. He waved the cucumber through the air, pointing it first toward the Hollys' back yard, then to his own house behind him. He turned his back and continued to point the cucumber to the right, then to the left. Perry waited for him to turn around again and face him. When he did, his lips were still moving busily. He stopped and broke into laughter with his mouth open wide. Perry did not have the faintest inkling of what he had been saying.

He liked Mr. Spencer. He seldom knew what he

was talking about, and Mr. Spencer seldom bothered to tell him. He made no concessions whatsoever to his young neighbor's deafness. He talked in his normal manner and, unlike most people, did not contort himself with wild gestures and silly lip shaping. Still, an understanding that neither of them could explain had always flowed between them. Perry had been watching him talk ever since he and Paul began toddling around their back yard and running to the fence when he leaned over to toss them a shiny hubcap or a length of rubber hose to play with. He had learned early not to concern himself with what Mr. Spencer was saying. He had a wart on his cheek that moved up and down when he talked, and watching that was entertaining enough, no matter what he was saying. Now, somewhere amid all that explaining and laughing—he did not know exactly where—he received an invitation to bring a basket and fill it with whatever was ripe and ready to pick. Perry went into the garage, found a basket and climbed the fence. Within a few minutes he was occupied with the red tomatoes, radishes, field peas and green peppers and did not wonder what had happened to Mr. Spencer. He had disappeared from sight.

Perry selected a final, perfectly shaped tomato and decided he had picked enough. He started for home. Mr. Spencer jumped out from behind a row of sweet corn. From the lift of his brows and the widening of his eyes Perry assumed he was asking a question. Making a quick guess, he nodded agreement. He had miscalculated. Mr. Spencer's face darkened with displeasure and apparently his mouth was expressing it. Quickly, Perry waved away his nod and substituted a frown and a violent shake of his head. Mr. Spencer regarded him dubiously for a moment, then turned and walked away. He was pointing toward the Etheridges' house as he walked. Presumably he was talking. His back was turned, however, and Perry could not be certain.

# 3

ALEXANDER MEANDERED along the hall, his head bent and his eyes scanning the front page of *The Atlanta Constitution*. He stopped in the kitchen doorway. Except for the sizzle of the bacon frying and coffee percolating, the room was silent.

Mamie was busy at the stove. The twins were talking with animation at the breakfast table. When he came upon them together as they were now, absorbed in what they were saying and oblivious to anyone else, he always had the sensation of watching one person making signs to his reflection in a mirror. This morning even the slouch of one of them, the foot hooked in the rung of his chair, the elbow propped on the table, the signing with both hands were duplicated by the other. Their brown eyes were bright. They could have swapped the wide grins that stretched their mouths, and he would never have known it. Their dark, wavy hair, like their tall, slender, straight bodies, had always grown uniformly and now looked as though they had walked out of Miller Goolsby's Barber Shop on the same day at the same minute.

They were not dressed alike, but that was no help in separating them unless he first knew who wore one thing and who wore the other. Even their signs appeared to be identical, which was unlikely unless they were merely echoing one another. He would never confess that at times he could not tell them apart. It was seldom necessary, for it was much simpler to wait for Paul to speak, then pretend he had known all along.

Mamie looked around from the stove and saw her husband in the doorway.

"Mornin', darling," she said. "I was about to send one of the boys up to see if you were still asleep."

He walked on into the room and peered into the skillet on the stove. "When are we going to have pancakes again?" he asked.

"When I lose about fifteen pounds and can wear every dress I own without holding my breath," she said, concentrating again on the bacon.

Alex turned to the twins. They were watching him, awaiting his attention. With the rehearsed precision of college cheerleaders, they greeted him with elaborate movements of their hands.

"Now don't pull that one on me again!" he said, dropping into a chair on the opposite side of the table. He unfolded the newspaper. "You left the hall light burning when you came in from Atlanta last night." Purposefully he avoided looking at them lest he single out the wrong one. "Looks like you'd notice if a light is on or off. Anyway, how did you get home? You didn't come in on Number 9."

They looked at one another and shrugged helplessly.

"And you didn't latch the back screen. It blew open and probably let in a houseful of crickets and mosquitoes."

They stared at him with blank expressions.

"Did you see Susie while you were in Atlanta?"

He received no answer.

"Well—did you?"

"Don't pay any attention to them," Mamie said over their shoulders. "They've been doing that to me ever since they came into the kitchen."

Alex spread the newspaper open again. He read in silence while the boys went back to their conversation. After a time he said, "I see the Russians say they're stopping the Nazis around S-M-O-L-E-N-S-K. But it depends on who you want to believe. Both sides claim they're winning."

Mamie turned from the stove. "I declare, Alex! It looks like out of that whole newspaper you could find something besides that awful war to tell us about every morning."

"It's the headlines," he said. "Look." He turned the paper around and held it up for her to see.

"I see, but that doesn't mean you have to talk about it all the time."

"Somebody better talk about it," he said, resuming his reading. "We're going to get in it."

"Stop saying that!" she exclaimed. "That war is none of our business."

"Then why do you think this country's turning out guns, tanks, airplanes and ships by the thousands?"

"For defense and for Lend-Lease to England and the Allies so they can get rid of Adolf Hitler for us."

"In the meantime, what are we going to do with all these new air bases and Army posts we're building and all these boys we're drafting and pilots we're training?"

"To defend the United States in case of attack," she said stubbornly. "Anyway, FDR won't let us get in the war. That's why I voted for him three times."

"He won't have any choice," Alex said with confidence. "This country's on a war economy, and if we don't get into the war, the economy will eventually collapse."

The twins had ceased their signing and were watching their parents.

"Mother thinks if she'll ignore the war, it'll go away," Paul spoke up. "But it won't. Dad's right. We're producing more war material than we can ship to England, and it's piling up. We've got to use it so we can replace it. Replacement is the key to a production economy. That's why Goodrich and Goodyear don't make permanent tires. They'd go out of business if nobody ever needed new tires. The only way you can use up a bullet is to fire it. The only way you can use up a bomb is to drop it."

Alex looked at his son with admiration and surprise. "Welcome!" he said. "I knew *something* would make you speak up. What brought on all this wisdom?"

"University of Georgia, Economics III, Dr. Edwin Elbert, professor. He says this country would still be back with the WPA, relief and the CCC if Adolf Hitler hadn't shown up on the scene."

"That's the worst thing I ever heard of!" Mamie said in horror. "The *idea* of giving Hitler credit for—"

"Hold it, Mother," Paul broke in. "Perry doesn't know what we're talking about."

Alex watched him turn to his brother, fascinated all over again by the change in his manner. He had been watching this same transformation take place for years and had never ceased to marvel at how the two of them seemed to blend into one person when they talked to each other. He studied their signs and shook his head in bewilderment.

"I've been watching them sign to each other all their lives, and I can't make heads or tails out of half what they say," he said to Mamie. "I wish I knew how they do it—or *what* they do."

Paul made a few more signs to Perry, then turned back to his father. "If I knew, I'd tell you," he said. He nodded toward his brother. "He would, too."

"I gave up years ago," Mamie said. She reached into the cabinet for a platter and returned to the stove. "I remember when they were little and I'd send Paul out in the yard to tell Perry something. Then I'd look out the window and it was as if he was telling him something else."

She came to the table with the platter. She wrinkled her nose at Paul. "And sometimes that is exactly what he *was* doing. Move the paper so I can set this down."

During breakfast Paul kept up a running account of his weekend in Atlanta while Perry glanced nervously at his watch from time to time and Alex wistfully eyed the folded newspaper which Mamie would never allow him to read at the table when they were eating.

"Unpack your suitcase before you go to work, Paul," Mamie said. "I've got to check through some of your clothes. Surely some of your underwear and socks have holes in them by now. I don't want you running around the University of Georgia looking like a sharecropper."

"What would you say if I didn't go back to school?"

"And why not, pray tell?" Mamie asked quickly.

Alex looked at him sharply.

"Because there's lots of high-paying jobs in Atlanta sitting there waiting for me to come get them. Boy! You can take your pick. Everybody's going into defense work now, and they can't fill all the jobs they leave vacant. Or I can go into defense work myself. You can't miss. Why, Smiley Finch could make thirty or forty dollars a week in Atlanta or Mobile right now, wheelbarrow and all, if he had enough sense to get off the train when it got there."

"You're not Smiley Finch," said his father. "Besides, you're on a student deferment that gets canceled automatically if you don't go back to school. Then you won't get a job anywhere except in the United States Army."

"Not if the draft board doesn't know I'm not in school."

Alex put down his fork. "Well, you just try not telling them and see where you end up," he said. "Behind bars, that's where. In case you haven't heard, the Selective Training and Service Act is the law of the land, and violators get prosecuted."

"Look, Dad, the Selective Service can't keep up with

everybody in the country. They don't know where you are if you don't tell them. I heard about a guy this weekend in Atlanta who registered for college this summer, then didn't go. He got a job instead and kept his student status, and nobody's any the wiser. It happens all the time!"

Alex exploded. "What kind of talk is this—you coming in here and telling me and your mother and brother you're thinking about beating the draft?" he exclaimed. "Now you try such a thing, and I'll notify the draft board myself. You ought to be ashamed of yourself to even let that kind of idea get in your head!"

"Don't get so excited, Dad," Paul said. "I didn't say I was *going* to do it, did I? Anyway, it's only from September to January. It's not the same as getting out of it permanently. Just long enough to make a little money and have a good time and—"

"That'll do, Paul," Alex said firmly. "I don't want to hear another word of that kind of talk in this house. Do you understand that?"

Mamie looked at Paul anxiously while he nodded at his father.

"All right, then," Alex said. "If you've been telling that to Perry, you turn around and tell him what I think of the idea in whatever language you use with him."

He got up and left the room.

"You haven't finished your breakfast, darling!" Mamie called after him.

"I've had enough!" he mumbled.

They listened to his footsteps going up the stairs. They remained silent until they heard him come down and the screen door close behind him as he left the house.

"Paul, I don't know what comes over you," she said, frowning at him. "You couldn't *possibly* have expected your own father to approve of such wild and ugly schemes as you dream up! And neither do I. Why do you keep doing these things? It's not as if you don't know better."

"Mother, just relax a minute," he said. "Everybody manipulates that draft board around to—"

"You're not everybody. You're Paul Harrison Holly from Bentley, Georgia, and whether you appreciate it or not, that's a lot to be proud of and a background to respect. You've been raised to know the difference between right and wrong, and if you make ten million dollars before January, it wouldn't mean a thing to me and your daddy or Susie and Perry and Ferebe if you didn't make it honorably."

She looked down at her plate, then pushed back her chair. "I think I've had enough, too."

She disappeared into the hall.

Paul turned to Perry and raised his eyebrows. "There goes another beautiful idea up in smoke," he said.

They left the house together and walked uptown.

"They think I mind getting in the Army," Paul said, "but I don't. As a matter of fact, I'm looking forward to it. The Army moves around and does things. It's exciting. It can't be boring in any way I can see. The only thing I don't like is that you can't go with me."

"I never did get to go to school with you, either," Perry replied. "This is another one of those things."

"No, this is different. In the Army you don't get to come back home for Thanksgiving, Christmas, spring holidays and summer vacations. We won't see each other regularly any more. I don't like that part of it."

They stepped off the curb uptown and walked out to The Well in the center of Chiles Street. They stopped.

"Look, Perry. How about letting me have five dollars until Saturday?"

"You haven't paid me back that last five yet."

"I know. I'm trying to save enough to register and pay my fees at school."

"That's not the real reason, is it?"

"No—and you know it," Paul said good-naturedly. "I spent more money in Atlanta than I intended to. See, I met this girl that was really something. She had an apartment and her roommate was out of town. So—well, it just took a lot of money, that's all."

"What do you need five dollars for?"

"To live on—what else? I'll pay you the whole ten dollars Saturday."

"You can't. You won't get but twelve."

"I'll stay home all next week. Then I won't need any money."

"Why don't you stay home this week instead?"

"I can't. I've got a date with Dicey Ann Darby tomorrow night, and I can't get out of it."

Perry considered that for a moment, then weakened. "I'll let you have two dollars, but that's all," he said reluctantly. "Just don't spend much money on Dicey Ann. Things don't cost much in Bentley."

He took two dollars from his wallet and gave it to his brother; then he went on across the street in the direction of the cotton mill. Paul turned and walked out North Chiles Street toward Sinclair's Service Station, where he was employed for the summer. Actually, it was more of a grocery store than a service station. It did not even sell Sinclair gasoline. Hutch Sinclair merely happened to be the proprietor.

Fat, sloppy Josh Bullock had selected Clay Tinsley's Grocery & Meat Market on the corner of Madison and Chiles as the starting point for that particular day's idling. Unless he got an early start, it was not the best of choices, for it faced the east, and the sun in his eyes was a detriment to any detailed monitoring of happenings on Bentley's main thoroughfare. This morning, the sun was already above the Security National Bank on the corner across the street. He stood at the front window of the grocery store with one foot resting atop a sack of flour and watched the twins at The Well in the middle of the street.

38

"You sure can't tell which one of them Holly boys is deaf and dumb when you see them together like that," he said idly to Clay Tinsley, who was leaning against the cash register, also looking on.

"Their own daddy gets them mixed up," Clay said. "Before the deaf one went off to school at Cave Springs, Mamie took him to Atlanta to a clinic three times a week and took the other one along because she didn't have anywhere to leave him. Then he started acting as deaf as the other one and kept everybody mixed up all the time. The doctor was half through a medical test once before he discovered he was examining the wrong one!"

"I just don't see how they do it," Josh said, still watching them. "I don't see how they can even tell theirselfs apart from each other."

"That's easy," said Clay. "The one that gave the money to the other is the deaf one. The one that took it is the one who can hear. He's always got his hand out trying to get something from somebody."

"His daddy told me he makes A's in college."

"People like him usually do if they want to," Clay said. "One of my boys went to school with him at the University before he joined the Navy. He says he's got his fingers in all kinds of pies up there and is forever trying to work a deal with somebody." He fell silent and watched one of the twins disappear from sight alongside the bank. "The draft will get him before long, though, and the Army will take all that out of him," he added.

"You see that Army convoy going through town yesterday?" Josh asked, without moving.

"I couldn't very well miss it. The only way it can get through town is on Chiles Street right past this store."

"They stopped outside of town for a while, and old man Easley that's got that big chicken farm down in Newton County pulled up and asked some of the soldiers where they was headed. They wouldn't tell him. When the Army lines up three hundred trucks and loads them up with soldiers and takes them to a secret place, you can be pretty sure something big's about to happen."

"It was a training exercise," Clay said. "The Army's got a little maneuver area the other side of Monroe where they go and pitch tents and spend the night and come back the next day. And there weren't three hundred trucks in the convoy. There were twenty-six. I counted them with my own eyes. How come you didn't see it go through?"

"I was down at the depot, I guess. That's how I found out that Holly boy makes A's in college."

# 4

State Highway 11 runs the length of Georgia from the dark swamps, pine trees and turpentine country in the south to the green mountains, trout streams and sparkling lakes in the north. Along the way it slices Bentley in half and bears the name of Chiles Street from one end of town to the other. The Well stands in the intersection where Madison Road crosses Chiles Street and is the most famous spot in town. It is an institution, the town's legend and tradition. According to local belief, it marks the place where back in the seventeen hundreds two trade routes met and crossed. Because it was a favorite overnight stopping place, the town grew up around it. That belief ignores the organization of Walton County in 1818, the great Land Lottery of 1820, and the 250 acres deliberately set aside for a town, but how could it be a legend otherwise?

Sheltered by a white latticed well house with a pointed shingled roof, The Well resembles a gazebo. A pulley, rope and bucket hang inside, but they are decorative and commemorative rather than functional, for The Well has been sealed since the middle of the last century. Once it marked the exact center of town, but no longer. In any event, the town radiates out from it. It is the marker from which distances are measured and by which people orient themselves.

It is a conspicuous place to hang posters, advertisements, handbills and placards, but a town ordinance prohibits it. It is a convenient outlet for scribblers with an urge to print unprintable words in public places. On Halloween nights past, revelers have painted it with riotous colors from fire engine red to hysterical yellow. Many years ago they managed to move the well house into Miss Puss Gregory's front yard. When the authorities finally tracked it down, they found Miss Puss inside it, seated in her favorite porch chair, rocking back and forth happily. "I've always wanted one of those," she said wistfully as she watched the workmen load it onto a truck and drive away.

Flouting all ordinances and threats, "BEAT NEWTON" appears in crude red letters as regularly as winter and the high school basketball season come around. One year the Town Council, thinking to anticipate basketball enthusiasts while at the same time hoping to preserve the dignity of the town's most revered landmark, hired a commercial artist in Monroe to paint the same message on a professionally printed sign. The day before the game they hung it with care on the side of The Well that faces south, the direction from which the enemy approaches on game day. On the morning of the game the sign had disappeared, and the familiar "BEAT NEWTON" was scrawled as usual across the side of The Well. Since then, the Town Council includes the price of a bucket of paint in its annual budget, paints over the slapdash lettering after the game is over and worries no more about it for an entire year.

Its central location is irresistible to campaigning politicians, itinerant evangelists and local fund raisers selling cookies, Christmas wreaths and raffle tickets. Gene Talmadge made a speech at The Well in the 1932 gubernatorial campaign, the year he carried Walton County over Abit Nix by four to one. The motor cavalcade taking

Eleanor Roosevelt to Monroe in 1938 stopped at The Well to allow her a chance to see it and presumably hear about it, but she did not get out of the car. The Well is Bentley's substitute for a courthouse square or a town plaza and is vastly less expensive and simpler to maintain.

It was only natural and almost inevitable, then, that when Bentley gave an official send-off to its young men who had been drafted into the military service, The Well was the place to do it. Among those called from Walton County in October, six were from Bentley, none of whom was well known. Two came from families in the Mill Village and three from outlying farms. The sixth was one of the Forester boys from over on Design Street, who drifted in and out of town too often to cultivate many close associations in the community. The crowd that came to see them off, therefore, was not a large one—the boys' families, a few scattered friends, some onlookers en route to work, the four members of the Town Council, including Samuel Pickett, mayor, owner of the Quality Furniture Store, member of the school board and sundry other committees around town.

The people were quiet and their mood somber. They stood about in separate clusters talking among themselves or saying nothing at all, looking curiously from one group to the other and occasionally peering to the north out Chiles Street for sight of the bus. The send-offs were never formal and ceremonious. Sam had ruled out speechmaking from the beginning, on the theory that the very presence of the town officials, friends and well-wishers spoke eloquently enough for Bentley's appreciation of its young men's service to their country and was, in a sense, a speech within itself.

On this morning, therefore, Mayor Pickett and the Council members moved from group to group chatting with the inductees and their families while waiting for the chartered bus carrying other inductees to come from Mon-

43

roe. When the bus pulled to a stop at The Well, they shook hands with each of the six men, then moved back to a respectful distance and stood while their families told them good-bye and saw them aboard. All of them waved the bus around the curve on Chiles Street as it headed south toward Highway 12, Atlanta and Fort McPherson, the induction center for the area. After brief farewells to the families who lingered behind, Sam Pickett and the members of the Town Council angled across the street and down the block to Glen Coker's Downtown Drug Store for coffee.

Popular sentiment favored younger men on the Town Council, and the incumbents concurred with enthusiasm. Sam Pickett, aged sixty-four, was the oldest. Charlie Downs, aged fifty-two, was the youngest. But the electorate did not support their sentiments with their votes, and the Bentley Councilmen got older and older. They were such fixtures on the municipal scene that it never occurred to the voters that any one of them would have campaigned with vigor for his own opponent if only he could find one to run against him. When one of them grew sick and tired of the whole business and threatened to resign, he was always brought up short by the requirement that his resignation would force Sam Pickett to appoint a replacement to fill out the unexpired term, and Sam was too good a friend to burden with a problem such as that.

"Things change, don't they?" Glen Coker said thoughtfully. He moved a chair from the next table and sat down to drink coffee with his friends. "You remember all that carrying on last year when the National Guard unit at Monroe got called up? Everybody was laughing and hollering and cuttin' the fool like they were going off to summer camp again. And that first bunch of draftees acted the same way—like it was the Fourth of July or Bentley Day. I was standing out front awhile ago looking at those boys leave, and it sure wasn't like that today."

44

"It sure wasn't," Sam Pickett echoed. His expression was troubled. "And the sad thing about it is that it's never going to be that way again. The war's getting too big. Somewhere along the line when I wasn't looking, Hitler spread out all the way around the Mediterranean to Libya into Syria and Iran and Egypt. Now when did he do that?"

"You just named it, Sam—when nobody was looking, that's when," said John Reynolds, publisher and editor of *The Bentley Weekly Enterprise*. "That's how Hitler's been so successful: not enough people were looking at him when they should have been. And don't kid yourself that this country can't get caught the same way. We think we're safe with the Atlantic Ocean between us, but the Atlantic Ocean can be crossed."

"Hitler hasn't been able to cross the English Channel yet, and it's only twenty-one miles," Charlie Downs said.

"True. But his Luftwaffe can still pound the daylights out of England from the sky. He still thinks he can soften up those islands to where he can walk in and take over when he gets ready. Maybe he can, even though the Battle of Britain last year was supposed to have settled that, more or less."

"You make it sound mighty gloomy, John," said Henry Carter, Real Estate, Insurance, Finance. "If we keep sending enough stuff to the Allies, maybe we won't have to get in it."

"That won't keep us out. It's our war, too, and I just hope we don't get caught with our pants down. We've got to— You've got a customer up front, Glen."

Glen Coker got up from his chair and moved to the front of the store.

The man standing by the cigar counter appeared to be middle-aged. He was lean, and his skin was weathered by the sun and wind. He wore blue denim overalls and a gray work shirt with the collar buttoned. A rim of white underwear showed at his wrists. He was nervous.

45

"Is the Town Council meeting in here?" he asked, looking over Glen's shoulder at the coffee drinkers beyond.

"Not exactly," Glen said. "Some of the Council members are back there drinking coffee, but they're not having a meeting."

"Is it all right with you if I talk to them?" the man went on, with no change of expression in his face.

"I don't know why not. I'm not on the Council. I'm Glen Coker. This is my store."

The man looked at him as if for the first time. "I know who you are," he said. "I been in here before to get prescriptions. My name is Albright. I got a place up the other side of Social Circle. I'm a farmer."

"It's nice to see you again, Mr. Albright," Glen said, extending his hand.

Mr. Albright ignored Glen's proffered hand and stepped around him to the table in the rear.

"How come you drafted my boy?" he asked the seated Councilmen, none of whom had seen him approach. His question was earnest and searching.

They looked up at him in surprise, then at each other.

"We didn't draft him, Mr.— I met you out at The Well a few minutes ago. You're Mr. er—"

"Albright."

"Have a seat, Mr. Albright," Sam said, reaching over to the next table for a chair. "We're having a cup of coffee. Just sit there and have one with us."

The farmer sat uneasily on the edge of the chair. He took off his tattered black hat and held it by the brim with both hands. Glen went to get a cup of coffee.

"We're not the draft board, you see," Sam went on. "We're the Town Council, and we came to tell your boy and the others good-bye, because we're proud of them and we appreciate what they're doing."

"I need him at home," Mr. Albright said dully, with no indication that he understood Sam Pickett's explanation. "His mother can't help out any more. She's got all these things wrong with her insides and has got to be operated on as soon as I can get enough money together to do it. She stays in bed a lot, and my boy and me has been looking after our two younguns, who still go to school. They're too little to help out, and I don't want 'em to have to help out. I want 'em to go to school and learn to do somethin'. So I need my boy at home."

"You ought to talk to the draft board, Mr. Albright," Charlie Downs said helpfully. "They're the only ones who can help you out."

"That's in Monroe, ain't it?"

"Yes, but we've got a man here in Bentley who's on it. Reeves Buckley, down at the bank. He can tell you what you can do or can't do."

Mr. Albright's eyes widened. "Oh, I couldn't bother Mr. Buckley," he said. "He's too busy to talk to me."

"No, he's not," John Reynolds said. "Reeves Buckley's a fine man. He's never too busy to talk to anybody. One of us can fix that up for you easily. Didn't anybody explain draft deferments to you, Mr. Albright?"

"Not that I know of. I heard about things like that, and my boy mentioned it when he got his draft notice, but I told him he's got to do what the Government in Washington tells him to do. I've always tried to learn my kids they got to obey the law. Now I own up to the fact that I don't understand all the laws, but if they're laws I want my kids to obey them. Their mother and me don't want them to get in any trouble. We want them to do what's right."

He looked down at his hat. He turned it in his hands and picked off an imaginary fleck from the sweatband. He looked up and directed his eyes to Henry Carter. "Do you know how I can get my boy back, Mr. Carter?" he asked.

Henry was startled. "You know my name?"

"Yes, sir. You hold the mortgage on my place."

47

Henry turned away suddenly. He swore under his breath.

"I never did want him to go," Mr. Albright was saying. "But I didn't know how it would actually be until that bus pulled out. His mother wasn't out there. She couldn't get out of bed this morning. She wanted to come more than anything in the world, and she tried, but I made her go back to bed. I got the lady down the road to come up and feed the younguns and get them out to the school bus stop on time. Now I got to go back and see about my wife and see what she needs and fix her something to eat and look after the younguns when they get home from school. They'll be hungry. I got to see about them. And I got to see about the livestock, and by then it will be dark, and I haven't even been out in the field today. Nothing's getting done and— I just need my boy back." His voice cracked.

"How about your boy himself, Mr. Albright?" Charlie Downs asked. "Did he *want* to leave? I don't have any kids of my own, but I can see how a young boy might want to leave home when his mama and daddy want him to stay."

Mr. Albright stared at his hat. "I don't know," he said. "He never did say. I just don't know."

"Well, you know, it might be that this is a good thing for him. You don't ever know for sure. I graduated from The Citadel in Charleston a thousand years ago. I got a commission as a second lieutenant, and all I could think about was being an Army officer for the rest of my life. My daddy had a business he thought I should learn and get into, and he talked me out of going on active duty. I thought the world of my daddy, but to this good day, I don't feel right about listening to him on that score. I'd rather be in the Army right this minute than sell all the Gulf oil and gas in Georgia. So maybe getting your boy back will be good for you, but not for him."

Mr. Albright had no response for Charlie Downs's remarks. An uncomfortable silence ensued. He looked around the table.

"Any of your boys got drafted yet?" he asked them at large.

"Mine are all girls," John Reynolds said with a smile. "But Glen Coker's boy was drafted a few months ago."

Mr. Albright looked around at Glen, who was standing behind his chair. "I guess you know what it's like then, Mr. Coker," he said.

"Yes and no," Glen said. "Our situation wasn't like yours exactly. Hart went to Emory University for a year, then quit and got a job up in Chattanooga. He got drafted from up there. He's in Camp Chaffee, Arkansas, now. He never did work for me in the store, though—not since he was in high school and worked after school and on Saturdays. His mother carries on something awful about him being away in the Army, but I think Hart likes it himself. I don't think it's hurting him any."

"Henry Carter and I have draft-age sons," Sam Pickett said. "We both know their number's coming up, but we don't know exactly when."

"It's going to get around to all of us one way or another," John Reynolds said, pushing back from the table. "I'll go call Reeves Buckley for you, Mr. Albright. He's no miracle worker, but you ought to talk to him just the same."

# 5

ALEXANDER JAMES HOLLY was fifty-four years old. His hair was graying around the temples, and he was thickening around the middle. Mamie reminded him more often than he cared to hear that he should watch his diet. He was five feet nine inches in height, which she claimed was not tall enough to carry much weight without looking paunchy and squatty. Standing in the doorway of the twins' bedroom looking at Paul's wide shoulders, slender figure and long legs as he bent over the bed folding a shirt made him feel exactly as Mamie feared: paunchy and squatty.

The radio on the desk by the window was too loud.

> My mama done tole me
> When I was in knee pants
> My mama done tole me—*son!*
> A woman's a two-faced . . .

"We'd better get one thing straight, Paul," he said. "We don't excuse your getting expelled from the University in any shape, form or fashion. It's the worst thing you've done yet. We've never had anything like this happen in this family, and we don't know how to explain it to people."

"Tell them I got expelled," Paul said without interrupting his packing. "That's what happened, isn't it?"

"I didn't come in here for you to get smart with me,"

Alex said sternly. "You've embarrassed this whole family, and I want you to know that."

"How can I help but know it? You've told me that ever since I came home." He finished folding the shirt and tried to fit it into the suitcase on the bed. Then he unfolded it and laid it out on the bed to try again.

"And I'm telling you again!" Alex said harshly, his voice rising. "And I'll tell you as many times as I feel like you ought to hear it. Do you understand that?"

Paul stood up straight and turned around. He took a deep breath. "Yes, sir," he said slowly and with tired resignation. "But I'm not the first University man to spend the night in the girls' dorm. It happens all the time. I just got caught, that's all."

"That doesn't make it all right. Your mother's too embarrassed to go out of the house. She imagines everybody in Bentley knows about it, and they probably do. But aside from all that, the tuition and fees and money for books and room and board have gone down the drain. We can't afford to squander money like that."

"I paid for more than half that myself. Don't worry. I'll pay you back."

"I don't want you to pay me back. But even if you paid for every cent of it, you can't afford to waste that kind of money. I was hoping you'd be mature enough by now to know that."

He dropped into a chair by the window.

> Mairzy doats and dozy doats
> And liddle lamzy divey
> A kiddley divey too,
> Wouldn't you?
> Mairzy doats and dozy doats . . .

Alex reached across the desk and turned off the radio. "How can you listen to that stuff?" he asked.

"It's Number One on the Hit Parade this week."

"I don't see why."

He sat quietly for a time. "Well—I don't guess there's any use in going on barking at each other," he said. "But I wish you hadn't got Perry all tuned up to go to Atlanta with you. You won't be able to look after him for long. You're on borrowed time yourself. Besides, you're going to have trouble finding a job for yourself with your low draft number and all."

"I'll find something. And Perry doesn't need as much looking after as you think."

"He'll need somebody to help him find a job. He can't walk into an office full of hearing people like you can and tell the first person he meets who he is and what he wants."

"It's been done before. Other deaf people find jobs. Perry can do the same thing. He can do lots of things."

"I know he can—if somebody has the time and patience to show him how. *Show* him, not tell him, and lots of places won't do it. He can't pick up a piece of paper and read all the requirements and qualifications and directions and instructions as easy as you can. Reading is hard work for him, and it takes him a long time. Perry's a special problem wherever he works. He needs special attention, and most employers don't have the time for it. Most places with vacancies won't take his application. And even if they do, they can't call him on the telephone about it, and he can't call them. He has to go back in person. Atlanta's a big place, and he can spend a half a day going across town to ask one question that you can ask in a two-minute phone call."

"The Association for the Deaf can help him," Paul said. "They have an entire department that steers deaf people to likely places and takes their telephone calls for them."

"Yes, they do, but he has to go around to see them in person, too. You can check on six applications while he's checking on one. You ought to think about things like that. Everything's complicated for Perry. Nothing's simple

—not even renting a room or ordering a meal or getting change for a dollar bill. I wish you wouldn't try to take him with you. He's doing all right."

Paul sat down on the edge of the bed. His mood softened. "Perry's not happy here, Dad," he said earnestly. "Just because he doesn't raise a ruckus and give you a hard time doesn't mean he's happy. He's lonesome. He doesn't have anybody to talk to, to associate with—no friends, no companions. He's the only deaf person in Bentley. Don't you see what kind of fix that puts him in? He can't make small talk with anybody. He can't even say, 'Boy! It's really hot today!' or 'Where are you going?' or 'That's a good-looking suit you've got on' because nobody would know what he's saying. What would you do if you couldn't talk to anybody about *anything*?"

"Perry can talk to people when he wants to."

"He talks when there's something specific that must be said," Paul said. He was emphatic. "That's all. Did you ever think about how many times a day you say things just to be polite or to fill in a gap? Perry *lives* in a gap."

"He certainly talks to your mother and me when he feels like it."

"Sure he does. But for crying out loud! You've got to talk to somebody besides your own parents."

"He doesn't give the people in Bentley a chance," Alex said. "He stays away from them so he won't have to talk to them."

"That's because they make him do all the work. They won't talk his language. They won't even try. They expect him to talk theirs. They think all deaf people can automatically read lips, but you and I both know they can't. Perry reads about half and guesses the rest. So he gets tired trying. It's easier to stay to himself."

"They do the best they can," his father said.

"Maybe—but I doubt it. Anyway, it's not the same as when he talks to other deaf people. He misses them. He can't even ask a girl for a date around here. Now you've got to admit that when you're twenty-one years old and never have a date with a girl, things are in pretty bad shape. It's not natural."

"He's been getting along fine at the mill," Alex said. "He's told me so more than once. I see his foreman every now and then—a Mr. Hardin, I think. He says Perry is doing all right."

"I guess he is—by himself," Paul said. "He stands there all day long watching those spindles, taking off the bobbins and carting in empty ones from the supply room. And nobody says a word to him unless the machine breaks down or the yarn gets tangled or he gets the wrong color by mistake, and only then because they have to. When he stops for a break or to eat lunch, they smile at him and nod pleasantly, but they don't strike up a conversation with him. It's hard work, see, and it's easier not to. So he goes off to himself and sits down alone so he won't be a burden to them. If you call that getting along fine, then maybe it is. I just don't agree, that's all."

"He's never complained to us about it."

"Perry's not a complainer. And Dad? That whistle is making a wreck out of him. It's like a knife sticking in his head every day at noon."

"I thought he had adjusted to that."

"He can't. It's impossible."

"Well—I've never kidded myself into thinking that things are easy for Perry, here or anywhere else," Alex said. "They never have been."

"And they never will be, Dad. Not here. They'd be better if he could blow off steam every now and then with somebody who could blow it back to him. Somebody besides me—some other deaf people. He was happier all those years at Cave Springs than he's ever been here, because he could talk to people. They don't need a language —they just talk."

"We've always done our best to make things as normal for him as possible," Alex said. "You know yourself

54

that one of the strictest rules of this house has always been not to make a special case out of him. Why, I used to tan his britches just like I tanned yours when he needed it. We still treat him as normal as we can."

"Do you know that deaf people feel as normal as you and I—until they get around hearing people? Perry doesn't get a chance here in Bentley to ever feel normal."

"Well, Son, all that might be true—and it probably is. But you're going at it the wrong way, and at the wrong time. You're going off half-cocked yourself, and I don't like to see Perry get swept along and get all mixed up, too. We're about to get in a war, and you don't know what it's like in wartime. The country goes crazy. Everything changes. I'd feel a lot better about Perry if he stayed here with us where he knows everybody and we can look after him. I know he's an adult, but that's how I feel about him, and I can't help it."

"Please don't worry about him, Dad," Paul said. "I'll look after him."

"No . . . you don't have to do that," Alex said softly and slowly. He lapsed into silence. He turned and looked out the window down onto the roof of the porch. The old hickory at the corner of the house was losing its leaves rapidly now. They were scattered at random and in patches along the sidewalk and across the grass that was losing its color.

"How do you mean?" he heard Paul say.

"I'll look after him myself," he said, turning back. "I'll take him to Atlanta if that's what he wants. You go on and do—do whatever it is you're going to Atlanta for." He stood up. "And I *will* worry about Perry. I always have. Just because I don't do a lot of sympathizing and holding his hand doesn't mean I don't worry about him." He moved toward the door. "How could I keep from it?"

"I'm sorry, Dad," Paul said. "I didn't mean to stir up a lot of problems."

Alex looked back at his son and sighed. "No—I don't

guess you did," he said. Then he left the room and went down the stairs.

In Cutler's Café on the east side of Chiles Street the noon rush hour was over, and the café was empty except for Giles Cutler, proprietor, who sat on a high stool back of the cashier's counter totaling invoices, and buxom, gregarious, middle-aged Clara Odum, who was clearing off a table in the rear.

"I just don't think Minnie Varner is looking good," she was saying across the width of the café. "Did you notice how her face is all sunk in? And I just don't like her color at all. It's too pasty and pale to suit me. She just sat here and picked at her food like a bird. I told Claude he ought to take her to Dr. Jesse for a complete checkup and some tests to see what in the world is wrong with her. He says she won't go and that she's just feeling under the weather, that's all."

She gave the table a last swipe, picked up a trayful of dirty dishes and started for the kitchen. She looked out the front window before she went through the swinging doors.

"Here come those Holly boys," she said. "I heard that one of them got expelled from the University, but I can't tell by looking which one."

"I didn't mean to stir up a hornet's nest," Paul said to his brother after Clara Odum had spent an undue amount of time taking their order while picking at him for information about his trouble at the University. "But it just seemed like something both of us could do. I was looking forward to getting an apartment together as much as you were. I'm already in enough hot water with Mother and Dad to take you over their protests. Look. Next Tuesday is Armistice Day, and you'll have a holiday. You can come in on Monday night and stay until Wednesday morning and catch the early train home. We'll kick up our heels. We can at least do that much."

"Do you need any money?" Perry asked.

"I always do, but I'll make out. I got a partial refund from the University that'll hold me until I get a paycheck. I didn't know I'd ever turn down any money—if that's what you're offering me—but you'll need it when you move to Atlanta. The thing that gets me is that we're always telling each other hello and good-bye. Now here we go again. I never do get to see you long enough. Do you remember once when I got sick and nobody could find anything wrong with me, and Dr. Jesse told Mother to take me to Cave Springs to see you? When we got there, it turned out you had been sick the same way just as mysteriously—"

"And we both got cured on the spot," Perry finished for him. "That happened twice. But speaking of sickness, you never did pay me back for that dose of castor oil I took for you when we were about seven or eight years old."

Paul shook his head. "You're wrong. I paid you back that time Mother sent you upstairs to stay in your room for something you did, and I stayed in your place while you went down to the river."

Clara Odum came with their lunch.

"I ought to put Mrs. Odum's mind at ease and tell her why I got expelled," Paul said. "I can beef up the story and make it a crime of passion and violence. She looks like she could use a good tale to stick her big, long nose into." He made his signs broad and gave them flourishes while Clara hovered over them arranging the dishes and watching him curiously.

"I just don't see how you can tell what each other's saying," she said.

"Then by the time she gives it her own twists and interpretations, she'll have a first-rate scandal that will keep her busy tongue flapping for weeks," Paul went on.

When she turned to go, both the twins were laughing uproariously.

# 6

THE WAR CAME HOME to Mamie Holly when Paul's draft notice arrived in the mail. She knew what it was before she opened it, for she had been expecting it and looking for it almost daily. Yet not until she held it in her hands and read its words did its significance actually take hold of her.

"Greetings:
Having submitted yourself to a local board composed of your neighbors for the purpose of determining your availability for training and service in the land or naval forces of the United States, you are hereby notified that you have been selected for training and service therein. This local board will furnish you transportation to an induction station. You will there be examined, and, if accepted, you will then be inducted into the land or naval forces . . ."

"Well, well, well, it finally happened," Alex said when she telephoned him at the depot.

"You sound real pleased."

"I guess I am in a way. It's more a feeling of pride, though. Like when I was able to say we have a married daughter or that we have two grandchildren. I like the idea of being able to say we have a son in the Army. When does he have to report?"

"December the eleventh. I've got to call Ferebe and

58

see if she can track him down and tell him. I don't know the name of that paper company where he went to work, and when Perry was there Tuesday he hadn't found a place to live. I hope I don't act like a big crybaby about all this."

"Now, honey, when have you ever acted like a crybaby?" he said pleasantly. "You'll do fine just like you always do. Imagine that! Private Paul H. Holly, U.S. Army. That sounds right nice, doesn't it?"

Mamie called Ferebe in Atlanta. She inquired about the children.

"They're all right now," she said. "Maggie had a cold and ran a fever for a couple of days, but it didn't amount to much. Ellie's driving me crazy, though. He thinks he can climb out of his playpen, but he only gets halfway out, then falls the rest of the way on his head. Ell says I ought to put a ball and chain on him and turn him loose. I'm thinking about it."

Mamie gave her the details of Paul's induction notice, and Ferebe promised to find him somehow.

"How do you and Daddy feel about his going?" she asked. "Ell will probably envy him."

"Your daddy's as proud as a peacock. I'm not sure myself, but it has to be done, and a lot of hand wringing won't change anything. You won't believe how some people act. Eleanor Pike went around talking about how frail J. D. is until she got him to believing it himself. J. D.'s their middle one—a year older than the twins. Dr. Jesse examined him and couldn't find a thing wrong with him, and she carried on something awful about how he was getting too old to know what he's doing, for she *knows* J. D. is 4-F. She's been sending him to Atlanta to a nerve specialist ever since! Isn't that the most ridiculous thing you ever heard of?"

"It takes all kinds, they say. I've been intending to call you, but we've been in a turmoil around here," she said.

59

"Ell left the telephone company two weeks ago and went to work at a new research laboratory, Globe Research, Inc. They do defense work exclusively. It's a grand job and definitely a step upwards. He's in their communications research division, naturally. They're just opening it, and he'll be in on the ground floor of the whole operation. They've promised to let him have his own projects instead of assisting on somebody else's. The telephone company offered him a raise if he'd stay, but Globe topped it. Besides, it's pure research, and that's what he's been wanting. We're so excited we don't know what to do!"

"Why, darling, that sounds perfectly marvelous!" Mamie said. "I'm so thrilled for both of you! Your daddy will be, too. You tell Ellison how proud of him we are."

"He says he feels more worthwhile now that he's doing something for the War Department. I don't think he could be any prouder if they had made him a four-star general."

"Oh, don't let them do that!" Mamie said. "One in the Army is enough for one family. Your daddy would join the Army or Navy if he could get in. He keeps up with the war in Europe as though it's his own personal responsibility."

"I wish he'd explain it to me. I get lost."

"So do I. I feel ashamed of myself for not keeping up. One of these days I'm going to corner him and make him bring me up to date—the way H. V. Kaltenborn does."

She was as good as her word. One night, after they had finished supper and Alex was twirling the dial on the radio that sat on top of the refrigerator, she stood over the sink washing dishes.

"Turn that off," she said abruptly. "I want you to tell me all about the war. I'm lost and Ferebe is too. We're mad at Japan about something, and I don't know what. I've been too busy hating Hitler and Mussolini to worry about anybody else. Now you just sit down there and tell me while I wash the dishes. You won't even have to dry them for me."

He turned off the radio and leaned against the refrigerator. "You know, Mamie, you're the limit. The absolute limit," he said. "You read the paper every day and you listen to the radio all the time. Now how come you don't know about Japan? FDR cut off the trade with the Japs some time ago and froze all their assets in the United States. Now I don't see how you could have missed all that."

"I heard *something* about it, but when the radio's on I'm always doing something else, and I guess I didn't pay close enough attention. And too many other things in the *Constitution* always get my attention. I read this morning about Isobel Waring getting married for the third time! I grew up with her in Madison. She must have eighteen stepchildren by now. I can't figure out what happened to her. She was a plain Jane if ever there was one."

"Did she marry money?"

"*Money?* From what I can gather, she gets richer every time she sheds a husband and marries another."

"See what you missed?" Alex said. "You don't have but one husband—a poor one. You'd better start shopping around before Isobel gets any farther ahead of you."

"Alex! You're just *awful!* But why did we cut off trade with Japan?"

"Because they've been land-grabbing out in the Far East—Dutch East Indies, Malaya, Indochina—and cornering all the rubber, tin, quinine and I don't know what all. We're trying to shake it loose by not letting them have the things they need from us—fuel, primarily. Now they're threatening some other countries where they can get it. We're telling them to stay home and leave all those other countries alone, because we don't like aggression. And they're telling us, in effect, that if we'll resume trade with them they won't need all those other little countries. We're at a standoff. In a nutshell, that's what it's all about. So the next time you hear something about 'sensitive negotiations' or 'the crisis in the Pacific,' you can shake your head wisely and talk like an authority on international affairs and impress all your friends. Now, did you get all that?"

Mamie got it, but she did not recognize the situation as anything more than an economic problem that would work itself out as such things always did. She could not worry about it seriously, for she had her hands full worrying about the Nazis. And why not? The war in Europe had changed the face of the nation in which she lived.

For more than a year new defense factories and plants had been sprouting up from the landscape as though the ground underneath had been fertilized. And still they continued to appear, larger and more mysterious, turning out arms and munitions in unthinkable quantities. Across the South huge Army camps and air bases were appearing in the unlikeliest of places, exhausting local labor sources and drawing in thousands of outsiders who had never before been south of the Mason-Dixon line or east of the Mississippi River. Along the Gulf Coast and around on the Atlantic side, shipyards were working under floodlights to maintain twenty-four-hour schedules and turn out ships for the Navy. Throughout South Carolina, Alabama and Georgia, textile mills were running double shifts and still backlogging orders for fabrics to be turned into olive drab and navy blue uniforms, ship canvas, blankets, parachute silk and Army tenting. Even Bentley's small cotton mill had converted its production into Navy blue serge for uniforms.

The South, however, was not unique. If any section of the country had not been changed by this new obsession with things military, no one knew where it was. Schools and colleges were offering military-oriented courses. Science laboratories and research foundations were taking on national defense as a primary project. The railroads were adding personnel and equipment and reorganizing their yards and terminals to handle the crush of traffic generated by the nation's convulsive defense efforts. Farmers were increasing their acreage under cultivation to meet the demands of the expanding armed forces. Meanwhile, up and down Main Street everywhere retail merchants, beauticians, doctors, lawyers, dentists, garage mechanics, landlords, restaurant and hotel operators were working industriously to take care of the people's needs, which were becoming greater and more numerous by the day. People had money now, and they were spending it. This was prosperity, and it was glorious.

They were riding a boom, and they recognized it as such; but despite the good things it produced for them, they were uneasy with it. They regarded it with suspicion, for booms are temporary and inevitably must be followed by a letdown, whether gradual or sudden. What then? The Depression, unemployment, soup kitchens and bitter hopelessness were still recent and ugly memories they would like to forget but could not. No one knew how long the new defense prosperity would last or what to expect afterward. Sorting mail in the post office or manning a teller's cage in the bank might not have been the best-paying job in the world, but it had been steady and promised to last a long time. Had they been too hasty? Could they go back? Had they burned their bridges?

No one could alleviate their real and practical concerns, so they pushed on, clinging to an ever-fleeing idea that things might stabilize into some kind of normalcy. They did not want their world to tumble down around their heads. Neither did they want to enter the war merely to hold onto the Good Life, which they had to confess they were enjoying, regardless of the cataclysmic horrors that were making it possible.

Yet they were going to war, and they knew it. They did not know when or where or because of what specific incident, but any talk of staying out of it was empty, and any thinking that the war would end without American intervention was wishful. Even those to whom the Atlantic Charter was but a vague abstraction regarded the change of mood, interests and activities around the country as evidence that the war was moving from a threat into a reality awaiting its turn.

Thus, with their minds tuned in on the war, their work geared to its pace, and their future dependent on its outcome, they could not have foreseen that they would be looking in the opposite direction when war actually came.

# 7

ON SUNDAYS when the stores were closed and Chiles Street was all but deserted, fat, sloppy Josh Bullock was forced to do his idling according to a carefully worked out schedule. By two o'clock or maybe two thirty the after-church crowd in Cutler's Café had already eaten and departed, and the place was quiet and dull for the rest of the day. Glen Coker opened his Downtown Drug Store for two hours in the afternoon, but not until four o'clock. That allowed Josh enough time during the interval to meander down to the depot and supervise the arrival of No. 7 eastbound and stay to oversee its departure, even when it was late. And it was late today.

He stood on the station platform, hands in his pockets, jingling coins and absently surveying a baggage wagon stacked high with trunks, boxes, cartons, metal cylinders and two crates of baby chicks. The day had an idle Sunday afternoon look about it that no other day in the week could parallel. It existed for its own sake, taking its ease and refreshing itself in comfort and a sense of well-being. The sun was bright and the day was warm for December. The wind was cool and blew gently through the clump of cedars outside the cotton mill. On the opposite side of the tracks the kudzu vine that smothered the embankment like a thick green quilt moved silently with the wind.

The mail truck stood in place at the edge of the platform, its gray canvas bags locked and heaped on one end. The mail clerk stood in the wide doors of the freight room smoking a cigarette and talking to the freight agent inside.

At the opposite end of the depot Smiley Finch rounded the corner and pushed his wheelbarrow out onto the brick platform. As he approached, Josh examined his cargo with passing interest. This time it appeared to be scraps of weathered lumber and two or three lengths of rusty tin gutter. Smiley winked and grinned at Josh as he passed.

"Working on Sunday, Smiley?" Josh asked.

"Workin', workin', workin'," Smiley mumbled happily. He winked and grinned again and followed his wheelbarrow down the platform to the freight room, where he turned and entered.

Josh looked down the tracks toward the trestle at Highway 11 and listened for the train. Hearing nothing, he turned and stepped back to the depot and the big windows that jutted out from the building to frame the dispatcher's desk on three sides. He peered inside at the clock on the wall above the telegraph table and at Emory Haynes, who sat reading a newspaper. He stepped to the door and stuck his head inside.

"Hey, Emory! You heard anything yet?" he called out.

The telegraph key was still. Emory's back was to the door. "I already told you it was twenty minutes late out of Milstead," he said without looking around.

"Yeah—but it's already thirty minutes late in here," Josh said. "It's nearly three o'clock."

"Okay—it's nearly three o'clock. You meeting somebody on the train today?"

"Naw."

"You going somewhere on it?"

"Naw. You know I'm not going anywhere."

"Then what are you so worried about it for?"

Josh closed the door and returned to the edge of the platform to await the arrival of No. 7 eastbound.

Alexander Holly came in from the freight room. He looked at his watch.

Emory lowered his newspaper. "Goochie McDaniel must be taking another one of his naps," he said.

"Looks like it. Anything special in the wire traffic?" Alex indicated the pieces of paper skewered in disarray on the stick file alongside Emory's old L. C. Smith typewriter.

"Nothing," Emory replied. "Same old stuff." He put his newspaper aside, clasped his hands behind his head and leaned back in his chair. "I guess it's quiet all up and down the line. I think the operator in Covington has been practicing his code, or maybe he's real bored. Anyway, he's been sending war news just to have something to do."

"And he'll get himself in trouble just like you're going to do with your jokes one of these days," Alex said, taking the dispatches from the file.

"I don't know if he was getting it out of the newspapers or off the radio," Emory went on. "It's all laying around there on the table somewhere, if you're interested."

He got up from his chair, walked to the window and looked out at the track and Josh Bullock's immense rear end. "How do you suppose—"

"Where's the rest of this one?" Alex interrupted.

Emory turned around. "Which one?" he asked.

"The one about a Japanese attack."

"Oh—I don't know. Maybe that's all of it. I just took a sentence here and there on some of them. That might be one of them. I got tired." Something about Alex's puzzled expression stayed his attention. "Why?"

"How long ago did this come in?"

"I don't know, Alex, unless I wrote the time group on it. He's been sending that stuff on and off ever since noon. What's so special about that one anyway?"

67

"If you received it right, it looks like Pearl Harbor's been attacked."

"Pearl what?"

"Harbor."

"Oh. Was that in some of the dispatches?"

Alex did not answer. He stepped over to his own desk and picked up the telephone. Emory was watching him with curiosity.

"Hello—Mamie? Turn on the radio," he said. "Emory picked up something in the wire traffic, but it's not enough to make sense. It's something about the Japanese bombing Pearl Harbor. There might not be anything to it, but turn on the radio and see. . . . *Pearl Harbor* . . . It's in Hawaii. . . . No, it's a Naval base. . . . Ours . . . the United States . . . That's right. . . . right . . . Call me back when you find out. . . . No, I'd better not. I've waited this long for Number 7, so I might as well stick it out and protect my investment. Be sure and call me back now. If this is what it sounds like, it can be serious."

Abbie Reynolds thought the house was getting cold. She kept thinking she would turn up the radiator, but she could not find a good stopping place. She was two-thirds through *The Keys of the Kingdom* and could not put it down. Beyond question it was the best thing A. J. Cronin had ever written. What was more, the Brahms piano concerto on the radio was complementing the story perfectly. It was a CBS broadcast from Symphony Hall in Boston. Even the telephone had been mysteriously silent since noon. So with the book, the music, all the girls out of the house, and John stretched out on the sofa in the back sitting room sound asleep and dead to the world, she was reluctant to interrupt her delicious Sunday afternoon to turn up the radiator.

Mrs. John Reynolds was enjoying herself so much, therefore, that she felt her privacy was being invaded when the Brahms was cut off abruptly to be replaced by a dramatic, urgent voice with a special news bulletin. She laid the book in her lap without closing it and listened while waiting for the Brahms to continue. At eight or eight thirty that morning Hawaiian time, according to the announcer, the Japanese Air and Naval Forces had attacked the American Naval Base at Honolulu. Details thus far were incomplete, but it was known that several United States battleships and destroyers had been sunk. Japanese aircraft had also inflicted heavy damage on the United States Army installations at Hickam Field, destroying many American airplanes on the ground. Heavy strafing had taken place at Schofield Barracks and at other installations where American military interests were centered. The number of American casualties was mounting. It was feared that they would be in the hundreds, possibly the thousands. The entire area around Pearl Harbor was in flames and covered over with black smoke billowing hundreds of feet into the air. A clear picture of exactly what had occurred had not yet emerged from the wreckage and destruction. . . .

Abbie listened with growing horror, not assimilating all she had heard. She tucked the flap of the dust jacket into the book to mark her place and leaned forward in her big overstuffed chair with her ear closer to the radio. *Americans? Japanese? Honolulu?* The announcer was saying that President Roosevelt was at that moment in emergency session with his Cabinet in Washington. Meanwhile, no high-level official in the White House, the State Department or the War Department could be reached for comment. Secretary of State Cordell Hull had been engaged in a series of talks with special envoys from Japan for the past several days in an effort to negotiate an amicable settlement for the crisis in the Far East. More news would be broadcast as it became available. . . .

Excited and frightened, Abbie got up from her chair and hurried through the hall to the back sitting room to wake her husband. She shook him by the shoulder. "John! Wake up, honey!"

He stirred, muttered and groaned, but he did not open his eyes.

"Something's happening that I don't understand!" she exclaimed. "It's on the radio. Wake up and listen! I'm scared!"

He opened his eyes and looked at her, but he did not see her. "What is it?" he asked. He let his eyes fall shut again.

"I'm not sure," she said. "Something about the Japanese bombing our Navy in Hawaii. Please wake up, honey. *Please.*"

"Where?" he asked sleepily.

"In Honolulu. They sank some of our ships, and they've been bombing some other places out there. They think maybe thousands of Americans have been killed."

Slowly he opened his eyes, this time with a kind of comprehension. "Honolulu? *Hawaii?*"

He sat upright and swung his feet to the floor. He bent over and reached for his shoes. "See what you can get on the radio there," he said.

She crossed the room and turned on the console Majestic in the corner and waited for it to warm up and the dial numbers to light. "What number is WSB in Atlanta? I never can remember. I've got the radio on in the living room, but I didn't pay any attention to what station."

He was lacing his shoes and ignored her question. "Do you know those sneaks have been sitting right up there in Washington talking to Cordell Hull about a peaceful settlement, and all the time they knew this was going to happen! Those yellow sneaks! Those slant eyed yellow sneaks!" He stood on his feet.

"What are you going to do?" she asked.

"How should I know," he said, smoothing down his hair, "but I sure can't sit around here barefooted while those Japs start a war with us."

---

Emma Horn sat in her front room and rocked. She still wore her church dress. It was rayon crepe, buttoned up the front and figured with gray-and-black squares that jiggled when she sat in church and stared down at it too long. One of her lean, bony hands clutched a small, white handkerchief; the other caressed the gray-and-black squares across her lap to keep away the wrinkles. She was waiting for Delpha, but she was not sure she was coming. Sometimes she and Cleatus came in on Sundays and brought all the children. Sometimes she came alone. Sometimes not at all. Just in case, however, she always kept herself looking nice on Sunday afternoons while she waited.

As she rocked she looked at Asa's photograph hanging on the wall above the bed and remembered the day she had turned the collar on that white shirt he was wearing. He had asked her to do it, but she did not know it was to get his picture taken until he brought it to her on her birthday. She wondered how Asa would look now, if he would look as old as she did. She had trouble thinking of herself as old while he was still young.

The little black radio on top of the sewing machine was turned up to full volume, but it was not loud. Elvin had checked the ground wire and aerial for her and found nothing wrong, so he thought maybe one of the tubes was weak. She did not know where to take it to have it repaired, and Elvin had never offered to do it for her. Today it did not matter. The static was bad, and she was not really listening, anyway. The only reason she turned it on at all was to get some of the quietness out of the house.

On 'Struction Street outside she could hear children laughing and yelling. A young man and his girl friend walked past the house, but by the time she could adjust her glasses to see who they were, they had passed from view. Delpha and Cleatus were always saying they were going to take her to Monroe one day and get her a new pair of glasses, but with seven little hungry mouths to feed, a tenant farmer like Cleatus just naturally never had any money left over to spend on old folks.

Her eyes strayed over the white counterpane on her bed, then to the lace curtains on the side windows beyond. Next door Sissy Carpenter had pulled down the shade in her front-room window, which she did when the evening sun came in too bright and she wanted to take a nap. Sissy worked hard all week long and needed to rest on Sundays or whenever she could. Dr. Jesse and Miss Mattie were good to her. They paid her more money than any other white folks paid their colored help, and they didn't tell her how to run the house. She didn't even ask them what they wanted to eat for breakfast, dinner or supper. She had never asked Dr. Jesse anyway, and she didn't see any use asking Miss Mattie just because she married Dr. Jesse.

While she looked at the window next door, the shade flew up and Sissy Carpenter's big, wide face appeared for a moment, then vanished. Emma turned toward the front window and saw her coming through the yard. The door opened a crack.

"Miss Emma?" The voice was soft, almost a whisper.

"Come in, Sissy. I seen you comin'."

She stepped inside. "I was afraid you might be taking a nap, and I didn't want to wake you," she said apologetically.

"I been dozin' right along," she said. "I guess I jes' rock myself to sleep like a little baby when I set in this chair too long." She laughed softly. "Set down, Sissy. I ain't seen you in near 'bout a week."

Sissy Carpenter was brown, big boned and had a comfortable, confident look about her. In her early fifties, she was probably the most handsome colored woman in Bentley. She nodded toward the radio, crackling and sputtering in the corner. "Did you hear the news?" she asked, lowering herself into a cane-bottomed chair by the kitchen door.

"No—I don't do much news listenin'," Emma replied.

72

"They is always talkin' about things I don't know nothin' about."

Sissy listened to the radio for a moment. "They're talking about it now," she said, "We're in a war, Miss Emma—a real war."

Emma brought her rocking chair to a standstill and looked at her keenly.

"*Who's* in a wah, Sissy?" she asked.

"We are—the United States."

"The *United States?* Who wif'?"

"With the Japanese. It's been on the radio. They dropped bombs on our Army and Navy in Hawaii. Lots of our soldiers and sailors have been killed. They sunk some of our ships and tore up lots more. It's bad. Real bad."

"Hawaii? Ain't that out in the ocean?"

"Yes, but it belongs to the United States. Nobody knows much about what's happened yet. It's still going on. You see . . ."

She repeated the news in as much detail as she knew while Emma leaned forward and took in every word she could understand.

". . . and I was afraid you might not have heard," Sissy said in conclusion. "Everybody at church tonight will be talking about it, and you ought to know about it before you go."

Emma resumed her rocking. "Asa wanted to go to that other wah when Delpha an' Elvin was little babies," Emma said, her eyes beginning to glow in reminiscence. "Ooooo, he want to go *so* bad, but they say they don't need him. He talk to a man in Monroe—a white man—and he say he oughta stay home and look after his wife and chillun. He stay home aw' right, but he sho' did want to go to that wah."

"You can't never tell. Elvin might have to go to this one," Sissy said. "He's about the right age."

"If Elvin want to go to the wah as bad as his daddy want to go to that other one, tha's aw' right wif' me,"

Emma said. "His daddy never did do none of the things he really want to do. Maybe Elvin can." She smiled wistfully. "I sho' hope so," she added. "I sho' hope Elvin get to do like he want to do some time."

Chiles Street had come alive. Three or four cars were parked in front of the Downtown Drug Store and that many or more at Cutler's Café across the street. A few were scattered elsewhere along the block. People stood about on the sidewalks in pairs and little knots. Some met and stopped in the street or leaned into open car windows. There were not many, but more than was customary at five o'clock on Sunday afternoon when they were usually at home taking another look at the Sunday paper, picking around in the refrigerator at the remains of their big Sunday dinner, visiting across their yards with their neighbors, or sneaking in still another nap while waiting for Jack Benny to say "Jell-O Again" and for Charlie McCarthy to trade insults with Edgar Bergen.

Giles Cutler often wondered why he bothered to keep his café open on Sundays after the church crowd had eaten and departed. No one came in except perhaps a train crew to drink coffee, maybe a passing truck driver and a straggler here and there at loose ends with time on his hands. Today Giles was not doing any more business than usual, but he had a much larger crowd while he did it.

They sat at the counter and nearby tables reviewing events as they knew them to that moment. They were excited, grave and angry as they tried to backtrack and understand how in the world the entire Japanese Navy could have come halfway across the Pacific Ocean in plain sight and get close enough to Hawaii to bomb it without somebody in the United States Navy knowing something about it. They were far from confident that they would not bomb the West Coast next. Why not? With half the U.S. Navy at the bottom of the ocean, what was to stop them? They speculated on what FDR would do the next day, but of course, he had no choice. He had to declare war. There was no way out of it. All the boys who had been worrying about when their draft numbers were coming up could stop worrying. Their numbers had come up. All of them. They hoped the U.S. Army was in good enough shape to fight off the Japs if they invaded California, and they sure better be, because the Navy could not help them much now.

Across the street the Downtown Drug Store was also alive with people, but no one was buying anything. They went in and out, joining whatever discussion was in progress inside the store or on the sidewalk out front. They swapped accounts of what they had been doing when the thunderbolt struck and how they had reacted. They traded versions of the news according to which radio station and commentator they had heard. Some claimed to have seen all this coming for a long time. Others said they sure hadn't, and you could have knocked them over with a feather. Now if Adolf Hitler had done something like it, they wouldn't have been surprised, but they sure hadn't figured on Emperor what's-his-name. All of which just showed them how you can't trust a yellow Jap.

On both sides of the street they speculated on the new rules, regulations and precautions that would most certainly go into effect immediately. They sized up their own military potentials plus those of their sons and brothers. They talked anxiously of their businesses and how they might fare in case of an all-out war, which now seemed all but inevitable. They talked and traded places with each other by ones and twos, carrying rumors and fragments of information from one group to the next.

Their homes could no longer contain them. They had received a jolt that after two hours or more still vibrated and showed no signs of settling down. They needed to know how their friends and associates were taking that same jolt. They wanted to know what they had heard, what they thought, what they predicted, how they felt. They wanted to confirm and compare their own ideas and emotions with someone outside their own families. Probably more than anything else they wanted someone to erase their disbelief and convince them that the Japanese attack on Pearl Harbor had actually happened.

With the passage of time, the high school boys' hangout had always shifted from place to place without rhyme or reason. Since school had begun in September, they had been congregating at the bus station, of all places, out on South Chiles Street, four blocks from uptown. Today they had already assembled when the news came. Though they recognized the gravity and far-reaching implications of the Japanese sneak attack, the excitement it generated contained a drama and even a glamour that might have escaped their fathers. They had watched Errol Flynn fly victoriously through the Battle of Britain. They had cheered Tyrone Power while he flew air cover over Dunkirk and returned safely to Betty Grable. The good guys always won, and never in humdrum fashion.

Even so, they realized that war was a serious business. They knew that even if they never wore a uniform or saw a bullet fired, the war would come home to them personally. With absolute certainty they knew, even if they did not articulate it, that they would wake up tomorrow morning in a world that would not be the same as it had been this morning when their parents had cajoled and threatened them out of bed and marched them off to church. They were not certain what to do about it, however, except talk. News or no news, they could always do that.

"I always thought wars happened in picture shows and history books—and to somebody else."

"Yeah. I'll bet my dad's at home right this minute having a purple tizzy. He's got a war map on our kitchen

76

wall with pins sticking in it. I hope he saved one to stick in Hawaii."

"If this war lasts until I get out of school, I'm sure not going to do like my dad did in France. He was a foot soldier in the trenches. That's not for me. I'm going in the Navy."

"If I do what my old man did, I won't get any farther than Atlanta. He never did go anywhere except to Camp Gordon. All he did was answer bugle calls, roll up the sides of his tent every morning and wrap puttees around his legs, and he's been in the American Legion ever since."

"I can't decide whether to fly for the Army or the Navy. The Navy's got the best deal, but too much water."

"You ain't gonna fly for nobody! You've got to go to college first, and this war will be over and done with before you get out of high school—if you ever get out at all, that is."

"If you wanta know the truth, every one of you guys is going to be drafted in the Army as a private—a foot soldier."

"Not me. I got flat feet, and I'm blind in one eye. Besides, I'm afraid of guns."

"Yeah. You and that soldier over there asleep with his head on his barracks bag."

"The war doesn't seem to be worrying him very much."

"Maybe he told Mr. Nicholson to wake him up when it's over."

"What I want to know is when did we get mad at Japan?"

"Today."

"You think we'll have school tomorrow?"

"You crazy or something? One of those Jap bombs would have to fall on top of Miss Mattie's desk before they'd close down that chicken coop."

"I'm going home and listen to the radio. Lowell Thomas has probably got this war figured out a lot better than you guys."

"You got your history theme ready? Mr. Whitworth said he'll knock off five points automatically on any that's late."

"Maybe he'll get drafted before breakfast and not be there himself."

"He claims he's 4-F."

"That's for sure—in the head."

While Alexander Holly replayed the war news to Perry as it came in, Mamie telephoned Ferebe in Atlanta to see if her family was all right. She was delighted to find Susie there.

"I can't explain it, but I just didn't want to stay by myself," she said. "So I brought my things to spend the night. Ell's going to drop me off at the streetcar line on his way to work tomorrow. All that Pearl Harbor stuff almost scared me out of my wits. I still can't believe it."

"I'm glad you're there, darling," Mamie said. "We've been worried about all of you. Have you seen Paul?"

"He was here until a few minutes ago. He wouldn't admit it, but I think he didn't want to stay by himself either. And Mother? He told us Perry was here last weekend. That's twice he's been here within a month and didn't get in touch with me or Ferebe. That's not fair!"

"Don't be upset. It doesn't mean a thing. He and Paul have been doing like that all their lives. They get off by themselves as if the rest of us didn't exist and make big, dark secrets out of where they've been and what they've been doing. Perry had a marvelous time on both weekends, and we're thrilled he could come. You don't know how much better I feel knowing you're all together today. We don't know what will happen next. Does Paul think today's news will make any difference in his induction?"

"No. He's still planning on going out to Fort McPherson Thursday. Ell said if he was in his shoes he'd go down and enlist tomorrow."

"I saw Millie Carter out on the sidewalk this afternoon. Andy called them from the University and said that's what he's going to do the first thing tomorrow morning. Your daddy's been listening to the radio all afternoon and telling Perry what he hears. You wouldn't think he would have so much trouble with his signs after all these years, but he tries, and I've been pitching in to keep Perry up to date. Emory Haynes called about six o'clock. The head office had sent some security measures against sabotage to be put in effect immediately, and your daddy had to go down to the depot. I had the strangest feeling when he left. It seems so unreal to be worrying about sabotage here in Bentley, of all places. The head office is sending an inspection team out over the line tomorrow to give assistance."

"Ell got called back to the lab, too. Some new plan they had to start."

"Let me talk to Ferebe now, darling. I'll feel better after hearing all your voices."

After she had reported her conversation to her husband and son, Alex said, "I wish all of them were here in this house with us right now. But that's kind of crazy, isn't it?"

"Not in the least," Mamie replied. "Are you afraid, Alex?"

"Why, yes, I suppose I am. I'm uneasy, at least. After all my predictions about getting into the war, this still shakes me down to my shoe tops. Things are going to be different from now on, Mamie. We've got to expect that. They'll probably never be the same again, even after it's all over. We've got to expect that too."

"Just so it doesn't change us, and I don't see how it possibly can," she said. "We've had to get used to a few things in our day, and we'll have to get used to the war now. I don't know what else we can do. Just so the children can always have a place to come back to if they need to or want to. Don't you think that's important?"

"The most important of all," he replied.

Mamie's gaze turned to Perry, who was looking at the Sunday magazine section of the newspaper. A shadow crossed her face. "I wish he didn't want to go to Atlanta," she said.

"So do I, but we can't stand in his way. He'll probably want to leave more than ever now."

Lights burned all over town that night, but few people could be seen out of doors. Except for the sounds of an occasional automobile passing through on the highway, Bentley was silent and withdrawn into itself. The Downtown Drug Store had closed at six o'clock on schedule. Giles Cutler locked up his café and went home two hours ahead of his regular closing time. No passengers got off or on No. 9 eastbound at seven twenty. After it departed, Emory Haynes put on the night-light in the waiting room and made his way on foot up Depot Street toward home. At the Trailways Bus Station Mr. Nicholson, the agent in charge, looked out over the empty station and the darkness beyond the circle of light out front and wished he could go home to his wife and children.

Reverend Charles D. Clapper, pastor of the First Baptist Church on North Chiles Street, had hastily revised his sermon that afternoon for the evening service. He was standing in his pulpit looking out at the few members of his congregation who had come.

"The best thing we can do on this day of tragedy and uncertainty is to carry on normally insofar as we can," he explained. "We do not know what tomorrow will bring, but in the meantime, let us continue with our regular evening worship service. Maybe it will help us to keep our feet on the ground and calm our anxious hearts and minds. . . ."

The Macedonia Baptist Church on West Madison Road held evening services as usual. Not many people came, but a passerby could not have detected that by the volume of the singing.

"It sound mighty like we gonna git in a wah," Reverend Freeman L. Lincoln, the pastor, told his congregation. "Now if we *do* git in the wah, that mean we gonna haf' to fight, and none of us don't like to fight. But if tha's what we haf' to do, tha's what we haf' to do. *And we gonna do it!* You jes' tell Jesus why you haf' to fight in the wah, and he'll probably say, "Tha's aw right wif' me, 'cause I know all about wahs and how people is always a-fightin' in 'em.' Jesus know how it is when you haf' to do things you don't like. Jesus he know 'bout terrible things, too."

Reverend Forrest Lindley, aged forty-six, father of five, pastor of the First Methodist Church on South Chiles Street, stepped out of his study into the sanctuary and moved directly to the pulpit. Only a scattering of his congregation was present—ten or twelve at the most. He looked down at them and smiled.

"Good friends, I know what it cost you to come tonight," he said. "I had to tear myself away from the radio, too. It's been an afternoon of horror for all of us. And maybe we've been too caught up in it to stop and pray just at a time when prayer is needed most. Suppose we pray now while you remain seated."

He waited until the people bowed their heads and settled into an attitude of prayer. Then he lifted his head and raised his eyes to the ceiling, and the words came:

"Dear God, tonight we're shocked and hurt. We're bitter and disillusioned. We're frightened and bewildered. We're worried and sad. We're angry and vindictive. All of

81

our feelings seem to be negative. Our hearts and minds are in a turmoil. Tell us what to think. Tell us how to feel. Tell us what to do. Take each of us by the hand and lead us. Guide our every step through whatever lies ahead. This we ask in the name of our Savior, Jesus Christ, and for His sake. Amen."

The people raised their heads and sat back in their pews.

"I can say many things, but I won't say them," the pastor went on. "I think we should all go back home now. That's where we belong. It's where our hearts are. Go home to your families. They need you just as you need them. It's dark tonight, and we can't see. Tomorrow our vision might be no better, even in the light of day. Ask God for courage and wisdom to face it. Go now in the knowledge of His love and understanding. God bless each of you and yours. Good-night, good friends."

# 8

AT A PRESCHOOL MEETING of her high school teachers on Monday morning, Miss Mattie Cofield Randolph, Principal, revised the day's schedule. President Roosevelt was scheduled to address a joint session of Congress at noon, and the lunch hour was to be extended long enough for the students to stay home and listen to him on their radios.

"You must encourage them to listen," she instructed her teachers. "Impress upon them that this is the first time in history an entire nation can listen to its President and Congress make a formal declaration of war at the time it is *actually happening!* Why, I break out in goose pimples to think what a rare opportunity it is for all of us. Of course, they'll all want to talk about these horrible events this morning, and I think we should encourage them. After all, it's history in the making. Nobody is talking about anything else."

Miss Mattie was right. The people's tone, however, had changed during the night. From what they heard and thought they heard, understood and misunderstood, they had managed to separate most facts from most fiction and put the bits and pieces together in a semblance of order and supply them with a background. In the process of assembly, their shock and disbelief had given way to anger. Their emotions spilled over like hot lava and flowed in all

83

directions. They were intemperate, unreasoning and not always well informed.

Chiles Street opened for business as usual, but the stores, shops and offices were no more than gathering places for people to talk and wait with dreadful anticipation for President Roosevelt's declaration of war at noon. Before they unlocked their front doors, however, businessmen found themselves facing a new problem for which they were not prepared. Young men were beginning to leave town. They left their jobs after hurried explanations to their employers, who could not in good conscience condemn their actions despite the work left undone in the wake of their sudden departures. They went up to Monroe to the courthouse where the Army and Navy maintained a joint recruiting office. They did not know if they would come back to work or not. Two or three packed their suitcases and went in to Atlanta, prepared not to return at all but to stay and enlist in the Army, Navy, Marines or Coast Guard, whichever would accept them for duty.

Their employers watched them go with anxiety tempered by a certain pride and not a little envy. They scratched their heads and tried to think what to do tomorrow and the day after. Today was no problem. Nobody was doing any business anyway. Josh Bullock had never been so busy idling. His choice of locations was unlimited and overwhelming, and all of them were good.

Merchants and dealers took anxious looks at the stock levels of their inventories, wondering exactly where and when the crunch would be felt first. Sam Pickett and the Town Council met to draft an open letter "To All the Citizens of Bentley" asking them to be calm and remain at their regular places of duty until the Government had time to inform them where they could serve best. It was important to maintain stability at home and carry on as normally as possible, for all of them would undoubtedly be called on to make sacrifices and work long hours to win the victory that must now be their primary goal.

At noon they heard it all. They knew what to expect and something of the way it would come about. What they might not have foreseen, though, was that their own participation would be quite so personal and their own involvement quite so complete. They listened, scarcely breathing. The stirrings in them could have been an awe of what they heard. The tingles could have been a patriotic fervor. But whatever it was that moved inside them, the citizens of Bentley, Georgia, were of one accord, at one time, in one place, and the place was 652 miles to the north. Yet they never left home.

Ten black limousines following one another onto Capitol Plaza . . . Secret Service men riding the running boards . . . crowds of onlookers . . . the President wearing his familiar Navy blue cape . . . waving and smiling but restrained . . . Senators filing into the House chamber . . . Supreme Court justices in their black robes . . . Cabinet members . . . high-ranking military officers . . . packed spectators' gallery . . . Mrs. Roosevelt wearing a silver fox fur . . . Mrs. Woodrow Wilson, a link with the past and another war . . . the President in formal morning attire . . . Speaker Sam Rayburn . . . Vice-President Wallace . . . a hush in the historic chamber . . . the President . . . a black, loose-leaf notebook, the kind carried by any schoolboy anywhere . . .

"Yesterday, December seventh, nineteen forty-one—a day which will live in infamy—the United States of America was suddenly and deliberately attacked by naval and air forces of the Empire of Japan. . . . I ask that Congress declare that since the unprovoked and dastardly attack by Japan . . . a state of war has existed. . . ."

President Roosevelt spoke for six minutes. Afterward, the Senators and Congressmen supported him, with the sole exception of one dissenting vote. The entire action had consumed less than a single hour.

The President signed the bill into law at a few minutes past four o'clock in the afternoon, twenty-seven hours after the first bomb exploded on Pearl Harbor, over three hours after his address to Congress and the nation. Not until then was the United States legally at war. To the people across the land, however, the war actually began while Marine Captain James Roosevelt, with care and concern, maneuvered his father from the speaker's rostrum into his wheelchair for the trip back up the aisle and downtown to the White House to help the country face only God knew what.

# 9

ATLANTA WAS AS EXCITED and stirred up by the declaration of war as any other city in the United States. But it had not convulsed itself into a red, white and blue hysteria since noon the previous day for the most reasonable of reasons. It had already hit a wartime stride. For more than a year it had been building toward it, sensibly, with intelligence and systematic vision. Its vitality flowed with energy like the waters of a great river that had been dammed up, then released through controlled channels to provide power where it was needed for the greatest good of the most. The city was in constant motion, organized and moving with purpose and a fixed sense of direction. Atlanta would not have been Atlanta had it not recognized what needed to be done and set about doing it. That was the spirit with which it rebuilt itself after General Sherman put the torch to it and marched on to the sea, leaving it for dead.

The city crawled with tractors, bulldozers and construction crews, clearing, digging, moving the earth, changing the landscape and its purpose for being. In the northeast part of town, on the site of old Camp Gordon, a World War installation long since abandoned to weeds, bats and spiders, the Army was constructing a hospital, an octopus with many tentacles, huge enough to receive and care for its soldiers in whatever state of health and condition they might turn out to be. Close by, the Navy was building an air training station where its fledgling aviators could learn the rudiments of flying before going on else-where to learn something more specialized and ultimate. To the southeast, fifteen hundred acres of farmland were being transformed into a colossus of warehouses to contain the new Quartermaster Depot and more supplies than any man down on Peachtree Street ever dreamed could exist in one location for one purpose. In the southwest long troop trains were shunted onto the spur at Fort McPherson, often in the dark of the night, to unload or take away hundreds of enlisted men and officers who were being sorted out, processed and made ready to train for war, if war should turn out to be the country's fate.

On the face of it, this was not the city of Atlanta or even the State of Georgia at work. It was the Federal Government. Atlanta merely happened to be a convenient site on which the United States Government chose to expend its time, energy and money. But even a Gargantua such as the United States Government could not have achieved its purpose without the willingness and resources that Atlanta held out to it on a silver platter. Its industry would retool for defense; its power would provide energy for it; its labor force would provide manpower for it; and its corporate management would fuse it into one effort and point it in one direction.

Federal agencies were moving into downtown office buildings by the score, replacing commercial tenants, while the railroads, communications, power and labor forces were straining to keep abreast of the increasing demand for theirs. The Chevrolet and Fisher Body plants near the Federal prison had converted many of their facilities to defense production, while many smaller, local businesses were turning their skills to producing anchor chains, sea chests, valves, hinges, heavy iron castings, steel plates, hair-trigger equipment, and even soup bowls for the Navy.

Draft quotas and volunteer enlistments made it difficult to meet commitments. To plug the gaps and supply the greedy needs of the war that was sure to come, strangers with strange names, strange accents, strange manners and customs were streaming into the city from the North, West, Midwest and from rural Georgia itself. They were absorbed so completely into the life stream of the population that few Atlantans had time to realize that their numbers were becoming vast enough to constitute a social revolution. Atlantans had been at war for a long time. It was just that they had been calling it by another name.

This was Atlanta on the day America officially went to war.

On the following day Susie Holly got off the streetcar at the corner of Alabama and Broad Streets. It was noisy with automobiles honking, stopping and starting; with policemen's whistles and screeching tires; with pneumatic drills and newsboys shouting headlines; with buses hissing up to corners and trolleys clanging through intersections. Everywhere people were hurrying, crossing streets, waiting for lights, dodging oncoming traffic in the streets and each other on the sidewalks, disappearing into buildings, rushing to work, intent on where they were going and acutely aware of exactly how much time remained for them to get there. Except for a few American flags along the street, today could have been any day last week or the week before that. Susie felt a letdown, a disappointment.

She was not certain what she had expected to find. Yesterday had certainly been an abnormal day. In the morning a charged expectancy had hung over Atlanta. She felt it and even saw it in the faces and movement of people in the streets, in the elevator, in the corridors of the building where she worked. After the President's declaration of war, the charge had ignited and exploded into an excitement that approached hysteria. Whatever the pretense, work ended for the day. The corridor outside her office teemed with people coming and going, rushing, talking, shouting, hailing friends and strangers alike, trading quips and sallies, laughing as though they were celebrating a victory rather than a tragic defeat. Their mood was curious, yet strangely understandable and even contagious. They were riding a tidal wave of emotion. She recognized that, and she knew that in time a leveling off would occur. Perhaps it had already happened. She was unprepared, nevertheless, for the morning to appear so uneventful and like all the others that had preceded it.

Mr. Kirkland, manager of the Piedmont Hosiery Company, was already at work when she arrived in the office. She stepped to the open door of his office and looked in.

"Mornin', Mr. Kirkland," she said.

Mr. Kirkland, efficient, professional and impersonal, looked up from a mass of papers on his desk and smiled briefly and pleasantly. "Good morning, Susie," he said. "How are you?"

"All right, I guess," she said. "But I don't know if I can get any work done this morning or not."

"Don't you feel well?"

"Oh, yes, sir!" she said hastily. "I feel fine, but it's the war. It's so exciting and—and so *historic!*"

He looked surprised and said, "Yes. I suppose it is, isn't it?"

She hesitated, waiting for an opinion or at least an observation, but he had already returned to his papers.

"I'd better get to work," she said awkwardly. She felt as though she had been talking to herself.

Emily Lanier had come in while Susie was talking to Mr. Kirkland. She had hung up her coat and was examining her face in a compact mirror. It was a pretty face to examine. She was brown haired, hazel eyed, mannered, gracious, poised and all that romantic notions decreed Southern belles should be but seldom were. Furthermore,

90

she was not at all oblivious to her own charms. Indeed, she worked to improve them with the diligence of a speed typist preparing herself for the national finals.

"Mornin', Susie," she mumbled. "I overslept this morning and had to finish my makeup on the bus. If my mother knew that, she would skin me alive!" She snapped the compact shut. "Susie! You promised to get rid of that upswept hairdo. You're too short and too blond and too—"

"And too fat," Susie interrupted. "But I don't care. Everybody in the dorm at college used to tell me until I got sick of hearing it that I was too short and wide to wear sloppy Joe sweaters and saddle oxfords, but I wore them just the same. Anyway, I don't see how you can come in worrying about hairdos this morning with the war to talk about. It was so thrilling and stirring on the radio last night. They kept playing 'Anchors Aweigh,' 'When the Caissons Go Rolling Along' and 'The Halls of Montezuma.' And didn't you just love Gabriel Heatter's newscast last night?"

"I didn't turn on the radio. Buddy and I went to the picture show."

"The *picture show?*" Susie was incredulous. "How on earth could you sit still in a picture show? With so much carrying on about the war and all, I mean."

"It was hard to sit still, all right. Charles Boyer was playing at Loew's, and he gives me the flutters. The only trouble is that when the lights came on, I had to look at Buddy again."

"Is Buddy going to enlist?" Susie asked, uncovering her typewriter.

"He doesn't have to. He's going to get drafted. The way he kept looking over his shoulder last night, I think he expected them to come get him in the middle of the picture show."

"If I was a man, I'd enlist in the Marines," Susie said.

"But since I'm not, I'm going to get me a war job at Fort Mac or the Naval Training Station or some place where I can help out with the war."

"Doing what?" Emily asked with indifference.

"I don't know, but good heavens! It's bound to be more helpful than typing up invoices and orders for argyle socks. I heard some city official on the radio last night—it might have been the mayor—say the war is everybody's business, and it'll take all of us working together to see it through to victory. I'm going around to the Red Cross tonight when we get off and see what kind of volunteer work they'll let me do. Then I'm going down to the USO and sign up to help out wherever they need me. I read about a new place over on Peachtree Street called War Workers Volunteers where they will find all kinds of jobs for volunteers. I'm going to register with them too."

"Sounds like you're going to be up all night," Emily said. She yawned, gave her hair a fluff and, with no enthusiasm, uncovered her own typewriter.

"What if I am?" Susie said with defiance in her voice. "My own brother, Paul, is going into the Army on Thursday, if not before. I get goose pimples just thinking about it. He's the only one in our family who can get in the service. Perry would if he could, bless his heart. So I intend to do as much as I can wherever I'm needed."

"Bravo!" Emily said. "Hand me a sheet of carbon, will you, Susie? It's too early in the morning for me to go into that gloomy supply room and try to find some of my own."

"Nobody seems to be worrying about the war this morning," Susie said unhappily, leaning across the desk to hand the carbon paper to Emily. "A man on the streetcar was working a crossword puzzle. Another one was sound asleep, and two women behind me were talking about how you marinate a beef brisket before you roast it in a three hundred and seventy-five degree oven for an hour and a half. I just thought everything would be changed this morning. After all, the United States has been at war over seventeen hours."

Had Susie stood atop the tower of the Million-Dollar City Hall and looked down over Atlanta, she would have seen a change that was as forceful as it was abrupt. Army and Navy recruiting offices were jammed with applicants, while men stood one behind the other in long lines stretching through the doorways and onto the sidewalks outside, waiting to get in and sign up.

# 10

FORT MCPHERSON is an Atlanta institution, as deeply embedded in the city's consciousness as Grant Park, Stone Mountain and the Chattahoochee River. It sits on the official boundary line of the southwest city limits, but it is surrounded by Atlanta on three sides and East Point on the other, making it an urban military installation. Not even local residents are always positive where Atlanta ends and East Point begins, for one pours into the other without interruption.

The Central of Georgia Railroad comes in from Newnan on the southwest and works its way north through College Park, East Point, past Fort McPherson and on into downtown Atlanta. It is paralleled by a single street twisting along with the tracks and changing its name each time it crosses a municipal border. Outside the Army post, it is Lee Street, heavily traveled and commercial, edged on one side by railroad tracks and telephone poles and on the other by garages, warehouses, used car lots, cafés, beer taverns, rooming houses and grocery stores with gas pumps in front and living quarters above.

Paul Holly had been in that section of Atlanta many times, and while he was aware of Fort McPherson and the considerable length of Lee Street it dominated, he had never been on the post nor had he been curious enough to wonder what it was like within. It was a landmark on the scenery, a convenient point of reference when giving directions, as useful in that sense as the State Capitol, Five Points or the campus of Georgia Tech.

He was unprepared, therefore, when he walked through the main gate of Fort McPherson to find an enclave that was separated from Atlanta by more than a gatehouse and a chain metal fence. He discovered another world alien to Lee Street outside. It was well defined and logical, clean and precise, orderly and regulated. It was of a piece. It followed a pattern. It made sense. He liked what he saw and how it made him feel.

He liked and somehow understood the stiff, unsmiling Military Policeman who stopped him at the gate, glanced at his papers, and, with polite detachment, gave him directions to the Induction Center. He admired the exactness of the white multiwindowed buildings that framed the streets and the hygienic sweep of the mathematical distances that separated them. He was intrigued by the uniformed soldiers he saw going in and out of the buildings and whom he encountered on the sidewalks. He was taken by the impersonal air and brisk efficiency with which they went about their affairs. He looked on with a kind of wonder at the freakish jeeps, oversized trucks and ungainly weapons carriers passing along the pavement and crossing intersections ahead, loud, rumbling and blasting, their drivers intent and serious but not necessarily grave. Paul Holly felt curiously at home.

He stopped and watched a formation of sixty or seventy men approach on the street, a solid olive drab block, gliding in unison as if borne on the smooth, polished runners of a single sleigh. As they came nearer, he marveled that he was looking at sixty or seventy humans submerging and combining their separate identities to create a symmetrical monolith that stopped and started, moved forward and backward, divided and reassembled itself according to the split-second decisions and hair-triggered commands of their corporal, who marched alongside them attached to the monolith like a handle. The corporal maneuvered the formation around a corner as deftly and with as much confidence as the drivers of those jeeps and weapons carriers steered their vehicles to wherever their business demanded they go.

Instinctively, Paul stood straight and breathed deeply as a quiet thrill swept through him. He sensed that in the moving block of soldiers he had witnessed an achievement that was ultimate, an end within itself. In a flash he got a quick glimpse of what the armed forces of the United States—or of any other country—was all about. The insight exhilarated him, and his own insignificance became a thing of importance. He walked on toward the Induction Center buoyed with a sense of expectancy. This was the United States's fourth day at war, and he was to be part of it.

On the Monday following their attack on Pearl Harbor, the Japanese had bombed Clark Air Field, an American installation in Manila, destroying B-17s, burning out hangars, fuel supplies, living quarters and killing a number of Americans and Filipinos. They attacked the United States–controlled islands of Midway, Guam and Wake and sank two British battleships in their assaults on Malaya and Hong Kong. So rapidly did the fighting erupt in far parts of the world that Germany's and Italy's declaration of war on the United States went almost unnoticed.

The Induction Center was crowded, noisy and alive with the bustle and activity that Paul had expected to find throughout the post. It teemed with men of indeterminate ages, all in civilian clothes, some carrying zipper bags or suitcases, all of them carrying long, white windowed envelopes. They were short and tall, fat and slim, young and old, handsome and ugly, tanned and pale, elegant and seedy, flashy and nondescript, robust and puny. Had the United States Army driven trucks into downtown Atlanta and with a giant net scooped up at random all the men along Forsyth and Decatur Streets, whoever they might be, its catch could not have yielded a more varied assortment of the American male.

They fidgeted with nervous energy, talked to one another with forced high spirits and excessive bravado. They laughed cooperatively and boisterously at each other's sallies whether they were funny or not. They waited in lines, curious, bewildered or frightened, some of them silent, straining to hear what was happening at the desks they were inching toward. They sat at long tables, frowning over blank forms they were required to complete, questioning one another and comparing their entries for reassurance. They milled about haplessly carrying papers in their hands, not quite willing to trust the signs with arrows on the wall that told them what to do and where to go next. Soldiers moved in and out of the room on their errands, occasionally pausing to bellow, "QUI-YUTTTTTTT!" They did not move as briskly as their colleagues outdoors, but with enough authority to inspire awe in the inductees, who watched them with open curiosity and newfound vested interest.

A soldier instructed Paul to join one of the lines. He took his place behind a short, overweight man with milk-white skin, dark hair, fat jaws and thick-lensed spectacles.

"I have an uncle who is a captain," he was saying pontifically to the man who preceded him in the line. "He told me personally that the Army needs officers with my qualifications—accounting and financial background—and I'll admit that I've not done badly in that field. I think I will be able to pass the tests to qualify me for a commission easily enough."

He rocked back and forth on his heels and peered smugly at the little man, his audience, who stared at him with envy. He, too, was bespectacled and milky skinned, but he was thin, emaciated, withdrawn and apparently too nervous to talk except to respond with an occasional awe-stricken "Gee!"

Two men had joined the line behind Paul.

"I got glaucoma in both eyes and a heart murmur."

"Then how come you're not 4-F?"

"That's what I'd like to know! Some quack doctor out in Druid Hills said I was 1-A!"

"Why didn't you appeal?"

"I *did*, and the board agreed with the doctor!"

"Why don't you write your Congressman?"

"*Write* him? I called him on long distance, but some fathead said he wasn't available. I just hope my health holds up—"

Across the way in a parallel line, one inductee was more jubilant than most. "Boy! This draft thing played right into my hands!" he exclaimed. "I been trying to figure out how to get rid of my wife, and the draft board comes along and gets rid of *me!* How's that for luck?"

Directly behind him a grouchy man made no attempt to hide his displeasure at the draft board's whimsical choices of inductees.

"They promised me my number wouldn't come up for maybe a year," he griped. "I don't belong in the Army, anyway."

"Ah do," said his neighbor, a sleepy-eyed, indifferent sort. "It's a family tradition. The Hawleys all fawt in the Civil Wah right heah in Atlanta."

A well-tailored man, brisk with authority and brandishing a beautifully tooled leather briefcase, ignored the line, went directly to a desk, was turned back, and to the room at large posed the question of where he might go to telephone his office. Those standing near him laughed loudly. "Whatcha gonna tell them—that you won't be back in the office this afternoon?" they hooted.

Paul watched a tall, slender, fluttery young man turn away from a desk. Delicately he touched his brow with long white fingers and looked as though he might faint.

Then Paul found himself standing before a desk looking down on a small, lean, wiry sergeant with skin that had been weathered by the sun and wind and cured to the consistency of tough rawhide. His sandy hair was thin and cropped so closely that he appeared to be bald. He extended a clawlike hand with tattooed knuckles for Paul's papers. Without speaking, he read the induction order far longer than its content would seem to warrant.

"Where you from, Holly?" he asked. His voice was hard and scratchy.

"Bentley."

"Where's that—Ohio?"

"It's about forty-five miles from here. Between here and Augusta."

The sergeant groaned. "This ain't true. I *know* it ain't true. Another Georgia Cracker!" He put his elbows on the desk, leaned his head into his hands and covered his face. "I thought we'd already signed up every Cracker in Atlanta this week. They been swarming in here like flies ever since them Jap slanty-eyed snakes shot up Pearl Harbor. Looks like some of you could of joined the Navy."

He opened a drawer in the desk, counted out some papers and shoved them across the desk. "Set down at one of them tables over there and fill out these forms. Print—don't write. And don't leave no blanks."

"Yes, sir," Paul replied, gathering up the papers.

"You don't have to call me *sir*," the sergeant snapped. "Don't nobody get called *sir* in the Army unless they're commissioned officers. I'm a *non*commissioned officer. Now I wanna give you some advice."

"Yes, sir?"

"Keep your head up and eyes open, or you'll get your head blown off," the sergeant said, waving him away.

On Saturday afternoon Paul was self-conscious in his Class A olive drab uniform. It was glossy with newness and stiff with unfamiliarity. Even on the Company street, where every man in view was dressed exactly as he was down to, and including, underwear and shoelaces, he felt conspicuous.

His blouse with the high lapels and four brass buttons down the front—all fastened and gleaming—encased him like a bandage. His high-topped G.I. shoes were as bulky as the box they came in. He had not yet discovered a comfortable angle to wear the ridiculous little OD cap that, judged by the evidence all about him, could be stretched into an infinite number of sizes and highly original configurations. The drill corporal had told them to "put 'em on and forget 'em," which a number of the men seemed to have done. Yet Private Paul H. Holly, U.S.A., 38062848, was at least three paces out in front of a tremendous majority of the bewildered, fumbling soldiers of Company D, 3rd Recruiting and Processing Battalion, Fort McPherson, Georgia. Through an oversight, perhaps negligence or a breakdown in the Quartermaster Corps clothing issue procedures, his uniform fitted him perfectly.

"Hey, Holly! You going into town?"

"As fast as I can get a ride," Paul replied.

He glanced over his shoulder and quickened his step. It was the big, friendly oaf from the swamps down in the turpentine country who slept in the next bunk with dog tags that clanked like chains in the night and woke up half the barracks each time he turned over or let out a hurricane-sized breath. He overtook Paul with ease.

"You want any company?"

Paul looked dubiously at the big man. He was built like a horse. His uniform covered him like a squad tent. "You mean you?" he asked.

"I ain't never been to Atlanta," he said. "My daddy tole me to be sure and look at the Capitol and Grant Park and mail him a picture. I don't know where they're at."

"Well, you see, Jabers, I'm supposed to meet somebody downtown. You know how these things go."

They stopped at the gate and showed their passes to a belligerent Military Policeman, who seemed convinced they were forgeries.

"My friend here, Private Dazel Lee Jabers, needs some directions," Paul said. "Maybe you can help him. Being a stranger here myself, I don't know east from west."

He hurried through the gate, leaving Private Jabers talking to the Military Policeman, who was too awed by his size not to listen. On Lee Street outside, Paul joined a line of soldiers along the curb to wait for some generous motorist to pick him up. While he waited, three city buses went by, all marked and headed for downtown Atlanta. Their passengers looked through the windows at him and his freeloading associates with sympathy, approval and fond admiration.

Paul stood on the corner at Five Points, breathing deeply and with satisfaction. He was exhilarated. He had been coming to Atlanta all his life, each time in total anonymity among the thousands of city residents and tourists on the streets. Now he had an identity. In the midst of the swirl of shoppers, sightseers and pleasure seekers in that busiest section of downtown Atlanta, he was set apart from them in a specific category, identifiable on sight. By no stretch of his ego could he consider it a rare or exclusive category, but it gave him a visible justification for being. He squared his shoulders and straightened his blouse to line up the row of brass buttons with his necktie. His uniform became gently comfortable and lost much of its strangeness.

He went to a telephone booth and called his parents. His mother was uptown shopping, and he talked to his father.

"We'll probably be reassigned next week," he told him. "Fort Mac is only a processing center. They promised us we'd be able to get in touch with our families before we get shipped out. Tell Perry we didn't know until after inspection today that we could get off the post tonight, or I would have fixed it for him to come see me. I sure would like for him to see me in my uniform."

"No more than he'd like to see you," his father said. "We're real proud of you, Son. What do you think about the Army by now? Do you like it?"

"You know, Dad, a peculiar thing happened to me. The minute I walked through the Main Gate Thursday I liked the Army. It was automatic. They've been running our legs off from before daylight until after dark. I've got a GI haircut, and my arm's sore from shots for everything but chapped lips. These sergeants chew on us all the time for breathing and being alive. They must have invented cussing right here at Fort Mac. Some of these Old Army men are downright eloquent when they start turning the air blue with cuss words. I'm going on KP duty tomorrow. That's a sixteen-hour detail with no letups. But don't feel sorry for me. I only wish I had discovered the Army earlier. I think I've found a home."

# 11

A NEVER-ENDING SUCCESSION of rumors blew through Company D like a capricious wind, unpredictable but always blowing. The men quickly accepted them as a built-in feature of military life, as inevitable as the bull roar of the sergeants and the leather lungs of the drill corporals. Some rumors were persistent and others were one-time affairs with brief life spans. One particular rumor was repeated so often in so many places its sources became unimpeachable and its contents indisputable: one-half the Company would be assigned to Fort Devens, Massachusetts, and the other to Fort Ord, California.

In its ignorance of Company D's plans for the war, however, the Army assigned the entire company, plus two men whose names appeared on the roster by mistake, to Fort Knox, Kentucky. The men would be granted no furloughs prior to their departure on December 23. Time was too short, and none of them had been in the Army long enough to earn one. Off-post passes were a tiny, remote possibility, but it was an outside chance that the men immediately ripened into a sure thing.

"I don't see why they can't let him come home for just a few hours before he goes," Mamie said. "It's not very far, and he can get back to the Post in an hour or so if they need him."

Alexander tried to console her with a broader and more practical view. "The Army can't make one set of rules for the boys who live forty-five miles away and another for the boys who live four hundred," he said.

"I know you're right, but just two days before Christmas! You would think the Army could wait for just two more—" She stopped and threw up her hands. "There I go being a silly mother, and I promised myself not to be."

"Maybe we can do the next best thing," Alex said. "Why don't you call Ferebe and Ellison and see about all of us getting together at their house before Paul leaves? Maybe he can get off for a few hours at least."

Mamie thought that was a grand idea and by the following morning had arranged it with everybody but Paul. He could not actually promise to be present for a family gathering the evening before his shipping date, but he offered some encouragement.

"Paul? If they won't let you off the Post, will they let us come see you?" his mother inquired anxiously. "We've just got to see you before you go."

"Oh, sure. There won't be any problem," he said. "Lots of guys' families come see them. They take them to the Company Day Room or to the Battalion Recreation Hall or to the PX restaurant—lots of places. Let me know when, and I'll meet you at the Main Gate and sign you in."

"Do you mean we could have been coming to see you all this time?"

"It's only been a week, Mother."

"Is that all? It seems so much longer—but all this is so strange to me."

"Is Perry coming?"

"Certainly Perry's coming! He's dying to see you in your uniform. And so are we. We can't picture you in one of those caps and all that brass trimming. Are you getting enough to eat, darling? Some of the boys I see look so thin."

On the theory that it is easier to cancel plans than to make them at the last minute, Mamie set to work. Christmas would be three days early for the Holly family this year, Christmas tree, Christmas gifts, Christmas dinner and all.

"We've already put up our Christmas tree," she told Ferebe. "Your daddy and Perry went down to The Well and picked it out a few days ago. The Kiwanis Club was selling them like they always do. Perry decorated it, and it's one of the prettiest we've ever had. But, you know, we can't find that tinsel angel Susie made back in grammar school. We've turned this house upside down. I do hope it didn't get thrown away with the wrappings last year. Anyway, we'll take all the presents from under our tree and bring them to your house and put them under your tree—if I ever get them wrapped, that is. You can hide Maggie's and Ellie's until Christmas morning if you want to. Tell Ellison to arrange to get home early that day."

"He'll do his best," Ferebe said. "But he doesn't work on an assembly line that stops at a certain hour each day, you know. Research labs don't work that way. I'm convinced that nobody in the lab owns a watch. They don't know day from night. Don't worry about it."

"I won't," Mamie said. She laughed. "Of course, you know that's not true. I'll probably worry everybody to death before we get through. But I want things to be just right for Paul's last evening with the family."

"You make it sound too final, Mother."

"Oh. I didn't mean to sound like that. Now, I'll bake the turkey here and bring it with me. Clay Tinsley had some pretty ones this year. I'll make the corn-bread dressing and cook it in your oven when we get there. Can you think of anything else? Would you like for me to bring a fruitcake? I made two this year, but my heart wasn't in the job. It seemed so trivial with the whole country upset by the war and worrying about what's going to happen to all the boys. But goodness! I already had the ingredients on hand, and I couldn't let them go to waste."

Susie was reluctant to promise that she would ask for the afternoon off.

"You must try, Susie," her mother insisted. "Just tell Mr. Kirkland that your brother is in the Army and is being transferred to Kentucky and we don't know where he'll go after that or when we'll see him again. He'll understand. Your daddy and Perry are going to take the afternoon off."

"*My* daddy? Alexander James Holly is taking a whole afternoon off?" She was delighted. "I can't believe it! Who's going to make sure all the trains get through Bentley while he's gone?"

"Josh Bullock, I guess. Or he might make all the trains wait until he gets back."

"Mother, I know I'll cry," Susie said. "I know I will, seeing Paul in his Army uniform and thinking about him going off on a troop train to the war and all. I don't see how I can possibly tell him good-bye. I'll cry all over the place."

"What's wrong with that?" Mamie said. "I'm planning on crying, too. Susie, haven't you seen Paul at all this past week?"

"No. I called out to the Post one night and left my number for him to call me. He called the next day. I was hoping he would ask me to come out there, but he didn't."

"He's probably been too busy to have company," Mamie said.

Ferebe Holly Hampton was staggered by the number of cardboard boxes, handbags and happily wrapped Christmas presents carried by her parents and brother when they got off the train.

"You look like you're moving!" she exclaimed during the greetings.

"Isn't it awful?" Mamie said happily. "I was afraid we'd crush the bows if we put the Christmas presents in a box, so we decided to carry them like they are. Where are the children?"

"They're at home with Susie. She came out right after lunch." She pointed to a cardboard box tied with stout cord that Perry carried in his arms. It was the largest package on the lot. "What's that?" she asked.

"That's the turkey," said her father. "And it's a first-class packing job, too. I did it myself. You could smell it all over the train. One man came down the aisle and said our coach smelled like the dining car."

Perry stood by and looked on with amusement.

"Whew! I guess we did look like a bunch of Gypsies getting off that train," Mamie said, settling into the back seat of Ferebe's car with Perry. "Now, what have you heard from Paul? I held my breath every time the phone rang this morning. I was scared to death it would be him saying he couldn't get off."

Ferebe turned on the ignition and started the engine. "He can't come," she said, maneuvering the car out into the traffic. "He called awhile ago and said their schedule's been changed to this afternoon. He tried to call you, but you must have already left the house."

Mamie gasped. "Do you mean he's leaving *today*?"

"He was ordered to report with all his equipment ready for shipment at five o'clock."

"Can't we see him before he leaves?" Mamie asked, scarcely breathing.

Alex took his watch from his pocket and glanced at it. "It's two twenty-four now," he said. "Maybe we can still make it. How far is it?"

"It wouldn't do any good," Ferebe replied. "Paul said they couldn't have visitors after they were put on alert."

"Maybe we could just drive out to the siding where they're loading the train," Alex suggested, not ready to give up. "Maybe we could at least see the train and watch it leave."

"We can't, Daddy. The trains load and unload inside

the Post. They won't let us in the gate without Paul to sign us in."

"Oh." Alex leaned back in his seat. "I was hoping we might . . ."

Mamie was horrified. "But we've got to see him, Ferebe," she said. "He can't go off like this without our seeing him."

"It looks like he can," Ferebe said.

"But why? He told me it was tomorrow. Why would they change it?" Mamie said.

"Who knows? The Army works in mysterious ways. There's a family in our neighborhood whose son was at Fort Mac, and he didn't even get to call and tell them he was leaving. The first they knew about it was when they got a postcard written somewhere between here and Michigan—or maybe it was Minnesota."

"It's not fair for the Army to tell the boys one thing, then do another!" Mamie went on.

Ferebe shrugged. "You know what they say—all's fair in love and war."

"Ferebe Holly!" Mamie was shocked and indignant. "How can you be so flippant about a thing as serious as this?"

"I'm not being flippant, Mother," she replied. She shifted gears into neutral and coasted to a stop at a traffic light. "After all, Paul's only going to Kentucky. That's not exactly the other side of the world. You're acting like you'll never see him again."

"You ought not to talk to your mother like that," Alex said, an edge coming into his voice. "She's upset, naturally—and so am I, if you want to know the truth."

Mamie began to cry. After a moment she took her handkerchief from her purse and blew her nose. She raised her head to see Perry watching her, his eyes troubled and questioning.

"Perry!" she cried aloud. She reached across the seat

and squeezed his arm. "You don't even know what we're talking about," she said gently and with remorse. "We didn't mean to ignore you, darling. We'd never do such a thing. You know we wouldn't."

He was studying her lips. He shrugged helplessly.

Quickly she translated her words into signs, then tried to explain the cause of their concern. She did not know the sign for Kentucky, nor was she fluent enough to explain the uncertainty connected with Paul's unexpected departure. The Army, the war, the upheaval—all those things had struck them individually and for the first time. They generated a shock and anxiety that she was not equipped to transmit.

"Help me, Alex," she pleaded. "I can't make him understand."

Alex partially turned in his front seat and tried. Perry was forced to watch him from an oblique angle, and he could not make out what his father was saying.

"I can't turn around far enough in the seat to tell him," Alex said. "Can't you tell him the Army sent Paul away sooner than we had expected?"

"I did, but that's not the whole message. He still doesn't understand the significance."

Alex turned again and got Perry's attention. "I'll write it down for you at Ferebe's house, Son," he said with his hands.

Perry watched him, then turned to his mother, puzzled. Mamie repeated Alex's signs.

"Won't we see Paul today at all?" he asked.

She shook her head.

"When will we see him?"

"Maybe he'll get a furlough when he finishes his training at Fort Knox. If he can't come home, we'll go see him wherever he is. So don't you worry about it."

"I wanted to see him in his uniform."

"All of us did. But war changes everything. Paul belongs to the Army now. He has to do what they say and when. We have to fit ourselves into the Army's plans, not vice versa. We're just as disappointed as you are, but we'll only make things worse if we don't accept that and do the next best thing."

"I should have come in to see him," Perry said. "If I had known this would happen, I could have come to Atlanta anytime. It's all my own fault."

"No, it isn't, darling," Mamie said. "Paul wanted to see you as badly as you wanted to see him. He thought it would work out just as you did, but it didn't. We mustn't blame anybody. We've all got to be ready for the unexpected. Ferebe told your daddy a minute ago that Louisville is not on the other side of the world, and she's right. All of us will see Paul. Don't be too upset."

"This might not have been the Army's doings at all," Alex was saying to Ferebe. "This could be a railroad routing problem. There might be priority shipments somewhere along the line that need the right-of-way. Or the rolling stock might be committed to other places, and so on. It happens all the time. The Army might not have had anything to do with it at all."

Mamie repeated that to Perry. He watched her intently, then turned and looked out the window. He asked no further questions.

Susie met them at the door with Ellie in her arms and Maggie at her feet. She was weeping.

"I promised you I'd cry," she said after straightening her makeup.

"But you didn't promise you'd cry all afternoon," Ferebe said, hurrying from the room to see why Ellie was screaming elsewhere in the house.

Later, Perry was entertaining Maggie in the living room with his signs. She thought it was a game, and for her benefit he turned it into one. Alex was wandering in and out of the house and into the back yard trying to figure out what to do with himself.

"I'm going to look for another job," Susie said when she and her mother were alone in the kitchen.

Mamie turned on the oven and set the temperature gauge. "What kind of job?" she asked.

"Oh, I don't know. Some kind of war work. With Paul in the Army now, I think I ought to do something too."

"Even in a war people still have to wear socks and stockings, don't they? Somebody's got to sell them."

"Maybe so, but it doesn't have to be me. Mr. Kirkland says we're headed for a silk shortage, and when that happens I'll be out of a job, anyway."

"What kind of war work would you do?" Mamie asked, her interest deepening.

"Lots of things," Susie said. "Girls are replacing men in war plants, working on assembly lines and doing mechanical things. Some of them even drive trucks."

"Susie, you can't do anything like that. It's not your kind of work, darling."

"I could learn it. That's what the rest of them do."

"Well, bless your heart. I think it's wonderful that you want to do it, but surely there must be war jobs more suited to your abilities and temperament. You're not the type for manual work. It just doesn't fit you or your natural interests. You're certainly not mechanical in the least, and there's no reason why you should be. Couldn't you get a secretarial or clerical job in the office of a war plant, say?"

"Probably at Fort Mac or the Naval Training Station. They're advertising for people. I'd be working directly with the soldiers or sailors, and that's more of a war job than I've got now."

"I don't suppose it would do any harm to look around," Mamie said. "But be careful what you pick." She put the pan of corn-bread dressing into the oven and turned back to her daughter. "Don't let me forget the time," she said, glancing at the clock above the refrigerator. "Nothing's worse than dressing cooked as dry as a bone.

**111**

Now, tell me what you've been doing. With so much going on, I seem to have lost track of everybody."

"I'm taking a First Aid course at the Red Cross. When I finish, I'm going into the instructors course."

"That's marvelous, darling. You'll be a grand instructor. I *know* you will. Abbie Reynolds is talking about starting up a First Aid course, and they're asking for volunteer workers in the county offices in Monroe. I'll probably start doing something like that. Where have you been going and who have you been going with? Have you been dating anybody?"

"You know I haven't."

"Why would I know it?"

"I never have, except on extraspecial occasions," Susie said. "Why would it be different now?"

"But here in Atlanta you must have had lots of opportunities to meet young men."

"I don't, and that's just it," she said. "That's one reason I want another job. At work I see Mr. Kirkland, Emily Lanier and those two gripy old maids who haven't smiled in years. That's all. So I don't get a chance to meet anyone or have a date. And with all the boys off in the service, things will get worse—unless I go to work at Fort Mac or the Naval Station. That's where the boys are."

"Susie!"

"Don't be so shocked," she said with a smile. "How else can I meet them? I wasn't exactly surrounded by boys at the Georgia State College for Women, and Bentley wasn't crowded with boys who paid any attention to me."

"Now, Susie, you went to lots of nice things in college and in Bentley, too. I remember how pretty you looked in that pink chiffon I made for your senior dance. There were lots of things like that."

"Not lots, Mother. *Some.* I went to special things, but I never had dates where boys took me riding in a car or swimming or to the picture show in Monroe—just the two of us. None of them hung around on the front porch or followed me home from school. I certainly never had a steady boyfriend. I'm twenty-four years old, and I want to meet some boys. So if they're not available where I am, why not go to Fort Mac or the Naval Training Station where they are?"

"Susie Holly, you'd better not let your daddy hear you talk like that! It sounds so—so common. It's not the way for young ladies to talk—or to act. You've been raised to know better."

"Yes, I have," Susie replied. "I must always be a lady, and that's what I've always tried to do. But when you're as fat as I am, that doesn't get you very far."

"Susan Meade Holly, you are *not* fat," Mamie said with firmness. "I don't want to ever hear you say that again."

"Then what am I—skinny?"

"Suppose you are a few pounds overweight? I've had that problem all my life."

"But in your case it wasn't so important."

"And why not, pray tell? Do you think I enjoyed it?"

"Being Margaret Meade Harrison of the Madison Harrisons probably helped you endure it."

"What's that got to do with it? You're a Harrison, too."

"But I don't have a houseful of colored people to wait on me, closets full of dresses, coming out parties in Macon and Atlanta and a mile-long veranda full of eligible young men to choose from."

"Susie, what on earth are you talking about? I was twenty-six years old when I married your daddy. Does that sound like I was rushed off my feet? I bought so many bridesmaids' dresses your Granddaddy Harrison used to say he was afraid he wouldn't have any money left to buy me a wedding dress if I ever needed one."

"You never lacked for boyfriends."

"I always lacked the right one until your daddy came along, and he had no connection with Madison and that mile-long veranda, as you call it. You'll meet the right man, darling. Everybody does. Ferebe did."

"Ferebe? Why wouldn't she?" Susie was beginning to sound bitter. "Homecoming Queen and what-all at the University. Brown hair, blue eyes. That figure. After two children, she can wear a cotton sack and look like Ann Sheridan."

"You're a lovely, charming young lady," Mamie said gently. "You're gracious and genteel. People love you. All those things are important."

Susie's temper flared. "Mother, why must you always try to make things look so rosy?" she snapped. "Did it ever occur to you that there just might be a situation every now and then that's not as peachy-keen as you paint it?"

"Susie? What's got into you? I was simply telling you that you're—"

"Why can't I gripe *just one time* without you trying to smooth it out and explain it all away?" she asked angrily. "Why don't you try griping, too, sometimes? It might do you good!"

She turned and ran from the room.

Ellison called around five thirty to say he would not be home until late. He did not know how late. Ferebe was incensed.

"Ell, you know you can make arrangements to come home on time if you'd only do it," she said. "I don't know what the problem is this time, but it's always something. I don't think you're being cooperative."

"It goes like this," he said wearily. "When you work under a Government contract, you've got to make Progress Reports to the Government whether you've got anything to report or not. For some reason known only to God and the United States Government, this report has to be in the mail tonight before we leave this place. Otherwise, we'll

114

lose the war and live under a totalitarian regime for the rest of our lives."

"You must have known about the report before today," she argued. "If it's due today, why didn't you plan for it and not wait until the last minute?"

"You don't understand, honey," he said. "We haven't had time to do anything about it until today."

"Apparently you don't have time today, either—not if you have to stay until midnight to do it."

He sighed. "One of these days I'm going to figure out how much the life of a project is lengthened by all these interruptions to make reports. And the absurdity of it is that, regardless of what the report says, nobody in Washington can do a blessed thing about it except perhaps cancel the contract. And they won't do that, because they don't want Georgia Congressmen and Senators climbing all over them."

"Can't someone else do the report? You're not the typist down there. Or are you?"

"You don't need to get cute about it," he replied. "No, I'm not the typist. But it takes other people to provide the input. Anyway, Ferebe, stop trying to figure out how Globe Research, Incorporated, should run its business. You don't know the first thing about it."

"It's not fair, Ell, and you know as well as I do that this could have been avoided. Mother, Daddy, Perry, Susie —all of us have everything planned. Maggie's got on her green sateen dress and Ellie looks darling in his little blue suit your mother sent him. It looks like a party, and I just don't know how you can't come home for it."

"I've been trying to explain why. Has Paul come yet?"

"He's not coming. He shipped out this afternoon. That's already cast a shadow over things, and now you do this. It seems you could make an exception to your precious routine—if you have one—just once in your life. But aside from this special occasion, you've got two children who are getting accustomed to going to bed every night without seeing their father, and that's bad. I don't know how Globe runs its business, but I think I could organize the work load better than whoever does it down there. No wonder the Government wants reports from you. They're afraid you won't get the work done at all."

"Listen, honey," he said. "Just get off your high horse long enough to see my side of what's happening. It is my job, you know."

"And this is your home, too!" she snapped and slammed down the receiver.

She stormed into the kitchen, where her mother was seated at the breakfast table staring out the window into the driveway.

"Let's get it on the table and eat it!" Ferebe commanded shortly.

Mamie looked around in surprise and quick alarm. "What on earth?"

"Oh, it's Ell and that job of his. He's not coming." Her blue eyes were bright with anger. "Where's Daddy?" she asked between clenched teeth. "Somebody's got to carve this turkey—unless we'd all rather pull it apart, and I could do just that with no qualms."

"I'm so sorry about Ellison," Mamie said. "I'm sure it's not his fault. But Ferebe! Calm down! I think your daddy's out in the back yard." She shook her head and sighed ruefully. "Paul gets shipped away before we can see him, and Ellison's not coming home for dinner. Then Susie's off somewhere sulking at me. Now you come raging in here like a lion. Even if I'm able to eat, I don't know if I'll enjoy it—not with you girls acting like this."

"Well, go see if you can make Perry mad at somebody, and we'll make a clean sweep of it!" Ferebe said. She went to the back door and flung it open. "Daddy!" she shouted without searching for him. "Will you come in and carve this stupid turkey?"

116

# 12

MAMIE HOLLY HUNG up the telephone. Alex was listening to the twelve o'clock newscast, while waiting for her to put dinner on the table.

"I'd like to have a quarter for every time Pet Wilkerson has asked me to pour at one of her teas, then never gets around to having the tea," Mamie complained wearily. "She's always going to use her grandmother's old bone china she got in England when she was a bride or the Wilkerson family silver that was handmade in Salem back in the year One. Why, nobody's set foot inside Pet Wilkerson's house since her mother died thirty-five years ago."

"What's the occasion for this one?" Alex asked idly.

"What do you think? The DAR as usual, and if it wasn't that, it would be the UDC. She was carrying on something awful about how she and Mollie Satterfield were the only members present at the last chapter meeting. Mollie had prepared a paper on the architecture of Faneuil Hall in Boston, but there was no one to read it to, because Pet had helped her write it. She thinks I owe it to all the Meades and the Harrisons and to my children to be active in the chapter again. I know Mama would turn over in her grave twice if she knew how I had neglected both the DAR and the UDC all these years. And I didn't really intend for it to happen that way, but I guess raising four children crowded it out of my mind. I can't honestly say I've missed any of it."

"It might not be a bad idea to get your hand in again," Alex said. "You can't deny that you enjoy historical places and things."

"How can I get my mind on the DAR and the UDC *now* with this dreadful war and all? They seem so unimportant! Pet went on and on about how the war is all the more reason the ladies should stand together in a show of strength for our principles and to emphasize the patriotic values on which the DAR was founded."

Alex turned off the radio. "You know, Mamie, Pet might not be as goofy as she looks and sounds," he said. "I know how the DAR and the UDC run around acting like silly old ladies—which is what a lot of them are—but those patriotic values she was talking about can't be sneezed at. That's what this war is all about, isn't it? All of us might be better off talking about them sometimes instead of keeping them to ourselves. I feel and think lots of things I can't put into words. But maybe if I was around people who talk about them, I'd loosen up and start talking about them myself."

"Maybe so," Mamie said. She had lost interest in the topic.

"And Pet might be right about the children, too," Alex went on. "They might be interested in such things if you were interested yourself." He stopped and laughed. "Isn't this the limit?" he said. "*You're* the one with the ancestors. I don't know who any of mine are except Papa's Aunt Pinky, who lived four miles south of Gainesville—or was it north?—and the only things I remember about her are that she had big feet and dipped snuff."

"I wouldn't care if you didn't know your own name. You couldn't be a better ancestor for our children if your family tree filled up the genealogy files at the Georgia Historical Society. Move back so I can set the table."

"Has Perry finished packing?" Alex asked.

"I told him to stop until I come upstairs and check his clothes. His face has been sparkling like a Christmas tree ever since he came home from Louisville last week. Those three days with Paul plus quitting his job at the cotton mill have him so excited he can't stand still. He's been right on my heels following me around the house and talking my arm off. I can't get a thing done. He asks me questions when my hands are in the dishwater or when I've got my arms full of something and I can't say a word." She smiled happily. "Even though I wish he could stay at home, I'm so thrilled for him I don't know what to do!"

"Are you sure you don't want to go with us?"

"You'll both do better without me. I'd find all kinds of little things to worry about and drive you both crazy. And it'll take up too much of your time to deliver me to Ferebe's and pick me up. Besides, I promised Bessie Melton I would help her gather the names of Bentley's servicemen for an Honor Roll to be hung on The Well. After we do that, we've got to find somebody to design it and paint it. We don't know how much money to ask the Town Council for. Minnie Varner's on the committee, too, but you can't count on her. She does things in her own sweet time and when the spirits move her."

Alex drove Perry to Atlanta the following day. At the headquarters of the Georgia Association for the Deaf he registered with the job placement division. From a list of organizations that employed handicapped people, Perry selected the Federal Civil Service as the best prospect for a war job, which was the only kind he would consider. Alex helped him complete the laborious, detailed application forms. The Association referred him to the home of a couple named Maxwell, who rented rooms and served meals to deaf people only. They had raised a deaf son and were fluent in sign language. They introduced him to a young man who lived there. The others were away at work. Immediately Perry liked the Maxwells, the atmosphere of the house, and the room they offered him. He took the room and moved in.

Alex helped him with his trunk and bags, then sat down to talk before he drove away and left him.

"Mr. or Mrs. Maxwell will call the Association and give them your address and phone number," he said. "If the Government doesn't have a place for you, the Association will help you find another. Don't get too impatient. It takes a lot of red tape. While you're waiting, and as soon as you get your feet on the ground, go back down there and put in some applications at other places. Are you sure you've got enough money—cash—to make out?"

Perry nodded.

"Leave your account in Bentley until you get settled here and find a local bank you like. Then ask Reeves Buckley to transfer your account. It'll make check cashing easier for you. If you run into any kind of trouble about money—any kind of trouble at all—be sure and let me know. You've never tried to cash checks in strange places before."

He got up to leave, but he did not go. "You know how to get in touch with Ferebe and Susie. Let them know where you are, and try to see them as much as you can." He looked about the room. "Did we forget anything?"

"No, sir. Everything's here. If it's not, I can get it later."

Alex started for the door and turned back. "Are you sure you'll be all right, Son?" he asked.

"I'm all right, Dad," Perry replied, smiling. "Don't worry about me."

"I'm not worried exactly. But we never left you anywhere before except at Cave Springs, and that was different. You're on your own this time."

"I'll still be all right."

"Your mother and I are real glad you want to get into

some kind of war work. We're as proud of you as we are of Paul for being in the Army." He looked toward the door again. "I intended to call Ferebe and Susie and at least say hello, but it's getting too late now, and I don't like to drive on the highway after dark. We didn't have any spare time, did we?"

"It's been a busy day, all right. I appreciate your helping me out like this. You made it easier for me."

"That's what I wanted to do." He walked to the door. "Well—I guess I'd better be getting on home," he said with reluctance. "The Maxwells sure seem like nice people, don't they?" He studied the room. "This is a nice room, too. With those three windows you'll get good cross ventilation when the weather gets hot."

Outside, Perry leaned through the open window of the car and extended his hand. Alex grasped it, then released it to say a final word.

"We know how hard it is for you to write, so we won't be expecting a lot of letters," he said. "We'll be in touch through Ferebe and Susie. But sometimes when you're not real busy we would like to hear from you. And come home as often as you can."

He put the car in gear, then released the steering wheel.

"If it doesn't work out for you, Son, you can always come back home. Don't ever forget that."

Perry patted his father on the shoulder, backed away from the car and waved him out of sight.

# 13

BENTLEY RAN OUT of young men sooner than anyone had predicted. It was generally recognized that a war takes whatever it needs from a nation, and the people were prepared to give what it needed at whatever the costs. In Bentley, however, they were stunned by the swiftness with which they gave their youth. By the end of March they were gone. It was as though someone had lined them up at The Well on Chiles Street and marched them out of town.

In the first few days of the war their rush to sign up in the Army, Navy, Marines and Coast Guard had amounted to an exodus, but the outward flow slacked soon after and became a trickle of one here, another there until no one was left to go. Even when a draft call had swooped them up and whisked them away in appreciable numbers, the gaps they left behind were individual. Their departures had been single events to be suffered or cheered, opposed or encouraged by their own families, friends and employers. Not until the migration had been completed and the town drained of all single men between their late teens and mid-twenties did the people come to view it as a whole. Their most precious resource, the one they had known must be tapped first, had been depleted.

Not all the young men donned uniforms. Some had

122

physical impediments or continuing ailments that made them unacceptable to the armed services, and they were rejected. From down on 'Struction Street and Tin Can Alley a few Negroes were turned away because they could neither read the instructions handed them at the recruiting centers nor write in the blank spaces of the bewildering forms they were told to complete. But they did not come back. They stayed away to find new jobs in new places, so in a sense the war had taken them too.

The youth shortage made itself felt immediately at Clay Tinsley's Grocery & Meat Market on the corner of Madison Road and Chiles Street. Horace Epps, aged twenty-five, had worked in the store for six years. On the day war was declared, he came to work as usual, opened up the store and made it ready for business. He moved the crates of milk and butter in from the alley, sorted out the fresh vegetables and arranged them in their stalls, took the money from the safe in the rear and counted it into the cash register at the checkout counter, swept the sidewalk out front, filled a few gaps in the shelves, turned on the overhead lights and unlocked the front door, ready for the day's customers. He worked alongside Mr. Tinsley until after one o'clock. Then he told him good-bye and boarded an afternoon bus for Atlanta to enlist in the Army, Navy or Coast Guard. He was not sure which it would be. Clay was left to run the store alone. Horace's departure had been abrupt, but so had the attack on Pearl Harbor.

Clay could find no replacement for Horace, and neither could he do some of the work Horace had always done. He could not do the lifting required to move the heavy sacks of flour and weighty cartons of canned goods from the stockroom to the shelves at the front of the store. He was sixty-five years old, had suffered three heart attacks, and had developed a spinal disorder that became agonizing if his back was subjected to undue strain.

"If I just had somebody to lift some of those heavier

cartons down from the stacks onto the floor where I could get under them with that pair of trucks, I could roll them up front and stock the shelves easy enough," he said. "Horace used to take care of the stockroom, and I never had to worry about it before."

Within the first two or three days after Horace's departure, Clay's shelves were yawning with empty spaces, and he was forced to open the cartons in the stockroom and leave them there. When a customer wanted a jar of peanut butter or a bottle of vinegar, he either sent him back in the stockroom to rummage around and find it or, if he could spare the time, went for it himself. When the carton lost enough weight for him to lift at no great risk, he took it up front and stocked the shelves with what remained. He hated to do business that way, and he was embarrassed. His customers deserved—and had earned—better treatment from him.

"I wish I could close up the store and go home," he told Alva Thomas, lifelong friend and proprietor of Thomas Mercantile Company next door. "Sometimes I get so tired I can't hardly move. And I get all mixed up trying to do what I ought to do and can't. I'd like to go home and stay."

"Then why don't you just do it, Clay?" Alva asked. "If anybody in this town has got the right to take it easy, it's you. You've been right here on this corner for forty years. That's long enough. You ought to sell out and take it easy."

"Can't do it, Alva," Clay said. "Nobody wants to buy a grocery and market these days. If there was another one in town, I might just sell out my stock and close up. But I'm the only one in town except Hutch Sinclair out on the highway, and he doesn't carry a full line. People have to have something to eat. But I probably wouldn't do it anyway. With two boys in the service and a son-in-law getting ready to go in, I wouldn't feel right sitting at home doing nothing. I just couldn't do it."

His wife rearranged her home schedule so that she could help out a few hours each day and make certain Clay did not get into a rush and try the heavy work. In the course of her duties, assigned and assumed, she did make an overall improvement in her husband's business that she considered of major importance and long overdue. She chased Josh Bullock out of the store.

"You oughta be ashamed of yourself loafing around with the war going on and every place in town crying for help," she scolded him. "Why don't you get yourself a job? I don't see how you can watch Clay and me struggling with all those boxes and sacks while you loll around not turning a hand."

"You see, I'm not familiar with the stock, Mrs. Tinsley," he said lamely.

"Well, you ought to be!" she snapped. "You've been lazying around in this store looking at it long enough to know every label on every can and bottle in the place. Now you get out of here, and don't you come back unless it's to buy something, and even then you'd better make it short and sweet."

Clay was uneasy. He did not go so far as to claim an abiding friendship with Josh, but he had no reason to think of him as an enemy either. Besides, Josh did buy his groceries from the store. He wondered if his wife had not been too hard on him.

"Humph! You won't go bankrupt because of what Josh Bullock *doesn't* buy," she snorted. "If you never have any more than him to worry about, you won't have any worries to worry about at all."

Charlie Downs had never wanted for help at his Gulf Station on North Chiles Street. He could always find somebody to fill a gas tank, check the oil, wash the windshield and change a tire. And what if they did get restless or dissatisfied and wander off to another job? All Charlie had to do was wait for the next kid, white or colored, to happen along, then put him to work. When they stopped happening along, though, Charlie was forced to do the work himself. He made out with an unfortunate succession of high school boys, but they were not available until the middle of the afternoon when school turned out. Until then, he had to make out the best he could alone. He was hard put to attend to that and to his fuel oil business at the same time.

"I've never seen anything like it," he said one morning early in April. The Town Council had concluded its business, and its four members were lingering in the Town Meeting Hall upstairs over the City Hall and fire station. "I can't think of one single man between eighteen and twenty-six left around here except that Varner boy, who's been an invalid all his life."

"How about that Baxley boy west of town? He's still around," said Henry Carter. "At least I saw him Saturday. He was uptown with his daddy, and he had on civilian clothes."

"I said *men,* not a mama's boy sissy like him," Charlie exclaimed. "He was in the station one day, and I said, 'When's your draft number coming up, Virgil?' and he said, 'I've got a deferment because I've got to stay on the farm and feed the soldier boys.' " Charlie raised his voice into a mocking falsetto and made a fluttery motion with his hands.

The others laughed.

"Maybe we'll be stuck with Virgil around here for the rest of the war, but we're going to lose some others," John Reynolds said.

"Who've we got left to lose?" Sam Pickett asked.

"When the pinch really comes, the Selective Service will raise the age limit. In the meantime, some of these young kids will grow into draft age. We've got a long ways to go yet. The war's barely getting started. The United States hasn't even had a chance to fight yet except out in the Pacific. The Japs have been in Manila for almost three months, and there's not the least sign of getting them out. We can't leave them there. General MacArthur left and went down to Australia because he knows we're about to lose the rest of the Philippines. The Japs have spread out all over Asia, and they're going to stay spread out until somebody chases them back home. And that's just the Pacific. We haven't done anything on the ground in Europe yet. We've put some troops in Ireland, and they haven't fired a shot yet. We haven't even warmed up. So steel yourself for Bentley to send some more boys off to war."

Henry Carter got up and stretched. "You know, sometimes this U.S. Government doesn't make one grain of sense," he said. "Everybody's hard up for help these days, and how many Japanese-Americans do you suppose they interned out on the West Coast—a hundred thousand? Whatever the figure, look at all the able-bodied manpower not doing a thing but sitting on their tails in those internment camps. Lordy mercy! They locked up farmers, mechanics, doctors, laborers, lawyers, schoolteachers—"

"Just a minute, Henry," Sam said. "You seem to be forgetting they're all Japs."

"Every one of them was born right here in the United States."

"They're Japs just the same, slant eyes and all. We can't let them run around loose. When they started rounding them up, they found out that their truck farms were right up next to air bases and Army posts and defense plants where they could see everything going on. There's no telling how much military information they had been sending back to Tokyo. Would you hire one of them to work for you?"

"I might," Henry said. "It takes four families to run my place up at Good Hope, and I've just got two left. Only one of them can work, and three of their kids are too little. I'm not sure they'll be able to get all the tobacco planted

127

this year. Old Pinch and Aunt Cordy can't work any more. They're too old and feeble."

"Are they still alive?" Sam asked in wonder. "I thought they'd been dead a long time. How old are they? Ninety? Ninety-five?"

"Nobody knows—not even them." Henry put on his hat. "You know, they've lived on that place in that same house since before I was born, and to this good day I've never heard them say *my* house or *our* house. When they're talking to me, it's always *your* house. Before my daddy died, they said *your daddy's house*. All their lives they must have been living a day at a time, wondering if they might get thrown off the place any minute. I wonder how long you have to live somewhere to feel like it's your own."

"Well, what do you know about that? Your daddy would have got rid of you and your brothers and sisters before he would have thrown Old Pinch and Aunt Cordy off that farm."

"I know," Henry said. "I've been living around niggers all my life just like you have and Charlie and John and everybody else. They're as much a part of me as you are, and I still wonder what goes through those black, kinky heads sometimes." He turned to go. "I'll see you later, Sam," he said. "Let me know what Frank Masters says. I still think he's the man for the War Bond Drive. He's got so much money he doesn't have any patience with people who don't cough up as much as he thinks they should. Maybe we need somebody like that to shake them loose."

Sam Pickett sat at the table and watched the Councilmen leave. He sat in silence wondering about the war. Even while the killing was going on around the world and while three-fourths of Bentley was worrying about whether their own sons would get killed, somebody still had to be moving heavy boxes, pumping gas, planting tobacco and looking after people who were getting old. He gathered up his papers, stuck them into his pocket and went out the door.

Downstairs he stuck his head inside the door of the City Hall office.

"Where do you keep the broom, Vernon?" he asked. "I've got to sweep out."

Vernon Robinson, City Clerk, looked up from his desk. "Don't worry about it, Sam," he said. "I'll get it later."

"No. We're the ones who made the rule that everybody using the Town Meeting Hall has to clean it up afterwards, and we can't break our own rule."

# 14

To THE PEOPLE across the land the war was a seizure. They were possessed by it. It took over completely, the captor of their thoughts and ruler of their actions. They gave themselves up to the surge of their emotions and the stirring of patriotic fervor that guided their days and disturbed their nights. They wore their hearts on their sleeves. Any public assembly for whatever purpose—concert, play, ball game, movie, dance, worship service—was a patriotic rally, and none got under way until after the audience had stood on its feet and sung the national anthem. American flags wafted overhead on the facades of buildings, along the curbs and sidewalks. Schoolchildren recited the Pledge of Allegiance each morning before classes began. A formidable, gray-bearded, stern, red, white and blue old man pointed a long finger at them from Army and Navy recruiting posters everywhere reminding them "Uncle Sam Needs You!"

Service stars appeared in the front windows of people's homes. Whatever the content of radio programs, a moment or two was set aside in which to exhort their listeners to save, to sacrifice, to give, to help. They responded within the limits of their understanding and capabilities, with little or no analysis of what they did or why they did it. If it was for the war effort, it could be nothing but good. They collected scrap metal, tended their Victory gardens, staffed Civil Defense centers, taught First Aid classes, donated blood, organized war bond rallies, worked in hospitals, raised their own production quotas, fought absenteeism in war plants, served on volunteer committees, helped newcomers find places to live, washed dishes at the USO, rode to work in car pools, waited in line for whatever they purchased, practiced blackout and evacuation procedures, dimmed their lights to conserve energy, parked their automobiles and rode streetcars, improvised substitutes or did without the most ordinary taken-for-granted items when they disappeared from the shelves of their favorite shops and stores.

Everybody did something. In Bentley, as elsewhere, idleness was immoral and unpatriotic. Mamie Holly went to Monroe on Tuesdays, where she served as a Red Cross nurse's aide in the County Hospital. Several Bentley ladies did volunteer work for the county in the hospital, the Public Library, the Courthouse and on whatever board or committee needed an extra typist, file clerk or envelope stuffer. By coordinating schedules, they formed carpools on their days. Mamie took turns driving with Martha Buckley, Lucy Pickett and Ethel Robinson from across the street. Some of the wives worked in their husbands' businesses to help alleviate the manpower shortage. Olivia Coker taught a First Aid class. Bruce Hensley from the cotton mill formed the men of Bentley into a Civil Defense organization and trained them for fire fighting, emergency disaster procedures and enemy aircraft spotting. Alex Holly enrolled in that. Bessie Melton operated a Red Cross blood bank in Dr. Jesse Randolph's office, where she worked. Miss Mattie helped after school and on Saturdays. All of them served on one or two of the many committees for the township, the schools, their churches and clubs. It was everybody's job to be on the alert for an ill soldier or sailor in town, or a service wife with small children who was having difficulties at the depot or bus station.

Pet Wilkerson met the trains regularly with a thermos jug of coffee, iced tea or lemonade, which she served to soldiers, sailors and Marines who got off or who were waiting to get aboard. She gave each of them a wallet-sized card with the Pledge of Allegiance printed on one side and excerpts from the Declaration of Independence on the other. Decorated in red, white and blue, it was a gift from the Colonial Dames of America. In the blank space on each card she wrote in thin, Spencerian script, "With our deep gratitude to you from the citizens of Bentley, Georgia."

The Town Council prepared a short brochure welcoming the transient servicemen to Bentley and hoping their stay would be pleasant. Along with a brief history of the town, it listed the facilities and services available to them plus schedules, addresses, telephone numbers and the names of people to be contacted for whatever they might need or want. School and church groups, ladies' clubs and civic organizations, Boy Scouts and Girl Scouts all took turns at the depot and bus station distributing them to servicemen passing through.

One morning Alexander Holly received notification that an eastbound troop train was to be shunted off onto a siding in Bentley for about two hours in the late afternoon. He called Mamie and told her. Immediately she telephoned Hannah Beasley and Martha Buckley, and by noon the three of them had organized the entire town into one huge hospitality committee.

"Nothing to it," Hannah reported afterward. "All we did was telephone somebody in every club, school and church in town and ask them to tell their members to bring something to eat down to the train—just anything. Rosanna Titsworth said she almost didn't have time to fix anything, because she stayed busy answering the telephone. She was called by the elementary school PTA, the high school PTA, her circle at the Methodist Church, the Garden Club and the UDC. Anyway, we got those long tables from the Fire Station—the ones we use on Bentley Day—and strung them out along the station platform. We got all the dishes and silverware from both church kitchens. Everybody cooked something and brought it and laid it out. Those boys swarmed down off that train like a plague of locusts and cleaned it all out, down to the cracks in the bowls and the burnt patches in the bottom of the pots.

"I felt sorry for a poor little second lieutenant. I thought he was going to cry. He was the troop train commander and was worried to death about the mess sergeant up front with all his men cooking up a storm for the GIs' supper. He was afraid nobody would eat it. I told him to save it for tomorrow—the train was going all the way to San Francisco—and he said three crates of lettuce gets wilted after it's chopped up!"

No one could recall what had occupied their thoughts and sapped their concerns before the war started. In retrospect their problems prior to then seemed to have been minor and transitory. To reconstruct their troubled state of mind in those days was all but impossible.

"I never dreamed it would be like this," Millie Carter said to Elizabeth Holder one day in the Five and Ten Cent Store, where Elizabeth had been working full time with Sim since Pearl Harbor. "Henry never did get called up in the other war. He expected to, and we stayed half ready for it, but it never happened. I was upset and concerned about that other war—I *must* have been—but it was nothing like this. The only way I can keep my sanity is to remember all those poor people who've lost someone already and realize how fortunate we are that Andy's alive. How's Dalton?"

"He was fine the last we heard. The Navy doesn't stay in one place, you know, and it's hard to keep up with him. Sometimes I think we'd be better off not to know where he is at all. I died a thousand times a day during the Battle of Midway. Sim did too—he just didn't carry on about it like I did. I know you'll be glad when they get through that horrible mess in the Solomons."

"Of course I will, but Andy will just have to go in somewhere else. You know how the Marines do. Then we'll sit here and go through it all again."

To parents, wives, brothers, sisters and friends, the war had become a state of mind, an attitude, a way of thinking. They could not go to it, fight it, win it or lose it; but they could touch the edges of it and send pieces of themselves to it via a lanky youth in ill-fitting khakis or a baby-faced sailor who should have been sitting in Miss Mattie's classroom after school doing penance for an infraction of the rules.

Mothers and wives hoarded their sugar and butter ration stamps until they had enough to buy the ingredients needed for baking the kinds of cookies and cakes their sons and husbands liked best. They packed them in heavy boxes with the same care they would have packed Swedish crystal. They double wrapped them in the thickest brown paper they could find, tied them with stout cord, addressed them in bold, black letters and suffered the reprimands of the postmaster, Tinker Ashley, for not wrapping them more securely, then mailed them to APOs and FPOs around the world. They clipped items from newspapers, articles from magazines, sequences from "Gasoline Alley," "Dick Tracy," "Moon Mullins," "Barney Google," a handful of crossword puzzles, a few editorial cartoons and mailed them overseas. They sent church bulletins, Bentley Day programs, baseball scores, football schedules, snapshots of the family, letters from aunts and cousins. They mailed books they thought their boys would like, magazines and papers they had always been accustomed to reading, table games they could play in their tents, puzzles they could work when alone.

And they wrote them letters. They wrote even when

there was nothing to write about but the war itself. They wrote that Daddy's just getting over a cold; Mary Ellen made all A's on her last report card; the weather has been beautiful; the dogwood and azaleas are prettier than they've ever been; Mr. Spencer got twelve quarts of honey from his beehives; the chokecherries, plums, figs, Concord grapes and crab apples are piling up on the back porch waiting to be jellied and preserved; the rains were heavy this spring, and Miley's Creek overflowed twice. Do you remember the lilac bush in the corner of the yard where Annie used to make her playhouse? We found a nest of baby mockingbirds in it last week, and we've been as excited as a couple of wide-eyed kids ever since. Your daddy says tell you he's never seen so many carp and black bass in the Alcovy River as this year, but that's because you're not here to help him catch all of them. Mrs. Brown asks about you regularly and says she still intends to write you a letter. Everybody's fine. Don't worry about anybody at home. Just take care of yourself and come home safely. That's the most important thing of all.

Some people complained about inconveniences brought on by the war, but their complaints were petty, on the surface, of the moment and meant nothing even while they uttered them. They were interpreted accordingly. For Clara Odum, at Cutler's Café, however, the war was a cruel and unnecessary burden laid on her by a heartless and dictatorial President who had wrapped the entire country around his little finger. When he said froggy, everybody jumped—if they knew what was good for them.

While she was willing enough for somebody to put Hitler and Hirohito in their places, she did not see what they had to do with her personally or with Bentley, the state of Georgia, or for that matter, the United States. Let the Europeans fight their own war, and who cares what those Japs do off on the other side of the world? If Franklin D. Roosevelt was so worried about all those foreigners, why didn't he go fight them himself? What right did he have to take Albert out of the University, where he was doing so well, and send him off to New Guinea, where he would probably get killed? He didn't care what happened to all the American boys, as long as his own sons were safe, and every one of them was. Nobody could make her think otherwise.

"Clara, people come in this café to eat and not to hear you sound off about FDR," Giles Cutler told her repeatedly during slack hours when they were alone. "So just take it easy and get off the subject. I've told you a thousand times I'm paying you to wait tables and not visit with the customers."

His reprimands had no effect on her. Her son, Albert, was a radio operator, a combat crew member aboard B-24 bombers in the Southwest Pacific, and she seldom let the customers in Giles Cutler's Café forget it.

"I can mention boys from right here in Bentley sitting behind big desks in swivel chairs with plushy jobs, and they don't even know there's a war on," she told them bitterly. "Just because their daddy's got the right connections to get them a commission, they're too good for that high and mighty Roosevelt to send them off like he sent Albert. Of course, Albert hasn't had a daddy since he was ten years old, so he doesn't have any connections, and Roosevelt sends him out to do the dirty work."

Through the years Giles Cutler's customers had built up a certain immunity to Clara Odum's incessant talk. It came with the Plate Lunch Special. For the most part it was small talk, often gossipy and harmless, and usually boring. The regular diners and coffee drinkers had developed their own systems for dealing with her. They knew when to listen, to respond or to ignore her altogether. They were finding it increasingly difficult to do the last. She was touching too many raw nerves.

"Go down to the bank and get Mr. Buckley to explain

136

some of those draft deferments him and that draft board hands out," she said. "*Vital war work!* Ha! That's a laugh. Most of them are about as vital as Smiley Finch. And somebody ought to take another look at the 4-Fs, too. Hang a cotton sack over their shoulders, and most of them could pick three hundred pounds a day if somebody stood over them and made them do it. I'm telling you, they can go chase Hitler all they want to, but personally I think they're chasing the wrong man. They ought to do a little chasing right up there in Washington, if you ask me!"

She became too much for Miller Goolsby. He came across the street every morning from his barber shop for coffee at whatever time he could get away, except on Saturdays when the farmers and the school kids came in for haircuts. One day after he had suffered through a diatribe against President Roosevelt about the way he was killing American boys, Miller pushed his half-empty coffee cup away from him and slapped the counter with the flat of his hand.

Clara was cleaning off the counter with a damp cloth.

"Okay, Clara!" he said loud enough to attract the attention of the other coffee drinkers lined up along the counter. "I heard all I wanta hear outta you about President Roosevelt and this war! Albert ain't fightin' it by himself. There ain't nothin' happened to him—or to you—that ain't happened to most people here in Bentley and the rest of the United States!"

Clara was startled into ceasing her work. She stood motionless, staring at him.

"For your information, I got two boys in this war," he went on. "I know some people who've got three, and I read in the paper about a family that's got five—and somebody is shootin' at every one of them, too. Now nothing's happened to Albert yet, and I hope it don't, but it might, just like it might happen to my boys and that family with five." He pointed a threatening finger at her and raised his voice

137

even more. "If I hear one more peep outta you about President Roosevelt and how he's a criminal and all that kind of hogwash, I'm gonna get the authorities on you, and don't think I can't do it! They got officials in Atlanta that takes care of people like you that go around downing the war effort and talking against it!"

He spun around on his stool, got up and stomped out of the café, forgetting to pay for his coffee.

Giles Cutler had been out of the café at the time and was unaware of Miller Goolsby's outburst. A few evenings later he stopped in at Glen Coker's Downtown Drug Store on the way home to pick up a prescription. While watching Glen paste a label on the bottle and mark the price on it, it came to him that he had not seen him for some time.

"You and Olivia haven't been in for Sunday dinner in a long time," he said pleasantly. "Somebody been inviting you out—or did you quit eating?"

"No—we've been staying at home, I guess," Glen said evasively.

Giles watched him keenly. "There's not anything wrong, is there, Glen?"

Glen handed the prescription to Giles and leaned on the counter. "I'll be real frank with you, Giles, and I've been wondering if I ought to tell you this or not, but it's Clara Odum. I think you ought to do something about her. Everybody's used to her talking all the time, but this is different. She's poison, and she's vicious with all her talk against Roosevelt and the war. Olivia and I try to ignore her, but she won't let us. She always brings up Hart's name and tries to compare him to Albert and, of course, Hart always loses out. We don't like that kind of talk about our own son, and we don't like that kind of talk about the war, either. I'll tell you this, Giles, because you and I have been good friends a long time. Clara's running your business away, but that's not the worst part. Whether she means to be or not, she's being subversive and seditious." He smiled. "She probably doesn't know what those words mean, but she can get herself in a peck of trouble if somebody wants to push it. And if she does, it sure won't help you any, either."

Giles was upset. "I didn't know it was all that bad," he said. "I talked to her a time or two and told her to quiet down, but I didn't realize it was like that. Do you suppose anybody else feels like you do?"

Glen lifted his eyebrows and cocked his head to one side. "Well—you could think about who's stopped coming, and that would be a clue. Ellen Presley comes down here for coffee instead of going next door to your place like she used to. She told me the other day she's got to where she doesn't like to come in your place where Clara is. There must be others who feel the same way."

That was enough for Giles Cutler. The following morning between the breakfast rush and the midmorning coffee trade, he sat down with Clara in the back booth.

"I'm going to put it to you as plain as I can, Clara," he told her. "You straighten up and shut up, or I'm going to fire you. It's just that simple. You're costing me business, and that's ground enough to fire anybody. But that's not all. I'm not going to have you or anybody else in my place of business talking subversively about the United States. We're having a war, and nobody likes it, but we're having it just the same. Lots of boys are getting killed, and lots of parents are going around half out of their minds with worry. Albert's a fine boy, but he's no better than the rest of the boys wearing uniforms. And all your talk about President Roosevelt doing *anything* to Albert *personally* makes you sound like you've gone crazy. Insane. Now, do you want to be the town crazy lady?"

He did not wait for her to reply. "Well, that's exactly what you're going to be if you don't stop all this talk—the town crazy lady. And you're going to be the town crazy lady without a job, too, because if I fire you nobody else in Bentley will hire you."

Clara broke into tears. "You just don't know how it is,

Mr. Cutler," she moaned. "You don't have any children, and you don't know—"

"Save it," he said shortly. "Go walk up and down Chiles Street and tell all the people who do have children just how it is. Tell Glen Coker, Henry Carter, Sam Pickett, Clay Tinsley, Alex Holly, Emory Haynes, Forrest Lindley, Tinker Ashley, Charles Clapper, Marsh Inman and the people out at the cotton mill and all the farmers in Walton County and all the niggers down on 'Struction Street. And be sure and cry when you tell them. It'll make them feel worse, because I'm sure none of them have any idea how terrible the war is."

He stood up abruptly and looked down at her. "You got any questions?" he asked.

She had buried her face in her handkerchief. She shook her head.

"Okay—either get back to work or get out of the place," he said. "You know the terms."

He turned and went back up front to the cashier's counter.

At the end of the week, Clara quit.

"I just can't work in a place where I'm not allowed to open my mouth," she explained to Giles. "I thought we still had freedom of speech in this country, but I guess I was wrong."

He counted out her week's pay on the glass-topped counter. "I don't know about the rest of the country," he said, "but you haven't got any freedom of speech in this café—not for the kind of speech you put out."

# 15

EMMA HORN RAN THE IRON to the end of the white tatting that edged the white pillowcase and shook her head with disapproval. It was not straight, and it did not lie flat. She took it into the kitchen, dampened it, then came back and ironed it again. Miss Caroline was particular about the linens on her big tester beds with the high posts and lacy canopies on top. She did not want any crooked tatting on her pillows. Whether they were on the bed she and Mr. Frank slept in or in one of the rooms where the Masters kept their company, she wanted all her bed linens to look fresh, straight and nice.

Carefully and slowly she guided the tip of her iron around the tiny ringlets and curliques and across the slender threads that held them together until she worked her way to the end once more. After she had finished, she put on her spectacles and moved to the window, where she held the pillowcase up to the light. It looked fine now. Alongside its mate on the bed they both looked fine. She folded them carefully and added them to several other pairs amid the snowy stacks of tablecloths, dinner napkins, towels and bed sheets. She turned back to the basket of sprinkled laundry. It was almost empty now. Miss Caroline was coming for it at six o'clock. She could rest her feet for a few minutes and still have time to do Mr. Frank's shirts before she came. He did not have many this week.

She took the yellow telegram from the end of the ironing board and lowered herself into her rocking chair to study it again. She recognized her own name at the top and Elvin's somewhere amid the jumble of words below, but little else. She leaned over the arm of her chair and craned her neck for a better view of Sissy Carpenter's side window. She was disappointed that she saw no sign of life, but she was not surprised. It was still early. Sissy seldom came home until after the supper dishes had been washed unless Miss Mattie and Dr. Jesse ate supper away from home. She looked out the front window. Everybody in the neighborhood worked until dark or after, but sometimes they came home early. Three or four children ran past the house, laughing and playing. They looked too young to read the words, anyway. She continued to puzzle over the telegram alone.

Two words at the bottom on the right-hand side of the sheet was probably the name of who sent it, but it was not a name she had ever seen before. She picked out a few words —"WE," "YOU," "SON," "AND." None of the others— and some of them were long words—suggested any meaning to her. She stared at the several lines for a few minutes, then put the telegram aside with reluctance. She went back to her ironing.

Maybe Elvin was coming home to see her. He had been away about a year now, and she had never seen him wearing his uniform. He sent her a picture of himself once, and she could see it now, stuck in the edge of the mirror over the dresser. His cap was cocked on one side of his head, and his necktie was folded and tucked inside his shirt. He was grinning big like Asa used to grin when he felt real good about something. He had written her two letters. They were short and slanted downhill across the paper in a big scrawl that gave Sissy trouble when she read it aloud to her. She complained that Elvin ought to know how to write a better hand than he did. The letters lay in the box with her best handkerchiefs. When Elvin got on her mind more than usual and she got to wishing she would get another letter from him, she took them out and looked at them from top to bottom as though she were reading the words.

Maybe the telegram told when he was coming. Some of the white boys that went away to the Army and Navy came back to Bentley to see their mamas and daddies. She saw Mrs. Satterfield's boy uptown on Chiles Street one day, and once Mr. Sam Pickett's boy, Alan, spoke to her. He wore shining gold and silver things on his shoulders and on the front of his jacket. She saw others, but she was not always sure if they were Bentley boys. It was hard to tell when they wore their uniforms. It would be nice if Elvin could come back to Bentley and walk around uptown on Chiles Street so everybody could see him in his uniform, too. She smiled at the thought. She glanced at the grinning face at the edge of the dresser mirror and continued to iron Mr. Frank's shirt.

She had finished the last shirt, buttoned the collar, folded it and laid it on the bed when Miss Caroline arrived. She looked stylish as she always did, no matter what kind of dress she had on. She wore a coat today, and it was stylish like her dresses, a soft blue, the color of her eyes. "Too bad I'm so short and dumpy and you're so tall and slender, Miss Emma," she often told her. "This dress I've got on would be just right for you." Emma liked to hear her talk like that, but she was thirty years too old for Miss Caroline's dresses, whether they fitted her or not. She wished she would offer some of them to Delpha, though.

Caroline stood over the bed admiring Miss Emma's work. "It's just beautiful!" she exclaimed. "But it always is. I told somebody last week at the Garden Club that I always hate to move my own laundry from Miss Emma's bed, because it's so fluffy and white and fresh the way you fold it and stack it and arrange it in neat rows. You make it look prettier than the linen department at Rich's. Did you have trouble with that green twill? I don't know where that funny-looking stain came from. I must have brushed up against something, but I can't remember being close to anything that color."

"No'm. It don' give me no trouble," Emma said. "It come out jes' fine. I jes' rub it a little wif' my han's, and it come right out." She stood by, warmly happy as always at Miss Caroline's compliments. "You gonna haf' to git Mistuh Frank some new hank'chiefs, though. He got three or fo' that gittin' thin and wore out like—less he got lot mo' in his drawah at home."

"I'll check and see," Caroline said, still admiring the laundry. "I'll declare! You're the only person in the whole world I'd let touch this luncheon cloth, Miss Emma! Lord only knows how old it is. My mother got it from her mother, who got it from her mother, and goodness knows how long *she* had it. It's Belgian linen and the most exquisite thing I own. Why, I wouldn't even let myself wash it." She picked up a stack of shirts. "Here now. I'll take these. You put everything you can in the basket, and I'll hang my dresses in the back of the car." She started for the door. "No—you stay in the house," she said. "No use for you to do all that walking. Just go ahead and put the things in the basket, and I'll be right back and get them."

She went in and out the front door until Emma's bed was empty. She stood and made a final survey to make certain she had overlooked nothing.

"Oh—I almost forget to pay you," she said, opening her purse. "I've been up to Monroe all afternoon working with the ration board. Never in my life have I ever seen records in such a mess! Honestly! I don't see how they can keep up with all those points and stamps and coupon books. Anyway, I've got to get back home and look after my own house. Seems like I'm always somewhere else." She was fumbling in her purse. "Yesterday Reeves Buckley talked me into working on the draft board records. I de-

144

clare! I don't know what those men do with their time. They meet for hours on end and, when they're through, somebody still has to— Oh, here it is! I was afraid I had left my wallet somewhere. Now let me see—"

"Miss Caroline, I want you to read sumpin' for me," Emma said.

"Why certainly, Miss Emma," Caroline replied pleasantly. She laid some bills on the dresser, then spread them out and counted them again. "I hope it's not long. I don't know where the time goes—"

Emma thrust the telegram into her hands.

Caroline glanced at it quizzically, then at Emma. She read the telegram, held it closer and read it again. She did not move. She stared at the yellow paper in her hand and raised her head slowly.

"Miss Emma, don't you know what this says?" she asked. Her eyes were filled with horror.

"No'm. They ain't been nobody to read me the words," she replied. "I keep lookin' out the window for somebody, but they ain't nobody home."

Caroline shook her head in disbelief. "How long have you had it?"

"I don' know. I find it in the screen do' when I go outside to see how the weather look."

"*This* was sticking in your screen door?"

Emma was becoming alarmed. Miss Caroline was acting like the telegram said something bad.

"Didn't *anybody* knock on the door and hand it to you or say *anything* to you about it?"

"No'm," she said weakly. Cold fear clutched at her now. "Miss Caroline, do it say sumpin' bad? Do it?"

Caroline turned her face away quickly and covered her mouth with her hand. "Oh, no!" she breathed softly. "No, no, no—"

"Wha's the mattah, Miss Caroline? I see Elvin's name on that paper. What do it say about him?"

Caroline collected herself and faced the old woman

again. "Sit down, Miss Emma," she said gently. "Sit down in your rocking chair right there, and I'll read it to you."

Emma Horn dropped into her chair. She sat forward, her back as straight as a plank, clutching the armrests, watching Caroline Masters. She was afraid to breathe.

Caroline tried to steady her hands. "This came from the War Department in Washington. It—it says:

THE SECRETARY OF WAR DESIRES ME TO EXPRESS HIS DEEP REGRETS THAT YOUR SON, PRIVATE ELVIN HORN, 19604044, DIED OF NON-COMBAT WOUNDS ON 17 JULY 1942 IN LONDON, ENGLAND, BRITISH ISLES. LETTER AND DE-TAILS FOLLOW.
                    THE ADJUTANT GENERAL

She looked up. She was sitting on the edge of the bed. She had no recollection of having moved. Miss Emma's eyes were leveled on her. Her face was a mask. She sat with her body rigid, her bony, black hands gripping the arms of her chair.

"What do it say, Miss Caroline?" she asked in a low voice without expression. Her lips scarcely moved. "You tell me what it say."

Caroline gathered her courage. Her heart was beating fast. "It says Elvin died, Miss Emma—in England—on July seventeenth."

"How come he die?"

"He received some kind of wounds, but it doesn't say what kind," Caroline managed to reply. "They're writing you a letter that will explain the details."

Emma still had not moved. Her face still had portrayed no emotion. The two of them sat in dreadful silence gazing at one another, neither able to find the right words to say.

After a time Emma found her voice. It was quivering. "Who killed him?" she asked.

"It doesn't say."

"Were he killed in the wah?"

Caroline lifted the telegram and studied it needlessly. She knew that "non-combat wounds" meant Elvin had not been killed in action. She also knew by the intonation of Miss Emma's question that if he had died in action as men at war do die, his loss would be no easier for her, but it would have been for a reason, for a cause. Whether or not she understood that cause, she would find a pride in Elvin's contribution to it. She watched the old woman lean forward expectantly. Caroline Masters decided she could not rob her of her pride. She had little else.

"Yes, Miss Emma," she whispered. "Elvin was killed in the war."

Emma Horn's expression changed almost imperceptibly. Something akin to understanding appeared on her black face. "Elvin's daddy, he want to go to that other wah, and they wouldn't nobody let him," she said. "Elvin he want to go to this wah, and he do it. He do jes' like he want to do."

"You can be proud of him for going."

"Yessum—I'se proud of him, but I don't know why somebody kill him," she said. "He write me two letters. He say he work in the kitchen where all the soldiers eat, and he like it real fine. But he don' kill nobody. I don' believe Elvin kill nobody."

"That's the terrible thing about wars. Men kill each other when they don't want to."

Emma began to rock slowly.

Caroline knew she must say something else, do something special for Miss Emma. She had received a death message. Her son had been killed. It was a time for weeping, for heartbreak, for grief out of control, for nonrational behavior, even hysterics. Yet they both sat talking calmly, almost with detachment. And Miss Emma was rocking.

"Why don't you cry, Miss Emma?" she heard herself

say. "You don't have to wait until I leave. Don't mind me. Go ahead and cry. It might do you good."

"I'se gonna cry," she said quietly. She continued to rock. "I'se gonna cry 'til I cain't cry no mo'. Inside me it hurt real bad right now. My heart, it feel real heavy like a big rock. I'se gonna cry aw' right."

Caroline turned away and wiped her eyes with her bare hand. It was almost dark outside. The room was dusky with shadows. She got up from the edge of the bed and looked for a lamp to turn on. Finding none, she turned on the ceiling light, an unshaded bulb hanging from a single strand of cord.

"Can I make you some coffee or a cup of tea?" she asked. "You might feel better with something warm inside you."

"No'm. I don' believe I kin swallow very good right now."

"I'm going to drive out and get Delpha," she said.

"Oh, Delpha, she don' come see me 'til Sunday. She always too busy 'til then. She haf' to work with Cleatus."

"I'm going to get her and bring her back here anyway," she said. "And I'm going to bring Sissy Carpenter, too."

"Sissy she haf' to wash the supper dishes 'fore she come home."

"Don't worry about the supper dishes. I'm going to bring her home." She was looking down on Emma's frizzled gray hair. "Isn't there someone else I can tell about Elvin?"

"I reckon everybody will hear about it. Sissy, she'll tell people."

"I hate to leave you by yourself. Would you like to come with me to get Delpha?"

"No'm. I reckon I better stay heah," she said. "I jes' don' wanta go nowhere right now. Seem like I oughta stay home." She looked up into Caroline's face. "You don' haf' to do none of them things for me, Miss Caroline." She got to her feet. "You go on home and see about Mr. Frank's supper, an' you gotta put away all yo' clean laundry."

"I'll get home soon enough," Caroline said. She went to the front door and stood with her hand on the knob. "Will you be all right while I'm gone?"

"Yessum. I be aw' right. You jes' go on and don' worry 'bout me none."

Caroline opened the door and looked back. Emma was standing like a statue. Her eyes were glistening.

"Miss Emma?"

"Yessum?"

Then she broke. Her tall, lean body seemed to crumble. She bowed her head and covered her face with her hands. She sobbed aloud.

Caroline shut the door and hurried back to her. "Oh, *Miss Emma!*" she cried. She put her arms around her and held her close. The gasps and jagged breathing shook both of them. Caroline patted her shoulder and guided her gently back into her rocking chair.

"What I oughta do, Miss Caroline?" she asked in a hoarse, muffled voice.

"Nothing," Caroline answered, her voice trembling. "Not a blessed thing but cry. Just go ahead and cry until you can't cry any more. That's all you ought to do."

A few minutes later she was in Downs's Gulf Station.

"Give me some gas, Charlie," she said, opening the door and getting out. "I'm going to use your phone while you're doing it." She started away.

"What's up, Caroline? You act like something's wrong," he said.

"There is," she said, turning back. "I just came from picking up my laundry at Miss Emma Horn's. The poor old soul had a telegram she had been trying to figure out for hours. It was from the War Department. Elvin got killed."

"Elvin Horn got *killed?* How?"

"The telegram didn't say. It said 'non-combat wounds.' He was in London."

"I wonder what happened," Charlie said. "Do you suppose he was sick?"

"Surely they would have said something about it if that was the case."

"I guess he could have got in some kind of accident—a car might have run over him or something like that." He rubbed his chin. "Mmmmmmmmm. Probably he got in a fight and somebody stuck a knife in him."

"Charlie! That would be awful! Imagine going overseas to a war and getting killed like that. She'll get a letter with the details later, but until she does, you ought not to talk like that. She thinks he got killed in the war. I didn't have the nerve to tell her he probably didn't—not the way she thinks, anyway. Maybe we ought to leave it that way."

"You can't keep things like that a secret," he said. He shook his head wonderingly. "Whatdya know about that? Ole slowpoke, shuffling Elvin Horn who used to work right here in this very station—when I could keep him on the job, that is. He's the last person in town I would have figured to get killed overseas."

"He's also Bentley's first casualty in this war, though."

"Well—I'm not sure you can classify this one as a war casualty," Charlie replied. "But whether it is or not, Bentley's first war death has to be the laziest nigger in town. Doesn't that take the cake?"

"How about the gas? I've got to go after Delpha and take Sissy Carpenter home to look after Miss Emma. I had to go to Monroe two days in a row. Right now I've got to call Frank and tell him to feed himself because—Oh! I forgot all about that car full of laundry. I guess I'll have to go home first, anyway. Might as well fill it up."

"No—no, just hold it!" he protested. "This stuff's rationed, and I've got to stretch it out for people who haven't got an X card for two cars like you and Frank do. They don't understand how you get away with it when they have to limp along with an A card and three gallons a week for *one* car. And if you want to know the truth, neither do I. I'll give you five gallons, and that's all."

She ignored him. "I'm going to wring somebody's neck down at that Western Union," she said. "The *idea!* Leaving a death message, of all things, sticking in the screen door for an old woman who lives alone and can't even read!"

"Probably whoever delivered it can't read either," Charlie said. "The Western Union is probably scraping the bottom of the barrel like everybody else."

John Reynolds gazed out the front window of *The Bentley Weekly Enterprise* onto Chiles Street, oblivious to what he was actually seeing. Suddenly he spun his chair around. He had made up his mind.

"Dicey Ann? Tell Fletch to bring this week's layout back up front," he said. "We can't run that Elvin Horn story like it is."

Dicey Ann Darby rose from her desk with liquid motion, touched her red hair prettily with her fingers and started for the rear door. "He's not going to like that," she said over her shoulder.

"He doesn't like anything anyway," he said, too preoccupied to give Dicey Ann's spectacular exit the attention it deserved.

Fletcher Ford, typesetter, stormed through the door, his hands full of news copy and his face full of disapproval. He was ready to argue.

"I've already got that page set up, John," he protested. "If you want this paper out tomorrow, you'd better leave it alone. Dicey Ann tells me you want to change that piece on Elvin Horn. What's the matter with it like it is?"

"We can't refer to him as Bentley's first war casualty,"

John said. He hoisted one foot onto the seat of his chair, hooked his arm across his knee and leaned back. "It's not a casualty. He got killed in a fight—a barroom brawl. I read the letter. That could have happened to him in Monroe or Atlanta or right here down in Tin Can Alley."

"Yeah, but it didn't," Fletcher said. "It happened to him overseas in the U.S. Army, and his mother got a telegram and letter from the War Department about it. Didn't that guy at the Fourth Army Headquarters tell you on the phone that if it happened in a theater of operations during wartime, it's technically a noncombat casualty?"

John waved his hand impatiently. "I know all that, Fletch," he said, "but it's still not right. It doesn't sound right. It'll get misinterpreted. A real casualty is when somebody is killed or wounded by the enemy. His hometown is proud of him and honors him with plaques and ceremonies. Before this war's over we'll probably have some genuine casualties from right here in Bentley. Somebody's going to get shot down by the Germans or Japs or get taken prisoner or get wounded or be missing in action on some godforsaken island nobody ever heard of. I'm talking about some of our own hometown boys. We can't put Elvin Horn in that category. We just can't do it, and that's that."

"His name is printed with all the other boys in the service right on the Bentley Honor Roll that's hanging on the side of The Well right this very minute. And it's there because he's a bona fide soldier in the U.S. Army—or he *was*, that is. How're you gonna get around that?"

"I'm not going to get around it. It's in the story already. In war, casualty's got a special meaning. What I've got to do is change the tone of the story and take out reference to casualty."

"The story is technically right as it is."

"Maybe. But the *Enterprise* doesn't have any technical readers. We can't make a war story out of it, that's all."

"What about his mother? I hear she thinks it was an honest-to-God casualty."

"She does," John said, nodding his head. "And from what I heard of the memorial service, the Reverend Freeman L. Lincoln treated it as one. They tell me the Macedonia Baptist Church was packed to the rafters. Sim Holder was there. He said he'd never seen so much carrying on—as if they were making a hero out of Elvin."

"Well, those people do that to anybody that dies and has a funeral! I wouldn't let that worry me. You know how they like to go to funerals and raise the roof. But at least that ought to give you a clue to what they'll be expecting to see in the paper."

"Well, they won't see it in the *Enterprise*," John said. He took his foot out of the chair, pulled the chair up to the desk and held out a hand. "You might as well quit trying to save your makeup, Fletch," he said. "You're the typesetter—I'm the editor. Now give me that story. We've got to shake a leg if you want to get it set up by noon."

"It's already set up, John! That's what I've been trying to tell you! Are you still going to run it on the front page?"

"No. Move it to the 'News from Bentley's Servicemen.'"

"That servicemen's page is already running over! We've got letters from everybody and their dogs this week all the way from here to Timbuktu, and all of them are as long as your arm. I always thought when you went off to war, you wouldn't have much time to write letters. This war doesn't seem to slow down any of the Bentley boys, though. Why don't you cut some of them down sometime? That's what an editor's for. They're all too long."

"Can't do it," John said. "When their mothers or daddies give me their boys' letters to run, they raise Cain if I leave out one tiny word. Then when I run the letters the boys write directly to the *Enterprise* their mothers and daddies ask me for the originals, which I always give them, and every word of *them* had better be printed, too. And that's okay. It's not asking for much, and I'm glad we're able to do it. What's more, I'm going to keep on doing it. If the paper shortage keeps getting shorter, I'll cut down somewhere else, but not those boys' letters. These people are proud of those boys, and I don't blame them. If some of my girls were boys and in the service, I'd be proud of them, too."

Fletcher gave in. "Well—it's your paper," he said, "but it looks like they'd think up something interesting to write about every once in a while. That Yancy boy wrote his mother from some place in Alaska and listed everything he had to eat in the mess hall, including the salt and pepper. Now you've got to admit that's not very hot news from the trenches."

"So what? It all adds up to news from Bentley's servicemen, and that's what the name of the page says it is. I do think you and Dicey Ann could watch their spelling just a little bit closer than you do, though. And that reminds me: Rosanna Titsworth called the other day raising Cain about the way you hyphenated her name last week. You and Dicey Ann watch what you're doing."

"Okay. What do you want me to move to the front page?"

"Respace what you've got and use fillers from the 'Personal Locals,'" John instructed him. "And if you need any more of those, I'll get Dicey Ann to call Mollie Satterfield or Hannah Beasley and see where they've been this week. One thing will lead to another. If all else fails, I can always ask Josh Bullock who got on and off the train yesterday."

Fletcher fumbled through the news copy in his hand, withdrew the Elvin Horn story and handed it to his employer. "Here it is, but hurry it up, willya, John? I haven't got all day. I've never seen anything like it," he muttered.

154

"Another nigger gets killed, and it turns into a special deal. How did all this get off on the wrong track, anyway? I heard that Mrs. Frank Masters was the one that started it."

"No. She happened to be there when the telegram came, but the letter didn't come until later. Sissy Carpenter read the letter to Miss Emma and dressed up the story. Caroline Masters has too much sense to do a thing like that."

The "News from Bentley's Servicemen" page of *The Bentley Weekly Enterprise* on Thursday contained a news release from the United States Marine Corps about Andrew H. Carter's promotion to First Lieutenant on Guadalcanal and another from the U.S. Air Corps about Private First Class Spec 3 Matthew Lindley's completion of a radio-communication school at Scott Field, Illinois. A letter from Sergeant George Haynes told how it was to spend (censored) days on a troop ship en route to (censored) with (censored) men crammed aboard and how good it felt to set his feet on solid ground when they landed in (censored).

At the top of the page was a snapshot of Aviation Cadet Marshall Inman, Jr., in the open cockpit of an Air Corps AT-6 training plane. The caption announced his recent graduation from flying school and commissioning as a second lieutenant at Victoria, Texas. Machinist Mate 2nd Class Alan Pickett wrote about his three days' liberty in London, where he ran across Staff Sergeant Hart Coker at the American Red Cross near Piccadilly Circus. They caught each other up on the hometown news from Bentley, and they both admitted they got kind of homesick.

In a letter to his parents from Fort Knox, Kentucky, Pfc Paul Holly observed that the Armored Force was *the* choice part of the U.S. Army and he felt sorry for all the other boys who were in some other branch. Jeff Goolsby wrote that the coolest day in Darwin, Australia, made

155

Georgia's hottest day seem like wintertime. He had already decided that when the war was over he would come back to Bentley and sit on the Alcovy River under the biggest oak tree in Georgia and maybe never get up again. Edwin Satterfield was in Officer Candidate School in Miami Beach and said that living in an oceanfront suite with three other officer candidates in the Roney Plaza, attending classes in the Pago Pago Club and eating his meals in the converted grand ballroom of the Versailles Hotel, crystal chandeliers and all, was not as glamorous as it probably sounded.

Petty Officer Horace Epps had been accepted for pilot training in the Navy's Air Training Program but had not received his orders yet, so he did not know exactly where he would be sent. He had heard that it would be Ottumwa, Iowa, but that did not necessarily mean anything. Meanwhile, he sent greetings to all his friends in Bentley.

At the bottom of the page a short news item stated that Mrs. Asa Horn (colored), 'Struction Street, Bentley, had been notified by the War Department that her son, Private Elvin A. Horn, age twenty-eight, had been fatally wounded in an accident in England, where he had been stationed with the United States Army. He was survived by his mother, and by a sister, Mrs. Cleatus Underwood of the Jack's Creek community. A memorial service was conducted at the Macedonia Baptist Church with the Reverend Freeman L. Lincoln officiating.

Most subscribers to *The Bentley Weekly Enterprise* thought it was nice of John Reynolds to soften the account of Elvin Horn's death. He had done it to spare Miss Emma's feelings, and why not? They all knew the truth, anyway, and what purpose would it have served to spread it out in print? John Reynolds might get a little rambunctious from time to time, cut the fool a lot and appear to take some things lightly, but when you came right down to it, he was as solid as a rock. In the twenty years since his daddy left him that newspaper to run, nobody ever got their dander up or their feelings hurt by anything they read in the *Enterprise*. The way he handled that Elvin Horn business just proved all over again that, white or colored, John was considerate of everybody's feelings.

Many of John's nonsubscribers, which included the majority of Bentley's colored residents, were also pleased that the *Enterprise* did not print the truth about Elvin Horn. At the same time there was a grumbling among them that, had he not been colored, the article would have been longer and would have been given a more conspicuous place in the paper.

Sissy Carpenter lost no time putting a stop to that kind of talk. "You just hush up your mouth right now," she told several of them one evening in front of Cuby Jackson's Café and Domino Parlor. "Mr. Reynolds was being good to Miss Emma and Elvin and to all the colored people, and he didn't have to be."

"Why, I heah Reverend Lincoln say wif' his own mouf' that they ain't no colored folks gonna ever git they name on the front page of the Bentley paper."

"I don't care what Reverend Lincoln said," Sissy snapped. "You're going to get all of us in trouble down here stirring up everybody like you're doing. Now you know what you've got to do to get along with the white folks, and I'm telling you right now you'd better do it!"

And they did it. They could still complain to their heart's content, however, about Sissy Carpenter and her high-and-mighty ways. They did not complain because she was siding in with the white folks necessarily—she did that all the time, anyway—but because there was not a colored person alive on 'Struction Street or Tin Can Alley who was a match for Sissy Carpenter when she decided they ought to do something and told them to do it.

# 16

PAUL HOLLY CAME HOME on furlough in August. He had finished his training in tank warfare at Fort Knox and had been held over for a specialized course that lasted another few weeks and that he was not permitted to discuss with his family. He had only a week, and how to divide his time between Bentley and Atlanta was a problem he was not able to solve to anybody's complete satisfaction.

"I'll settle it by staying where it's the coolest," he said teasingly to the entire family, who had assembled in Bentley for Sunday dinner the day after he arrived home. "Was it always this hot in Georgia?"

"Listen to the world traveler!" Ellison Hampton hooted. "You'll think Georgia is in the Arctic Circle if the Army sends you off out to one of those jungle islands where the natives are born naked and stay naked all their lives because it's too hot to wear clothes."

"I doubt if I'll have to worry about that," he said. "All the guys in the last two classes went in the opposite direction—to Europe."

"Are you sure you'll be sent overseas, Paul?" asked his mother with apprehension. "Don't they keep some of the boys here to train the others?"

"Sure, they do, but they won't keep this one," he replied with assurance. He laid his fork on his plate and leaned back in his chair. "I figured it all out right after I got off that train in Louisville. The guys they keep for instructors are always from the top of their class. I knew how to get in that category, and I knew how to stay out of it. I knew exactly when to be sharp and when to be dumb. You don't get medals for going through a training course. Everybody comes out the other end of the chute the same —just another GI. I passed the course with flying colors, but I took pains to stay out of the top of my class." He snickered and winked at Perry. "Take my word for it. They won't be keeping me at Fort Knox for an instructor or anything else."

Alex sat at the head of the table and listened to his son. A shadow crossed his face. "That doesn't sound right, Paul," he said. "It's never right to do less than your best in whatever job you're doing. You should never hold back."

"I didn't hold back," Paul replied. "I just didn't blitz as many of my classmates as I could have. Look, Dad. I don't mean to sound like a blowhard, but I'm *good* at all that stuff we had to do. It comes natural with me. I did most of it standing on my head. I'd get out on the gunnery range and have the time of my life while lots of the other guys worried and got nervous and all tensed up. It was like that all the way through. It drove some of those clucks crazy. You wouldn't believe how they sweated out some of those exercises and field problems. Some of them would even get *sick*. I liked it. I ate it up. But I learned it so I can fight in a war, not teach it to somebody else. I'm a good soldier, and the Army gets its money's worth out of me. You don't need to worry about that."

"I'll bet you didn't win Fort Knox's award for modesty this year," Ferebe said lightly. "But you never won it in Bentley either."

Paul turned to his sister, unperturbed. "You go right ahead and be your same old sarcastic, clever self," he said.

159

"You're probably still as cute as you've always thought you were. But I wasn't just sounding off. An important thing has happened to me. You know the old business about a square peg in a round hole? Well, I've either become round or the hole has become square—I don't know which—but I *fit*. I don't know about you, but that's a brand-new feeling for me, and I like it."

Susie was seated across the table from Perry and translating the gist of the conversation into signs for him.

"Ya'll are going to have to stop talking," she said. "I can't eat and talk to Perry at the same time, and I'm so hungry I'm scared. I'll bet Mother used up every ration point in this house to cook this dinner."

Mamie laughed happily. "I almost starved your daddy to death saving them up. I started saving as soon as we found out when Paul was coming. Now listen to me, everybody. We've all got to figure out who gets Paul when and for how long. He only has until Saturday."

Perry rapped on the table. All eyes turned to him. "Paul's going back to Atlanta with me tonight," he said. He was happy, and his face portrayed it. "He's going to stay with me, and tomorrow morning he's coming out to the Quartermaster Depot to see where I work and what I do. Then I'm going to take the afternoon off."

"Tonight?" Mamie gasped. "But you just got here yesterday afternoon, Paul! We've hardly seen you!"

"Neither have they," Paul replied, nodding toward the others. "I'll come back later in the week. Is Dicey Ann Darby still around?"

"She got married," Alex said. "Some soldier down at Fort Benning. Old Cy's been raising Cain about it. She never had seen the boy but twice before she married him. He's an Italian from New York or somewhere up there. That didn't set well with Cy either."

"The war must be making people lose their minds," Susie said with disapproval. "A girl in one of my First

Aid classes writes to a soldier she's never laid eyes on, and she claims they're going to get *married!* Can you *imagine?* But listen, Paul—save me a time to take you out to dinner or lunch while you're in Atlanta. I want to be seen in public with a serviceman in uniform. It's the thing to do nowadays."

"We're planning on your coming to our house too," Ferebe said. "Maybe you can spend the night with us. You can pick the night."

"I'll cook you my specialty—spaghetti and meatballs," Ellison offered. "I guarantee you'll sop your plate and be crying for more after it's all gone."

Alex looked to the other end of the table at Mamie and shrugged. "You see, Mother?" he said. "You and I are going to have trouble working our way into Pfc Holly's busy schedule this week."

She sighed. "Well, it certainly looks that way," she said, too pleased to conceal it. "But it's so grand for all of you to be here together now that I'm not going to worry about this week at all. Goodness! I just can't remember the last time all of us were in this house at the same time. It's just marvelous! I think even Maggie and Ellie realize what an extra-special occasion it is, don't you, Ferebe?"

Perry could hardly take his eyes off his brother. He watched him with pride, admiration and not a little envy. Paul caught his gaze as their mother was talking.

"Look here, Perry," he said. "How about you going back to Fort Knox for me, and I'll work for you at the Quartermaster Depot for about a week? I'd like to wear some of those new clothes you were flashing around when you came to Louisville—and that suit you've got on now."

"What will I do when I have to talk to somebody?"

"Go on Sick Call. Tell them you've got laryngitis and lost your voice."

In the days following, Mamie fretted and worried that Paul might get caught up in his own pleasures, lose track of the time and not come back to Bentley at all before he returned to Kentucky on Saturday.

"He doesn't *have* to come back," she said to Alex. "He could easily leave from Atlanta. He took all his clothes with him."

"He didn't bring enough to leave any here. Anyway, he brought them to wear, didn't he? He'll come back. He wouldn't go off overseas without coming back to see us, not with the war and all. You're worrying about it too much."

He had sought to waylay her anxiety, but he had increased it instead. As he talked, she had an uneasy feeling that he spoke with no confidence and had been trying to convince himself. To their immense joy and relief, however, Paul returned on Thursday afternoon and stayed until Saturday morning, when he got aboard No. 6 for Atlanta, where he would change trains for Louisville.

In the meantime Mamie washed and ironed his khaki uniforms and, according to Paul, made them look better than the GI laundry ever did. She was insistent upon his choosing what they should eat so she could cook it for him. Alex grilled him about Army life, his training routine, the weapons and equipment he had learned to operate and handle. Both of them clung to his every utterance and considered it time lost when he was out of their sight.

Saturday morning came too soon, and the three of them sat in the dispatcher's office at the depot waiting for No. 6 westbound to arrive.

"How will we know where you're going and when you actually leave the country for overseas?" his father asked.

"You won't," Paul said. "They'll start censoring our mail at the POE, and I won't be able to tell you where I'm going or when or how."

"I'd probably worry myself to death if I knew," Mamie said. "I know you're not a good letter writer, darling, but the war makes everything different, and you're going to have to do better."

"There's something I want to say to you, Son, before Number 6 hits the switch plate out at Turtle Hill and everybody starts running in and out of here," Alex said. "You're a trained soldier now with a specialized skill, and in spite of what you were telling us Sunday about how easy it's been for you, I know you worked hard and applied yourself to the limit. You'll keep on doing that. I don't have the slightest doubt about it. I know what's inside you. I've always known you've got what it takes. When you got in the Army, I told you we were proud of you. We still are—only prouder."

He stopped, cocked his head, held up his hand and listened. Mamie and Paul watched him curiously. They could hear nothing.

"Now! That was well timed, wasn't it?" Alex said brightly, getting to his feet. "She just crossed Turtle Hill switch plate. Here she comes." He looked at his watch. "Two minutes. We might as well get on outside."

On the drive back up Depot Street Mamie wiped her eyes. "I'm glad I could save all this until after he left," she said. "You know, the Army hasn't taken any of Paul's swaggering ways out of him, has it?"

"No," Alex said thoughtfully as he turned onto Chiles Street. "And that might be a blessing. It might be the thing that will save his life."

In early September Mamie and Alex received a post-card from him. He was at the Port of Embarkation in New York.

"I went down on Times Square last night," he wrote. "For a farewell glimpse of the United States, that one is hard to beat. I'm fine. More later. Love, Paul."

They heard nothing more from him until November when, soon after the Allied landings in North Africa, they learned that he had gone ashore with the American forces at Algiers. From the moment they read his letter, which was painfully brief and scarcely told more than his new address, now an APO, the war took on a closer and deeper

163

meaning for them. It was theirs now, in fact as well as in theory, as they had realized from the beginning it must someday become. It had entered their home on Madison Road and taken up residence, a dreadful living presence, unwanted and unwelcome, stalking their days and troubling their nights. It possessed them. The war was in other places, too—in the steamy jungles of New Guinea, on the high seas of the North Atlantic, even in the frozen stretches of the Aleutian Islands—but the Hollys' personal war was being waged on the hot, dusty, windy deserts of North Africa.

With the collapse of the French Resistance at the start, the takeover of Algeria and Morocco had been swift and relatively easy. But then the war became tough and bloody. The fighting was fierce, and losses on both sides were heavy. Advances were slow, and sometimes the front lines hardly seemed to move at all.

Mamie and Alex followed the North African campaign in the newspapers and on the radio with their hearts in their mouths. Names of places they dared not try to pronounce became familiar to them. They located them on a map they never folded and put away out of sight. They watched the U.S. Army fight its way westward into Tunisia to be thrown back by the Germans. They cheered Field Marshal Montgomery's Eighth Army as it pushed westward across the desert in pursuit of the sly, wily General Rommel and his Afrika Corps. They measured the miles that separated the American forces from the British and tried to estimate when they would meet and trap the Nazi forces in between. They did not know where Paul was in all the fighting, but they examined action photographs in the newspaper through a large magnifying glass, searching the dirty faces of any American soldier within camera range on the chance that one of them might be their son.

With the same grim intensity and anxiety, the attention of other families in Bentley was fixed on an island in the Pacific named Guadalcanal, where the U.S. Navy and the Marines were fighting desperately to wrest it from Japanese control. The jungle battles were grisly, casualties were sickeningly high, and the fighting stretched on week after week. The Japanese had taken Bataan from the Americans back in April, and in May General Wainwright had surrendered his troops at Corregidor. Not until summer at the Battle of Midway had the United States won a decisive victory in the Pacific, but the triumph faded as the fighting afterward got bloodier and bloodier.

Christmas was a troubled blur to the Hollys. Susie and Perry came home on the train Christmas Eve night and returned to Atlanta Christmas night. Perry had heard from Paul more often than his parents had, but inexplicably he relayed little information to them. Susie had received calls from the Army and Navy for job openings, but each of them had been outside her range of skills. She was unhappy and still waiting.

With their minds the captive of the North African campaign and Paul's safety, the traditional Christmas tree in the living room and the traditional turkey dinner with Grandmother Meade's wedding china, silver and crystal were almost perfunctory. When the four of them sat down in the dispatcher's office at the depot to wait for the Atlanta train, they scarcely realized that Christmas had come and gone. They had been in the war one year and eighteen days.

After New Year's when Roosevelt and Churchill met in Casablanca, their hopes and optimism received a boost. The significance of the meeting did not come through to them, but the big-faced President with the wide, contagious grin and the Prime Minister in his roll brim hat and cigar clenched between his teeth were reassuring sights in their morning newspapers. They sat with General de Gaulle and General Girard in the glaring sun before a backdrop of dazzling white Moroccan buildings, looking for all the world as if they knew exactly how to finish the war and finish it victoriously.

Mamie and Alex saturated themselves with news from North Africa. No tidbit was too small for their consumption. No event was too insignificant to escape their analysis. The news was comprehensive and instantaneous. The mail, however, was slower and came later. Much later. The time in between was agonizing. And they received precious little mail while they agonized.

"Do you think he's all right, Alex?" Mamie asked one evening after supper, desperate for confirmation of everything she wanted to believe. The radio was turned on to "Fibber Magee and Molly," but neither of them had been listening. "I get just as worried when the casualties are light as when they're heavy," she said. "Even among the light casualties, there's always the awful possibility that—"

"He's all right," Alex broke in hurriedly. "But he ought to have his britches kicked for not writing more than he does. And if he'd walk through that door this minute, I'd kick them—hard."

"He's always done like this," Mamie said defensively. "You remember when he was at the University how we used to tell ourselves that no news is good news."

"I remember, but this is different," Alex said. "Tunisia is farther away than the University of Georgia, and he's in Tunisia for different reasons. We can't pick up the phone and call him if we want to talk to him, and he can't come busting through the front door when we're not expecting him and when he ought to be back at school studying. He's probably sitting over there somewhere in Africa right this minute without a scratch on him, but how are we supposed to know that? *He* knows he's all right, so what are *we* worrying about? Oh, we don't need to worry about Paul Holly! He can take care of himself. That's why I'd like to kick his britches from one end of Chiles Street to the other."

Mamie smiled fondly. "Well—that's the way Paul is," she said. "He wouldn't be Paul if he wasn't that way."

"Stop trying to smooth it over, Mamie!" he said sharply. "You know as well as I do that he's not treating us right. He doesn't care how we feel or what we think."

"Alex! That's an awful thing for you to say! Things are hard enough without your taking that attitude!"

"And he's making it harder for us," Alex went on. "He's not in this war by himself, you know. We're in it, too, whether he realizes it or not. It's time he woke up and looked around."

"You're making it sound like we haven't heard from him at all."

"Three times," he said flatly. "And one of them was only to tell us his APO. Everybody in Bentley hears from their boys more than we do. Emory Haynes hears from his boy almost every week. Paul just doesn't care, that's all, and you might as well face it."

"Please don't, Alex," she pleaded. "Please don't talk like that. I haven't drawn a free breath since we found out he was in Africa, and you're not making things easier."

"Well, you're not going through anything I'm not going through," he said. He picked up the map and glanced at it idly, then laid it aside again. "I think somebody would have told us by now if he wasn't all right," he added hopefully. Then after a moment, "Don't you?"

"That's what I keep telling myself," she said, "but the time differences and distances are so great, I can't help but wonder if something's happened and we haven't had time to hear."

They listened to the news on the radio wishing they did not have to turn it on at all. They brought in *The Atlanta Constitution* from the front porch each morning and checked every headline in the first section before they could breathe easily, talk normally or swallow the first sip of coffee. They saw the Western Union messenger on the street with telegrams in his hand and tried not to wonder

167

if they should hurry home in case one of the messages was for them. They froze in position when the telephone rang. Their hearts jumped if a strange automobile stopped or even slowed down in front of their house. They opened their mailbox at the post office, eager for a letter from Paul but afraid to look lest there be nothing. They read the ever-lengthening casualty lists in the newspaper trying to convince themselves that Paul's name could not possibly be among them if they had not been notified first.

"You know what we're doing, Mamie?" Alex said. "We're learning to live with fear, and we haven't caught the knack yet. That's what it is—fear. We've never had to deal with it except in small, short doses. Now we're getting a big dose, and we don't know for how long. We're going to keep on being afraid until the war's over and Paul's back home again. To make it worse, we can't do anything for him. Not one blessed thing. Everything's out of our hands. The only thing we can do is be afraid and learn to live that way without letting it get us down."

They could not bring themselves to give a precise name to their fears. It was unthinkable that Mamie should say openly that maybe Paul had been killed and they had not yet been notified by the War Department. Alex dared not speculate that Paul might be lying unconscious in a field hospital with a leg, arm or half his stomach blown away. They both knew that at any minute of the day or night he could be reported killed, wounded or missing in action, but those were words they could not force past their lips. Not saying them seemed to keep the possibility at bay and the actuality remote.

Reverend and Mrs. Charles David Clapper, First Baptist Church, received one of those dreaded telegrams in May. Their son, Mitchell, a B-25 pilot in the Air Corps, had been shot down out of the skies over the Mediterranean on the day British and United States troops entered Bizerte and Tunis, and victory in North Africa was virtually complete. Mitchell had grown up in Bentley and had been a junior at Mercer University in Macon when he joined the Air Corps as an aviation cadet.

"I've just about cried my eyes out," said Mollie Satterfield. "Right over my back fence I watched that little boy grow up. He got into every kind of meanness you can think of. Oh, I had to watch him like a hawk. I never knew what might be going on in my own back yard. He and Sonny Ashley used to steal the peaches right off my tree just as they were ready to pick and I had all the jars ready to put up preserves and spiced pickled peaches. They would throw them at passing cars, at each other and other children, and I'd have to go out and chase them away. Before the day was over, though, he might climb over the fence—he never used the gate—and come visit me like nothing had ever happened—the cutest thing you ever saw in your life! He always came over to see me when he came home from Mercer. He turned into a fine young man, but I'll confess there were times when I would not have bet a quarter on it. And to think he used to be our *paper boy!*"

Bentley's worst fears came to pass and became an awful reality in the death of Mitchell Clapper. He was the town's first combat casualty of the war. There were few families it did not touch and disturb deeply. He represented all of them in a way they would never have chosen, and the Clappers' tragic loss was also theirs. From the Pacific, the Atlantic, the South Seas, the Equator, the North Pole, the Mediterranean and the Far East, the war came home to Bentley. Chiles Street had become ten thousand miles long.

Reverend Forrest Lindley, pastor of the First Methodist Church, offered to conduct a memorial service for Mitchell in his father's own pulpit at the First Baptist Church.

"I guess you'll have to, Forrest, because I could never get through it myself," Mr. Clapper responded gratefully. "It's a fine thing for you to do."

"Well, Charles, maybe you and I are like doctors,"

Mr. Lindley said. "They go around looking after people when they're sick and in pain, and when they get sick themselves, they look after each other."

The First Baptist Church was packed. People stood around the walls and in the vestibule. It seemed odd for Mr. Clapper to be sitting down front with his family instead of standing in the pulpit he had occupied since before some of them had been born. His bald head with the white fringe around it was an unfamiliar sight from the rear.

"Mitchell Clapper gave his life for a cause he believed in," Mr. Lindley told the hushed gathering. "He would much rather have lived. He wanted to finish his education, embark on a career, marry, raise children, have a home, be happy. Those are not unreasonable wants, nor are they unattainable for most young men who want them. In essence they are the ingredients of the cause for which he died. It sounds almost too simple, doesn't it?

"The gift of life is a precious gift, and the right to live it with freedom to come and go as we like, to work where we choose, to worship as we please, to say what we think, makes the gift all the more precious. It makes it all the more imperative that we guard it and protect it. Life is precious to all of us. It was precious to Mitchell Clapper. Maybe the cause he died for, then, was the Cause of Life.

"We don't have to believe in the institution of war itself to believe in the causes for which they are fought. But somehow, man in all his imperfections insists on selecting war again and again as the means to uphold those causes he believes to be right and just. If, in the sight of God, those causes *are* right and just, maybe someday He will show us a way to uphold them by right and just means. We have to hope for that. We have to pray for it.

"We have lost a fine young man. The gap he leaves will not be filled. Every person occupies his own niche in this world. It's peculiarly his, and when he vacates it, it remains empty. But the rest of us will go on—his parents, brothers, sisters, friends, his sweetheart—because life on this earth does not end for all of us at the same time. Captain Mitchell Clapper, United States Army Air Corps, lived twenty-three years. That's not very long, and we tend to think that his life was cut short, that it ended prematurely. But maybe not. Perhaps the purpose for which he was put among us has been achieved. Perhaps his life was fulfilled. We don't know. But we do know that he lived for his dreams and his aspirations, and when the time came, he died for them. Can any of us do any more than that?

"So we must thank God for this young man and for the family that gave him to us, to the nation and to history. In return, we give God and this family our hearts. We wish it could be more."

The town pulled itself back together and went on about its business. The Thousand Years of the German Third Reich had been cut off in Africa and the Middle East. The price had been high, but everybody knew it would be. Still, it was over and done with; the killing had ended for the time being, at least in that part of the world; everybody could stop and breathe easy for a spell now.

Then two months later, in July, the Allies landed in Sicily.

# 17

PERRY HOLLY HAD BEEN CAPTIVATED by his surroundings from the first day. The warehouse was a vast sweep of concrete and steel girders. It was cool and inviting, brushed with shadows the color of dusk. While he waited for the next pallet of labeled, taped, stenciled containers to be towed into the Checkout Station, he looked down through the canyon of boxes and crates to the wide rectangle of daylight at the opposite end of the building. The two men at the Receiving Station were thin silhouettes in the distance framed by the big open doors and a background of blue sky.

From where he sat at a high desk inside wide doors that yawned onto the loading platform outside, the warehouse always had an appearance of quietness. Movement was slow and orderly. A tug pulling several loaded pallets would bend itself around a corner and jolt its way along the center aisle, then come to a slow, easy stop at the Checkout Station. A train of empties or half-loads would cautiously roll across the center aisle en route from one side of the warehouse to the other. Men with clipboards wandered in and out among the high stacks, studying labels and writing on their papers. Usually they worked alone but sometimes in pairs, and they, too, moved slowly and with deliberation. Even the forklift trucks that took away entire columns of boxes or put new ones in place handled their loads gently and with leisure. The tempo increased in the early morning, late afternoon and at lunchtime when the men hurried in and out of the building; but it was their numbers, not their speed, that suggested sound. Altogether, the unhurried activity inside the warehouse was pleasant. It was nothing like the frenzied turning of the thousands of spindles in the cotton mill that shrieked at him and gave him headaches, frequently turning into nausea. Yet, the activity was enough to stave off the lonely silence that weighed him down when nothing moved.

He looked outside and across the way to the next warehouse. Another stood beyond it, another across the street, and still others end to end. At least a dozen warehouses similar in design, red brick and massive, and many lesser buildings were geometrically spaced over fifteen hundred acres, all sliced through with miles of broad, paved streets and cut through the middle by a double railroad track. This was the new Army Quartermaster Depot that within months had grown up out of the flat farmlands south of Atlanta, changing its rural sleepiness into a busy, urban sprawl. Thousands of people had left their farms, their regular jobs, their hometowns to converge on the new giant installation and work with the Army to keep American soldiers supplied with the clothing and equipment they needed to fight a war.

When Perry left the desk and stood in the big entrance to the warehouse, he could see the wide expanses between buildings, sodded with new grass and bordered with long strips of concrete sidewalks. Best of all, he could see space. The sky, the sun, the rain—whatever met his eyes—the distance and openness gave him a sense of freedom. Back inside, the serenity and bigness of the warehouse gave him a release as fulfilling. Two years in the stifling, oppressive heat of the cotton mill, where the least draft of air would break the fragile cotton yarn, and shut away from the outdoors by glazed windows to shield the wispy thread from the stark destructiveness of the daylight, now seemed like an illness from which he was convalescing.

To deepen his sense of well-being and give him a comfortable feeling of security, he no longer had to fear the cotton mill's whistle. The whistle had been a torture instrument that inflicted its horrors each day at noon for thirty seconds of total agony. Daily as twelve o'clock approached, he tried to keep his eyes from the watch on his wrist, but he was powerless. When the whistle sounded it jabbed into the sides of his head like a dull, rusty-bladed knife and scraped the sharp edges of every bone in his face, rasping, grating, screeching and zigzagging with sadistic glee.

Once the whistle had malfunctioned and blown for almost two minutes. When it stopped and his senses returned, he found himself on the floor, huddled against the wall, his arms covering his head as if warding off blows. Two fellow workers were standing over him. They helped him to his feet and led him outside into the fresh air. His spindles had become snarled and someone had turned off his machine. After lunch he returned and worked to untangle the yarn and make his machine operational again, too embarrassed to look to the right or to the left. He had no system of communication through which he could explain to his co-workers how the pain had blinded him and closed off every avenue of behavior that was rational.

His father and mother knew about the whistle, but they did not know the extent of the pain it caused him. Paul had more of an understanding than anyone else, but even he could not know. The mill whistle could be heard from anywhere in Bentley. People set their clocks by it, went home to dinner by it, terminated visits and business

174

calls by it; and whether he was standing before his spindles or on the far side of town at the Clegg Line, he could not protect himself from its ragged scraping. Every day before noon during his first few days at the Quartermaster Depot, he tensed himself and made ready. Within the first week, however, the whistle released him altogether, and he relaxed in the confidence that he need never again suffer its cruelty.

Mr. Knox touched his arm and pointed to a tug coming toward them with several pallets stacked high. He picked up a clipboard, affixed a sheaf of checkout sheets to it and walked out onto the floor. Perry took his own clipboard and a bundle of colored gummed labels and string tags from a box and followed him.

They waited while the driver halted the tug at the wide yellow line where the words "STOP HERE" had been painted across the concrete floor. Mr. Knox smiled and waved at the driver and set to work reading labels, comparing them to the checkout sheets on his clipboard and making notations as he went along. When he had completed the first pallet, he handed the sheets to Perry, who studied them, then wrote a series of numbers on them with a black marking pencil. He counted out a number of green stickers, wrote numbers on them and pasted them onto the cartons. After he had tagged all the cartons on the pallet, he verified the count against the totals on the checkout sheets and moved on to the next pallet, where Mr. Knox handed him some more sheets. They repeated the process until the entire load had been checked, after which Perry waved the driver through to the loading platform outside. Then the two of them returned to the desk to log the shipment on a master sheet and reconcile the totals with the figures given them by Shipping and Receiving.

On a busy day when the tugs were lined up waiting their turns at the Checkout Station, they might follow the same routine for two hours without a break. The work was simple enough, but it required all Perry's attention while he was doing it. Once after he had waved a load through, Mr. Knox looked up from his clipboard, raced to the door and signaled the driver to stop. He motioned Perry to him. He placed a forefinger on an entry on the checkout sheet and raised his eyebrows in question. Perry did not understand. He studied his lips as they moved, but he could not read them. Mr. Knox took the colored stickers from Perry's hands and selected a red one. Then Perry understood. "Ctn 17-264-6" should be removed from the shipment. Had he pasted a red sticker on it? He had not. He had misread Mr. Knox's penciled notation. As he became accustomed to his handwriting, however, he learned that most of his notations were standard phrases to be recognized on sight.

Numbers were easy for him. A number could have but one meaning. It was constant. It did not change according to the context in which it appeared. Words did, though. The same word written in two different places often carried two different meanings. He was never confident with words. He guessed at their meanings, oral and written, more often than even his own family realized. In the Quartermaster Depot his difficulty was compounded by the Army's specialized vocabulary and its official abbreviations and its strange way of turning sentences around and taking key words out of their normal sequence. None of that was to mention the bewildering thickets of little words in which he found them, if he found them at all. When he was working, therefore, he was forced to concentrate with an intensity that allowed for little daydreaming.

While he was collating the completed checkout sheets and totaling the quantities on an adding machine, Mr. Knox picked up the telephone and spoke into it briefly. He hung up the receiver and scribbled a note to Perry: "The Major wants to see me." Then he was gone.

Mr. Knox was good to him, and he was patient. Not all the deafs employed by the Depot were so fortunate. Over lunch or on the bus to and from downtown, they talked of their own supervisors, who were ill-tempered and fussy, impossible to please and who obviously regarded their deaf subordinates as nuisances they were forced to tolerate, impediments to their own work. Deaf people required special instruction for simple tasks that hearing people could learn to do in half the time with hardly any instruction at all.

Curtis Ivey, who had completed two years at Gallaudet College in Washington, D.C., and who worked in Building 411, told his friends of two days when he was completely idle because his supervisor did all the work himself rather than attempt to explain it to Curtis. Bryan Landers, whom Perry remembered from his school days at Cave Springs, told of his supervisor, who got so angry at him that purple veins stood out across his forehead while his mouth opened and closed successively for what seemed like five minutes. Bryan never did learn what prompted the outburst.

Mr. Knox was middle-aged with a kind face and gentle manner. He prided himself on a passable knowledge of the manual alphabet, which he had learned in his younger days for no more reason than a person learns the words to a catchy ditty. If they were sitting at the desk with nothing to do, he insisted on using it when conversing with Perry. Hand spelling was tedious and stretched conversation to unbelievable lengths. Perry had learned it at Cave Springs, but he had seldom used it since. Mr. Knox might have been surprised had he known that his young charge was no more proficient in the manual alphabet than he himself was. Still, Perry was grateful for his willingness and labored attempts to talk to him even when talking was not required. Cheerfully and industriously he spelled back to him whether he knew the correct spelling of a word or not.

He continued his work until he had reconciled all the totals and the sheets were ready for Mr. Knox's initials in the corner. He clipped them together and put them into the metal tray at the corner of the desk. He was warm with satisfaction over a job completed. He wondered if since morning he could have checked out any carton that might contain a pair of boots or a combat jacket or a web belt or a helmet liner or a mess kit or even a little OD colored packet of thread, needles and buttons that would find its way into Paul's hands. Probably not. Still, he could not help but indulge himself occasionally in the whimsy that a box or crate he had checked out would find its way to an Army Quartermaster Depot overseas and from it Paul would be issued a G.I. blanket, say.

Content in the possibility, he tidied up the desk. He was a happy man. He had responsibility, and he loved it. He did nothing mechanically or unthinkingly as he had done at the cotton mill. His actions were not governed by the whirring of a machine or by the length of an electrical cycle over which he had no control other than a switch labeled "Off" and "On." His work now required him to read, think, to discriminate, to act as he, Perry Mills Holly, evaluated the task to be performed. Granted, he worked within a strict set of procedures and had no authority to vary them, but he worked at a pace dictated by a human being, not by an inanimate, unthinking machine that told him what he must do and when he must do it.

Several times each day he delivered finished work to the front office and picked up work to be done, plus a bewildering mass of Army memorandums and directives he was expected to read and do something about. He made his pickup and delivery trips on his own schedule according to his own decision. Each step in his daily routine, however small and trivial, provided him with a freedom of choice that was exhilarating. He was a useful

178

citizen with a useful occupation, a vital link in the long, long chain of supplies and equipment that reached halfway around the world and made it possible for Paul and thousands like him to fight the war.

He got up from the desk and wandered out toward the loading platform. He stopped at the entrance and glanced down the length of the warehouse. A two-pallet load of wooden crates was coming toward him. An orange metal tag hanging from the front of the tug bore the black letters "CHECKOUT."

He peered toward the opposite end of the building, hoping to see Mr. Knox approaching. He saw nobody, not even the men at the distant Receiving Station. As the tug drew nearer, he moved back to the Checkout Station to ask the driver to wait until Mr. Knox returned. It would not be long. He had been in the Major's office for about fifteen minutes, and he never stayed any longer than that.

The driver stopped his tug at the yellow line and dismounted. He was not one of the regulars. Perry had never seen him before. He lifted his hand and waved. The driver did not look at him. He leaned over the tug and busied himself making an adjustment in the position of the seat, seemingly unaware of Perry's presence. Perry waited for him to finish with the seat and face him.

When he did, he glanced at his wristwatch and spoke two or three words. Or was it only one? His lips moved too fast, and his upper lip scarcely moved at all. He was big, rough hewn and unsmiling. He regarded Perry with indifference and fumbled in his shirt pocket for a package of cigarettes. Without thinking, Perry lifted his hands to explain, then dropped them. The driver would not understand signing. He made a quick move toward the desk for paper and pencil, but the driver was speaking again. He pointed toward the big clock over the entrance, then turned and walked out onto the loading platform.

Perry glanced at the clock. Noon was approaching.

179

Probably the driver did not want to delay his lunch hour. Anxiously he searched the aisle for Mr. Knox again, but in vain. He could see the driver outside on the platform, his back to the door, blowing cigarette smoke into the wind. The sensible thing to do—the only thing—was to write a note of explanation and take it to the driver. He had never checked out a load by himself, nor had Mr. Knox given him authority to do so in his absence. Besides, he was by no means certain that he knew enough about Mr. Knox's work to do it for him. The job required close and precise meaning. The words on packing labels were as exact as numbers. They allowed for no reasoning, estimating or guessing. He did not trust his own facility with the English language to see himself through so final an operation as checking out two or three dozen wooden crates of Army supplies and equipment headed for soldiers who were dependent upon them in some faraway place across an ocean.

Back at the desk, he started to write a note to the driver, but he stopped. He could at least get everything ready for Mr. Knox to begin his checking when he returned and perhaps save a few minutes' time. He studied the load number on the pallet and found the checkout sheets to match it. He rechecked the identifying numbers twice before he affixed the sheets to the clipboard. He stuffed some string tags and several marking pencils in the pocket of his shirt and returned to the floor. While he waited for Mr. Knox, he looked through the checkout sheets to occupy himself and began trying to match an entry to a label on a crate. He succeeded. He rechecked his work and convinced himself that he had made no error. Then why not check it off the sheet and tie a green tag to the crate? It would be one less for Mr. Knox to worry about. For the third time he verified his findings, then checked off the entry and tied a green label to the crate.

He moved on to another entry and another crate,

then to another. He worked slowly, reading and rereading and, if he did not recognize a word, matching it letter by letter on the sheet and on the label. The work was absorbing as he moved from crate to crate, but it was laborious. Many of the entries were nonsense syllables that communicated nothing, and his only course was to find nonsense syllables that were identical, pair them up and check them off. Even after he had completed a check and moved on to the next, he found himself returning to recheck once more for insurance.

He stopped to rest his eyes and survey what he had done. He was appalled by the number of wooden crates with green tags on them. A quick panic swept over him. Suppose there were steps in Mr. Knox's operations that had not been visible on the completed checkout sheets and that Perry knew nothing about? He had developed but little assurance in his own competence, and it fled him now. For all his checking, double-checking and verifying, he was left stranded with no confidence in the accuracy of anything he had done. His palms grew sweaty. He felt a fluttering inside his stomach. Perhaps he should stop now and wait. It was not too late to write that note to the driver. He had not intended to go so far. If Mr. Knox had to undo all his work and redo it, the time consumed would be more than—

The driver appeared in the doorway. He stood for a moment and looked inside the warehouse. Then he disappeared.

Perry returned to work. He glanced at the clock on the wall. It was five minutes until noon. The fluttering in his stomach increased. His hands trembled so that he could hardly make a firm mark on a green tag. Once he stopped, laid his clipboard on a crate, took out his handkerchief and mopped his face and dried his palms. He looked again for Mr. Knox, praying that he would come before he unwittingly finished the load.

At last he finished the first pallet. He stood back and breathed deeply with relief, but not for long. Another pallet remained to be checked. With great effort he kept his eyes off the clock.

The driver appeared again. This time he came inside the warehouse and watched Perry without speaking. His impatience was obvious. Perry could feel his stare, but he pretended not to notice his presence. Eventually he returned to the loading platform.

Perry tried to work faster. If the driver returned a third time and the load was not ready to tow away, his impatient silence might turn into something considerably more unpleasant. But he knew no way to speed up the operation. He had to read each word and come to some kind of terms with it, for words were not like pictures. They did not convey their own message or tell their own story. A word meant nothing unless you could paint your own picture to go with it, not unless you could create an entire environment in which to set it. And that was the most impossible of tasks. Words stood alone. They were their own pictures—pictures that portrayed nothing except the meaning some person assigned to them arbitrarily.

The driver returned a third time. He moved to the first pallet and examined the green tags on the crates. He walked around the pallet on which Perry was working, examining it critically. He moved to Perry's elbow and looked down at the clipboard. Most certainly he was talking, but Perry did not look at him to see. As he moved away, Perry saw from the corner of his eye that he was pointing to the big clock above the entrance again.

Perry worked on and somehow tied the last green tag to a wooden crate. He looked back through the checkout sheets, scarcely breathing. On the second page he found an item that he had not checked. At the end of the line was a word that said nothing to him. He spelled it out: "d-e-l-e-t-e-d." It had a vague familiarity, but no more than

182

the hundreds of words in books and newspapers he was forced to skip because no image had been assigned to them. The fluttering turned into a knot as he flipped the other sheets, hoping to find the word repeated in a context he recognized. He did not find it. Whatever the word meant, surely it must explain why he had not checked the entry. He counted the crates on both pallets again and reconciled their totals with the checkout sheets. Everything tallied.

He wiped his palms on the side of his trousers and took out his handkerchief to dry his face again. Frantically, he looked back down the aisle for Mr. Knox. He saw only some blurred activity at the Receiving Station at the other end of the building. He stepped back to the desk and thumbed through a stack of previously completed checkout sheets hoping to find "d-e-l-e-t-e-d" somewhere among them, anything to give him a clue. Nothing. Sick at heart, he counted the crates for the third time. He did not know what else to do. Nothing had changed.

The driver returned. He was angry. His face was red and his eyes threatening. He was talking, shaking his head, waving his arms, pointing to the clock, to his wristwatch, talking, talking, talking, apparently unaware that his words were wasted, that no one heard them.

Perry knew he could wave him through. After all, a green tag had been tied to each crate in the load. But how was he to account for "d-e-l-e-t-e-d"? If the driver would only stop talking. If he would get that angry scowl off his face. If he would ask a question. If he would smile or look moderately pleasant. If he would appear to be waiting for an explanation. Perry's stomach was burning.

He turned once more to search for Mr. Knox.

The driver was pointing to the tug and the entrance now. He went on talking, talking, talking.

Suddenly, Perry stepped back and waved him through the Checkout Station onto the loading platform.

He had no explanation for his actions. He did it because he could think of no alternative. He could not explain the delay to the driver. He could not even apologize. At the moment he had no desire but to see the rear of the last pallet disappear through the big door.

The scowl on the driver's face grew uglier. He sliced the air in a quick gesture of disgust and mounted the tug. He towed the pallets out of the warehouse while Perry watched numbly.

He made his way back to the desk and fell into his chair, limp and spent. His shirt and undershirt were wet and cold. He wiped the perspiration from his face and hands again and spread his handkerchief across the corner of the desk to dry. He felt no relief, no triumph, no sense of accomplishment, no satisfaction in a job completed. He felt nothing but a cold, clammy fear that he had done nothing right. He did not look down the aisle for Mr. Knox now. He did not want him to come back. Not now. He did not want to see him.

But Mr. Knox did come back. He was preoccupied, and his eyes were troubled. He nodded to Perry, took a sheaf of papers from a drawer and started reading through them line by line. Perry looked on, not wondering or caring what he was searching for. No doubt it was connected with the Major's summons to the front office, but he could not bring himself to be concerned. He waited.

When Mr. Knox had finished and returned the papers to the drawer, his face brightened. He was his pleasant self again.

Perry stared at the checkout sheets in his hand. They were wrinkled where he had gripped them. Along the edges the type was blurred with sogginess. He laid them flat on the desk and tried to smooth them. When he caught Mr. Knox watching him with mild curiosity, he took a deep breath and laid the papers in front of him.

Mr. Knox glanced at the top page, then at Perry, with surprise. He began to study the sheets. Perry's insides

184

congealed as he watched his supervisor read number after number, line after line, sheet after sheet. He tried to read the expression on his face, but he saw neither approval nor disapproval. He waited for a question, a request for clarification along the way, but none came. He prepared himself for whatever the consequences might turn out to be for exceeding his authority. He waited. At last Mr. Knox reached the bottom of the last page. Quickly he scanned all the sheets and came to the bottom of the last page again. Perry held his breath.

He looked up at Perry and smiled. He lifted both hands in a gesture of approval. He clapped Perry on the back, once, twice, three times. His smile turned into a wide grin.

Perry stared at him in disbelief. Mr. Knox was talking. Suddenly he shook his head, stopped and picked up a pencil. He scribbled some words on a pad and shoved it across the desk. "Good work. You know as much about this job as I do. Thanks."

Perry sat numbly for a bit; then he pushed back from the desk and bolted for the door, the outside and the fresh air.

He and Mr. Knox ate lunch together. It was too late for him to meet his deaf friends in the cafeteria as he usually did. Throughout the afternoon his spirits were high. He knew an exhilaration that came from the satisfaction of a job well done, and he could share it with no hearing people. He kept it within himself until he met his deaf friends at the bus stop after work. Of course they would understand.

On the bus ride into town his elation remained unabated, but the significance of what he had done got lost in the telling of it. His friends watched everything he said and nodded with approval. Yet they tended to regard his accomplishment as only slightly out of the ordinary. He was disappointed. He was to meet Susie for dinner, though, and she would understand what the day had meant to him.

# 18

THE MAN ON THE ELEVATOR was small, thin and pale. He stood alone in the corner and watched her through dark-rimmed spectacles. Susie would not have looked at him a second time had he not greeted her. His face was narrow and his features pointed. His smile was friendly but not personal.

"Good evening," he said. "It's unusual to find only two people on the elevator this time of day, isn't it?"

He was about her own age, twenty-six or twenty-seven at the most. His dark suit hung carelessly on his spare frame. A disarray of papers stuck out of a side pocket in his jacket. He was bareheaded, and his thin hair flopped loosely across the top of his head.

"It will probably fill up before we get down," she said, looking at the arrow sweeping around the arc above the door. She turned back to him and noticed a slouch in one shoulder. Maybe he was stooped.

They descended the rest of the way in silence. No one else had got aboard.

The door slid open, and she stepped out into the lobby. Behind her she heard a heavy thud and a light metallic clink. She turned back. The man had fallen to the floor of the elevator car. He was crumpled forward on his knees and was trying to push himself up with his hands.

"Oh!" Susie hurried back inside. "Are you hurt?" She bent over and grasped his arm to help him.

"No, I'm all right, I think," he said. His spectacles had fallen off. He looked up at her with eyes that now seemed tiny and blank. "I'm sorry—and a little embarrassed," he went on. His hands were searching the carpet around his knees. "Do you mind helping me find my glasses? I'm almost totally blind without them."

She released his arm and found his spectacles on the far side of the car.

"They're not broken, are they?" he asked anxiously.

"They're all right." She handed them to him. "Here. Let me help you get up. What happened?"

"It's the brace on my left leg," he explained. "It's been loose for several days, and it finally gave way. I should have had it looked after as soon as I noticed it."

He sounded almost British, but then she decided it was probably a New England accent of some kind. She helped him to his feet. When he had steadied himself, she released him. He did not move. She watched him expectantly.

"I'm sorry again," he said. "I can't walk without support of some kind. I don't like to be any more bother than I've already been, but can you help me out into the lobby where I can sit down?"

"Why, certainly! Here, lean on my arm—or I'll hold yours—or however you do it. You tell me what to do."

They made their way through the door out into the lobby. He dragged his left foot, and each forward movement was accompanied by a light clink of metal.

"You're very kind," he said. "This happened once before when I was alone, and I crawled on my hands and knees to a chair. It might look strange for me to crawl out of an elevator in a public place, though."

People were coming out of the other elevators and rushing through the lobby toward the front entrances of

the building. A few looked at the pair of them with passing interest and hurried on.

"I'm taking up too much of your time," he apologized. "Sit me down somewhere and leave me. I'll be all
right. Maybe I can fasten the pin back temporarily—at
least enough to get me home."

Susie's eyes were sweeping the lobby. She was per-
plexed. "That's funny," she said. "I never had noticed it
before, but there's nowhere to sit. Not even a bench." She
looked back at him. "What do you think we ought to do?
Would you like to go back to your office, where you can
call someone?"

"Everybody's gone. I was the last one out, and I don't
have a key. I really should use my cane all the time. A bit
of misplaced vanity on my part." He smiled.

He searched the faces as they went by, but he recognized no one.

She waited.

"Well—if you can help me out to the curb, I'll flag a
taxi. You can lean me up against a lamppost and be off
about your own affairs."

Susie was dubious. "Taxis are hard to get this time
of day, and especially with share-the-ride restrictions. You
have to be going in the same direction as the other passengers, or they won't pick you up. But come on, and
we'll see. Maybe I can telephone someone for you."

He considered that for a moment. "I can't think of
who would be at home right now."

She helped him across the sidewalk through the passing crowd to the curb. "A cabdriver will never see you unless you're out in the street," she told him. "When we
get you settled, I'll see if I can get one for you."

"Please, Miss—you've done more than enough, and I
can't detain you any longer," he said. "You look as though
you might have a date, and you can't keep him waiting.
Just leave me by that lamppost."

"Oh, I couldn't do that!" she said. "You might still be standing there when I come to work tomorrow morning."

She maneuvered him a few feet along the curb. He hooked an arm around the lamppost. She could feel him relax.

"Here. Now, how's that?" Susie still held to him.

He laughed. "This is the classic pose for a drunk, isn't it? Hanging onto a lamppost. You don't need to hold me up," he said. "I won't fall now. I insist you go on. Your boyfriend might be—"

"What part of town do you live in?"

"Close to Emory University, but please—"

Susie was already off the curb, beyond the parked cars and out onto the edge of the street. The traffic was heavy and impatient, but it moved swiftly, and in each spurt of automobiles she hoped to find a taxicab. She looked in both directions, but the only cabs in sight were at the corner, where they flowed almost regularly across the intersection. She watched them anxiously, hoping one would turn the corner and come in her direction. None of them did.

She looked at her watch. She did not like to keep Perry waiting. He would be kind and understanding, which was all the more reason she did not want to keep him waiting. If she left now, she could make it to the Ansley on time. On the other hand, a few minutes' tardiness was generally excusable, for nobody was ever punctual down to the minute and second. She tried not to be concerned about Perry. When she looked at her watch again, another fifteen minutes had gone by. A five- or ten-minute walk to the Ansley would make her that much later. She took another look for a taxicab and, seeing none among the automobiles and buses, returned to the man at the lamppost.

"This is the wrong place to flag cabs," she said to him.

"We'll do much better at the corner. Let me help you—if it's not too far—and we'll have better luck."

"No. Definitely not," he said. He spoke kindly and softly but with determination. "You leave me here and go on to your date."

She regarded him with new interest. "I didn't tell you I had a date, did I? You mentioned it before."

"You didn't have to tell me. It seems right that you do, somehow. You've got that air about you. Besides, your dress is too pretty to be wearing downtown in an office building unless it's for something special."

"As a matter of fact, I do have a date," she said. "And I am late, but he'll understand when I tell him what happened. He's—" She stopped. She had started to explain, but she liked the picture that had obviously formed in his mind. "But whether I'm late or not, I can't walk away and leave you hanging onto a lamppost."

"Yes, you can. When you get to the corner, perhaps you can find a policeman who will give me a hand. He'll know what to do."

"But what if I can't find one? They're all directing traffic at this hour."

"If you don't, perhaps you won't mind telephoning a precinct station and detailing my predicament. They'll send someone to rescue me."

Susie could not make up her mind. "I feel *awful* leaving you like this. It's inhumane."

"My name is Robert Shaefer, and I work on the twelfth floor—Southern Trade, Incorporated," he said. He was dismissing her. "I'll get in touch with you tomorrow—if you'll tell me your name and how to find you."

"Well—if you're absolutely certain you'll be all right," she said with reluctance. She gave him her name and where she worked.

"Have a good time this evening," he said. "I mean a *really* good time." He smiled at her. This time the smile was personal. She found in it a message for her and nobody else.

She walked toward the corner and, despite the distressing situation she had left unresolved, hurried along to meet Perry with a spring in her step and a heart that was light, frothy and happy.

Perry could scarcely contain his own pride as he told her of his experience at the warehouse that morning. Susie was understanding, and what escaped her in his signing, which went too fast at times, she found in the enthusiasm in his face and manner. He finished and sipped his drink.

"That's not all I want to tell you," he said, setting the glass back on the table. "I've got a girl friend."

"My heavens! Aren't you the newsy one!" She lifted her glass. "Let's drink to her. Then tell me about her. I can't wait."

"Her name is Lydia Regan, and she comes from Abbeville over in South Carolina," he said. "She works at General Motors and lives downstairs at the Maxwells'. She's about my age and is real pretty."

"Is she deaf?"

"Partially. But enough that she went to a school for the deaf like I did. She signs more than she talks aloud."

"How serious is this?"

"I don't know about that, but we have a good time together. We go swimming out at Piedmont Park and take a picnic sometimes. We've been to the zoo and the Cyclorama at Grant Park, and we're always stopping somewhere to watch a softball game. She likes football, too. And we're going to some of Georgia Tech's home games this fall. One Saturday afternoon we went downtown and window-shopped, browsed through the stores, bought a sack of peanuts from a street vendor and went in Walgreens for a coke. We had more fun than you can imagine. She dragged me to a picture show one night but you remember, I never liked picture shows. I get tired of watch-

191

ing people jumping around and chasing each other when I don't know what for. Of course, she couldn't explain it to me in the dark. Then one day we went to the High Museum of Art and—"

"Heavens above! Don't you ever stay home?"

He shook his head and laughed. "I had almost forgotten what it was like to do things with other people," he went on. "After I came back home from Cave Springs, I was by myself all the time except when some of you came."

"Perry, that's the most wonderful thing you've told me since the time you came home from Cave Springs when you were in the first grade and taught me to tell the story of 'Chicken Little' in signs. You remember how you got so mad at me because I was so dumb and slow to catch on?"

"You deserved it," he said, grinning.

"Perry, does Paul ever write to you?"

He nodded.

"I've never had one line from him. Neither has Ferebe. And poor Mother and Daddy are beside themselves. They hear from him once in a blue moon. I feel so sorry for them I could die. What does he say? What does he do? What does he write about?"

Perry sat motionless for a time before he lifted his hands to reply. "He tells me about the war—as much as he's allowed to tell. I can't make out some of his scribblings, and he uses a lot of words I can't connect with anything. It takes me a long time to read his letters. They mix me up sometimes."

"I'm not trying to snoop," Susie said "but if you'll let me, I can read some of them for you. I know you and Paul have always been going off to yourselves and having big secrets and not telling us where you've been or what you've been doing and making big mysteries out of everything, but I'll keep my mouth shut if you ever want me to read one of Paul's letters for you."

"I'll think it over," he said, a faraway expression coming into his eyes. "I get a strange feeling about Paul fighting in a war in Europe. I feel like I'm there myself even when I don't know what he's talking about in his letters. I study all the war pictures of the Fifth Army, and I can't fit him into any of them. There's nothing real about any of it. Yet I feel like I'm in the middle of it myself right along beside him."

"It's always been that way with both of you, hasn't it?"

"Yes, but he has always been somewhere I had been myself and could understand. The war's different. He might as well be on the back side of the moon." He smiled. "But I'd feel like I was there too, wouldn't I?"

# 19

He came into Susie's office the following day after lunch. She was surprised at how small he was. She had been thinking he was taller. He walked with a slight limp, and she saw that the drop in his shoulder was not a slouch but that he was stooped, after all.

"I hope your employer won't mind my stopping in for a moment during office hours," he apologized. "I remembered your name and the floor but not the name of your company. I knew I'd recognize it on sight, though."

He appeared to be wearing the same suit, shirt and necktie, but she decided he might be one of those men whose personality puts a stamp of sameness on everything they wear. He walked with a cane this time.

"It's my insurance," he said. "It's rather like carrying an umbrella when it's not raining, but it is comfortable and reassuring."

He asked her to meet him after work for dinner. They would go to a Chinese restaurant he knew and liked; that is, if she liked Chinese food and, of course, if she was not busy that evening.

"I don't have a thing to do, and I love Chinese food," she said quickly. "I haven't had any in *ages*."

After he had gone, she telephoned the Red Cross to say she would not be able to work her shift at the blood bank that evening.

"Will wonders never cease!" said Emily Lanier. "I can't believe that anything could possibly interfere with the war effort. Are you giving up the war for the duration?"

"Certainly not, silly!" Susie said with a giggle. "I can work at the blood bank anytime, but how often do I get invited out for dinner?"

He met her in the lobby and told her he had picked out a charming Chinese restaurant not too far away. She said walking was fine with her, if it didn't bother him.

"This cane probably performs another service for me," he said after they were settled at a table. "With so many men in uniform these days, people tend to raise their eyebrows at the sight of a draft-age man who is not. I carry my explanation in my hand."

"I wish my brother had some visible sign like that," she said. "He's deaf, and of course you can't tell that by looking. Does it bother you about not being in the service?"

"To an extent. But the feeling is not new—only the situation. I've never been able to do many things other boys did. You become philosophical about it. Some things you can't do, so you accept that condition. You probably understand that. With deafness in your immediate family, surely you appreciate the problems of handicapped people. In terms of their relationships with other people the problems are much the same, regardless of the nature of the handicap."

"We never think of Perry as handicapped—not consciously, I mean. He's a member of the family who happens to be deaf. After he's been away from us awhile, we have to get used to talking to him again, but it doesn't take long. We all have ways to communicate with him without making the correct signs."

"I hope nobody in your family ever lets him think you pity him," he said. "That's humiliating."

"Oh, no! My mother and daddy never would let us do that. While we were growing up, he fussed at us, and we fussed right back at him. I saw my daddy give him a spanking once. I went off and cried, because Perry couldn't. He had tears in his eyes, but he couldn't make any sounds. I thought my daddy was the cruelest man ever born until afterwards when I was out in the yard and happened to walk past the garage. He was inside doing something to the car. Tears were rolling down his cheeks. He doesn't know I saw him, and I'd die before I'd let him know."

Seated in the Chinese restaurant, he surveyed the place with satisfaction and watched her eagerly for signs of her approval. She obliged him, but she did not tell him that she came to the same restaurant sometimes when her money was running out, for the prices were low and the servings enormous.

Robert Shaefer had been a victim of infantile paralysis when he was six years old and had worn a brace on his leg ever since. He grew up, an only child, in Manchester, New Hampshire, and had completed two years of college at Amherst. When his parents died in an automobile accident, he dropped out of school.

"I didn't have to," he said. "With their insurance, the sale of the house and property and two or three small investments, I could have finished college comfortably and perhaps even established myself in something afterwards. But I think I used their deaths as an excuse not to."

"Why would you do that?"

He toyed with his water glass. "I've never really had the nerve to explain it to myself," he said, spinning the glass slowly and examining it intently. "I think it was because by dropping out of college, I didn't have to commit myself—at least not then and there."

"Did you commit yourself later?"

"No. I was studying political science, and don't ask me why. It was not what I wanted. I didn't mind it, but the field didn't interest me. Two more years and I would have had the degree and been forced to do something with

196

it. I think the reason I chose it was because it involved a lot of reading, and I could do it alone—no labs, no teamwork, none of that. It's not an exact science, you know. It's got no yes and no answers. I liked that part of it, too. It's such a slippery, shadowy subject no one can tell whether you're good or bad in it."

"What did you want, then?"

"Music." He continued to study his glass. "I hear it, feel it, play it and write it. But I can't release it—not all of it. It explodes inside me. I'm a good pianist, and I've written sheet after sheet of good music, but I'm still cooped up with it inside my head. I recognized early that I would never be equipped to set it free without advanced and expert instruction—the best. I applied to Juilliard, Eastman, the New England Conservatory and some lesser ones. All of them turned me down. They said I did not meet their standards musically. So I continued on my own, even while I was at Amherst, thinking my time would come later. It never did."

The waiter brought their dinner, and she listened with proper interest as he explained some of the dishes she might not understand.

"My parents never took my music—or my dedication to it—seriously. They were happy for me to have a nice pastime to compensate for the things I couldn't do, but their interest went no further than that. The best thing I ever wrote was a sonata. After I had finished it, I invited them to sit down and listen as though they were attending a formal recital. I planned it, rehearsed it and got ready for it as though I were to perform on a stage. Before I had finished playing, my father went back to reading his newspaper. My mother listened to all of it, or at least she watched me play it, but at the end she got up and left the room. 'That's longer than some of your others, isn't it?' she said over her shoulder. I was sixteen years old. I've never played any of my music for anyone since."

Susie was touched. "But everybody doesn't have a real feeling for music," she said helpfully. "My own daddy's not musical at all. He even sings off-key in church."

"But it wasn't only my parents," he went on. "I was seldom asked to play in public—school programs and things like that. I rationalized that by the fact that I did not participate in many school activities."

"You didn't give it up altogether, did you?" she asked. "I mean, you must think you've got real talent or you wouldn't be so serious about it."

"I have no doubt about my talent," he said matter-of-factly. "I didn't give up music. I can't. It won't let me go, even though I haven't touched a piano since I've been in Atlanta—about two years now. I play in my mind. On the bus in the mornings while everybody else is reading, talking or napping, sometimes I see the notes on a sheet of music and feel my hands on the keys, and I play the entire pieces from beginning to end. If I make a mistake, I go back and correct it. Sometimes I start back at the beginning until I make it successfully past that mistake. Once I played a piece twice and went past the corner where I was supposed to get off the bus. I don't have a piano. I don't have room for one, and I couldn't afford it if I did. Do you like music?"

"Yes, I do. But I don't know anything about it, except I like some pieces and some I don't."

"That's all you need to know," he said. "It's like looking at a picture. It appeals to you or it doesn't. You're not required to analyze your reasons. On the other hand, if a picture or a piece of music is explained to you, your appreciation is heightened, and you might grow to like the very thing you rejected in the first place. Would you like to hear me play sometime?"

"Oh, I'd love to! Will you play some of your own compositions and explain them?"

198

He was silent for a moment while he gazed at her. He did not appear to be considering her request at all. He was pleasant and relaxed and apparently was looking at her because he enjoyed looking at her. She felt comfortable in the silence.

"Yes," he said after a time.

They had more coffee as she told him about Bentley, her family, the Georgia Railroad, The Well, Georgia State College for Women in Milledgeville, the house on Madison Road where she grew up.

"The Bentley Historical Society started a project once to identify all antebellum homes—and one or two colonials —and mark them for historical purposes, but I don't think they ever went through with it. They had their eyes on ours, among others. There aren't many—not since General Sherman got through burning them."

"Is it large with white columns?"

"Heavens no!" She laughed. "You probably read *Gone with the Wind*, too. It's just that it's probably an authentic example of houses of that era. Mother takes great stock in historical things and thinks they should be preserved. I agree. If people didn't think that way, many of those lovely old homes, churches, and bricked wall gardens with grilled iron gates in Savannah and Charleston might not be there today for everyone to enjoy. The South might have already lost much of its charm."

They ordered more coffee and sipped it as he told her what it was like to live in the industrial town of Manchester. He told her of Boston on the south where he could go for concerts, plays, museum exhibits, of the White Mountains and Hawthorne's Great Stone Face on the north, of the granite quarries and textile mills scattered throughout the state, of the miles of vacationland, indescribably beautiful in the fall when entire mountains were afire with gold, red, yellow, orange and other rich colors that man had not yet learned to duplicate. His fa-

199

ther had been a printer, starting out working for a large printing company in Portsmouth. In Manchester his success had been moderate and comfortable. Neither he nor Robert's mother claimed a long New England ancestry, nor were they particularly intrigued by early American history, the evidence of which lay all around them.

"They were good people, respectable, intelligent, but I'm afraid they would not have adapted easily to your Southern openness and friendliness," he said. "You probably would think they were unsociable, but they weren't. It was just that their circle of friends and acquaintances was rather small, and all of them respected one another's privacy. That's what they all liked and wanted, so that's what they all got—by tacit agreement and custom."

"People in Bentley would think you were peculiar if you didn't know everybody in town and weren't happy to see them every time they came in sight."

"That's characteristic of Southern towns," he said. "Atlanta's too big a city for that, but there's some of it here, too. Quite a bit, in fact. In the dry cleaner's or grocery store or even the post office out in my neighborhood, those people will visit with you at the drop of a hat, even when they're busy."

"Do you like it that way?"

"If it's not overdone," he said. "When I began to understand one of the reasons for the difference, at least I accepted it. Keep in mind that in New England we go around bundled up to the ears for months on end. You don't stop and visit on the sidewalks or in your front yards or over your back fence when you're as cold as a block of ice. Freezing temperatures are not conducive to chitchat. Your immediate goal is to get in out of the cold. For most of the year down here that's no concern. You move slower, because you'll get too hot if you move fast; and as long as you're moving slower and the other people you meet are moving slower too, it's easier to talk to one another than not to. But don't forget that the way people live in New England requires a certain cooperation and understanding among themselves also."

"I hadn't thought about it like that," she said. "What did you do when you weren't writing music or playing the piano?"

"I read. I'm a voracious reader. I'll read anything. I must have inherited my father's love and reverence for books, although he admired the craftsmanship that went into their manufacture, while I admire the contents more. At any rate, he taught me to respect books. Once I turned down the corner of a page in a book to mark my place. He lectured me at great length about mistreating books— the thing we leave behind us for the next generation and the next. I'm glad he did. I treat a tattered or damaged book as gently as you probably treat a wounded animal or pet."

"It's funny you would make that comparison," she said. "I was always in trouble at home for bringing in stray dogs, hungry cats and birds with crippled wings."

"I knew that," he said. "Your concern for me yesterday was a good demonstration."

"You're not a wounded animal."

"In a way, I am. You didn't know me. You had a date. You were in a hurry. Yet, when you saw I was in trouble, that took priority."

The waiter approached their table. He was apologetic. It was time to close.

They looked about the restaurant in surprise. The place was empty except for an old Chinese man removing the cloths from the tables.

"I can't believe it!" Susie exclaimed. "What have we been doing?"

"Talking, and I can't think of an evening I've enjoyed more," he said. He looked at the check and handed the waiter a bill. They got up to go.

"In your biography you didn't tell me why you moved from New Hampshire to Georgia," she said.

"That's easy," he replied. "Probably the most uncomplicated thing I ever did." He stopped at the cash register for his change before they stepped out onto the sidewalk. The street was all but deserted. "It was the weather," he continued. "I hated the long winters in New Hampshire. I couldn't enjoy the very things that make it attractive to many people—the snow, the skiing, sledding, ice skating. When it was icy and snow lay deep on the ground, I had trouble getting around. My crutches would slide out from under me. I used crutches until I was twelve or thirteen years old. Or my feet would slip, and I'd fall and sprain an ankle—always something like that. I could never move fast enough to keep warm. So during winters I virtually hibernated. In the springs when I ventured out again, it was as though I were recovering from a long illness. After my parents died, I came south where it's warmer. I selected Atlanta because it's a city with all the advantages, although I'll have to say that it's not sleepy and dripping with the honey chile, magnolia atmosphere most people associate with the South."

"Do you like it?"

"It's beautiful. The sun knows exactly where and when to shine through all those magnificent trees—sycamore, poplar, pine, crab apple, persimmon, tall oak—and it knows exactly how to filter its light on the yellow jasmine, trillium, honeysuckle, red woodbine, and always the dogwood and azalea. You see? I know the names of them. I get completely intoxicated by what I see."

"Goodness! Maybe I'd better take another look at it for myself!" she said. "Have you got any friends in Atlanta?"

"Not really, but it's my own fault. People are nice to me. Sometimes I eat lunch or dinner with someone from the office, but that's about all. I spend a lot of time in the libraries, and I like the museums. I go to an occasional concert when I have enough money for a ticket. I went to the Met when they came to town last and saw *La Bohème*. It was glorious. They've stopped coming now until after the war."

They arrived at her streetcar stop and stood on the corner waiting.

"I talk incessantly when I get an opportunity," he said. "I must be making up for lost time. If I were around more people more often, I would spread it out and not unload quite so much on one person."

"I loved it," she said. "I loved every minute of it."

He saw her aboard her streetcar, then walked off down the street to catch his bus.

# 20

THE PEOPLE AT HOME anxiously followed two wars and uneasily kept their senses alert in case a third broke out elsewhere. And throughout it all were the servicemen, the soldiers, sailors, Marines and a sprinkling of their counterparts from Allied countries, whom few people could account for but accepted, nevertheless, as necessary members of the constantly moving population.

In Atlanta, military uniforms were everywhere. The Terminal and Union Stations, the airport and bus depots teemed with them. People were accustomed to them on streetcars, in waiting rooms, in the apartment upstairs and the house next door. They became familiar sights lined up outside restaurants and cafés along Forsyth Street waiting to eat between trains, wandering aimlessly alone or in clusters on downtown streets, in Grant Park, around the State Capitol. On those spots where all Atlanta seemed to converge at one time—Five Points during rush hours, Decatur Street on Saturday night, Peachtree Street at Christmastime—the city resembled a huge military installation enjoying its off-duty hours.

Many of the men were stationed in Atlanta; others were passing through; still others came for a weekend or on three-day passes from Fort Benning, Camp Stewart, Fort Oglethorpe, the air bases at Valdosta, Moultrie, Albany and other installations that appeared so suddenly throughout Georgia that many people were not aware of their existence until they learned of them from a furloughed stranger in uniform.

The Red Cross fed them; the USO entertained them; theaters gave them discounts on tickets; museums, galleries, concerts, exhibitions admitted them with no charge at all; streetcars, trolleys and buses gave them free rides; restaurants served them nonexistent steaks; nightclubs seated them at unavailable tables; churches singled them out as honored worshipers; congregations divided them up and took them home for Sunday dinner; motorists picked them up off the curbs along busy thoroughfares and went out of their way to take them wherever they wanted to go. Matrons mothered them, their husbands protected them, their daughters danced with them, their young children imitated them.

Beyond question, Atlanta's love affair with the American serviceman was deep and abiding; and no matter who he was, a banker turned corporal or a grease monkey turned captain, its heart always had another corner in which to tuck him until time to send him back home, to another city, to another region, to another country, or even into the hands of the enemy himself. The people knew that it was a fleeting condition, a phase that would pass, that one day, for better or for worse, the strangers would leave, the uniforms would disappear, and Atlanta would return to normalcy, whatever that might turn out to be. But until then, the city's reigning celebrity was the man in uniform.

Susie Holly was conscious of them and, when she walked down the street with Robert or Perry, painfully so. She tried not to be and was ashamed of herself for it. It was not a matter of justifying to onlookers why young men of their age still wore civilian clothes. After all, Robert's cane and Perry's signing told the entire story.

But she felt left out. She looked into the faces of women and girls coming along the sidewalks, laughing, talking, somber, quiet, and she envied them. The corporals and colonels, the seamen and admirals with whom they walked arm in arm were their contributions to the war, their personal stake in it, and they wore them proudly as they would badges.

She overheard them on buses, in restaurants, in stores, and it was obvious that they had accepted their husbands' and sweethearts' military regimen as their own. She listened to their easy, natural use of military phrases and identifications with a kind of wistfulness. While their talk was not always incomprehensible to her, she had little reason to indulge in it herself, at least not with the same proprietary interest they had. She was on the outside looking in. She had Paul, certainly, but he belonged to everybody, not only to her. Besides, he was in Sicily. Sometimes she seemed to be the only woman in the State of Georgia not attached to a man in uniform; and except for the very young and the very old, Robert and Perry seemed to be the only men in the State of Georgia not wearing one.

"Doesn't it ever bother you because you can't join the Army or the Navy?" she asked Robert.

"You asked me that once before, and I told you. Are my civilian clothes making you uncomfortable?" He was rather curt.

"Oh, no! I didn't mean anything like that!"

"Then why did you mention it again?"

"I'm sorry. That first time slipped my mind. Perry and I talk about it sometimes. He says he'd love to be in the Navy."

"I'm not Perry," he snapped.

She avoided the topic from there on.

"I don't know who's overseas fighting the war," Emily Lanier said. "It looks like the whole armed forces is on Peachtree Street every time I go down there."

206

"They're making me feel like a slacker, and I'm going to do something about it," Susie said with decision. "I'm not going to wait on Fort Mac or the Navy or the United States Government any longer. They can hire somebody else. I'm going to get me a war job, and if the Piedmont Hosiery Company can't sell socks without me, they can go bankrupt and people will have to go bare legged."

To Emily's astonishment, Susie followed through on her promise.

"How did you know where to go? I wouldn't know where to start."

"Where to *go?* Listen, Emily, the big choice is where *not* to go. I never heard of so many job openings—ever. Have you looked at the classified ads lately? You won't believe it! Practically all the Help Wanted ads are for women. There are scads and scads of them for typists, receptionists, file clerks, switchboard operators, waitresses, salesgirls—take your pick. But there are also scads and scads of them for women truck drivers, drill press operators, welders, mechanics, construction workers, and even *bricklayers!* Can you imagine? Filling stations and parking lots are crying for women attendants. Any woman in town with a driver's license can be a cabdriver. And bus drivers! Wouldn't you hate to drive one of those huge buses? I knew there was a manpower shortage, but I never dreamed things were so desperate."

"Susie, you must be out of your mind going off down in that awful part of town to work!" Emily admonished her. "There's nothing down there but ugly old ironworks and machine shops and smoky tin buildings and railroad tracks. Think how it will be when you have to come home after dark."

"It's not all that bad. I can get on and off the bus a half block from where I work. Lots of girls work in that area. I can hardly wait to get started. The Dixie Metal Works takes Navy contracts—metal brackets and little doodads for ship interiors. Something *really* connected with the war."

"Why don't you just join the WACs or the WAVES and be done with it?"

"I would if I could lose fifteen pounds," Susie replied. She laughed. "I'm going to miss you, Emily. I just love talking to you all the time. You're so irreverent about things. If you're not tied up with Buddy Sunday morning, why don't we get together and have brunch somewhere? Say about ten o'clock, and neither of us will have to hurry."

"I'd like to, but I'm going to a cocktail party at nine, and it'll just be getting started by ten."

"At nine o'clock in the morning? A *cocktail* party?"

"It's some weird people Buddy knows. They work on the swing shift at one of the plants. They claim nine o'clock in the morning to them is like six o'clock in the evening to us. She goes out in the back yard and hangs her washing on the line at ten o'clock at night."

# 21

SUSIE COULD NOT MARK the exact day or week she fell in love. It happened too gradually and too subtly for that. All she knew was that she was in love with Robert Shaefer. Often she had wondered how she would feel when it happened, if she would become giddy and inattentive, rapt, lost in the clouds, blind to practicalities. She had seen that happen to her friends, and it seemed to be standard emotional behavior for heroines in stories, novels and the picture shows. She was quite unprepared, therefore, to discover her feet planted firmly on the ground and all her faculties intact. While she was aware that Robert did not fulfill her girlish ideal of the man who would be her Prince Charming, she could scarcely remember what that ideal had been. Robert had provided his own ideal and personified it all at the same time.

He stopped by her office a few times on his way to lunch, and she went with him. They ate at a drugstore near their building or in a cafeteria two blocks over. Sometimes they ate hamburgers at a hole-in-the-wall place that reeked with onions, mustard and meat cooking on a hot greasy grill. She paid her own check each time as she did with Emily or other girl friends. There was never a question about that. In time, lunch together became part of their daily routine.

In the afternoon they met downstairs by the elevators in the lobby and walked to their car stops together. His was two blocks beyond hers, but frequently she walked past her stop to his, then back to her own after he had gone. Occasionally they stayed downtown to see an early picture show or an exhibit of rare books at the Public Library or to hear a concert by the Atlanta Choral Guild, sometimes the symphony, and once they attended a concert by the Georgia Tech Band on the steps of the State Capitol. He did not like shopping, and after she had persuaded him to go with her to Rich's one evening, she never asked him to go along again. She cooked dinner for him in her one-room apartment. Afterward, she was strangely concerned about him as he walked off alone into the darkness toward the avenue and the car line. Long after she had rolled up her hair, got into bed and turned out the lights, she heard the tap-tap-tap of his cane on the sidewalk growing fainter and becoming absorbed by the night.

She began her new job at the Dixie Metal Works and was pleased with her decision to change. Mr. Pittman was rather gruff but not unkind. The other girls were her age or older, congenial, nice; some of them were service wives from other parts of the country, working only until their husbands were transferred elsewhere. Daily she experienced a thrill in knowing that the bills of lading, packing slips and invoices she typed were for Navy equipment that was actually going to war.

With all her satisfaction, however, she had not foreseen how much she would miss Robert. They continued to meet downtown after work. It was not until she began to realize that each of her days pointed to that moment when she got off the bus at the corner of Alabama and Broad Streets to find him waiting, slight, thin, hair blowing in the wind, lifting the end of his cane and waving it to her in greeting, that she discovered she was in love with him. She did not have to analyze the feeling or question it. She knew.

"Don't tie yourself to me, Susie," he told her. "You can do better. I'm not exactly the Victor Mature sort, you know."

"Well, my goodness! I'm not Jane Russell either! Ferebe nearly had a fit the last time I was at her house. She accused me of eating five meals a day."

"But you're not using your head," he said, his mood becoming contemplative. "I'm crippled, and when we're together, you're crippled along with me. We necessarily move at my pace, not yours. My restrictions are your restrictions. You're too active and lively for that. You're accustomed to doing what you want, when and where you want, on the spur of the moment, if you feel like it. With me you have to look ahead and calculate. How far is it? How accessible is it? How high is it? How steep are the stairs? More often than not it's easier to sit still and not move at all. It's more than physical limitations. It's an attitude, a system of thinking, a way of life, and it's completely alien to you. Do you know I've never climbed a tree? I've never scrambled up and down a riverbank. I've never been to a dance. I have no idea how it would feel to balance myself and walk on a single rail like you used to do down by your father's railroad station."

"Those are things I did as a child."

"But I didn't, and that's significant. When you and I look back, we don't see anything similar. You're gregarious. You've always loved people and loved to be with them. It shows in your conversations. You're constantly referring to people you knew in Bentley and in college and what they did and said or things you did together. I'd have to rack my brain to think of an interesting thing to tell you about anybody in Manchester and Amherst. They couldn't have been so dull as that. It's me—not them. They didn't interest me. I've always been a loner. I don't understand your sunny openness toward everybody you meet. Maybe I would if you felt obligated to be friendly, but you don't. You don't have a choice. It's the way you are. It's built in."

"Maybe I'm like my mother," she said. "She can't help it either. If you walk down the street with her, you'd think every person she sees is her best friend. None of it is put on. She likes people, and they like her too. You can tell."

"I have to work at being friendly, which probably means it's not real with me. With you, it's as natural as breathing. That's why I'm apprehensive about going home with you to meet your parents. Here in Atlanta we're on neutral ground. Atlanta belongs to neither of us. But that little town where you grew up belongs to you personally. When you see me in that setting, I might not be the same to you anymore. The risk frightens me. I'm afraid you might see that I don't fit into Bentley, with your parents—or with you. I don't want that to happen."

"My daddy was afraid of that. He was overawed by my mother's family and background and traditions and way of living, which apparently was pretty special. They came from different worlds—twenty miles apart—and they made it. It's unbelievable he ever thought it could be a problem. I don't remember ever reading in a book that two people have to be alike to be fond of one another. In fact, I've always heard that if people are too much alike they don't get along at all. I can't argue about the differences in us. We don't match. Not the teeniest bit. So I guess you'll have to go on being unfriendly, and I'll be friendly, and you'll have to go on walking with a cane while I walk without one. But I don't see why we can't do it at the same time in the same place—together."

"You're going to be sorry, Susie," he said. "I should head you off, but I don't want to. I should tell you to forget me and find somebody more like you are, somebody who can do the things you like, but I don't want you to forget me and find somebody else. So what are we going to do?"

"Do? We're going to Bentley as we planned," she said. "That's what we're going to do."

"Did you tell your parents everything about me when you went home?"

"Everything," she said. "They're having the piano tuned for you. That is, if Miss Pickney Jarrell hasn't lost her tuning tools again. She goes off and leaves them at somebody's house, then forgets whose house she went to last and has to phone all over town. Nobody plays the piano much anymore. Mother used to play for us and teach us songs when we were little. Ferebe and I took lessons, but our playing stopped when the lessons did. I can't wait to hear you. I told them you were a composer, and they're impressed. You've got to take some of your own pieces to play. I promised them you would."

"I will, but they might not like them," he warned her. "You might not like them. I'm not sure I like them myself. None of them say what's inside me."

"For instance?"

"Feeling. An overall, encompassing sense of existence that won't divide into parts or sections. If I could describe it in words, I wouldn't need the music. Music is subjective. It's tremendously personal. When you write music, you write big chunks of yourself into it. Yet it might not express the real way you feel, think, believe. It can be frustrating."

Susie did not understand. She supposed everyone had feelings and emotions they could not describe or express, but in her own experience they were always transitory. One summer she had seen a sunrise in the Great Smokies that was more beautiful than anything else she had ever seen. She was alone. The others were still asleep in the cabin. Later she tried to describe it to them, but for all her efforts she could make it sound no more special than all the ordinary sunrises everybody experiences. The missing part she could not supply was the lovely and tranquil, yet awesome, state of mind in which it left her. She had not been frustrated, though. The mood soon wore off and with it her desire to describe it.

213

Understandably, Susie's mother and father were looking forward to Robert's visit. Susie had never brought anyone home with her except her roommates and other girl friends from college, and never a young man. Bringing Robert was special to her, maybe a once-in-a-lifetime event, and they resolved to make the weekend as special as she apparently hoped it would be.

"We'll give him Paul and Perry's room," her mother said. "If you come on Number 7, that will give me time to wash the dinner dishes and straighten the kitchen and put a roast in the oven for supper—if I've got enough points left to buy one. Your daddy and I got steak hungry not long ago, and I used twenty-four points for the scrawniest T-bone steak I ever put on a table. And Susie? If you've got any sugar stamps you don't need, maybe I can make an applesauce cake. I made a box of walnut crunch cookies to send Paul last week, and I used all my stamps. I hope Robert likes desserts."

Her father, while trying to share her mother's enthusiasm, was troubled and could not conceal it. "You're not excited enough," he told her. "Are your mother and I reading too much into this situation?"

"No, Robert's the one," she said. "If I had gone shopping maybe I would never have picked him out, but I didn't have anything to do with it. When it happens it happens, and apparently nobody has any control over who it happens to."

"But you don't sound happy," he persisted.

"I'm happy," she said simply with no change of tone. "I'll admit it's not the feeling I always thought it would be. I thought I'd be dancing on the rooftops and carrying on like an idiot."

"I'd feel better about it if you did," he said. "Are you sure you don't feel sorry for him or pity him? I hate to ask you a thing like that, but you ought to know for yourself."

"I was at first," she said. "I felt so sorry for him I could cry. Then I got to where I liked him. He was interesting

214

and talked about things I had never heard anybody talk about before. He was different from anybody I ever knew. And he was always so sweet to me. Then I got to where I worried about him if the weather was bad and I knew he'd have trouble getting around, or if maybe he had walked too far and got too tired. If I didn't see him for a couple of days, I worried that he might be at home sick. Then when I moved down to Dixie Metal, I got to where I could hardly wait for the bus to get me downtown to meet him on the corner. Sometimes when he wouldn't be there and hadn't called to tell me, I imagined everything in the world happening to him. Things went on from there, and I knew I was in love with him, and I knew he was in love with me. He didn't even have to tell me."

"*Did* he tell you?"

"He didn't have to, but he did—in his own way."

"You're twenty-six years old, and we're certainly not trying to tell you your own mind," her mother said, "but he'll be a special problem for you, darling, and your loving him won't change that. As much as we all love Perry, there's not a member of this family who at some time or other hasn't been provoked and impatient when we've had to repeat things for him that really weren't important enough to repeat, or when we've had to slow down our talking when we were in a hurry, or when we've had to go looking for him all over the house and yard because we couldn't call him. Many times we've explained him to people and made excuses for him when we wished we didn't have to. We can remember time after time when understanding him and making ourselves understood seemed so impossible that we just wanted to give up. All of us are human enough to have been thoughtless on occasion, too, and let him see our irritation. We've lost our temper at him for things that weren't his fault. Of course, we've had the advantage of growing up with Perry, and it never occurred to us that the situation could be any other way.

"With Robert, though, the problems will come all at

once. It will require lots of learning and understanding and patience. Your freedom will be restricted. Your situation won't be like your friends', and sometimes the difference will seem almost cruel to you. You can love someone enough to spend your life with him, but your cup won't be running over every minute of every day. Sometimes you'll feel that it's almost empty. Just the normal adjustments of living together bring on problems under the most ordinary of circumstances. With Robert, you'll be taking on an additional one. A big one."

"But Mother, is his lameness any reason I can't love him?"

"No, no, *no*, darling!" Mamie exclaimed hurriedly. "I don't mean that at all. We just want you to look ahead and try to be ready for some of the things in store so you won't be hurt and discouraged or disillusioned when they come."

"There's another thing too, Susie," her father said. "It won't go away, and you ought to face it. Any kind of deformity is not very pleasant to look at. Any of them take some getting used to. You're going to have to get used to Robert's in a way you haven't had to yet. You'll see him without his braces, and you'll have to see one leg half the size of the other. Maybe you won't like that, but there it is. The way you describe his shoulder, it must be shrunken or caved in. However it is, you'll see that too. There'll come a time when you'll have to see him without his coat and tie and shoes and cane, and he won't look like he does now. You've got to be ready for that."

"I'm ready for it, Daddy," she said softly. She smiled reassuringly. "Don't you remember? I told you at the beginning that he's not much to look at."

# 22

THE RAIN CAME DOWN in sheets and waved across the station platform like a curtain blowing in the wind. Alex stood at the window inside the depot and looked out. It was cold for September, and except for the woodsy green of the random shrubbery and saplings scattered along the crest of the embankment across the railroad tracks, it looked like a winter day. The tall cedars by the cotton mill bent under the rain's attack. The sky was low and the color of slate. He took his watch from his pocket and looked at it.

"I hope this lets up by the time Number 7 gets in," he said. He checked his watch with the clock on the wall and returned it to his pocket.

"The sun might be shining before Number 7 gets in," Emory Haynes said. He typed a final word on a dispatch and tore it from his typewriter. "It hasn't even left Atlanta yet."

"What's the holdup this time?"

"What's the holdup *any*time?" he countered. He skewered the dispatch on the stick file and spun around in his chair. "Somebody ought to have their heads examined about these timetables," he said. "A train hasn't come through Bentley on time since the war started, but the timetables stay the same. Do you suppose anybody's crazy enough to think they're ever going to run on time when

217

every run is overloaded and bulging at the sides with passengers, mail, baggage, freight? Looks like somebody would figure out that it takes longer to load four baggage cars than it used to take to load two. And you can't clear a twenty-four-car hookup through the yards as quick as you used to clear twelve. Marvin—uh—Marvin—what's his name? You know—the conductor on Number 7? He says when it's time to pull out in Atlanta, passengers are still lined up back to the gate, and he can't give the high sign until they're all aboard. Looks like somebody would catch onto that and change the schedules to take care of it."

"It would be the same old story whatever the schedule," Alex said.

"It might help straighten things out, though. There's a lady from Monroe that climbed all over me the other day. Her husband was stationed over at Aiken and was supposed to meet her in Augusta. She said he only had a three-day pass, and she didn't want him to use all of it up in the depot waiting for her."

Emory had a good point, Alexander thought, but he did not know what anybody could do about it. The railroads were doing well considering what they were up against. The country was on the move. Nobody seemed to stay at home anymore, and to Alex they all seemed to travel by rail. They were moving to new jobs; wives were en route to join their husbands at new stations; parents were going to visit their children; servicemen were on furloughs; government workers were traveling on war business; families were hurrying to ports of embarkation to say hello or good-bye to someone; soldiers and sailors were being transferred to new posts. The eastbound trains were jammed, and the westbound trains were jammed. Even the north-south connecting line from Gainesville was jammed. Sometimes it looked as though all the people east of Bentley were swapping places with all the people west of Bentley.

Vacant seats had disappeared for the duration. Passengers stood in the aisles, in the vestibules and sat on their luggage if they could find enough floor space to put it down. A berth in a Pullman required a priority rating that was hard to come by and was useless anyway when all the berths had long since been taken. It was easier and more pleasant to go hungry for the length of a trip than to stand reeling and lurching in long lines waiting for a table in the dining car and a menu on which the scratched selections outnumbered those available. Conductors, brakemen, ticket agents, baggage handlers, waiters, and even innocent news vendors suffered the barbs and stings of irate passengers who apparently held them personally responsible for an overcrowded coach, a malfunctioning seat lever, a noisy, drunken sailor, a window that was stuck, a lavatory that had been occupied too long, a water cooler with no ice in it, or a schedule that did not coincide with their own desires and needs. In retaliation and self-defense the beleaguered railroad employees angered them further by asking if they didn't know there was a war on and moved to the next displeased ticket holder, who had a complaint perhaps different in substance but identical in spirit and absence of logic.

The railroads' equipment was showing its age. It was groaning and creaking under the impossible and still growing demands for longer runs, additional runs, heavier loads, more tonnage, better service and the greater urgency with which it all should be handled. They needed new and up-to-date equipment, but they could not get it. Materials and labor were too scarce. Steel, aluminum, chromium, iron, tin, wood, rubber, petroleum, textiles all had gone to war, taking along with them the men and women needed to forge them into a war machine. Any new rolling stock that came out of the factories was for use by the armed services or by industries engaged in direct war production. The military services ordered locomotives and switch engines, flatcars and boxcars, not to mention especially designed cars on which they mounted big guns and mysterious monsters heavily guarded and concealed from public view by tightly drawn coverings. The Army's and the Navy's needs took first priority, and nobody tried to argue about that.

Still, the railroads had to haul more passengers and freight than they had ever hauled before, and they were forced to use anything with wheels to do it. They had to make it do, for there was not any more where that came from. To keep operating at all was a continuous struggle. Overuse of rolling stock meant extra maintenance, which meant extra time out of service and in the shops, which meant additional manpower, which was as scarce as the materials they needed to work with and could not get.

All the while, the Government was taking crews, locomotives, baggage cars and hundreds of passenger coaches off their regular runs to move troops around the country, thereby turning an already crucial shortage into a nightmare for the railroads, who did their best to pacify their passengers with what they had left. The Government claimed priorities on rights-of-ways in all sections of the land to move critical military supplies, disrupting regular train service even further and leaving the railroads to move their regular traffic when they could. Terminal facilities were miserably swamped. They were strained to the edge of collapse simply by taking incredible numbers of passengers off trains and putting others on, never seeing any evidence in the numbers left over that anybody had arrived or departed at all.

And the people continued to travel north, south, east and west, hoping for the best in accommodations and scheduling while expecting the worst, and wondering how on earth a nation could have the know-how to turn out thousands of airplanes, ships and tanks and deliver them on demand anywhere in the world at exactly the time they

were needed, yet was incapable of running one steam locomotive and an ordinary passenger train on a simple, reasonable, slow-at-best schedule, or within a respectable distance of it, anyway.

Emory was still right. The man on the mail truck, the
men in the freight room, the man from the American Express, and the expectant passengers with tickets in their
hands had to be ready by two nineteen in case No. 7
should be on time. They knew it would not be, but they
could not take the chance. They got ready, therefore, and
waited. Two hours, maybe only one if they were lucky,
would go to waste for everybody involved in the arrival
and departure of Georgia Railroad's eastbound passenger
train No. 7. But nobody knew a remedy for the unhappy
situation outside of calling off the war itself, and who
could do that?

The wind was up when No. 7 finally did pull into the
station, and the rain was coming down harder, or maybe
its blowing and shifting made it seem to. Alex had been
waiting inside the freight room because it was on the end
of the depot closest to where Susie and Robert would get
off the train. He had also moved the car to the edge of the
platform at the end of the depot to shorten their dash
through the rain. In his hands he held a heavy canvas
service umbrella. As the train hissed to a stop, he opened
the umbrella and hurried across the platform to where the
conductor in his slicker coat and rain hat was placing a stool
at the foot of the steps. The conductor turned his face
upward and peered into the vestibule waiting for passengers to alight.

"Did you bring all this rain with you, Mr. Estes?" Alex
shouted by way of greeting.

The conductor turned and grinned cheerfully. "It's
with the compliments of the Georgia Railroad," he
shouted. "What brings you out in all this weather, Mr.
Holly?"

"My daughter and a friend. I hope they're aboard like they're supposed to be."

Despite what Susie had told them and how she had prepared them, Alex was not ready for Robert Shaefér. He had not expected him to be so small—at least not so short. When he came into view in the vestibule above, he appeared to be no taller than Susie, but it was difficult for Alex to judge with the rain in his face, the umbrella, the luggage, other passengers on the steps, the squealing, the hurrying. It was only a quick impression.

"The car's right over here at the end of the depot!" he called to them after they were off the train, had separated themselves from the other people and the greetings were over. "You go ahead, and I'll bring the bags. Which are yours?"

Susie pointed to them and turned toward the car with Robert. Alex picked up the two bags and started to follow them, then stopped. He had not noticed Robert's cane. Through the curtain of rain he watched them huddled together under the umbrella making their way across the platform, the cane preceding them like a divining rod. Susie was holding the umbrella above their heads with one hand. With the other she held Robert's arm. They were not walking fast. She was watching the wet platform and his feet, guiding him cautiously and anxiously as she would an old, feeble man. Alex was touched, but he was also saddened. Susie looked old herself.

He was coming up behind them when suddenly Robert's cane slipped and he fell. His body stretched forward while he tried to hold onto the cane and retain his balance. Susie was clutching frantically onto his arm while the umbrella flew out of her hand and was caught by the wind and the rain. It blew down the platform. With both hands she held to him, but she was too late. His weight pulled her down with him.

Alex dropped the two bags he had been carrying and rushed to help them.

They were a jumbled, struggling heap of coats, legs and arms on the wet bricks. While the water splashed about them, they raised their heads in shocked bewilderment. The rain beat on their bare heads and streamed down into their faces.

Alex reached for Susie's arm. "Are you hurt?" he inquired excitedly, helping her to her feet.

"I'm all right," she replied. "See about Robert while I chase the umbrella."

He released her and turned to help Robert.

"This is embarrassing, Mr. Holly, and I'm sorry," Robert apologized while Alex helped him to his feet.

"Don't worry about it," Alex said. "Accidents happen to everybody."

"Need any help, Mr. Holly?" It was one of the men from the freight room coming toward them.

"We're okay, Ed, thanks. Just a slight accident. Go on back inside."

"I don't know what good this will do now," Susie said, returning with the umbrella. "We're already soaked. Are you hurt, Robert?"

"I'm all right—I think. I haven't moved yet. Where's my cane?"

Alex found it and handed it to him. Water poured off his head and plastered his dark hair on his forehead down to his eyebrows. He looked smaller than ever now. He was also pathetic and sickly in appearance.

They made it to the car and sat inside, dripping, miserable and confused. Robert was still embarrassed.

"This is terrible," he said. "Now we're getting your upholstery wet. I feel like an idiot."

"You don't need to," Alex said, backing the car away from the platform. "And don't worry about the upholstery. It'll dry out."

Susie was in the front seat with her father. She was near tears. "My hair!" she groaned, as they drove up the hill on Depot Street. "I waited until this morning to have it fixed so it would be fresh for coming home. Now look at it! Mother's going to *die* when she sees me—and she's never seen Robert before!"

"Now you're both just fine," Alex placated her. "When we get home you can change clothes, and you'll look like you did when you got off the train. I'll tell your mother how pretty your hair looked. It was the first thing I noticed."

He looked in the rearview mirror at Robert. He was seated in the back plucking at his wet clothes.

"I'm sorry we couldn't give you a better welcome, Robert," he said. "The rain's been coming down like this all day."

"I'm the one to apologize for making that spectacular entrance," he said. "My cane slipped out from under me. I only use it for balance and emergencies. I shouldn't have put so much weight on it on that slick platform."

"The main thing is that everybody's all right," Alex said, turning onto Chiles Street. "Just look at this! The windshield wipers can't work fast enough to keep it off."

"This isn't fair!" Susie lamented. "It's not like I wanted it to be. All this rain and us falling down and getting soaked to the skin. And Robert even bought a new necktie. I've been telling him how pretty it is in Bentley— and I don't know what all. I feel like crying."

"It wouldn't help a thing," Alex soothed her. "Your mother will be glad to see you the same as if the sun was shining and you were dry as a bone. And Bentley is a pretty town, Robert—as pretty as Susie told you it is. She'll take you around when the weather clears, and you can see for yourself."

Mamie was too alarmed by Susie's and Robert's drenched, bedraggled condition to use much time on introductions and greetings. "I'm so sorry I don't know what to do," she sympathized. "Give me those wet coats, and you go on upstairs and change clothes. Susie, I fixed the

224

boys' room for Robert. The blue towels in the bathroom are his. I put yours on your bed."

After they had gone Alex followed her out onto the back porch, where she opened the umbrella and set it on the floor to dry.

"What did you think of Robert?" she asked him.

"I didn't get a chance to think anything," he replied. "Not with all the falling down and Susie's carrying on. I did feel sorry for her, though."

"Bless her heart. She did an awful lot of getting ready for this trip. She had it all planned and worked out. I know exactly how she feels. I think she had on a new dress. At least, I don't remember ever seeing it."

"They had to stand up on the train," Alex said. "A young girl offered Robert her seat, but he wouldn't take it. He did sit on the armrest part of the way, though. What do *you* think of him?"

"Me? My goodness! I barely saw him. They looked like you fished them out of a creek, so it wouldn't be fair to even have a first impression."

"Maybe—but you've got one anyway," he said half teasingly. "I could tell."

She busied herself with the umbrella, which needed no more of her attention. Then she stood looking through the screen across their yard into Mr. Spencer's garden.

"It's a shame it can't be pretty weather for them," she said. "I don't know exactly what Susie has in mind for them to do, but they certainly can't go anywhere in this downpour. I don't think any of her friends are in town right now. They're all so scattered, it's hard to—"

"What was it?" Alex broke in. He was persistent and amused.

She turned back to him. "What are you trying to get me to say, Alexander Holly?" she asked, feigning ignorance.

"Whatever it is you're thinking, Margaret Holly," he replied.

She stared into his eyes, now amused. "You know, you're really a terrible person, and I don't know what I'm going to do with you." She started for the door. "I think it would be improper for me to give my opinion this early," she said piously, stepping into the hall.

Later, the four of them sat in the living room, getting acquainted. "Bentley can't offer much in the way of excitement, Robert," Alex said. "About the most exciting thing that happens around here after the sun goes down is the arrival and departure of Number 14 westbound at six fifty. I'll be glad to take you down to see that, if you'd like to go." He laughed. "It won't come in at six fifty, though. The war knocked all the train schedules in the head. Sometimes I stay at home until she whistles on the grade out at Turtle Hill. That's when she starts clattering over the switch point, and that leaves me plenty of time to get down to the depot."

"Daddy, I don't think Robert would find that very interesting," Susie spoke up. "Not after that big splash we made down there this afternoon. Anyway, we'll be going back tomorrow when we leave—same place."

"Oh. Well, I thought he might be interested in seeing what goes on behind the scenes in a railroad depot," he said pleasantly. "But I might not even go down myself. Sometimes I don't."

"That's true," said Mamie. "If he's out of town or flat on his back with a high fever. Susie? Why don't you take Robert around through the house? There's nothing elegant about it, but he might find it interesting." She turned to him. "We think it's genuine antebellum architecture, but we're—"

"I've already told him about the house, Mother," Susie said.

"But he hasn't seen it," Mamie said. She turned to him again. "It gives you an idea of how ordinary people lived before the Civil War. All of them didn't live in columned

226

mansions at the end of an avenue of oaks. We had small farmers and planters back in those days, too. We have some old rosewood and mahogany pieces of furniture scattered around that came from the old Harrison home that you—"

"*Mother!* Robert doesn't want to see any of that old stuff!"

"Why not?" he said. "I've been sitting here looking out into the hall at that little table by the front door, wondering what function it was designed for."

Mamie was delighted. "Oh—you mean that console table?" She got to her feet and led him into the hall. "It was designed for just what you see—to be pretty. It's old but not particularly fine or rare. My Grandmother and Granddaddy Meade had it in the old family home down in Morgan County. It was one of the few things they saved when General Sherman came through and burned them out. It has a lot of meaning for me. I grew up with it. My mother had it in her front hall. When company was coming that I was especially fond of, I used to dress up my dolls and set them on that table to greet them when they came in the front door. I'm sure everybody gets attached to things like that for their own personal reasons. You probably saved some of your parents' things that would mean nothing to anybody but you."

"I'm afraid not," he said. "I sold everything in the house to a secondhand dealer, including all the linens, dishes, pictures on the wall—everything from the front of the house to the back."

"My heavens! Surely there was *something* you couldn't bear to part with," she exclaimed.

"No. To my parents all possessions were necessities, nothing more. If they happened to admire anything they owned, it was coincidental and secondary. Everything was totally without distinction. You could duplicate their furniture in any store anywhere—except the better stores, that is."

Alex had followed them from the living room. "If your parents were like mine, they couldn't afford to buy anything nice and fine," he said.

"It wasn't that," Robert said. "They didn't care. My mother never attached herself to anything in the house. Apparently, the pictures throughout the house had been hung to fill blank spaces on the wall and nothing else. Once when a wire broke and a picture fell to the floor, my mother swept up the shattered glass and threw the picture in the garbage can, frame and all. Her only comment was that she'd find another one of some kind. I must have been as indifferent as she was, because even before I got accustomed to the blank space it left, I couldn't remember what the picture was about."

"Our children are just the opposite," Mamie said. "They're familiar with everything in the house and are possessive about it. They know where it came from and where it belongs in each room. Even Paul—but he won't admit it. There's nothing here that's special and fine, but it's theirs, part of their growing up. They look back on it, and that's important. Of course, we get criticized here in the South for too much looking back, but I see nothing wrong with it. I don't apologize for it. It's just the way we are. Some people think it's embarrassing and a sign of weakness to be sentimental about places and things, but I don't. It's a sign you have a soft, mellow spot somewhere in your heart, and heaven knows we can use more of that nowadays with this terrible war and all."

Susie was embarrassed. "Mother, you're making us sound like Little Women and Little Men," she protested. "Robert was raised another way, and he might not understand what you're telling him."

"I'll confess I don't," he said pleasantly. "It sounds nice, though. It just happens that I've never done much looking back myself. I've never had the faintest desire to go back to Manchester or to Amherst, where I went to college. Maybe I missed something along the way. New England is beautiful and charming by anybody's criteria. I know that. Yet I don't miss any of it."

Alex stood by listening and decided that Robert had not missed anything along the way. If the truth were known, he probably remembered everything that ever happened to him and did not like what he remembered. That was why he never did much looking back.

In Mamie's determination to take Robert's lameness in stride, she became so conscious of it that she was as crippled as he was. She realized it would be wrong for his slight limp and his crooked shoulder to color her reaction to him as a person; and anywhere else, under any other circumstances—had he not been a friend of Susie's, say—she knew they would not. But this was not anywhere else. It was Madison Road in Bentley, and this was the man Susie had brought home for them to meet. She could feel sorry for him, as she most certainly did, but considering his somewhat special status at the moment, she could not help but be affected by his physical infirmities.

When he was seated in a chair, she worked desperately to ignore the metal strips appearing below the cuff of his trousers, running past his ankles, turning at sharp right angles under the arch of his shoe and holding his foot like a vise. When he pushed himself up out of a chair, she tried not to watch him plant his left foot slightly to the front and put all his weight on his right. She did her best not to hear the tapping of his cane across the floor or the faint creak of a metal hinge when he moved. Her efforts at unawareness, though, only increased her awareness that Robert Shaefer was crippled, could not move around well, required extra time to move around at all, and that Susie wanted to marry him. She was appalled at herself for allowing his physical condition and appearance to block her judgment of his good qualities, which surely he possessed in abundance. She was ashamed of herself for feeling a slight antipathy toward him because of it. Maybe if he didn't belong to Susie . . .

Alex found Robert agreeable and friendly enough, but he was inhibited by his size more than by his lameness. He was the smallest man he had ever known personally, but the infantile paralysis had no doubt affected his growth in other parts of his body as well as in his leg and shoulder. He felt genuine pity for him on that score, but it did not lessen an eeriness about his personality. He was also self-conscious in his presence as he had been with Ellison Hampton when Ferebe first brought him home with her. After all, he was more than a casual visitor and certainly deserved to be treated as someone rather special. Yet he did not want to overdo it. He never had approved of parents' making too much over their daughters' boyfriends regardless of their intentions and exact status.

In any event, he was not entirely comfortable with Robert. When he found himself alone with him for a few minutes, he asked Robert if he was too hot or too cool; he raised a window or lowered it; he thought up small chores in other parts of the house; he checked on the rain or called to Susie and her mother and asked who they were hiding from and why didn't they come be sociable.

While Mamie prepared supper, Alex went down to the depot, and Robert sat on the front porch watching the rain. Susie sat at the kitchen table reading one of Paul's rare letters. He was in Italy proper now, but he could not say where. They knew the Fifth Army was at Salerno, and Alex figured he had gone in on the beachhead. He and Mamie pacified their fears, however, by reminding themselves that some of the Fifth Army's troops were still south of Salerno. Paul could be somewhere in that direction behind the heavy fighting. In any event, he was all right, at least when he wrote the letter.

I didn't know you could get so tired and still stand on your feet. I took off my shoes yesterday for the first time

230

in four days, and I had to pry my socks loose from my feet. With your buddies getting shot up all around you, it's funny how you can think about such things as a hot shower and shaving. But I'm still here, and the next time you hear from me I'll be farther up the road, then farther than that. You just watch my smoke—I'm going to write you a letter from Berlin before I get through. I told you I was coming over here to win the war, didn't I? That's what I'm doing. I'll take a bath after it's over. . . .

When Susie had finished the letter and put it down, Mamie inquired about Ferebe and her family.

"She's fine, but Mother, she's getting so irritable!" she said. "Ell works all the time, and she fusses at him like it's his own fault. I don't see how he stands it, and he's so sweet about it. If he's not there, she fusses at me, and I know it's not *my* fault. Ell stays at that lab fourteen hours a day sometimes; then she fusses at him because he tumbles into bed as soon as he gets home. I told her she ought to be ashamed of herself. Lots of women's husbands are thousands of miles away and don't get to come home at all. She said she might adjust to that easier than expecting him home minute by minute every night and keeping Maggie and Ellie awake hoping they'll get to see him before they go to bed, never knowing when to cook supper or whether to cook it at all. She doesn't always eat with the children, thinking maybe Ell will come home later and she can eat with him. But then she doesn't think the children should eat without her, and she gripes about it all the time!"

"She's under a big strain, Susie," Mamie said. "Most people are under some kind of pressure nowadays. Wives of soldiers and sailors aren't the only women whose lives have been disrupted by the war. It hits everybody. Ferebe doesn't mean one-tenth of what she says. She's proud of Ellison and what he's doing for the war. She brags about his work more than he does."

"She ought to tell him so instead of jumping all over him."

"He knows it, darling," she said. "Don't get so upset. And Ferebe knows that keeping things going at home for him and the two children is her contribution to the war just as his is at the laboratory. Ferebe never has been one to go around making pretty speeches. They have a perfect understanding."

As they skipped from topic to topic, Mamie avoided Robert's name, trying desperately to think of a way to speak it casually and without self-consciousness. He lay underneath the thin skin of their conversation ready to surface at the slightest prick. She did not want to talk about him, but she knew he must be discussed, brought out into the open and dealt with for better or for worse. She wished Susie would refer to him in passing and at least acknowledge his existence. An offhand mention of his name might break the spell of his presence that hung over them and rendered her incapable of asking a question about him, making a harmless comment about him. But apparently Susie was as inhibited as she was. She seemed to be fully aware of her mother's reservations and did not want to hear them articulated and force an issue that might take care of itself if left unattended and given its own chance. She stepped around Robert's name as adroitly as her mother did.

Mamie heard Alex drive into the garage. He came in through the back door dripping rain. Mamie sent him back out onto the porch to take off his coat and hat. He returned carrying a package.

"Do we have time for a drink before supper, Mother?" he asked.

"A drink?" Mamie echoed in surprise. "You *know* we never have a drink!"

"Well, Susie never brings a young man home with her," he said. "Tooker Jordan was down at the depot, and

I asked him for a bottle. He said he had quit that business and is working for the war effort now because people won't give him any ration stamps for his merchandise, and the OPA wouldn't give him a priority on his materials. But he did happen to have a bottle left over from peacetime that he'd been wondering what to do with ever since Pearl Harbor."

"Alex! You ought to be ashamed of yourself doing business with someone like Tooker Jordan!"

"It's like Tooker told me—we're all in this thing together. I saw Robert on the front porch when I drove in. Go get him, Susie, and we'll see if we can lead your mother astray with a little dab of whatever this is that Tooker Jordan sold me."

Tooker Jordan's concoction was terrible, but it did loosen their tongues and relax them somewhat, at least during the first half of supper. Then the talk inevitably gravitated to the war. Alex was disappointed that Robert did not seem to know much about it except in outline, and he was resentful that his interest did not seem to go much deeper.

"I couldn't figure out what MacArthur was doing there for a while," Alex said. "I had been reading about bypassing the Japs, but it didn't make much sense until I got out a map and started figuring it out for myself. He's neutralizing some of the Jap bases and cutting them off from supplies without actually occupying them. He's starving them out. Our bombers probably use them for alternate targets if they can't get to their primary targets. That's pretty smart figuring, don't you think, Robert?"

"It sounds sensible," Robert replied without much spirit. "I haven't kept up with it enough to realize that was the situation."

Alex waited for more. Nothing came.

"Well, you've got to hand it to the Army and the Navy," he went on. "They know how to fight a war. And do you realize that the generals and admirals running things were just young fellows in the last war? They were pretty far down the ladder back then. They've learned their business from the bottom up, and my hat's off to them. Every one of them."

"That's their career—West Point and Annapolis," Robert said. "They've had their lifetimes to learn their business. They're supposed to know what to do. That's the nature of their jobs."

"Maybe. But they haven't had anything to practice on," Alex said. "When you stop and think about it, they had to learn all these things out of books. There's no way MacArthur and Eisenhower could have had any actual practice at whipping armies like Japan's and Germany's."

"You can't cope with a situation or rise to a crisis until the situation or crisis actually exists. That's what the generals and admirals have done. They have been doing the jobs they were trained and expected to do."

Alex was not pleased with what he had heard, but he did recognize an element of common sense in it.

"Okay," he said. "You can look at it that way if you want to. Anyway, I'm proud of the way they're fighting the war. It's what happens here at home that gets my goat. I read somewhere that one of the airplane companies had twenty-one thousand workers sitting around doing nothing because some of the finished planes have not tested out combat worthy, and they can't go ahead until they are. You would think they'd get rolling and fix up those planes, but they're sitting there drawing pay doing nothing. Twenty-one thousand people! There's no excuse for it. And some company out on the West Coast built some tanks that split wide open after they were finished because the steel companies had been selling them second-rate steel at first-rate prices. That's a terrible thing. It's happening everywhere—faulty ammunition coming out of the plants, defective parts for airplanes. Every time they track down the reason, it's always somebody trying to get rich quick. There's always a culprit somewhere in the background. The Government prosecutes anybody it can build a case against, but it really doesn't put a stop to it. The thing I don't understand is that nine times out of ten it's somebody whose sons are out there depending on fool-proof equipment to save their lives. Their *own* sons. I don't know how they can do it."

"Of course, dishonesty is nothing new in the United States or anywhere else," Robert said. "This only happens to be a publicized concentration of it perhaps."

"Maybe. But an all-out war like this ought to make the manufacturers get their eyes off the almighty dollar a little bit."

"It would take more than a war to do that, Mr. Holly. Wars don't change anybody. They only bring out the worst —and every now and then, the best—in people. Despite all the rationing and scarcity, you can buy anything you want on the black market right this minute—cigarettes, stockings, coffee, tires, radios, refrigerators. They're for sale everywhere. The war might have created the reason for a black market, but it didn't create the people who operate it. They've been here all along with a touch of larceny in their souls and a lot of upright, God-fearing customers eager to trade with them."

"Well, I'm sorry you don't have a better opinion of the American people than you do," Alex said. "Because we have some who are dishonest doesn't mean all of them are."

"I don't have a bad opinion of the American people, Mr. Holly. I only think that the fact of our being in a war doesn't change everybody involved into selfless, sacrificing patriots. Generally speaking, people don't change unless it's to their own personal advantage."

"We have a son with the Fifth Army in Italy," Alex said quietly. "We have another working for the Army in

Atlanta. We have a son-in-law doing communication research for the War Department in Atlanta. Susie, her sister and mother do whatever volunteer work they can. They all do more than I do. I don't know if the war has changed us or not, and I certainly can't think of any personal advantage we enjoy if it has."

Susie was horrified. "Robert wasn't talking about us, Daddy," she exclaimed. "He was speaking generally. Remember, he doesn't have anybody in the war like we do."

"Everybody's got somebody in this war," Alex said with emphasis. "Even Pet Wilkerson. She's not kin to anybody in it, so she went out and adopted the whole Army and Navy. She didn't have to do that, because she already had somebody in the war. There's no such thing as not having somebody in the war. In fact, everybody's in it themselves." He paused and let his words hang for a moment. "I thought everybody knew that," he added.

# 23

THE FOLLOWING MORNING was clear and sunny with a fresh, wet, clean smell from the rain. The ferny leaves of the spreading mimosa by the back porch glistened with clear droplets of water. Susie looked out her upstairs window onto the top of the garage at the patches of leaves from the walnut tree pasted scattershot by the rain onto the shingles. Across the wet grass the oleanders outside the Etheridges' dining room windows were deep and green with moisture. The big magnolia that shut out the view of their back yard glimmered like dark satin. It was all beautiful, and Susie was unhappy.

Last night had been embarrassing. After supper her father seemed to no longer feel it necessary or important to make conversation with Robert. She loved the way he had exerted himself to entertain him, talk to him, make him feel at home and at the same time like a guest. Now he had moved off into a distance from where he was still hospitable and courteous—she had never seen him act rude toward anybody—but he was not as outgoing and anxious to please as he had been. He moved about the house restlessly, checking windows, listening to the radio in the kitchen, talking to her mother, occasionally wandering into the living room and out again without lingering. He went upstairs early, reminding them to lock up the house and turn out the lights before they came up.

Her mother had refused to let her help with the dishes and occupied herself in the kitchen, leaving her alone with Robert in the living room. She also found an excuse to go to bed earlier than usual.

"The coffee's still hot, but be sure and unplug the pot before you go to bed," she told them. "And help yourself to some more of that applesauce cake. Your daddy and I will never eat it all by ourselves."

From the time of his arrival, Susie knew her parents had been uncomfortable with Robert, but she could point to nothing specific in their manner, action or speech to bear out that conclusion. She sensed it. She could not diagnose the reason, and she suspected they did not understand it themselves, but they did try to overcome it and relax and simply be themselves as they were with all the family's friends. She was grateful to them for that. At moments she thought they might succeed. Before supper was over, however, their discomfort had turned into disapproval, and an almost invisible coolness of manner set in. It was not deliberate, and she was convinced that they were unaware it was evident at all.

Robert gave no indication that he noticed. At least, she didn't have to worry about that. On the other hand, she kept reminding herself that since his own cynical views were the cause of it, there was no reason to shield him from their reactions. After all, they were her parents, and if they were displeased by his views, why shouldn't he know it? It was embarrassing, nevertheless. Robert was her responsibility. The entire situation was her responsibility.

When they were alone and she was brooding over the most effective way of taking him to task, he introduced the topic himself.

"Do you think I offended your parents at the table this evening?" he asked.

"You must have noticed, or you wouldn't bring it up," she said.

"I noticed a slight change in their attitude somehow, but I've known them such a short while it was difficult to know for sure. I've been unable to think of what I might have said or done that could have been objectionable." He did not appear to be concerned so much as puzzled.

"That's easy," she said quickly. "It's what you said about the war. That's the touchiest subject you could talk to Daddy about—unless you talk one hundred per cent for it, and you didn't. In his mind, you're either for it or against it. There's no middle ground."

"I didn't talk against the war."

"You might as well have, because he thinks you did. And you'll have to admit you didn't say anything to support it. He thought you were low-rating the American people, and as far as he's concerned that's low-rating the war, because the American people are the people fighting it. You shrugged off all that dishonesty about black markets and scandals in the war plants as nothing but people running true to form."

"But I was actually talking about human nature and how people act. We could have been talking about any situation—the Depression, an earthquake, an election. It so happened we were on the subject of war, that's all."

"No, it didn't *so happen*," she said. "The war is the biggest and most important thing he knows about right now. You didn't have to take issue with him or throw a wet blanket on everything he said."

"I was only expressing my opinions. I've always done that. Isn't that what people are supposed to do?"

"I guess it is, but not all the time and in every case. The roof's not going to necessarily cave in if you don't. You didn't have to tell him that General MacArthur and General Eisenhower are not doing any more than they're paid to do and expected to do. He thinks they're something extra-special, and for that matter, so do I. The men doing the actual fighting in the war have first claim on his affections. They're his heroes and lots of other people's,

239

too. I don't see anything wrong with having heroes. I'd hate to think everybody in this world was as dull and uninteresting as I am. Heroes give you somebody to admire and look up to. Didn't you ever have any heroes?"

"Not that I recall," he said.

"Not at *all*—not even Tom Swift or Babe Ruth or Charles Lindbergh? It might have been good for you if you had looked up to somebody. Even now it might help you."

He regarded her with new interest. "I believe you're actually irritated at last," he said with amusement. "I've never seen you irritated before. I've often wondered what it would take to ruffle you. You are irritated with me, aren't you?"

"Well—yes, I am," she said. "Daddy was being real sweet to you trying to talk to you. He had been doing that all afternoon ever since we got off the train. You could have met him halfway."

"You know what's happening to you?" he asked, a note of triumph in his voice. "I told you before we came that when you saw me with your parents in their environment, you might get a different picture of me, and that's exactly what you're doing."

"And you sound real happy about it—like you've been trying to make it happen and prove something. I think you decided before we came that you wouldn't try to fit in. You refused to play the piano for them without any apology or explanation. They had that piano tuned for you, and I had promised them you would play. You don't seem to realize they were paying you a compliment by asking you."

"Things weren't right," he said. "I told you that—them, too. I'm not a jukebox you put a nickel in and the lights come on and the music comes blaring out the speaker. Anyway, aren't you making too much of all this? Surely everybody who comes into this house doesn't act the same and talk the same and follow the same pattern."

She stared at him a time before speaking. "You know, I had never thought about it before but, yes, they do," she said. "They all act pretty much the same up to a point. You can say that about the whole town of Bentley, and that's what makes it a nice place to live. In a town this small, people can't stay out of each other's way like they do in a big city. They don't even try. They see each other all the time, because there's nobody else to see and nowhere to hide. So they do follow a pattern. They're interested in the same things, and they talk about them. They go to the same places, and they talk about where they've been and where they're going. They know the same people and they have the same interest in what they do, and they talk about them. They all do follow a pattern, if that's what you want to call it."

"That's too bad," he said. "It sounds dull to live so predictably and expect it of one another."

"That doesn't worry them as much as it worries you," she said. "They're not exactly characters out of *God's Little Acre*. They don't throw the dishwater out the back door, keep their washing machines on the front porch, park their pickup trucks in the yard and shoo the chickens out of the house when it's time to eat. They've been around—to school, to college. They travel. Take a look at the houses some of them live in, the farms and property they own, the clothes they wear, the cars they drive, the businesses they operate, the number of people they hire. Ignorant, narrow people don't do all the things they do. Not everybody's rich—only a few are. They feel downright sorry for people who live in big cities and have to ride buses and streetcars and elevators and wait for stoplights and drive miles and miles through heavy traffic to get to work, then do it all over again at night to get back home. And the best thing about the way they live is that it's what they want. That's what the war's all about—so people can

241

live the kind of lives they want without somebody trying to make them live another."

"Bravo, Susie!" he exclaimed. "I'm admiring you more all the time! I've never heard you be philosophical until now. I rather like it."

"But you don't really understand what I'm saying?"

"Not really, but I'm pleased that you're saying it."

"Looks like I've been wasting lots of words, then," she said.

His manner softened. "No, you haven't, Susie," he said. "I didn't realize I was being as difficult as you make me sound. Believe me, it was not intentional. Perhaps I should be more adaptable."

She seized on that. "Please try, Robert! Won't you, please? They're wonderful people, and they're doing their dead-level best to like you and understand you. Don't you think you can help them out just a wee tee-nincy little bit?"

All that had been last night. As she sat in the kitchen she could hear her mother moving about upstairs getting dressed for church. Her father had gone to the depot early, before she got up, as though it were a regular work day. Robert was still asleep, or at least he had not come out of his room. It was almost eleven o'clock, and that was overdoing it, she thought.

Her mother had laid the bacon in the skillet on the stove ready to light the fire underneath when he appeared. A carton of eggs waited nearby. She had buttered a pan of bread slices ready to put in the oven for toast. A cut glass dish filled with her clearest scuppernong jelly and another with her fresh fig preserves sat on the table with the cream and sugar. Before she had gone upstairs, she and Susie had sat at the table reading the paper, drinking coffee and talking. Susie had caught her mother glancing toward the door expectantly every now and then and pausing in mid-sentence as though listening for Robert's footsteps on the stairs. It did seem thoughtless and even rude to visit a family for less than twenty-four hours and spend so much of the time sleeping. She wondered if it was a regular weekend habit of his. Her father had always been an early riser and a little bewildered by people who were not. Paul used to say the habit his daddy frowned on most was sleeping.

After her mother had gone to church, Susie tasted the coffee. It had grown strong and stale. She poured it out and made a fresh potful. She turned the pages of the newspaper without concentrating on what she saw. At eleven fifteen Robert still had not come downstairs, and she felt like a prisoner caged inside the house while all that fresh air and sunshine were waiting outside for her to enjoy. She reassembled the newspaper, took down a cup and saucer from the cabinet, set them by the coffeepot on the table and went out onto the front porch.

It was a marvelous day to show off Bentley in its bright, sparkling cleanliness. She stood listening to the slow, drawn out, always mournful singing coming through the open windows of the Macedonia Baptist Church. She tried to separate Sissy Carpenter's deep, booming alto from the others, but she must not have been present. People on West Madison Road said nobody needed to ask whether or not Sissy Carpenter was in church, for they could hear her all over that end of town and on out past the Clegg Line.

She wandered out to the sidewalk and strolled down toward the Etheridges'. Their newspaper lay on the deep front porch that wrapped itself around three sides of the house. The Etheridges' was not the prettiest and largest house in town, but it was the most comfortable looking— white, two-storied, green-shuttered. The doors and windows were closed, the shades were drawn, and a stillness lay over the place. Apparently they had gone out of town. She tried to remember the name of Martha Lou Etheridge's husband. It was funny she would forget. Ferebe had been a bridesmaid and had worn the loveliest, most gorgeous, glamorous pale green dress ever made and carried a bouquet of the most fragile, exquisite camellias ever grown. She herself had been constantly underfoot running back and forth across the yard to admire Martha Lou's trousseau and examine each new wedding present as it arrived. She had even sat awestricken on her bed and watched her put on her bridal veil.

Across the street a strange man was cutting back a tangle of overgrown shrubbery by the side porch of the old Lassiter house. A youngish woman she had never seen before leaned over the railing and was talking to him. The Lassiters had not been the owners of that house for forty or fifty years. Since they moved away it had been sold and resold, rented and rerented to a long succession of families, many of whom no one remembered at all. Everybody still called it the Lassiter house, though, and few people could remember the Lassiters either. Mr. Etheridge was always wishing he had enough money to buy the house and tear it down.

Up ahead the wide, thick branches of the Carters' giant elm covered the sidewalk and the edge of the street like a green, vaulted ceiling. When the sidewalk was hot enough to blister your bare feet, it was the shadiest and coolest stopping place between uptown and home. She wondered how many times she had crossed the street rather than walk through the dark tunnel when she feared Andy Carter might be hiding overhead in the branches waiting to pour water down on the head of whoever was foolish enough to risk passing underneath. As she walked by the big white house, she noticed a pale square sticker on a beaded glass pane of the front door. It was bordered with red, white and blue. In the center was a large blue service star of darker shade. That was for Andy. She reminded herself to check and see if her mother and father had put one in their window for Paul.

She had not intended to walk to Chiles Street, but she was coming up on the back of Clay Tinsley's Grocery & Market before she realized how far she had come. In the alley back of the store, a misshapen, jagged gash in the asphalt was filled with dirty rainwater. Clumps of wireweed grew around it. She paused and looked the length of the alley. The shabby, faded, peeling backs of the stores looked junky and disreputable, with wooden crates thrown about at haphazard angles, garbage cans running over without lids and random piles of trash. On the opposite side of the alley was a line of the thickest cedar trees in town. Mrs. Bessie Melton hated cedar trees, but she had planted them anyway so she "wouldn't have to look at Bentley's ugly behind every morning while she drank her coffee and ate her slice of toast."

At the front of Tinsley's Susie started to turn around and go back home, but she went out into the intersection to The Well instead. Chiles Street had its regular Sunday morning gone-to-church look about it. Two or three cars were parked in front of Cutler's Café. No one was on the street except three lanky young boys in coats and ties standing around on the curb in front of the Downtown Drug Store. She suspected they were playing hookey from church. She tried to think back to who the boys were and if they were that young and skinny when she and Addie Sue Spencer walked down one side of Chiles Street even though it would have been more convenient to walk down the other, only so they could be scandalized and insulted by what the boys said to them, or by what they said to each other if they chose not to say anything to them at all.

She turned back toward home wishing she could stand around on the curb and watch cars and people pass. For some reason it was a privilege denied girls and women. She had always envied men and boys their right to stand for hours doing absolutely nothing but watching and talking and making funny jokes. She wondered if Robert had ever stood around idly on the street corners of Manchester alone or with other boys. Somehow the picture did not fit.

As she turned up the sidewalk at home, it struck her that a simple, everyday, effortless act such as standing around on a street corner was far more important than it appeared to be. It was not the actual standing around itself so much as the life you lived that enabled you to do it that made it important. She looked up at Robert's open window and would not have been surprised had Paul and Perry appeared, unhooked the screen, climbed out onto the roof and shinnied down the branches of the hickory tree at the corner to the ground below.

Robert was sitting at the kitchen table drinking coffee with the newspaper spread out in front of him. His cane was hooked over the back of his chair. He wore a necktie, but he did not have his coat on. She recognized the shirt as the same he had worn yesterday. It was rumpled, and the collar looked stale and untidy. He glanced at her, grunted what she assumed to be a greeting, then continued to read the paper.

"I was beginning to think you were going to sleep all day," she said brightly.

"No," he said without taking his eyes from the paper.

"We've all been up for hours. Daddy had already gone to the depot when I got up. Mother's at church. She wanted me to go, but I told her I'd wait for you to get up and cook your breakfast if you want any. Do you?"

"No."

"I guess it is kind of late for that," she went on. "Mother will be back and fixing dinner before you could finish eating it, anyway. Things are certainly pretty outside after the rain. I walked downtown to The Well. You should have been along. It's the town's most historic landmark. It's what started Bentley in the first place. You have to know that when you see it, or you'll think you're looking at a plain, ordinary well."

246

He lowered the paper and looked over the top at her. "Look, Susie. I'm no good at making conversation the first thing in the morning. It takes me a while to get going."

She stood across the kitchen by the stove and wondered if he would have said that to her daddy.

"Oh. I'm sorry," she said. "I just didn't realize that eleven thirty was the first thing in the morning."

He was reading the newspaper again and not listening to her.

She moved toward the door and stopped. "I've been thinking it over," she said. "There's a train at one o'clock, but it'll be two or three o'clock before it gets here. If you think you'll be able to talk to anybody that early, maybe we'd better get on it instead of waiting for the six o'clock, which will be seven or eight o'clock."

"All right," he said. He picked up his cup, took a sip of coffee and set it down again without looking in her direction.

At the door she stopped again. "Robert, did you ever stand around on the street corner in Manchester?" she asked.

"No."

"That's what I thought," she said.

She went upstairs to her room and stayed until she heard Robert come up and go into his own room. Then she went back downstairs to wait for her mother to come home from church.

Her mother was upset when she learned of their new departure time. "But darling, we'll barely have time to eat dinner," she said, tying an apron around her waist. "I haven't even started anything yet. I've got a chicken cut up for frying. Did Robert have breakfast?"

"No. I put everything away. He wasn't hungry. The train will be late. We'll have plenty of time for dinner."

"When are you going to show him around town? You wouldn't have much time if you tried to do it now. Won't it be peculiar for him to come visit us and see nothing but what's between this house and the depot? He might like to see the Wilcox and the Porterfield plantations. There's nothing lovelier in this part of Georgia than those two old places. They've been kept in their original condition, too."

"He can see them some other time," she said. "We just thought with the trains running so late there's no telling what time we would get back if we waited until six o'clock, and it might be better to go early."

Her mother watched her keenly. "That's not the real reason, is it?" she asked.

"Isn't that a good one?" Susie countered. She turned and began adjusting the tiebacks of the curtains nearest her.

"I guess it is. But Susie, there is something else, and if you want to tell it to me, I'll be a good listener." She moved to the hall door and closed it.

Susie turned from the window and stared at her. "Robert and I had words last night," she said. "I'm afraid we've had it."

"Oh? Maybe it's not as bad as you think. All couples go through this at one time or another. Maybe it's not fatal, after all."

"Yes, it is," Susie said with sadness, "and he's the only person who has ever paid any attention to me."

"When you get back to Atlanta, maybe things won't look so bad. I remember when Ferebe thought the world was coming to an end because she and Ellison had a spat. She didn't know how she could possibly live out the rest of her life without him. But he came back and—"

"Mother, you don't understand. It's not that way at all. We didn't have a falling-out. We're not mad at each other. We're still speaking. But I discovered this morning when I walked uptown that it's all a big mistake. It can never be, and what's more, I don't want it to be. He doesn't know that yet, and I feel *awful!* I feel so sorry for him I could die!"

Mamie dropped into a chair. "Oh, I see," she said in a whisper. She gazed at her daughter thoughtfully. "You'll find the right time and place to tell him, darling, and when you do, you'll say exactly the right thing." She brightened her mood deliberately. "Now, what you've got to do this minute is help me get dinner ready. Go tell Robert to pack his bag while we're doing it, and you get your own things together. Hurry back and lend a hand. We'll use my own wedding silver and china. After all, we do have company for Sunday dinner."

In the Union Station at Atlanta they threaded their way through the crush of travelers to the taxi stand at the front of the building. It was bedlam outside. People groaning under the weight of their luggage, small children, boxes, parcels, barracks bags, scurried about in all directions, dodging one another, talking excitedly, calling out greetings and farewells. Redcaps shouted their way through the swarms in and out of the station. The street was choked with automobiles, bumper to bumper, headlights burning, honking impatiently, shifting gears, racing motors, inching their way up to and away from the curb. An engine backfired. A bus idled noisily. The driver stood by the open door yelling out his destination. The angry blast of a policeman's whistle repeated itself again and again to pierce the din.

At the edge of a crowd of people all jammed together and working their way laboriously to the front, Susie and Robert stopped and set their bags on the sidewalk. Quickly more people came up behind them and on both sides of them to press toward the center of the crowd. At the curb the starter was calling out sections of the city and organizing the passengers into little groups to share the ride. Eventually they found themselves at the front of the crowd and standing on the curb.

"Robert, I've been wanting to tell you something," she said when she found a time she could speak without shouting. "I want to apologize to you from the bottom of my heart and with everything that's in me. I wanted to tell you on the train, but not while standing in the aisle with all those people's faces right up against ours."

"Apologize for what?"

"For taking you to Bentley," she replied. "It worked out exactly as you were afraid it would—and there wasn't anything I could do about it. Not a thing in this world, and I feel awful!"

"You shouldn't," he said. "I apologize to you for going. You tried, and your parents tried, but you couldn't make it work. The three of you were superb. You don't have the tiniest inkling of how superb you were, and that makes you all the more so. At dinner today I knew it was all over for you. You did nothing or said nothing to tell me. But I knew. I wanted to be wrong, but I knew I wasn't."

"But Robert, you've been so good to me, and you're being good to me right now. I feel *ungrateful!*"

He laughed outright. "Susie, do you know you're the only person alive who would say a thing like that—or think it? Don't heap blame on yourself. This trip to Bentley had to take place sooner or later. This was probably the right time for it."

"I wish you'd fuss at me and make it easier," she said. She drew in a quick breath. "Robert? What if I'm wrong?" she asked.

He laid a hand on her arm. "You're not wrong, Susie," he said. "I'd give my other leg to think you might be, but you're not. Don't argue with yourself about it. If it's right, you—Susan Meade Holly—will know it. If it's wrong, you'll know that, too. Don't torture yourself by analyzing it either way."

Anxiously she looked at the confusion of traffic. Down the street she thought she saw the outlines of a taxicab. "What do you think we ought to do?" she asked. "It doesn't seem right to get in separate taxicabs and ride away without something else. This is not the way these things happen. There's not any reason we can't see each other again, is there?"

"Not a one." He glanced at the impatient people churning around them, craning their necks for the sight of a cab, inching their luggage along the concrete with their feet, inadvertently jostling one another and apologizing. "I want to talk to you in some place where we can hear rather than in all this. Will it be all right if I wait for your bus as usual tomorrow?"

"Why, *certainly* it will be all right!" she exclaimed. "And if a cab doesn't hurry up and come along, I'm going to break down and cry right here in the middle of all these people."

"Excuse me, sir. Where are you going?" It was the starter at his elbow.

"Druid Hills."

"I've got three others for Druid Hills. I'll put you in the next cab. There's one turning in now."

They waited, and neither could think of a word to utter. The cab pulled up to the curb. Robert looked at Susie and extended his hand. "Good-bye, Susie," he said.

"Robert?"

She released his hand and watched him limp toward the open door of the waiting taxi. He carried his bag in one hand and his cane in the other. Before he got inside, he looked back at her and tried to smile. He was not entirely successful.

Susie was glad that it was dark. She cried into her handkerchief all the way home. The other passengers were courteous enough to pretend they did not notice. Or they could have been preoccupied or indifferent. In any case, she was grateful to them.

# 24

ROBERT WAS NOT WAITING on the corner when Susie got off the bus downtown. She stood and waited for him, glancing at her watch and scanning the rush of people coming along the sidewalk. He had never been late before, and this was the wrong time for him to be late now. Her First Aid class met on Monday nights. On Mondays they usually had a cup of coffee together, sometimes a quick sandwich or a hamburger; then she hurried home to change into her Red Cross uniform, brush up on the evening's instruction and be ready for her car pool to pick her up to meet her class.

She still felt wretched about telling Robert last night. The time and place had been terrible for a thing so important and sensitive, and she was afraid she might have been too blunt and unceremonious. At the same time she was thankful she had already done it. Otherwise, she would have worried herself sick all day rehearsing little speeches, phrasing and rephrasing, building her courage, dreading the ordeal, shrinking from it, imagining the worst possible scene as a result. Had she waited until today she might have lost all her nerve by now and convinced herself that she needed more time to confirm her own feelings. She turned mushy inside each time she dwelt on how sweet and understanding he had been.

Nervously and with growing impatience she looked at

the big clock on the corner across the street and watched the people coming toward her on the sidewalk. After a time, she decided she could wait no longer. She stepped out to the curb, ready to take her streetcar when it came along.

Her telephone was ringing when she let herself into her apartment. It was Emily Lanier. She was excited.

"When's the last time you saw or talked to Robert?" she asked.

"Last night. He went home to Bentley with me this weekend and was supposed to meet me downtown after work today, but he didn't show up. Why?"

"Then you don't know what happened this morning?"

"No. What?"

"The FBI raided that place where he works and arrested everybody in it—including Robert Shaefer."

"The FBI? Arrested Robert? What for?"

"This is mostly hearsay, but it's pretty straight. It was for espionage or conspiracy or sabotage—I'm not exactly sure," Emily said. "Anyway, it was one of those dramatic things that don't happen except in picture shows about spies."

"*Spies?* Emily, what are you talking about?" Susie asked, bewildered. "What's Robert got to do with spies? Are you having a drink—or two drinks?"

"Yes, indeed—bourbon—but that doesn't change anything," she replied. "And you'd better get one for yourself. I'll tell you what I know about it, which isn't much. I only know what people in the building have been saying all day. This girl in the—"

"Emily! Stop explaining and tell me what you called to tell me. I've got a First Aid—"

"Okay, okay—just calm down," Emily said. "This Southern Trade, Incorporated, turns out to be a dummy outfit. They've been collecting information from railroads and truckers and airlines about shipping—don't ask me what kind of information. That's all I know. Through some elaborate system of go-betweens that I don't understand, everything they collect ends up in the hands of the Germans and the Japs. I don't know which—they just said the enemy. They picked up some other people around town at the same time—the people who have been feeding them information, I guess. It's a big sensation all over the building. I don't know if it's on the news yet or not. I haven't turned on the radio. Turn yours on and see if—"

"All that doesn't mean Robert was involved personally," Susie said. She was doubtful and defensive at the same time.

"He works for the company, though, and that's what the company's been doing, so how could he not be involved? They arrested everybody in the place, even the girl who did the typing and filing. Did you know her when you saw her? I've been trying to figure out which one she could be. You know, we might have ridden on the elevator with her a thousand times. She might even have sat at the counter with us at the drugstore. Do you know which one she was?"

"No, and I think you've got this all mixed up. I don't believe one word you're telling me."

"You'd better believe it. I didn't see them being taken out of the building, but I went down the hall to the ladies' room this afternoon, and that tall, skinny girl who works in the stockbroker's office was in there. You remember the sickly one who looks like a turkey and is always taking nervous pills? She had on a *middy blouse*, of all things, complete with a big Navy blue bow! She walked in looking like she was about to throw up—"

"*Emily!*"

"Oh—well, she said she saw all of them down on the sidewalk. They were handcuffed—every one of them. I asked her if one of them limped or walked with a cane and was real small, and she said yes. So that's got to be Robert, don't you think?"

"Where did they take them?"

"To jail, I guess. Where else?"

"Which jail?"

"How should I know? I don't know anything about jails and who goes to which one. But if it was the FBI, it must be a Federal jail of some kind. The only one I know is the Federal Penitentiary down on South McDonough. But I think you have to be a friend of Al Capone's to get in that one."

"I wonder how I could find out."

"You could call the FBI if you really want to know, or maybe it will be in the paper tomorrow—" She caught her breath. "Susie, you're not thinking about going to see him, I hope."

"Why not? He's in trouble."

"But there's nothing you can do about that. Not now."

"You're assuming he's done something wrong, and I'm not. He could be as innocent as a newborn babe. He might not have known what was going on."

"Not *known?* Did he ever tell you exactly what his job was in that place?"

"He's a clerk—general office without any particular specialty. He's told me many times it's low level and unskilled. It's just a job. He's no more interested in that Southern Trade, Incorporated, than you are in the Piedmont Hosiery Company. So how could he be involved in the inner workings?"

"He got arrested, didn't he?" Emily countered. "Use your head, honey. Wherever he is, you can't go see him. You can't get mixed up in it. They'll be investigating everybody he knows. You take my advice and stay away and hope your name doesn't surface in all this. And it might not unless he tells them about you or someone else tells them. It's a chance worth taking."

"But Emily, you can't know somebody one day and

the next day pretend you've never heard of him because he's in trouble."

"You can, too, and you'd better do it. You don't understand what you're doing. Once they get your name, they'll swoop down on you like a swarm of bees and investigate you to a fare-thee-well. And they'll go out to Bentley and do the same thing to your mother and daddy and anybody else who ever heard of you. And don't forget Ferebe and Perry—they'll investigate them, too."

"They wouldn't do that; but if they did, what would they find out?"

"Nothing, but this will probably be in the papers and get a lot of publicity, and the fact that the FBI has been in Bentley asking questions about you in connection with the case will put doubts in people's minds that will stay there forever. Think about your family before you go traipsing off down to the jail. The FBI doesn't play games. They run down every possibility whether it looks promising or not."

"Emily, you're exaggerating the whole thing. And I'm already involved—with Robert."

"You and I know that, but the FBI might not. Let them find out for themselves and hope they don't. But for heaven's sake, you can't go marching into a jail and sit in the visitors' room talking through a little grill and looking pitiful like one of those long-suffering immigrant wives with a babushka over her head. Besides, what can you do for Robert?"

"Maybe nothing, but people in trouble need somebody, and Robert doesn't have anybody but me."

Emily gasped. "Susie? It's just now penetrated my thick skull," she said. "Are you in love with Robert?"

"I thought so until this weekend in Bentley, but I found out I'm not. It's a long story, but I'm definitely not in love with him."

"Good. That's all the more reason you ought not to go see him."

"No. It's all the more reason I should. Because I'm not in love with him doesn't mean I hate him. Last night I told him how it was with me, and he was the sweetest thing you ever saw. He's failed at everything he's ever tried. I'm one of the latest additions to his list. Whatever wrong he's done, I've got to make sure he can feel he's done one or two things that were right."

Emily was silent for a time. "Okay—have it your way," she said at last. "But before you do, why don't you bring your toothbrush and come over and spend the night. We can talk some more for as long as you want. Then maybe you won't do anything rash."

"I can't. I've got a First Aid class tonight, and if I don't get going, I'm going to be late."

"You're going to teach a class *tonight*? How can you keep your mind on the subject?"

"I'll have to. It's too late to find a substitute."

When Susie returned from her class, she turned on the radio and got ready for bed while she waited for the late news. Teaching her class had been more of an ordeal than she had anticipated. Her mind strayed from what she was saying even while she said it. She was embarrassed when some of her students startled her out of her reverie by asking for assistance with their leg splints. Usually she strolled among them making corrections and giving them guidance before they requested it. As she was dismissing the class someone reminded her that she had forgotten to give them next week's assignment. She had not thought to plan one.

The newscaster referred to the arrests as a "roundup of an espionage ring" and the "smashing of an extensive spy network that reached out into all parts of the city." Informants at war production plants, military centers, railroad, air and trucking facilities had been supplying shipping information and statistics to the nerve center of the operation, which was a downtown company under the vague disguise of a trade brokerage firm. There it was assembled, analyzed and disseminated to a higher level. Five men and three women had been arrested and were being held incommunicado in the Federal Detention Center at the Federal Building. The FBI would release no names for the time being.

Emily's warning came back to her. Her problem was solved for the time being. If Robert was being held incommunicado, they would not allow her or anyone else to see him.

# 25

FEREBE HAMPTON HAD BEEN TRYING to reach Susie since Ellison left for work, early as usual. She was not at the office, and she did not answer her telephone at home. The names of those arrested in the espionage ring on Monday were in the morning paper. It had been a one-edition sensation two days before when the story broke and the suspects were rounded up. The excitement had spent itself since. As war espionage was measured, this particular ring was not considered a major operation or a "big catch" for the FBI. The information they collected contained no vital military secrets as such. It was accessible in one form or another to any citizen willing to do the work of gathering it from the many parts of the transportation industry and assembling it into a meaningful whole of trends, volumes, tonnage, routings, schedules, highs and lows. Piece by piece it was worthless as war intelligence except to saboteurs, who had always been a constant menace. Collectively, though, it had a value.

The FBI called it Targeting Intelligence. In peacetime it had another name—Economic Surveys—and was traded willingly between friendly governments. In wartime, however, the same information took on grim significance. It was useful to any foreign government with plans, immediate, long-range or potential, of attacking another country.

With railroads, highways and airlines converging on it from all directions, Atlanta was the key transportation center of the South, hence of paramount importance to the defense of the United States. As such, the Government had designated it a Critical Defense Area long before Pearl Harbor. It was as vital to the prosecution of the war as a bridge spanning a river would be to a battalion of advancing tanks or marching combat troops.

Ferebe had glossed over Robert's name along with the rest and moved on to yet another grisly story of the German war in Russia with its unreadable names and incredible slaughter of ten thousand here, fifteen thousand there, all disposed of in one or two lines of neat type as expeditiously as the number of hogs and cattle shipped to the Chicago stockyards within the last twenty-four hours. At times she half resolved never to look at a newspaper again until the war ended. All the photographs seemed to be of men lying dead on beaches, tanks exploding, cities crumbling to dust under heavy fire, airplanes plunging to earth in flames, refugees with bundles fleeing under strafing, dirty GIs staring in horror at their buddies who had been blown to bits, ships burning and men leaping into the sea, flamethrowers broiling men in their caves. Death and destruction had become the norm. Horror had become commonplace. Insanity had become heroic.

She was convinced that from whichever side you viewed it—Allied or Axis—the world had gone mad. It had long since abandoned hope that it could save itself through rational, civilized behavior. Men were killing men by the thousands and gathering them up to identify and bury the best they could before moving on to kill more. They were shooting the arms, legs and faces half off each other and patching up whatever was left to send back to wherever they had come from in the first place and in one piece. The world was afire. The skies were black with smoke and red with blood. Factories, seaports, railroads, military installations and entire cities with people living in them were being pulverized. Even Americans were raining bombs on France, which was not the enemy at all but an old friend they were trying to save. In the rocky hills of Italy, where her own brother, Paul, was fighting, villagers were digging out from under the rubble that had once been their homes to welcome with open arms their liberators who had destroyed them. Ship was confronting ship on the high seas, and while surrounded by thousands and thousands of square miles of nothing but water, and with no one to look on, fighting to the death, then rescuing the survivors. Men were killing and getting killed on beaches and in jungles of remote islands that neither side actually wanted but could not permit each other to have. Men captured as many prisoners as they could feed, clothe and shelter, then killed the surplus.

As Ferebe was turning the page of the newspaper, not knowing whether to cheer or to weep, the name of that company where several of the suspects worked began to prick at her memory. She looked at the story again, read the address of the Southern Trade, Incorporated, and made the connection. She telephoned Susie's office. She was absent. The girl who answered the telephone had not seen her since she left the office Monday afternoon two days before. She offered no further assistance and seemed to be impatient to be rid of her caller. Upon request the girl gave Ferebe the telephone number of Mr. Pittman, the office manager. She telephoned him. He would be out of the office until at least three o'clock.

Ferebe tried not to be alarmed. Yet she hung up the receiver with foreboding. There could be no connection between Robert's arrest and Susie's absence, she told herself. She was being theatrical to speculate on the possibility. Susie could have taken time off for shopping and errands. She could be sick, but the telephone was at her bedside, and she could at least answer it. Unless . . .

Without allowing herself to pursue the thought, she

261

decided to take the children and drive out to Susie's apartment. The building was not large or important enough to have a name and telephone listing of its own, and she did not know the name of the neighbors or the manager, who lived on the premises. She called Maggie and Ellie in from the back yard and started getting them ready to go. Susie had told her last week that she had planned to go to Bentley for the weekend and take Robert. She had not talked to her mother since and assumed they went as planned. Her mother and father read *The Atlanta Constitution* every day and would surely see Robert's name on the front page with the others. She wanted to talk to Susie before her mother telephoned. She was surprised she had not called already.

"Maggie, see if you can tie that bow yourself," she said to her daughter while she put Ellie's shoes on him. "Just try it, honey—you might be surprised at what you can do. Sit still, Ellie—I can't do a thing with you wriggling all over the place—"

She stopped and took Ellie's foot from her lap. "Oh, no!" she moaned. "I must be going crazy!"

It was Ell's day to drive in the car pool, and she had forgotten it. She had no way to get to Susie's apartment. To make certain her mind was not deceiving her, she went to the back door and looked out at the garage. The doors were open and the car was gone.

The telephone rang. It was Polly Timmons, two houses down and across the street. She had received a telegram from the War Department. She was crying and talking incoherently, but Ferebe pieced out the essentials quickly. It was about Gordie.

"Oh, no, Polly! No, no, *no!*" Ferebe screamed. "I'll be right there, honey! Hold on to yourself. I'm coming! Hold on!"

She ran back to the children, too horrified to realize she was screaming at them until the startled, frightened looks on their faces brought her around. She forced herself to breathe deeply and compose herself.

"We've got to hurry," she told them. Her voice was trembling. She dropped to the floor and finished tying Ellie's shoe. "Randy's mother got some bad news about his daddy, and we're going to see if we can help them."

Polly Timmons was too stunned to do more than hand the telegram to Ferebe, and Ferebe was too stunned to do more than stare at it. She had heard of casualty messages and was acutely aware of the horror they contained, but she had never seen one before. Now she held a real one in her own hands and, while looking at it with her own eyes, found it to be unreal. It did not exist. There was no such thing as the yellow sheet of paper Polly Timmons had put into her hands.

THE SECRETARY OF WAR DESIRES ME TO EXPRESS HIS DEEP REGRETS THAT YOUR HUSBAND, LIEUTENANT GORDON DABNEY TIMMONS, USN, 256557, WAS KILLED IN ACTION IN DEFENSE OF HIS COUNTRY ON 12 SEPTEMBER 1943 IN THE HUON GULF IN THE SOUTHWEST PACIFIC OCEAN. LETTER FOLLOWS.
THE ADJUTANT GENERAL

She could think of nothing but that Randy had been learning to talk when his father saw him last.

"Where is the Huon Gulf?" she asked pointlessly and without meaning to ask. She knew that it was off the coast of New Guinea and that Gordon had been aboard a minesweeper out there. She had also read of a combined amphibious-paratroop attack on Lae and Salamaua on New Guinea proper. She and Polly had reasoned together that Gordie's minesweeper had been helping to prepare the way for the assault. Yet she still asked the question. She received no answer, nor did she expect one.

She was beginning to fear she was losing her mind. Only hours ago she had read in the paper that 100,000 Germans had been killed in Russia within a one-month period. That was more people than the entire population of Macon or Augusta or Columbus, and they had been wiped out in thirty days. She had accepted the figures with an impersonal kind of horror and moved on down the page. Now here was a single death—*one* person—that turned her numb with disbelief.

Polly held out her hand. Ferebe grasped it, then dropped it and put her arms around her. She wept openly and without restraint. She was not certain if it was Polly's or her own body that was shaking with sobs. Nor did it matter.

"I wrote Gordie a letter last night," Polly said into Ferebe's shoulder. "It's out on the mailbox now for the postman to pick up. I wrote him one earlier in the day and tore it up. It was too gloomy and depressing. He's got enough problems of his own without worrying about ours." She lifted her head. "I don't even know what Randy's doing."

Ferebe got to her feet. "I'll look after Randy, and I'll get the letter off the mailbox. If you'll let me, I'll call your folks and Gordie's too. Let me look after the house—everything. Some of the neighbors will want to know, and I'll call them."

Polly was helpless and agreed by not protesting. Ferebe went off in search of the children and left her staring into space. Later, people began to arrive, the telephone began to ring, and the children began to get noisier. To lessen the confusion, Ferebe took Randy home with her and the children.

The Hamptons' friendship with the Timmonses had started as a neighborhood association, then deepened into a more special and personal relationship. The four of them were near the same age with similar backgrounds and interests. Polly had attended the University of Georgia, where she and Ferebe had known many of the same people but not each other. Gordon grew up in La Grange and had graduated from Emory University with a reserve commission in the Navy. He had been called into active duty two months before Pearl Harbor, and Polly had seen him only once since. She and Randy spent two weeks with him in San Diego, where his ship came in for refitting. He was not coming home now, and when Ferebe stepped through her own front door, she was choking from a huge lump in her throat that would move neither up nor down.

The lump grew and became more obstinate each time Randy romped through the house like a wild mustang. After lunch when she put him to bed with Ellie for their naps and he fell asleep looking for all the world like a fat, dimpled cherub, the lump in her throat threatened to suffocate her. Exactly one-half of his world had disintegrated, and he knew nothing about it. Maybe he would never know. What could he know—that his life had changed directions before he knew it was headed in any direction to change from? For the rest of his life his father would never be more than a mild curiosity to him. The thought was sad. It was even sadder for Gordie to have loved a son who would have no feelings toward his father other than those taught him by his mother through the years, and those feelings could never be anything more personal than reverence, respect and admiration. It would be humanly impossible for Randy Timmons to ever love his own father.

She tiptoed to the door and saw that both boys were safely asleep. Then she went into her own room, sat down on the edge of the bed and wept. How could it make any difference in the outcome of this idiotic war whether Gordie Timmons lived or died? He was only one man with one wife and one child in one house in a peaceful, respectable neighborhood that he wanted to come back to more than anything else. That was the reason he left it in the first place. Was that a justifiable reason for killing him?

Susie came back to her abruptly. Susie had nothing to

do with the craziness of the war. She was no riddle, no enigma, no mysterious figure of intrigue. She was as open and apparent as a clean pane of glass. Then where was she? How did she ever get mixed up with that creepy Robert Shaefer? When Susie brought him to the house one Sunday afternoon, she had been appalled by his shrinking insignificance. She should not have been surprised, but she was. Susie had always dragged home the ones everybody else overlooked, shunned, didn't like or didn't know existed. Robert was yet another one. At least, she hoped there was no more than that to it.

Something was wrong. Susie was not thoughtless. Why didn't she get in touch with them? She must know they'd all be concerned about her when Robert's name appeared in the papers. What if she had had an accident in her apartment and no one knew it? Those things did happen to people who lived alone. She had already tried to reach Emily Lanier, but she was visiting her family in Waycross until Monday. She stared at the telephone and considered calling her mother, but she did not want to alarm her. There had to be a reasonable explanation for Susie's disappearance, and she wanted to find it herself rather than upset her parents.

She heard Maggie come in from the back yard. She was calling to her and crying. She had fallen and skinned her knee, but one of her friends had hurt her feelings. Ferebe diagnosed that as the real cause of her wailing and moaning.

"Well, honey, maybe she didn't mean it," she said. "Don't you ever say anything to your friends you don't mean? Now don't you worry about it, and don't you feel ugly toward Marcia about it. You know she is fond of you, or she wouldn't want you to play with her like she does. Suppose you stay in the house for a while, then when you go back outside you can pretend it never happened, and you both can have a good time like you always do."

While she was washing her knee and putting mercuro-chrome on it, Randy appeared in the doorway, bleary-eyed with sleep. He wanted to go home.

"Go finish your nap, darling, and we'll go home when you wake up next time," she persuaded him. She led him back into Ellie's room, but Ellie was awake by then, and she knew beyond question that two afternoon naps had ended. Within minutes both boys were on the living room floor playing with Ellie's toys. Maggie went into her own room and closed the door.

Ferebe sat down by the telephone in the hall and tried to think of someone to call about Susie. But unwittingly she found herself focusing on Ellie and Randy on the living room floor. They were struggling over a single section of a Tinkertoy. They had been playing with the entire set when for no visible reason both of them wanted the same elongated piece with a round knob stuck onto the end of it. Irrationally she wanted to scream at them. Why must you fight over one insignificant piece? Why can't you be satisfied with what you've got? A Tinkertoy is not worth fighting over! Not even the entire set of thirty or forty pieces, including the box they came in, is worth fighting over! *Why can't you just enjoy what you've got and let the other one enjoy what he's got? Why do you have to fight?*

She controlled an impulse to settle the squabble by taking the Tinkertoys away from them altogether. Instead, she quickly turned back to the telephone and called Globe Research and asked for Ell. He was in a meeting and could not return her call until a recess. When he did call back, she almost wept again, this time at the sound of his voice.

"Oh, Ell, you're the only thing I've heard all day that makes any sense."

"What are you talking about, honey? I haven't said anything yet."

"The sound of your voice is enough," she went on. "You don't know how glad I am just to hear—"

"Ferebe! What's wrong? What's going on?"

"That's what I don't know. Things quit making sense today."

"Now, now, now, take it easy and tell me what it is," he said gently. "It can't be all that bad. Relax and tell me. Go on."

She was ashamed of herself. "I'm a big crybaby, and that's not my nature. But things started going wacky today, and they haven't stopped—"

She told him about Gordie Timmons. "And do you know what Polly kept saying? She kept saying, 'There must be something besides this yellow piece of paper. There's got to be more than this to come back home. There's just got to be. This telegram can't be all that's left. There's got to be more.' "

"I'll come home as early as I can, honey," he promised her. "Tell Polly I'll come down as soon as I can. She'll understand." He paused. "Why does it always have to happen to the good guys?"

"Why does it happen to anybody? Do you think you can sneak out of the meeting early?"

"I'd like to, but I'm in charge of it. It'll probably go on the rest of the day. Some people from Washington are here, and we're spending all day telling them things they would already know if they'd read the reports we've been sending them. I'm telling you—when we win this war, we'll win it despite those pinheads in the Federal Government. No wonder Washington is crowded these days. They all—"

"Ell, there's something else driving me out of my mind," Ferebe interrupted him. "Do you know that Susie's boyfriend was arrested in that spy roundup Monday?"

"Susie's boyfriend? What boyfriend?"

"The one she brought to see us one Sunday—the only boyfriend she's ever had, as far as I know. Don't you remember? He was crippled and walked with a cane."

"Oh, him! How could he be a spy? Are you sure?"

Ferebe explained the circumstances up to that point.

"Have you been in touch with Perry? Maybe he knows where she is."

"I can't until tonight," she said. "I called his house and asked Mrs. Maxwell to bring him to the phone tonight, so I could ask him a question or two. I wish you could come home. I don't want you to do a blessed thing but stand here where I can see you with my own eyes."

"You know I—"

"I know, and I'm not going to fuss at you," she said. "Hearing you for a few minutes is good enough for me. Go on back to your meeting, darling. I didn't mean to add to your problems. Come home when you can, and I love you."

Ellie and Randy were at peace once more. She had no idea who was the victor. It was over, and that seemed more important than who won or lost. She dialed the Dixie Metal Works and asked to speak to Mr. Pittman. He was surly.

"I can't keep track of these girls even when they're present," he grumbled. "They're never at their desks. They're always running out for coffee breaks or to the ladies' room or getting sick, so how can I keep track of them when they're not here at all?"

"Surely you can check to see if she's on vacation or has the day off or has called in sick."

"I can. If the time and attendance sheets are posted up to date, which I doubt. They never are. Hold on."

She heard the telephone hit the desk with a thud. After what seemed to be an inordinate length of time, Mr. Pittman came back on the line.

"She's not on vacation or sick, and she doesn't have the day off," he said flatly. "That's according to the records, which don't mean much around here."

"Did she resign?"

"No."

269

"But she's not there?"

"No. Nobody's seen her since Monday."

"You mean nobody knows anything about her at all? This isn't making any sense. Doesn't *somebody* know something about her?"

"I told you—no. Is there anything else you want?"

"Do you mean that's all there is to it?" Ferebe asked.

"It's all I know. It's what you asked, isn't it?"

"As her superior, surely you have some responsibility for her presence or absence." She was becoming more exasperated than alarmed.

"I do," he replied wearily.

"Then how can you be so indifferent about why she's not at work?"

"I'm not indifferent. I just can't do anything about it. Now I've got to get back to work, Mrs. er—"

"I don't understand this, Mr. Pittman," Ferebe said, her voice rising. "Here's the entire country at war. People are getting killed. Guns and ammunition must be produced, and you don't seem to be the least concerned when your people don't show up for work to deliver your part of the war production—whatever it is."

"Look, lady," he said. "Don't try to tell me how to run the war. When these people don't show up for work, I do their work for them. They don't do it for each other. I do it. I never know where anybody is. How would you like to come down here and try to run an office with temporary help? That's what all of them are—temporary. Here today and gone tomorrow. If they smell a job with more pay at the new Bomber Plant or at Chrysler or Fischer's or at Fort Mac—anywhere—off they go. Some of them don't even give notice. They just don't show up for work the next day. Their boyfriends come home on furlough, and they quit their jobs to be with them for a week or ten days. They don't take leave with or without pay. They quit. Their husbands in the Army or Navy get transferred and—boom! Off they go! Some start to work one day and three days later drop out of sight with no warning or explanation. They turn up from nowhere, and we hire them, because we need bodies. Just bodies. Then they vanish into thin air. Some of them don't stay long enough for us to learn their names. Your sister is not the first girl to disappear from this company with no explanation."

"Well, of course, I didn't mean for you to go into all that—"

"Maybe your sister hasn't told you what we make in this plant as our part of the war effort," he continued as though she had not interrupted him. "Well, I'll tell you. Among other things we make a little metal gadget that wouldn't look like anything to you, but it's a bracket and fitting for fire extinguishers on Navy ships. Did it ever occur to you that fire extinguishers have to be fastened onto *something*—especially on ships trying to stay afloat under bombardment? Well, they do, and somebody has to make those little gadgets, and that's what we do. That's our contribution. We're proud of it, too. The Navy needs them, and we make them. It's important to us."

"Mr. Pittman, I'm awfully sorry that I spoke so—"

"We feel our responsibility for our war production, and we deliver what we can when we can. But we're always behind. We seldom meet a quota or commitment on time. We've never received an 'E' award for excellence in war production. We probably never will. Do you know why? Because this plant and this office is overloaded with people like your sister who don't take their responsibilities seriously enough to at least call in so we can cover their work for them before it gets out of hand. With us it's a fight to hold onto the contracts we've got. The only reason we hold onto them at all is because all the other companies have got their hands full and can't take on any more work. Whatever we deliver—even when it's short of our commitment—is better than nothing. Is that how we're supposed to be running the war?"

"Mr. Pittman, I'm trying to apologize to you and tell you that—"

"We're even too far behind to take holidays, but we have to take them, because we can't afford to pay the overtime it would take to run full schedule on holidays. In peacetime, lady, this company would have gone bankrupt long ago."

"Please understand that I wasn't being critical of—"

Mr. Pittman ignored her further. "We haven't had an able-bodied male around here who could walk up two flights of stairs without fainting since the day after Pearl Harbor. I'm the youngest male in the office section, and I'm sixty-three. I've got arthritis and can't move around very good. I get up from my desk only when it's absolutely necessary. I'm way over my head in this job, and I know it. I belong out in the plant. But all the men with experience in the company joined the Army and Navy or went on to big-time war production jobs, and I was the only person left to do the job. I'm trying to do it. I've got two boys in the service. One of them was with General Wainwright on Corregidor, and we hope he still is. So don't lecture me about the war and war work and what I ought to be concerned about and who I ought to keep track of. Whatever you do for a living—and I don't really care what it is—come on down here, and I'll be glad to swap with you. I'm sorry I don't know anything about your sister. I mean that. I'd like to help you."

He slammed down the receiver.

Ferebe's face burned. She wanted to dig a hole, crawl into it and pull the dirt in after her. She resented Object Lessons, especially when they were designated and presented as such, but she had received one, and she was too embarrassed to evaluate it. Maybe the embarrassment itself was the evaluation. Throughout the remainder of the day the sounds of Mr. Pittman's scolding haunted her. He had shamed her into her place and reduced her personal problems and concerns to self-indulgent whimperings. She resolved not to let Ell know of the conversation, and she could only hope that Susie would not hear of it from another source.

When the children got hungry and irritable, she gave them their supper without speculating on the possible time of Ell's arrival. She would wait and eat with him herself, even if it was two o'clock in the morning.

Mrs. Maxwell called while the children were eating. Perry was waiting by the telephone.

"I know this is an imposition, Mrs. Maxwell, and I won't keep you long," Ferebe said.

"Don't worry about it, Mrs. Hampton," she replied. "I waited until I had a little time before I called you back. Perry's waiting now. Go ahead."

"Will you ask him if he knows where Susie is?" she said. "Tell him she has not been to work in two days and nobody at the office knows how to contact her. She doesn't answer her telephone at home, either. Susie's our sister."

"Yes, I know," said Mrs. Maxwell. "Just one minute while I ask him."

Ferebe waited and was surprised how quickly Mrs. Maxwell came back on the line.

"He doesn't know, Mrs. Hampton. He hasn't seen her since a week ago Sunday. Let's see now—that will be two weeks this coming Sunday, won't it? He and Lydia—a young lady who has one of our rooms here—spent all day at her place. They had a wonderful time. He wants to know if anything's wrong."

Ferebe thought fast. She had no objections to Perry's knowing the real reason for her uneasiness, but she was reluctant to pass it through Mrs. Maxwell.

"No. No, nothing's wrong," she said, "but I hadn't seen or heard from Susie for a while, and now I can't get hold of her. Ask Perry if he knows the telephone number of her apartment manager or of any of her neighbors. Make sure he knows there's nothing to worry about."

Short silence again.

273

"No, he doesn't know," Mrs. Maxwell said. "I think he's getting a little worried, though. Are you sure there's nothing I can tell him? I'm not being nosy—it is *his* conversation, you know. You'd be surprised at the confidential conversations that enter my ears and go out my hands —my husband's, too." She laughed.

"No. Please assure him there's nothing to worry about. You might ask him when he's coming out to see us again. He hasn't been in several weeks."

While she waited, Ferebe wondered how many such conversations per day the Maxwells handled for their roomers and whether or not she herself would have enough patience for them.

"Mrs. Hampton? He wants to know if it will be all right for him to come out Friday night or Saturday morning for the weekend. He says he'll take the bus and you won't have to worry about meeting him or picking him up anywhere."

Ferebe was delighted. "Yes, indeed, it will be all right!" she said. "I'll probably put him to work too. You can tell him that. I've got lots of shopping to do, errands to run, places to go that have stacked up on me simply because it's almost impossible to get a sitter when you need one. I'll turn over my two children to him while I do some of them. They adore him. They're absolutely fascinated by the way he uses his hands to talk, and of course, he makes quite a show of it for them. After he's been here, they go around for a day or two waving their hands and imitating him. Tell him if I can get my husband away from work long enough, we'll dream up something special all of us can do together. And while you're on the line, how is Perry? Is he getting along all right?"

"Just fine, Mrs. Hampton," she said cheerfully. "I've been fixing a lunch for him to take to work recently—or whenever he decides he wants it. He gets tired of the cafeteria, you know, and he likes to find different places to eat

274

outdoors. Some of the others bring their lunches, too, he says, and they get together and eat. Is there anything else you'd like to say to Perry or ask him?"

"No, and you are so sweet to do all this. Tell him to bring any sugar stamps he doesn't need, so we can have a decent dessert. Mine get away from me somehow."

Mrs. Maxwell laughed again. "I'm afraid I get all their stamps when I get their rent. It's the only way I can fill their sweet tooths. I hope you find your sister, and I know you will. It looks like everybody's got so much on their minds these days they forget to tell each other what they're doing. She'll turn up. Don't worry about it."

After the children were in bed and while she waited for Ell to come home, Ferebe concluded that her parents had not seen Robert Shaefer's name in the paper, or, if they had, they knew where Susie was and had already talked to her. Otherwise, she would have heard from them. She decided to telephone them. If it was the former, she would not mention it. If it was the latter, they would volunteer the information.

"Ferebe, darling! It's so good to hear from you!" her mother said at the sound of her voice. "Is everybody all right?"

"Yes, we're all right. We had a blow today, though." She told her about Gordie Timmons.

"How dreadful!" her mother said. "Isn't that just awful? We met them once, if you'll remember. Please give Polly our very best, and do what you can for her, darling. It might seem to you that you're doing nothing, but at least let her know you care. We had something of a shock ourselves. Did you read about Robert Shaefer—Susie's friend—in the *Constitution* this morning?"

"Yes, and I've been wondering if you saw it."

"Yes, yes, we did. We were watching for it. Susie told us all about it yesterday, so we—"

"Susie? Have you talked to her?"

"Why, certainly, we've talked to her! She's right here this very minute. She came yesterday morning."

"Oh, no!"

"What's the matter?"

"Mother, I've almost been out of my mind all day trying to run her down! I could just— Let me talk to her!"

"Ferebe! What on earth? Susie? She wants to talk to you—"

Susie came on the line.

"Susie Holly! I'd like to wring your neck!" she stormed at her. "Why can't you tell somebody what you're doing, for pity's sake? You just wander off out of town like everybody is supposed to know where you are! Your boss doesn't even know where you are. I called him this afternoon and—"

"My boss? Mr. Pittman?" Susie screamed. "He certainly *does* know where I am! I called him yesterday afternoon and told him I was coming to Bentley, and he said, 'Yeah—okay,' and hung up. He didn't stay on the line long enough to know if I was dying or going off to join the WACs or what! He stays too busy all the time and hears about half what people tell him. I told him, all right, and he probably gave you a speech about not knowing where anybody is because nobody will tell him and—"

"I've been scared to death Mother and Daddy would see the piece about Robert, and I wanted to talk to you first. Don't ask me why. I just did. What did you go back to Bentley for?"

"It's hard to explain," she said. "I stayed awake half the night Monday trying to decide if I should try to see Robert or not. Emily Lanier had argued with me that I shouldn't. As it turned out, they weren't letting him see anybody, anyway, so I didn't have much to decide. Just the same, I had a guilty feeling that I ought to at least try. I always pass in front of the Federal Building on my way to work, and for some reason I pulled the cord Tues-

276

day morning and got off. I stood on the sidewalk across the street for I don't know how long—I was late for work—and had a terrible battle with myself. I came within an inch of walking into the Federal Building, but I didn't. Finally I decided to remove myself from the temptation altogether, so I came home. That's all there is to it. I'm coming back tomorrow."

"You don't sound very upset about it," Ferebe said.

"I am, though," Susie said. "I've been torn into little pieces about the whole thing. I never would have thought Robert could get mixed up in something like that, and I'm not sure even now that he is actually involved. I'm glad I came home. I've had two days to get my feet on the ground back here where things are sane and make sense. I know what to do now. Mother and Daddy know all about it. I'm definitely going to see Robert—I've got to—but I'll wait until the right time. I don't know when that will be, but it'll come along. I'll tell you the whole story when I get back."

"Well, if this doesn't take the cake," Ferebe said, far from pacified. "Apparently, I've been having my own private little mystery all day. Looks like you could have called me. Tell me one thing now. What's all this between you and Robert? Are you *serious* about him?"

"Suppose I am?" Susie asked loftily. "Would that be so impossible?"

"In your case, no," Ferebe said. "That's what I'm worried about. Are you?"

"No."

"Good!" she exclaimed. "Now I won't mind hearing the whole story when you get around to telling it to me. I guess I'd better hang up before— Oh, Susie? When you get back, will you write down the names and telephone numbers of everybody you know and give them to me? They might come in handy someday."

# 26

LED BY BRITISH TANKS, the Fifth Army entered Naples on the first day in October to find the lovely Neapolitan city of song and romance devastated and its harbor full of sunken ships. But Naples was back in Allied hands, where it had belonged all the time, and the Nazi army had been pushed that much farther back toward Germany, which it should never have left. For the Holly family it almost seemed that the war had ended altogether. Paul had stayed behind.

Mamie could not read past the first few lines of his letter:

Miracles do happen, I guess. Instead of getting ready to move north like I've been doing ever since I can remember, I'm getting ready to move south. A replacement wandered into the battalion with my name written all over him and became my best friend on sight. I'm waiting for orders to join an MP company somewhere south of here. So it looks like for a while I'm going to be one of those soldiers I've read about who takes baths, gets his hair cut, shaves, wears clean clothes, shines his boots and even works regular hours. Rumor has it that GIs even sleep on cots where I'm going, but I'll wait until I feel one under me to believe it. . . .

Mamie broke into tears. She cried aloud and could not stop. The telephone rang and she could not answer it.

She sat in the hall inside the front door with her lap full of unopened mail, crushing Paul's letter to her and letting the tears run down her cheeks and onto the front of her dress. When she felt the paper getting soggy, she dropped it onto the floor and continued to sob into her bare hands.

"Dear God," she breathed. "Dear, dear God—you did remember. . . ."

Her hands were wet as if she had held them under running water. She got up and went into the bathroom to dry them and wash her face.

"You just look *awful!*" she scolded her reflection in the mirror. Her eyes were red, and her face was streaked. "I don't know what you'll do if you ever get any *bad* news."

She bathed her eyes in cold water and patted her hair back into place. She had started through the house to telephone Alex when she remembered she had not read all of Paul's letter.

She hurried back into the hall and retrieved it. The ink had run and blurred some of the words along the edge of the pages. She read past them eagerly:

I've made some lifelong friends in my outfit, and I'll miss them. A bunch of guys were talking about this the other night, and we got to wondering if any of us would be friends under any other circumstances. We decided that none of us would have ever made it. We didn't match up anywhere—interests, backgrounds, educations, geography, what we want to do after the war—nothing. In fact, some of us didn't even like each other when we first joined the outfit.

Now don't get your hopes up about all this. It doesn't mean I'm headed for home. Later on I'll probably rejoin my battalion or another one like it somewhere up the line, and that's all right. It's the system, and I won't complain. In the meantime, I can't help but be a little bit happy that they've figured out how to run the war without me for right now and maybe a little while longer.

I never knew what war was like. But I guess nobody does until they're actually in one. You don't have time to think what it's all about or why it has to be fought. You're too busy doing that one job out in front of you at the minute and trying to stay alive while you're doing it. If you don't put that first on your list of things to do, it's Katie-bar-the-door. I don't know any GI who feels heroic. The job's too dirty, ugly and downright hard to get inspired about.

Susie wrote me about her boyfriend. She's got to be kidding! Where does she find all these people that nobody else knows? Ferebe sends me some cookies and candy all along, but she's like I am—not much of a letter writer. Take care of yourselves and don't worry about me. If things were any better for me, the medics would have to give me some gloomy pills to get my morale back down to normal. I'll send my new APO when I get it.

Love,<br>Paul

P.S. I'll miss you too, Censor. Or do you have a brother down where I'm going?

Alex was as happy as Mamie, but he cautioned her against too much optimism. "Naples is not as far up the Boot as you might think. There's still an awful lot of Italy between Naples and Berlin. Besides, a lot of priorities are going into the big buildup in England for an invasion. So the war in Italy might be due for a slowdown."

"I'm so happy right now that I'm not even thinking about how much longer it will go on," she said. "To think I can pick up the paper tomorrow morning without holding my breath while I see what's going on in Italy. Now if Susie can get that awful business about Robert Shaefer behind her and out of her mind, I guess I'd be the happiest mother in Bentley, Georgia—maybe the whole United States. I'd give anything in the world if she wouldn't see him again."

"She's got to, Mamie. She wouldn't be Susie if she

didn't. She can't scrub him out of her mind without doing something else. Some people might, but not Susie. Nothing is worse to her than the feeling she might have made somebody unhappy. She'll do anything at all to make it all right with them. All of those people at Robert's company have been indicted, according to the paper. I told her to wait until after that. I hope she did."

She did. It was amazingly simple. Susie telephoned the Detention Center and asked if there were any restrictions on visitors and the hours they were permitted to come. Apparently her question was routine, and her identity seemed to be of no importance or interest. Some of the prisoners had been interviewed by reporters, and the papers had published some photographs made around the Federal Building. There no longer seemed to be anything special or exclusive about any of them or the case itself.

Now she sat across the table from Robert in a plain, but not altogether unpleasant, room and talked to him with more composure and presence of mind than she would have thought possible. No guards stood in attendance. No grill or partition separated them. She had been required to leave her purse outside at the desk. In its place she had been given a piece of paper containing a list of its contents. She held it in her hand. Otherwise, she could have been sitting for a job interview in the personnel office of a factory, department store or military installation. Robert wore dark trousers and a bluish-gray shirt opened at the collar. She assumed it to be part of the prison garb. He hung his cane on the back of his chair as she had seen him do time and again. He brushed his hair back from his forehead and adjusted his dark-rimmed spectacles.

"I wanted you to come, Susie, but I knew you shouldn't," he told her. "When the guard brought me your name, I could have refused to see you. If I had wanted to strike a noble posture, I could have done that and let you think the absolute worst of me. That's brutal, but it could have some long-range advantages for you. That's Plot 3-C in a James Cagney–Pat O'Brien movie, I think."

"Robert, I'm not thinking about the absolute worst of you. I'm thinking about the good part of you, or I wouldn't have come," she said. "All this business you're involved in is terrible, and I can't imagine for one minute how you or anybody else could do such things. I never have felt right about not seeing you again after that night down at Union Station. It was all too abrupt. I felt other things should be said. But as time has gone by I can't remember what they were except one. I want to thank you for the past few months. No matter how things have turned out, that's when I saw the good part of you, and I'm sure there's more where that came from. I just wanted you to know that."

She looked down at her hands folded in her lap. "I guess that's all I came to say," she added. It had been surprisingly easy, although she was uncomfortable under his gaze.

"I didn't tell the FBI about you," he said. "Your name is on the record outside now, though. Doesn't that bother you? You might be investigated."

"I've already been investigated," she replied. "I was pretty dumb not to have realized that. They came to see me the week after you were arrested—two men. They were nice and gentlemanly. They knew about your visit to Bentley. They knew about Mother, Daddy, Paul, Ferebe, Perry, Ellison—all of us. They already had a background file on me from the papers I had filled out when I was trying to get a job with the Army and Navy. I explained my —my association with you. So my coming here didn't take a lot of courage."

"But I'm a subversive person," he said. "Doesn't that bother you?"

"It certainly does," she said sharply. "I don't know

anything more despicable than working against your own country, especially when it's fighting for its life. Did you know what kind of business you were in?"

"Yes, I knew," he replied.

"And you worked there anyway?" Susie was incredulous.

"It was a job. It paid me a salary. I went to work in the mornings and back home at nights. We compiled figures and never discussed what they were for. It didn't matter. I was not motivated by any ideology or politics. I worked for them in Boston. How I got started there is too involved to tell you. I was recruited—if you know what that means. I wanted to go where it was warm, and I asked them to send me to Atlanta. I knew about the office here. You don't know how it is to be cold all your life. I had been cold ever since I could remember. Looking back, it seems that I lived my entire life tied up in tight little knots. Coldness was a permanent condition with me. I could never relax. Somewhere along the line I suppose my insides grew cold and congealed too. They agreed to send me here."

She was touched. She did not quite understand the feeling he described, but there was something pathetic about the manner in which he described it. In her experience cold weather was to be enjoyed, especially if you were cozy around an open fire and looking at the weather through steamy or frosty windows.

"Couldn't you have come to Atlanta for another reason?" she asked. "Lots of people come down here for war jobs."

"You might say I came for a war job, too," he said. His smile was grim. "But that wasn't a funny remark, was it?"

"No, it wasn't. Don't you care who wins the war?"

"Why worry? The Allies will win it anyway. No enemy can stand up against the United States's industrial might.

It's overwhelming. The production of war goods in this country is fantastic, and it's still on the increase. There's no end to it. The supply is inexhaustible. The assembly lines can run forever. For each ship the enemy sinks, the Allies can replace it with two or three new ones. The enemy can shoot down a couple of B-17s, and the United States sends in an entire squadron of B-17s, right out of the factory. When an airfield gets bombed, the bulldozers and concrete mixers have a new runway ready almost before the wreckage has been cleared away. Guns, tanks, and ammunition are stacked sky-high all over the country waiting to be shipped out, and the stacks are getting higher and higher. It's like lining up all the Chinese people four abreast and marching them past a given point; they'll never stop marching past. So the war is all settled. It's only a matter of killing enough people and bombing enough cities to convince the enemy they've lost."

"You're so matter-of-fact about it! Don't you feel any remorse or regrets about what you've done?"

"I don't like to be in jail, if that's what you mean." He smiled. "I don't mean to be flippant. Yes, I feel a lot of remorse—on your account. You're too good a person to get mixed up with me. I should have got out of your way in the beginning. I knew that at the time. But I wanted to see you. I've wanted to see you ever since. You're the only person I've ever had any real feelings about."

"Did you really want to marry me?"

"I think so, but I knew all the time I never would. I could never live with anybody. That weekend in Bentley convinced me of that. In your family, and probably all families like it, everything belongs to everybody—the house, the meals, the furniture, the time, even each other. I wouldn't know how to share like that. And it's the only way you do know. So you see? You weren't the only one to have second thoughts that weekend. I'm glad you told me first, though, so I wouldn't have to tell you."

She hardly knew what to make of him. Except for the clothes he wore, he did not look any different from the way he had always looked. He talked the same. She detected nothing unusual about his manner. Yet it was unrealistic for him to be a prisoner charged with spying against the United States and not be different from the Robert Shaefer who had been a guest in her parents' home and slept in her brothers' room.

"This is the most peculiar conversation I ever had," she said. "You've committed one of the lowest of all crimes. You can't get one ounce of sympathy from anybody in the country. The newspapers call you traitors, turncoats and spies. You're in jail and are probably going to prison for several years. I'm supposed to feel contempt and hatred for you. You've been working against my brother Paul, who has been in combat getting shot at for over a year. Yet here I sit across the table from you talking calmly and feeling practically nothing toward you but curiosity. Does that make any sense? Or am I going crazy?"

"It's probably the best way for you to feel," he replied. "It's better than a lot of dramatics. You're too real to be dramatic. You deal with things as they are—and as you are. I wish I had met you years ago. Then maybe I wouldn't have lavished so much pity on myself all these years."

"Knowing me wouldn't have made any difference," she said.

"Perhaps it would have. You took me at face value, which couldn't have been very high, and before I knew what I was doing, I began taking stock of myself—the last thing I would ever have done on my own. Honestly, that is. You see, there's something contagious about you. You rub off on people. All your cheery, happy optimism and Good Will Toward Men began to do something for me. I began looking at how unhappiness was a self-inflicted way of life with me. But it was too late to do anything about it—for your sake, anyway. Maybe for my own, but not yours. I couldn't get away from Southern Trade, Incorporated, and I would not let you get in it with me." He stopped and lifted his eyebrows. "You might want to make a note of that. It's the only unselfish motive I've ever had."

"I don't believe that," she said.

"I know you don't, and that proves what I'm trying to say. You're totally unfamiliar with selfishness, so you don't recognize it when you see it. You can't begin to understand it in others. I'm selfish. Self-centered. Nobody ever mattered to me, except me—until I knew you. You're the only person I've ever cared about in my entire life, outside myself. I never even loved my own parents. They were fixtures like the sink, the refrigerator, the furnace. You need and expect certain things to make life livable, and they were some of those necessities. Nothing else."

She studied his face. "You're putting on an act," she said. "You're trying to be cold and impersonal, and I don't believe you feel that way. Are you bitter toward your parents now?"

"No. I don't feel anything toward them. I could have sold them along with the house and furniture and never looked back over my shoulder at what I had done."

"*Robert!* You *know* you don't mean that! That's the worst thing I ever heard anybody say! You sound like you don't have a heart."

He leaned forward. His expression deepened. A look of bewildered anguish appeared in his eyes. "I didn't think I did, Susie," he said. He was plaintive. "I think that's what I've been getting at. I was beginning to wonder if my left leg was the only part of me that was shriveled or was missing altogether."

Susie was horrified. "You couldn't *possibly* have thought such a thing," she said. "Everybody's got a heart —except the Tin Man in *The Wizard of Oz*. And he eventually found his."

Robert seized on that. "Where did he find it—and how?" he asked knowingly.

"Dorothy—the little girl—showed it to him. It was there all the time. Don't you remember?"

"Yes," he said. He lowered his eyes. "Indeed, I do remember." He spoke softly and she could barely hear him. His voice was husky. She looked away so as not to embarrass him.

"You showed me mine," she heard him say.

She turned back to face him.

"There was never a way we could have ended Happily Ever After, was there?" he asked. "If I had the gift of tongues, I would apologize to you as you deserve, but I don't know where to start and where to stop. But I know one thing. You're a magnificent human being, Susie Holly. If somehow, somewhere you don't get the absolute best this life can offer, then justice is a mockery. With everything that's inside me—whether it's a heart or not—I hope you find the best husband in the world and a houseful of children who'll love you as much as you'll love them—and how can they help it? And when you do—and you will—that husband and those children will be the most fortunate people God ever made. I can't tell you to forget about me, for I don't want you to forget me. I want you to remember me—the best parts, at least."

He reached across the table and took her hand. He squeezed it gently. Then he stood up abruptly. She looked at him in surprise.

"What will you do?" she asked. "The Tin Man went on to be happy."

"I don't know. I don't have a very happy feeling right now. Perhaps Whittier was right."

"About what?" she asked.

" 'For of all sad words of tongue or pen,
The saddest are these: "It might have been." ' "

He turned and left the room without looking back.

# 27

On the Sunday before Thanksgiving, Ferebe, Ellison and the children came to Bentley unexpectedly. Mamie was preparing dinner and complaining about the increasing length of Mr. Clapper's sermons. She thought someone should speak to him about how inconsiderate he was of the ladies who left roasts at home cooking in their ovens. It took too many ration points to buy a decent roast for them to be overcooked only because Mr. Clapper would not get to the benediction by twelve o'clock.

Alex was sitting at the kitchen table browsing through the Sunday edition of *The Atlanta Constitution* and comparing its size to its pre–Pearl Harbor bulk. Both the *Constitution* and the *Journal*, like their counterparts across the country, had dwindled in size. Not only had their editorial content been condensed and some of it eliminated altogether, but the paper on which they were printed was thinner now and of different quality. No one except possibly the people involved in its production considered the reduction of newsprint to be a major sacrifice to the war effort. Still, Alex felt slightly disoriented each morning when confronted with the strange new feel, weight and appearance of an ingrained institution that was as familiar to him as the view of Wylie Spencer's beehives from his back porch.

As he turned the pages, he wondered if there could ever be an end to the list of wartime shortages. Through necessity, Mamie had become a regular pack rat. Literally, she had become a string saver. She also hoarded paper sacks, cardboard boxes, rubber bands, paper clips and any length of elastic that had not lost its strength. She saved bacon grease, and it was a slow process, for she refused to cook more than one slice of that precious commodity for Alex's breakfast. When she went to the grocery store, she took her empty egg cartons to be refilled. A broken milk bottle was a near catastrophe. A lost bobby pin, straight pin or safety pin was not a casual occurrence. Alex himself used the same razor blade each morning until shaving became as torturous as surgery without an anesthetic; then he changed. But only then.

Newsprint was also a victim of the war. After all, it had its beginning in a forest, and the manpower, fuel, energy and transportation required to process it from a tree into words were among the most critical resources needed to prosecute the war. When Alex followed the process from a tree to a classified ad, he wondered how a newspaper ever fought its way into existence at all.

"Did you know Superman was classified 4-F by his draft board?" he asked from behind the comic section.

"How could he possibly be?"

"I must have missed it when it happened, but he failed his eye test on his preinduction physical. With his X-ray vision he read through the chart and the wall it was hanging on and through several other walls to another chart down the hall. The letters were not the same as on the chart he was supposed to be reading, and he failed."

"Well, I *never!*" Mamie exclaimed. "I stopped reading the funny papers when Skeezix Walters and Joe Palooka got in the Army. I had enough people to keep track of without worrying about them. You know they'll be in one scrape after the other, and I didn't want to have to bother."

"You're not doing your part, Mamie," he said. "Tillie the Toiler joined the WACs and is having all kinds of problems. Looks like you'd want to keep up with her. Daddy Warbucks is a general. He's in charge of everything."

"Naturally. You didn't expect him to be a corporal, did you? Go see who's at the door. I didn't realize it was locked."

With her preparations for dinner happily interrupted by the arrival of the Hamptons, Mamie decided not to even try to have it until after Alex went down to the depot and returned.

"I hope you're cooking enough for all of us," Ferebe said, lifting the lid off a pot and sniffing the contents.

"I always do," Mamie replied. "I don't think I'll ever learn to cook for two people. I still cook for a houseful; then we eat leftovers for the rest of the week, or until we can't bear to face them any longer. But Sunday dinner itself never changes. We still rush in from church, throw everything on the table, then watch the clock while we eat it. I declare—I'll never understand why your daddy feels that Number 12 can't arrive and depart without his presence. I think we'll start having dinner on Sundays after the train has left town and is at least halfway to Atlanta. Eating would be a lot simpler."

"You haven't changed either, Mother," Ferebe said. "You've been threatening to do that since the year One."

"And one of these days we'll do it, too."

"Or you'll change the Georgia Railroad schedules to fit your mealtimes," Ferebe said. "Now say the rest of it. The part about Daddy letting Emory Haynes look after Number 12 on Sundays."

Mamie laughed. "I just hadn't got around to that part yet. But Emory is perfectly capable of watching the train come and go. Really, that's all your daddy does."

Maggie and Ellie went with their grandfather to the

depot. Ellison read the paper, half participating in the conversation between his wife and his mother-in-law. After dinner the children entertained themselves throughout the house and on the back porch. The weather was not right for them to go outdoors. The four adults settled themselves lazily in the living room before an open fire. The day was raw and cold, as gray as dusk.

"We can't stay late," Ferebe told them. "We've got a bad tire. Ell has looked all over Atlanta for a new one, but unless you're willing to pay a king's ransom on the black market for a new one, they're not to be had. We don't want to have a flat tire on the highway after dark."

"I've decided to go into the Army," Ellison said without preface.

Without stopping to assess the gasp from Mamie and the look of surprise on his father-in-law's face, he continued. "That's what we came to tell you. It wasn't a sudden decision made in a gush of patriotism while the band was marching by or in the hysteria of a war bond rally. It's been a long time in the making."

Alex rubbed his chin with a forefinger and turned to Mamie, who was staring at Ellison.

"What brought all this on?" he asked. "You've never said anything about it before."

"Even before Ferebe and I started talking seriously about it, she knew as well as I did that it wasn't a question of yes or no. It was only a question of when. She understands what I'm doing."

He looked to her for reassurance. She nodded.

"I don't mean to sound thick-headed, but I don't understand it," Alex said.

"You don't have to go, Ellison," Mamie said. "My goodness! With two children and high-priority war work, you couldn't possibly be called in."

"We both know that, Mother," Ferebe said quietly. "He's classified 3-A, which is a perfectly valid, honorable and justifiable deferment. Nobody's forcing him to go. Nobody's even encouraging him to go. It's his own decision, but he didn't make it without me. He wouldn't give the Army a final answer unless I agreed, and I did." She smoothed her dress across her knee. "Who would have predicted that I would ever agree to Ell's going off to Lord knows where without me?" She sighed. "But everybody's doing strange things now." She got up from her chair and found her purse in the hall. She returned, sat down again, opened her purse, took out a package of cigarettes, lighted one and settled back in her chair.

Mamie had been watching her in wonderment.

"Ferebe! You don't smoke!" she exclaimed.

"I do now," she replied.

"When did you start?"

"Oh, I don't know—one day, I guess."

"Cigarettes are rationed, too," Mamie reminded her. "It seems like a funny time to start smoking when you can't even buy cigarettes. If you're going to start using something, why don't you start using something there's plenty of?"

"There's no such thing," she said. She blew out a heavy cloud of smoke. "I told you everybody was doing strange things. I just wanted to do something wild, and this is the wildest thing I can think of." She coughed violently and fanned the smoke away from her face. "Anyway, as we were saying, Ell's going into the Army, and that's that."

"Do you mean you've already signed up, Ellison?" Alex asked, his face a mixture of alarm and incredulity.

"No, sir. Not finally. I filled out some papers, but they aren't legally binding. It's in the Signal Corps. Nothing is binding in the Army until you actually take the oath. Meanwhile, I'm listed against a quota, and as long as my name is on that board, they can't recruit anybody else for that particular slot. They gave me a strict time limit on how long that can be. And unless I change my mind, the only thing left for me to do is raise my right hand, say 'I do,' and that's it. I've even had the physical to make certain I'm qualified."

"When's the deadline?"

"Wednesday."

"But that's the day before Thanksgiving!" Mamie said.

"The day before or the day after—it comes out pretty much the same," Ferebe said. "It so happens that the deadline is Wednesday."

Alex still had not assimilated all he had heard. "What about the research lab?" he asked. "You're not just another employee. They can't replace you off the streets or from a labor pool or by running a classified ad in the paper. What about all that?"

"It created a problem, all right—and a stir. Far beyond my own little bailiwick, as a matter of fact. Mr. Jeffers, the president, called me in and discussed it for quite a while. He didn't openly try to talk me out of joining the Army—that would be unpatriotic—but that was the purpose of the talk."

"He offered him a raise," Ferebe said.

"He did?" Alex's eyes widened.

"Yes, sir, and it was a good one," Ellison said. "Although my mind was already made up, he handed me a tough one there. Not only because of the money per se. But a promotion was staring me in the face and with it a big future, a big potential, an open stairway to the top, and I would have made it. I'm still wondering if I have the right to deny Ferebe, Maggie and Ellie all the good things that would mean."

"But Ellison, if the Government and the research lab need your know-how that much, maybe you should listen to them," Alex said, trying not to argue but to understand.

"I can't," he said. "Their viewpoint is as valid as mine. I've always known that. Over the long haul, and evaluating what I can do as a whole, I can make a much greater contribution to this country with Globe Research than with the Army. It's no contest. But Mr. Holly, this war has become very personal to me, and I've got to do something about it on a personal level. I've got to where I can't think of long-range results. Even when I do, it's not enough. At the lab I recently finished steering a project through to completion. My part of the job is over. I'm proud of what we've done and my part in it. Do you know how long it will take to translate it into something usable? Maybe— and only maybe—before the war is over. If not, then maybe it will benefit combat crews in the next war, God forbid. It has peacetime applications too. Airline pilots can benefit from it for years to come. Those are the kind of long-range results I've been .working for. They're too long for me to wait for.

"In the meantime, a bomber pilot doesn't worry about long-range results while he's plowing his way through weather, searching for his target and dodging flak. His concerns are more immediate and urgent. He's the guy I want to help—not his children and grandchildren. Somebody else will help them. They always do."

"But Ellison, your project—whatever it is—will help thousands of combat crews, won't it? Isn't that better than helping one at a time?"

"Yes, sir, it is. I'd be stupid to think otherwise. Mr. Jeffers says I'm shortsighted. I admitted it. So is every pilot, navigator, bombardier, tail gunner and radio operator who goes out on a mission. They can't think too far beyond the mission they're flying, or they might never come back."

"Will you be flying as a crew member?" Alex asked.

"I doubt it," he said. He laughed. "The Army is running true to form, they tell me. With all my know-how in air-communications, made to order for the Air Corps, they offered me a direct commission as a first lieutenant in the

Signal Corps on the ground. Within six months, after some basic military training and some military communication orientation training, I'll be ready to join a combat unit or whatever kind they decide I'll fit best."

"Oh, no, Ellison . . ." The words escaped Mamie's lips before she could check them. "Paul's already in it. Isn't that enough for one family?"

"Yes, ma'am, it is. Or it would be if somebody could figure out how to run the war by family allocations," he said. "One of my brothers is in the Navy somewhere in the Pacific. The other is in the Army Air Corps at Quanah, Texas, wherever that is. After I got off work Wednesday, we took the children and drove down to Griffin to tell my parents. Their reaction was the same as yours. Mama said she didn't think it was ever intended for one family to send all its children off to this war or any other war. Dad thinks trading communications at Globe for communications in the Army is only robbing Peter to pay Paul." He smiled. "I guess you could look at it that way."

"What about Ferebe and the children?" Alex asked.

"We'll be fine, Daddy," Ferebe spoke up quickly. "We've been over it again and again. We have friends all over Atlanta in our situation—husbands off in the service and wives at home with the children. It's become the norm. We've got our own house with friends and neighbors in a neighborhood we love. Everything is familiar, convenient and secure. The shopping center, the doctor, the nursery school, even the kindergarten, are within walking distance. Susie can get to our house within thirty minutes. Perry will come any time I ask him, and he'll stay for as long as I want him. You and mother and the Hamptons are only an hour away. Ell's salary in the Army will take care of us. We've figured that out, too. It's a pay cut, but we can make it. We'll get along fine. Don't worry about us."

Ellison had been watching her intently as she talked.

"What she says is true," he said. "Still, it's the one thing that makes the whole business all but impossible. It's not fair to her and Maggie and Ellie. It's not fair to leave her to fill my shoes as well as her own, and it's not fair to Maggie and Ellie to deprive them of a father for however long it turns out to be. It's not fair to the two of you, either. No matter how much we reassure you, you'll try to fill in for me, to be my substitute, to look after them while I'm away. Mama and Dad use all their gas coupons, plus what they can scrounge, running back and forth to Milledgeville and Newnan to see about Jim's and Dave's families. They'll add Atlanta to their itinerary to see about mine, the same as you will."

"We certainly won't consider that any kind of a burden, Ellison," Mamie said.

"I know you won't. Still, it's not fair to force that responsibility on you. It's mine, not yours. It's not fair to the Globe people who have staked time, effort, plans and money on me. It's not fair to anybody. But what *is* fair?"

"It's not just Ferebe and the children we're worried about, Ellison," Alex said. "We'll worry about you, too. We figured Paul was the only one of you boys that would be going. Of course, we knew Perry never would, and well— we never had thought about you going either."

"What happens after Wednesday?" Mamie asked. "Will you be in Atlanta for any length of time? At least until after Thanksgiving?"

"I don't know. Possibly I'll be around for another week or two or three. Then they told me I might be around only long enough to get some shipping orders and a railroad ticket to Fort Monmouth. They told me to pack a bag and be ready to leave, just in case. In other words, when I take that oath I won't have any choice when to leave town."

"You've burned all your bridges behind you, haven't you?" Alex asked.

"For all practical purposes, yes. I'm through at the

lab. All I've got to do is clean out my desk and tell the people good-bye. Ferebe and I spent all day yesterday going over bank accounts, household bills, insurance premiums, mortgage payments—everything. Tomorrow she's going out to Fort Mac for a wives' orientation where they'll explain the Army system of pay and allowances and allotments, her rights and benefits as a dependent, the services available to her on the Post while I'm gone and so on."

"My goodness! It all sounds so final!" Mamie exclaimed. "It gives me the shivers to hear you talk as if you're going away forever."

"We don't plan on *that*," Ellison said with a smile, "but while I am gone, Ferebe will have to look after things single-handedly, so she needs to know how."

"I wish you could bring the children and come back to Bentley and stay with us," Mamie suggested to Ferebe.

"No, Mother. Neither of us thinks that would be wise. It's important for the children to be in their own home, even if their father is not there. They'd be visitors anywhere else and feel even further removed from him. Anyway, Atlanta's our home, and that's where we belong."

Ellison got up from his chair and moved over to the sofa. He sat down again and leaned forward, elbows on his knees. "Mr. and Mrs. Holly, I want you both to understand why I'm doing this," he said. "I want to go into the Army for the same reason all those men swamped the recruiting offices the day after Pearl Harbor. Every time I see a man in uniform, I get a guilty feeling that he's doing something for me that I should be doing for myself. I see thousands of kids swarming around the railroad or bus station wearing uniforms that don't fit, hot, tired, dragging barracks bags across the floor or carrying them on their shoulders, and my own clothes get to feeling too pressed, too creased, too immaculate. They suffocate me. This is my war, too—my personal war as much as it is theirs. I feel left out.

"Things are out of whack for me. My work has lost

its challenge. My own house has become too comfortable and cozy. I'm misplaced. I'm aboard the wrong train. No matter what committees and boards I serve on downtown, how much blood I give, how many war bonds I buy, how many campaigns and drives I organize, it's either not enough, or it's not what I should be doing. I don't feel worthwhile any longer. It's a miserable feeling."

He leaned back against the cushions and stared at the fire. "This Gordie Timmons thing hit me harder than you might imagine. He was our friend, our neighbor, and despite his reserve commission in the Navy, there was no more reason for him to go into the service when he did than there is for me to go now. I feel useless since he got killed. I never see anybody my own age anymore unless they're in uniform. I never see my own friends. They're all gone. Everywhere I go, I'm the oddball. All the men are much older or much younger unless some servicemen are present. People look at me as if wondering why I'm wearing civilian clothes. And why not? I catch myself wondering the same thing about able-bodied men I see not in uniform. I see Honor Rolls of men in the armed forces every place. There's one on the Courthouse lawn in Griffin. I noticed yours on The Well. I see them in stores, clubs, office buildings, hotels. We've got one at Globe inside the front door. I look the other way to keep from seeing it. Sometimes I dread to leave the house where anybody can see me. That's no way to live."

He stopped for a moment, then added, "All that put together is the best explanation I can give. I hope it makes sense."

Mamie stirred. "I wish I could change your mind, but it would probably be wrong to try," she said. "It's hard to keep right and wrong separate sometimes."

Alex turned to his daughter. "How about you, honey? How do you feel about it—deep down, I mean?"

"I'd rather he'd stay home, but I know he can't," she

said. "I'm proud of him and what he's doing. It has to be done. It's that simple. Or maybe it's profound. That's Polly Timmons's attitude about it. She says Gordie had to be in the war, and if she didn't believe that she'd lose her mind. For her the war is over, and she says if she could turn back the calendar and do it all again, she knows they'd still do it the same way."

Alex got up from his chair and moved to the fireplace. He stretched his arms out before him and placed both hands on the edge of the mantel. With his weight on them, he learned forward and bent his head low. He studied the fire. The logs had almost burned down. Tiny flames darted along their remains. Only a random crackle penetrated the stillness of the room.

"You drove out here just to tell us," he said slowly, without moving his body. "And you drove to Griffin to tell your folks. Both trips on a bad tire."

"We didn't want to tell you on the telephone, Daddy," Ferebe said. "And it wouldn't fit into an ordinary letter. Besides, unless you and Mother come to Atlanta before Wednesday, Ell might not get to see you again for a long time."

"Why didn't you call us, darling?" Mamie said. "We could have come in on the train this morning and spent the day."

"We wanted to do it this way, Mrs. Holly," Ellison said.

Alex stirred. They watched him, waiting for him to speak.

"You and Ferebe are waiting for an answer of some kind from us," he said, looking around at Ellison. "It can't be our permission. You don't need that. What is it, son?"

"Your understanding, Mr. Holly," Ellison said. "That's all."

Alex looked back into the fire and was silent for a time. He stood up and smiled at Ellison. "Then God bless you," he said. "Both of you." He looked at Mamie, still smiling. "You didn't expect to hear me say that, did you, Mother?" he asked.

She smiled at him. "No," she replied, "but I expected you to think it."

Ferebe telephoned her parents Wednesday evening after she and the children returned from seeing Ellison off on the train for Fort Monmouth. Mamie was at home alone. Alex had gone down to the depot. An Army shipment of tanks was claiming the through right-of-way, and a regular freight train was being shunted off onto the Bentley siding until it passed through.

"Well, darling, I think it's perfectly marvelous how you prepared yourself and the rest of us for this," her mother told her. "And I know you'll use the same common sense in the decisions and adjustments you'll be making as time goes on."

"Telling Ell good-bye wasn't the brave, chin-up exercise I had associated with sending your husband off to war. He wasn't even wearing a uniform. He'll get those when he gets to Monmouth. It was more like sending him off to Washington again on a business trip. It will probably hit me about Saturday or Sunday when it's time for him to come home."

"Not only then, but it will come on you anew from time to time," Mamie said. "During Perry's first year at Cave Springs, even after I had adjusted to his absence, it would come on me sometimes with such force I felt like I was actually standing in front of the building kissing him good-bye again. You must be prepared for things like that."

"Actually, the leave-taking was rather frantic," Ferebe said. "The station was jammed as usual. It looked like every person in the place was trying to scramble aboard Ell's train. He had the good fortune to get a sleeper, so he didn't have to fight for a seat. He had to fight to get aboard, though. I was carrying Ellie, and he was leading

300

Maggie with one hand and carrying his suitcase with the other. Maggie was about to get trampled, so he picked her up and put her on his shoulders. It was so noisy, and we were so busy working our way through the crowd we couldn't talk. When we got to Ell's coach, the conductor was yelling 'All aboard.' He was gone before we knew what struck us. Maybe that's the best way. I hadn't been saving anything in particular to say at the last minute; yet I can't get over the feeling we left something unsaid."

"You probably did," Mamie said. "You'll have to write it in a letter. We were hoping Ellison could spend Thanksgiving Day at home, but we knew it might not be possible, didn't we? Still, we'd be thrilled to death if you'd bring the children and have dinner with us tomorrow. I bought the smallest turkey Clay Tinsley had, but it's more than your daddy and I can eat. If you'd rather, we can pack up our dinner and bring it all to your house. Or maybe you don't want to do either."

"You're real sweet, Mother, but we've got to start getting used to things sometime. Thanksgiving Day is as good a time as any. Susie said she might come out for the day. We've been in such a state I forgot to buy a turkey. Isn't that ridiculous? Look, I've got to go. I wanted to talk to you and Daddy. That's the real reason I called. I could have written you a postcard about Ell."

"Oh, Ferebe! Bless you, darling!" Mamie said. "Your daddy will be sorry he missed you. And Ferebe? Don't be too brave, and don't be too independent. Your daddy and I are right here, and we'll come running in a minute if you need us, or if you want us for no reason at all. That's what we're here for."

"I'm going to cry!" Ferebe said. "I know I am! But Maggie's doing something to Ellie or vice versa. They're having a knock-down-drag-out at any rate. 'Bye, darling. Hug Daddy for me, will you?"

# 28

SAM PICKETT, MAYOR, wanted to turn on the Christmas tree lights at The Well again. The other members of the Town Council were not in agreement.

"Now, Sam, we agreed right after Pearl Harbor to turn off those Christmas lights until the war's over," Henry Carter reminded him. "Every city and town in the United States has cut down their street lights and turned off their big electric signs to save energy and electricity. Peachtree Street in Atlanta is not half as bright as it used to be. Jacksonville, Miami and Savannah—every place on the East Coast—is under complete blackout. We can't do it."

"I agree with Henry," Charlie Downs said. "If the Statue of Liberty can get along without a light in her torch, we sure ought to be able to get along without our lights at The Well."

"Nobody says we can't get along without them, Charlie," Sam said with patience. "But people need cheering up. The war is getting worse and worse. Our boys are getting shot down every day over Germany and France, and if they're still alive when they hit the ground, they get taken prisoners. They're getting killed and wounded all over the world. It makes you sick in your heart to think about how we lost *three thousand* men at Tarawa, and that's just *one* battle. It's real hard to throw your hat in the air about taking another island from the Japs when so many of our own boys get killed doing it. It makes you want to say, 'Keep the island. It's not worth that much to us anyway.' Right here in Bentley we're on our way to having the highest casualty rate in Georgia based on our population. Mitchell Clapper and Marshall Inman killed, Albert Odum missing in New Guinea, Sonny Ashley wounded and in a hospital in Honolulu. Tinker told me that he and Janet can't get a priority to go see him. The town needs something bright to remind it how things used to be and how they'll be again some day. I thought maybe an old familiar sight like the lighted Christmas tree at The Well would help. How about it, boys?"

"We can't do it, Sam," said John Reynolds. "We just can't. I know the juice it uses is a drop in the bucket, but that's not the point. It's a symbol of what people should do. I'm against it." He rose to his feet. "I've got to get back to the paper. Fletch Ford claims we don't have enough newsprint for this week's edition of *The Bentley Weekly Enterprise*, and I've got to get back and make a liar out of him."

Henry Carter followed him out the door.

"Looks like you lost, Sam," Charlie said after the others had gone. "You had your heart in the right place, though. You know, it's a funny thing. Last year and the year before, every time I passed The Well and saw that dark Christmas tree I thought about the war. It was kinda like a big sign was hanging there saying, 'This Christmas tree is not lighted because we're fighting a war.' Everybody will have to wait until the war's over for the lights to come on again."

"I guess you're right, Charlie. It's really not a whole lot to ask them to wait for."

"Right. Except for what it means. Then it's a mighty big load."

For the third year the Christmas tree at The Well was

dark. Maybe next year they could turn on the lights again in the Annual Christmas Tree Lighting Ceremony. The combined choirs of the Baptist and Methodist Churches, the Choral Societies of the high school and elementary school would gather at dusk to sing Christmas carols. One of the ministers would say a prayer. The mayor would flick a switch. The Christmas tree would burst into hundreds of happily colored lights. The crowd would gasp and applaud. Everyone would start talking, laughing and shouting "Merry Christmas!" and in Bentley, the Christmas season would officially begin.

Speculation about a second front in Europe was growing. In November Roosevelt and Churchill had met in Cairo along with Chiang Kai-shek, who really did not matter. Indeed, his presence detracted from the importance and significance of the conference, for he had no power, nothing to contribute and attended only at the sufferance of the other two mighty leaders. One week later, however, Roosevelt and Churchill moved to Teheran for still another conference, this time with Joseph Stalin, and the world sat up and took notice. No one had any doubts that something really big was in the offing.

For two years the Russians had been fighting the Nazis in Eastern Europe. Stalin had long wanted the western Allies to open a second front and take the pressures off his own armies in the east. As the three leaders sat in Teheran, the people at home steeled themselves for an invasion of the Continent. They knew it had to be, and they waited for it with cold dread.

Meanwhile, Germany was taking merciless poundings from the skies. Electric plants, waterworks, steel mills, railroad marshaling yards, munitions factories, waterways, wharves—anything that could contribute to a war-making capability—was a target. In a single fifty-minute raid shortly before Christmas, seven hundred planes of the RAF Bomber Command dropped seventeen hundred tons of bombs on Berlin alone, once the lovely city of grand hotels and linden trees. No city could withstand that kind of destruction for long periods. Once the capital of the Third Reich had been bombed into nothingness, the war in Europe would end. Without its central brain and nerve center, the Nazi war machine would be uncontrolled, incapable of saving itself from complete defeat.

Ellison Hampton had been in the Army less than a month, scarcely long enough to earn leave time for the holidays. It was impossible for him to come home. Mamie could not bear to think of Ferebe, Maggie and Ellie squealing, laughing, opening presents and cluttering up the house on Christmas morning without him. Ferebe would not agree to bring the children home to Bentley, not even for the day. She had searched and searched for a Christmas tree, and in desperation finally purchased what she termed the scraggliest and last Christmas tree in Atlanta and got ready for Christmas at home with her two children.

Christmas fell on Saturday. Perry and Susie took a long weekend from work and came home together on the train Thursday night. Before dawn on Christmas morning, Alex, Mamie, Susie and Perry drove into Atlanta, roused Ferebe and the children from sleep and stayed all day.

"I've got to where I almost dread Christmas," Mamie said. "With so many boys away from home it seems forced. People don't seem to have their minds on it. They just go through it mechanically because that's what they've always done."

"That's what we're supposed to do," Alex said. "Don't you remember the old song from the last war, 'Keep the Home Fires Burning'? That's what everybody's doing."

"All the boys seem to get on my mind at Christmas more than any other time," she went on. "Yesterday while I was uptown, a soldier came along the sidewalk and said, 'Merry Christmas, ma'am.' Oh! I *almost* died! Just think how many of them are homesick and lonely like that."

305

"The ones I see in Atlanta don't look very lonely and homesick to me," Perry said. "They travel in bunches. I seldom see a soldier or sailor by himself. There's always two, three or four, and they always seem to be having more fun than anybody else."

"You ought to see them at the USO on weekends," Susie said. "They carry on like they're at an American Legion convention."

"When you're working at the USO, do any of the boys try to date you?" Perry asked.

"Sometimes, but it's always the wrong one. Some of them are terrible! They try to impress you with what big shots they are. One of them told me he was a major, of all things. He said he takes off his insignia when he goes off post so he can pal around with the men, because officers aren't supposed to be friendly with enlisted men. Can you imagine? One boy wanted to take me home. He was darling, and he was gentlemanly, too. You would have approved of him, Mother. I was about to agree until he told me he was married, and I chased him away. He said he was due to be shipped out to combat duty the next day and wanted his last night in America to be a memory he could carry with him. That's one of their favorite lines. Most of them are pretty nice, though. They're like the boys in Bentley or anywhere else."

"That's who they are," Alex said.

The weather was threatening, and they drove back to Bentley before dark.

"You'll never know what it meant to me for all of you to come," Ferebe told them as they were getting into the car. "The last time you came for Christmas dinner, the same two people were missing, and I was mad enough to chew nails because Ell didn't come home. I wish I was mad at him now. I'd give anything in this world to be hopping mad at Ellison Capers Hampton, Jr., right this very minute."

# 29

ALEX HOLLY WAS WORKING HIS WAY through a mass of dispatches, bills of lading, freight reports and muttering to himself about the Georgia Railroad's Traffic Manager, who apparently had the crazy idea that the Bentley yards were as large as Atlanta's and could handle as great a volume of traffic. He was allowing him no track or time to switch the freight off and onto the Gainesville line, and he would raise Cain with him if he did not switch it and move it on schedule.

"If he'd just get out of that chair long enough to ride out here and look at what we've got to work with, he might get a surprise," he mumbled, frowning at the dispatch in his hand. "Of all the stupid stunts, this one takes the cake."

He thumbed through the Gainesville freight log looking for a way to delay it long enough to get an eastbound shipment through. He thought he found one. He slid the telephone in front of him and picked up the receiver. The door from the waiting room opened, and a stout, elderly lady entered. He looked up and replaced the receiver. It was Emory Haynes's day to come in late, and Alex had been in the office alone all morning.

"Are you in charge of this depot?" the lady asked.

He knew from experience and the intonation of her question that another complaint was forthcoming.

"Yes, ma'am. Can I help you?"

"You certainly can," she said, drawing her lips tight as she said it. "I think you'd better come out in the waiting room and see for yourself. A colored soldier is sitting out there with a white soldier—in the *white* waiting room."

"I see," Alex replied, his mind still on the tangled routing out of Atlanta. "I'll come out and take care of it. Thank you for telling me." He turned back to the telephone.

Apparently the lady was not ready to leave. "I wasn't going to say anything about it and cause any trouble, but when he got a drink of water from the white water fountain, that was too much."

"Thank you, ma'am. As soon as I make this phone call I'll—"

"I don't know what things are coming to," the lady went on. "You hear all the time how colored soldiers from the North try to sit in the white sections of trains and buses and in the theaters, too. We had our Jim Crow laws a long time before the Army had colored soldiers. I can't understand why the Army insists on sending them down here to the South. They know what they'll be up against. We're not going to change our laws simply because a colored boy happens to be wearing a uniform."

"I understand that, ma'am," Alex said, his hand still on the telephone. "If you'll excuse me a minute, I'll come out and take care of—"

"I'm from Tallahassee, and I'm on my way up to Athens to visit my married daughter," she said. "I have another daughter, unmarried, who works in Jacksonville. She told me that colored soldiers even try to dance with white girls in the USO down there. She's one of their hostesses. Lord only knows what else they try to do. Give them an inch, and they'll take a mile, I always say." She paused and her eyes narrowed. "How come you didn't know that colored soldier was out there, since you're in charge of the depot?"

Alex released the telephone. "Has he been creating a disturbance or causing trouble for anybody?" he asked.

"Well—no, not exactly that," she said with obvious reluctance.

"Then that's probably why I didn't know he was out there."

"Now that you do know, don't you intend to do anything about it?"

"You reported the matter to me, and I promised to take care of it—after I make a phone call," Alex reminded her. "I don't mean to be impolite, but I can't do either one while I'm talking to you, can I?" He smiled at her.

She did not return his smile. Instead, she glared at him for a moment, then left the office.

Later in the morning Emory Haynes listened with fascination while Alex told him of the incident.

"Did he give you any trouble?" he asked.

"Not the least. He wasn't very happy about it, but I told him it was a Georgia law, and neither of us could do anything about it. So he moved."

Emory tested the key, found it in order and spun around to face Alex again. "The trouble is the Army is drafting more of them now, and the more they draft the more they're gonna send down here," he said. "I'm afraid we're gonna have trouble before it's all over. And that reminds me. Have you been hearing how Cleatus Underwood's been going through that ten-thousand-dollar G.I. insurance Emma Horn got for Elvin?"

"What's he bought now? The last I heard he bought a 'thirty-nine Dodge he doesn't know how to keep running."

"I don't know what all. Alva Thomas says Delpha comes in his store and buys the brightest, loudest dresses he's got, and one day she bought two hats at one time. She's always bringing those kids in and buying shoes and things for them—good stuff, too. Not cheap, low-grade things like they're used to. Reeves Buckley ought not to let Emma draw out that money every time she asks for it. He knows she's getting it for Delpha and Cleatus to squander."

"It's her money, Emory. If she wants it, Reeves has got to let her have it. He talked her into putting it in a savings account so it wouldn't be too easy to get her hands on it, but it's hers. She can have it anytime she wants it for any reason she wants it. I doubt if she knows how much money it really is. Emma doesn't know how to spend money or how to keep it, either."

"That's what's happening to lots of those people all over the country," Emory said. "They're getting things they're not used to having, and they don't know what to do with them. They're getting jobs they can't handle. They're going places they've never been, and they don't know how to act when they get there. They're making more money than they ever laid eyes on, and they don't know how to save it or spend it. You know who we've got to thank for all that, don't you? It's Eleanor Roosevelt, that's who. She keeps them stirred up all the time."

"I'm not sure what I think about Eleanor," Alex said, returning to his work. "But I wish she'd stop flitting around the country and stay home awhile. She's got a nice house up there in Washington if she'd just stay in it and realize it."

"Speaking of Roosevelt, Alex, do you think he's as sick as they say he is? I keep hearing rumors that he's actually dying on his feet. But if that's true, how come they keep on talking about running him for a fourth term?"

"Because we need a good President," Alex replied. "I don't think he can live through a fourth term. Just look at his pictures. He looks like he's a hundred years old, and he's only sixty-one. That job's killing him. He's got big, dark circles under his eyes, and his face is all wrinkled and sunk in. He's lost nearly all his hair. He looks sick all over. He's a big man, you know, and he's lost a lot of weight. But you can count on one thing—if he runs again, nobody can beat him, not here in the middle of the war. I kind of wish they'd let him off the hook this time. He deserves a rest. If a man's sick, you'd think they'd give him enough time off to get well, wouldn't you?"

Alexander Holly and Emory Haynes were not alone in their concern for the President's health. The Democrats themselves—and the Republicans, too, for that matter— had no doubts that he would win a fourth term if he wanted it. The real question was: could he survive it? From one side of the country to the other, the American people studied President Roosevelt in the newsreels, in magazines and newspapers, dismayed by what they saw. They saw a dying man, and they did not know how to save him, for they themselves were killing him.

He had led them to a point in their history a stranger unaware would never have believed. Life had become a fantasy, but they were too busy, too engrossed in the urgent matter of life and death to stop and realize that, by any known standards, what they were doing could not be done. They were on the victory road in a war of such incredible scope that by comparison the earlier war had been local. Close to 11 million men and women were in uniform at home and overseas. Twelve hundred military posts, camps and stations were operating throughout the country readying young Americans for every conceivable phase of warfare. In one year alone the Army Air Corps had graduated 65,000 pilots, 14,000 navigators, 14,000 bombardiers, 83,000 aerial gunners and 530,000 technicians of all kinds. From the wreckage of Pearl Harbor the Navy had built up a force of 80,000 ships of every description. Over 100,000 servicemen lay dead. More were certain to die. American troops were in Asia, Africa, Australia, South America, Europe, North America, even in Antarctica and on all the seven seas. There was almost no place left in the world for them to be. Yet they had not reached their destination.

Military operations of such wondrous dimensions

could have been no more than a matter of wishful thinking had not the people and resources at home been mobilized and marshaled on a scale equally unprecedented and ambitious. Fifty million war workers had produced more than 200,000 war planes, 80,000 tanks, 85,000 naval vessels and cargo ships, 300,000 artillery pieces, 15 million rifles, 6 million tons of bombs, 2 million trucks, 20 million small arms and 40 *billion* rounds of small arms ammunition.

Although the people were convinced they would win the war, the payoff was yet to be. It lay out there ahead somewhere at still another point in their history, this one inexact and yet to be reached. They could not afford to settle for less than a seasoned President with a sure foot, clear vision and a dogged determination to find it and lead them to it, and they already had one. Who would dare presume to take his place now? A fourth term as President of the United States for Franklin Delano Roosevelt was imperative, an oncoming tragedy they did not know how to stave off.

Ellison Hampton graduated from his field communications course at Fort Monmouth in April and came home for a ten-day leave. He was in marvelous condition, lean, tanned and considerably more cheerful, lively and relaxed than when he left. Ferebe was ecstatic about his appearance, but she did have to admit to herself that military uniforms and Lieutenant Ellison C. Hampton, Jr., were not intended for each other.

His was expertly tailored and fitted him perfectly. The insignia on the lapel of his green blouse, the buttons down the front and the brass buckle at his waist were glittering. His pinks hung straight without a break or wrinkle to precisely the correct length to cover the tops of his brown, plain-toed shoes. His visored green cap with the brass insignia on the front sat on his head at the exact square angle all officers and enlisted men had been in-

312

structed to wear theirs but seldom did. His uniform was faultless, and he wore it with ease, but in some uncertain way the two of them were uneasy with each other.

And it was a matter of supreme unimportance.

"You're you, and you're *not* you!" Ferebe gushed. "And I like you both ways! What happened to you? What did you do?"

With Maggie and Ellie climbing over him, tugging at him, hugging and kissing him, wearing his cap, playing with his insignia, interrupting him, he sat in the big gray wing chair in his own living room and talked around, over and under their squealing, babbling and squirming.

"I've never worked so hard in my life," he said. "And I mean physical, manual, hard labor, and most of it was outdoors—rain or shine, snow or sleet, night or day. The hours were regular. I ate and slept on a schedule. Most nights I fell into the sack too tired to turn over, but do you know what? Right this minute I feel better and more rested than I ever felt in my life."

She could not take her eyes off him. "I can't believe you're not going to jump up out of that chair and go running off to Globe Research Laboratory any minute now," she said.

"Not a chance. A man would have to be an idiot to run off and leave all this." His eyes roamed the room hungrily. "Are you sure this room was this small when I left? I was thinking it was larger."

He was due for reassignment, but he could do no more than speculate on where he would be sent. "I've narrowed it down to two places—the Atlantic and the Pacific," he said. "Then I eliminated the Pacific for the only reason I could dream up: I don't want to go there. That leaves the Atlantic. We're pouring men into England by the thousands for the big buildup. I've decided that's where I'm going. Keep in mind that any soldier worth his salt tries to develop his proficiency in second-guessing the

Army. It's a constant challenge to him, for it's a skill that has never been mastered. Now what else would you like for me to predict about my future in the Army, Mrs. Hampton?"

"Does it have to be overseas?" Ferebe asked.

"No, but it will be. We might as well be honest and face it. I'll probably be assigned to an outfit going in on the invasion, when and wherever that turns out to be. It's got to be soon before the British Isles sink into the ocean under the weight of all that equipment that keeps stacking up."

"Oh, Ell! You don't honestly believe that, do you?"

"If I get assigned to the ETO, it won't be to go sight-seeing."

"Everybody won't go in on the invasion. Somebody has to stay behind. Maybe they'll assign you to an outfit that's stationed permanently in England."

"If they do they'll be wasting a lot of training on me. That's a combat course I just finished. You ought to see me crawling along on my stomach in the rain and the dark, unreeling that wire and trying to find the place I'm supposed to set up a command post, in territory I've never seen and know nothing about except from a measly pocket map I'm trying to keep dry, while dodging the enemy who's somewhere out there but I don't know where. In one exercise they were firing over our heads. They claimed they were firing live ammunition. None of us were stupid enough to stand on our feet and put it to the test. So you figure it out. That's what this business is all about, you know."

"I guess it is," she conceded pensively. She brightened. "But I'm like Scarlett O'Hara. I'll worry about that tomorrow. In the meantime, you've got ten free days at home with us before you go anywhere at all. Not even to Griffin and Bentley. They're off limits. Everybody's coming to see you here—in this very house. After you called,

I got in touch with your folks and mine and arranged a schedule. It's on the calendar in the kitchen. I'll show you later. The rest of the time is ours—yours, mine, Maggie's and Ellie's. You're not getting out of my sight. Come on!"

It was a glorious ten-day leave. They visited friends, and friends visited them. The Hollys came, and the Hamptons came. Susie and Perry came at random times. Ferebe and Ellison took the children shopping, to the picture show, to hot dog stands, to Piedmont Park for a picnic, to Grant Park for an afternoon at the zoo, but best of all, they stayed at home with them and winked at the rules and schedules as they enjoyed their father's leave of absence from the Army.

Then it was all over, and Ferebe found herself standing in the railroad station with Maggie and Ellie. They were waving through the grilled iron gates at Ellison until he lost himself in a mass of khaki, olive drab and Navy blue, all moving away in disorder and hurried confusion along the platform to be sucked up in bunches by the waiting train. After the platform was deserted except for the workmen, and the red lights on the back of the last coach curved out of sight, Ferebe, Maggie and Ellie went back home.

# 30

THE COUNTRY WAS LIKE a steel coil ready to snap and spring loose at the terrible news of the invasion. It came shortly after midnight on a Tuesday in June, and if it caught anyone asleep, they could not have slept much longer. In cities, towns, villages and crossroads over the breadth of the land, anything that would make a noise was set loose. Church bells, school bells, train bells, factory whistles, locomotive whistles, fire whistles, air raid sirens, ambulance sirens, automobile horns, foghorns blasted the night.

Lights came on. Radios blared. People poured out of their houses into their yards and into the streets shouting the news to their neighbors. Hotels, nightclubs, taverns, restaurants, theaters, all-night stores and shops emptied themselves of their employees as well as their clientele, who rushed for the sidewalks and the outdoors, the only place big enough for their jubilation. In plants, factories and shipyards, workers left their assembly lines, their lathes and die presses, their paint buckets and welding apparatus and made for the parking lots or any space where the most people were likely to congregate. People streamed into churches and chapels and filled the pews to weep, to pray and to sit in silence with reverent dread.

Nothing resembling it had ever happened to them. Outwardly they appeared to be celebrating a victory, but underneath all that raucous, uncontrolled excitement lay a cold fear and a grim anxiety which gnawed at their insides, which was the price they knew they must pay for their optimism and hope.

Mamie and Alex Holly put on their clothes with scarcely a glance into the mirror to see if they were on straight. Mamie was still snapping the front of her dress when she joined Alex on the front porch. He had hoisted one foot up onto the railing and was tying his shoe. Porch lights had been turned on along Madison Road from the Macedonia Baptist Church to Chiles Street. They could hear doors slamming, car engines starting, people talking. They hurried down the steps and out onto the sidewalk. They had long since decided that wherever they happened to be and whatever they happened to be doing when news of the invasion broke, they would go immediately to the church. Mr. Clapper, Mr. Lindley and Reverend Lincoln had asked their congregations to come at whatever the hour. They walked up Madison Road to Chiles Street and went no farther.

People were gathered at The Well, and they were still coming from all directions as if drawn by a magnet. They poured into the street, ignoring an automobile at a standstill in the middle of the block, headlights burning, unable to go forward or move backward. They were not quiet, but neither were they noisy. Their conversations were not boisterous, but neither were they restrained. They had the awesome topic of D day to talk about now, and talk begat talk in the night on that tiny little stretch of Georgia State Highway 11.

"It won't be long now! Berlin, here we come!"

"We've *really* got old Adolf on the run now."

"Yeah, but he doesn't have anywhere to run to any more."

"How long do you think it will take to polish off the Nazis? Three months? Four months?"

"Four months? You crazy? It won't take that long.

We've been saving up for this one. Ike is throwing everything we've got into it."

"I'll bet a blackland farm we'll be in Berlin in thirty days."

"I wish it was all over. Bobby's in this one. He hasn't told us anything, but we know he is. He's been in England since February."

"I haven't drawn a decent breath for two weeks just waiting for this. I've been keeping the radio on, but I've been scared to listen to it. We haven't heard from Harold in three weeks."

"Poor Anne! I know she's at home walking the floor right this minute. And her with those three small children! Her husband is in the airborne infantry, you know, so he's *got* to be in the thick of it."

"I couldn't get Bert to come. He wouldn't leave the radio."

"Donald, too. He said he could pray any time, but the invasion wouldn't wait until he came down here, then back home."

"Isn't it a dreadful thing? I heard that Eisenhower planned to land one million men on the first wave."

"Poor Mr. Clapper!" Mamie said as she and Alex merged in with the crowd. "He's probably waiting at the church for everybody, and they're all down here."

"If nobody shows up, he'll come down here too, and it will all work out the same," Alex said.

Which is exactly what happened. Within minutes Mr. Clapper and Mr. Lindley appeared among the gathering. The fire truck pulled up to the edge of the crowd and turned its spotlight squarely on The Well. Mr. Clapper and Mr. Lindley stepped into its glare and held up their hands for silence. The talking subsided into a hubbub, then into a murmur and finally into absolute quiet. Mr. Lindley stepped forward and, with no introduction or explanation, lifted his face to the dark sky and began to pray for the safety of the boys in Normandy, for strong hearts and resolute spirits. After he had finished, he was followed by Mr. Clapper. At the sound of the last Amen, the two ministers moved out of the spotlight and lost themselves in the crowd.

The people dispersed in twos and threes.

"We'd better go, hon. Six o'clock comes early in the morning."

"I hope I can get to bed before then."

"Me too. About all we got on the radio before we came down here was the announcement of the invasion itself. There'll be lots more stuff by now. What network were you listening to?"

"CBS, I think, but it's on all of them."

While the first news of D day was coming in, Ferebe Hampton sat alone in her living room listening to the radio. She had turned on every light in the house except those in Maggie's and Ellie's rooms. While she wondered whether Ell was in Normandy or still in England, she wanted no shadows or darkness to clothe her fears. The house was close and hot, but she did not notice as she sat huddled in a corner of the sofa, afraid to let herself speculate on whether Ell was dead or alive, in one piece or several.

For the rest of the week radio networks canceled their commercials and much of their entertainment to bring in short wave broadcasts directly from the battle sites themselves with the actual sounds of the war as background to the horribly explicit accounts of the fighting and killing. Anyone within earshot of a radio became its prisoner. A new phase of the war in Europe was under way, and it was the final phase. It had to be. The Nazis were besieged from the east, the south, and now from the west. For help or escape Germany could turn in no direction but the north, where nothing lay except water, ice and emptiness. Hitler's

319

days were numbered. As the first excitement leveled off and the people steeled themselves for more bitter grief and sickening anguish to come, their oneness of purpose was more indestructible than ever.

Ellison Hampton was in Normandy. And he was all right. He had gone ashore at 0947 on the morning of the landings. He could not say exactly where he was. Ferebe did not even wonder. He was alive. He was unharmed. He was safe. That was enough. She held his letter in her hands for at least an hour before she could control herself enough to telephone his parents, then her own, and tell them.

# 31

NONE OF THE TOWN COUNCILMEN seemed to have their minds on the meeting.

"Okay, Sam, let's get this show on the road," Charlie Downs said. "What's on the docket for today? I've got to run into Atlanta this afternoon. I've got an appointment at the Capitol to get my fuel quotas straightened out. *Readjusted* is what they call it when somebody's listening."

"What are you up to, Charlie?" Henry asked with suspicion. "Who're you going to see?"

"I'm going to see somebody who can *do* something instead of telling me there's a war on and we all have to make sacrifices. You know, the next person who says that to me is going to get it right in the teeth, even if it's somebody's grandmother."

"Better be careful," John warned him. "You might get in trouble and end up with no quotas at all."

"I know what I'm doing. I've been watching the dealers in Madison, Covington and Atlanta rocking right along while I argue and plead and play nice guy with that OPA outfit in Monroe that doesn't know which end is up, and I've got my stomachful of it. People are always sounding off because their houses are too cold and somebody is getting pneumonia and all that malarkey. You tell me one sad story, and I'll tell you ten worse. And do you know what they do? When they can't get what they want from me, they get it somewhere else. I found out that all the noble Americans who make untold sacrifices for the war won't do without one solitary thing if they can figure a way to get it—by fair means or foul. If you call their hand, they'll say, 'If I don't take it somebody else will.' So after nearly three years of riding the short end of the stick, I decided to get on the long end."

"Well now, Charlie, that doesn't sound like you," Sam Pickett said. He was disturbed and alarmed. "You've always followed all the rules and the laws and have been a good, honest businessman and a hardworking member of this Council. I'd hate for you to spoil all that. I don't know what you're up to, but it doesn't sound right. It might not be the patriotic thing to do."

"I'm as patriotic as all my customers who'll fall all over themselves to take advantage of what I can do for them with my new quotas. You don't think everybody in this country plays by the rules, do you? If the people could be trusted, we wouldn't need any ration cards. The Government would tell people how much to use of what, and they'd use it—no more. If people followed the rules, the black market would go out of business. Al Capone said he couldn't have made the first nickel from his beer and gambling without the patronage of his customers, the honest American citizens. So—I'm going to get a 'readjustment' in my allotments, then come back and tell that OPA outfit in Monroe to take a flying leap. And everything will be nice and legal as the day is long!"

"It might be legal, technically speaking, but will it be ethical?" Henry asked.

"I don't know about that, but if it's unethical, so is the guy who's going to work it for me—and you elected him. But as I was saying, I can't sit around here chewing the fat all day. What's up for today, Sam? Are we going to do anything about that culvert over on Short Street?"

322

"We talked about that two weeks ago," John Reynolds reminded him.

"Yeah, but it's still not fixed. Bill Beasley was in the station yesterday, sore as a boil. He says he's going to break an axle crossing it and he's going to send the repair bill to the Town Council."

"Tell him to go around by Extra Street," Sam retorted. "It's not any farther."

"What if he wants to go from one end of Short Street to the other?"

"Let him walk! It's not very far. Why do you think it's named Short Street? But I haven't had time to see about it. Seems like all I do is go to meetings. You can name anything you want to, and if it's connected with the war, Walton County's got a committee for it. And I'm on all of them because I'm the mayor of Bentley. This is my last term, too, and you might as well know it now."

They laughed and hooted.

Sam ignored them. "Tomorrow I've got to go up to Monroe for the Walton County Resource Mobilization Committee, and the next day I've got to go back to a committee made up of the chairmen of *all* the wartime committees. I'm telling you, if committees ran this war we'd still be sitting back there at Pearl Harbor shaking our heads and wondering what to do. Everybody makes speeches and spends five minutes talking about how they're not going to talk very long because they know everybody's busy and has so much on their minds. Any one of them can talk Clara Odum into the ground any day in the week."

"That's pretty tragic stuff you're putting out there, Sam," John Reynolds said.

"It's not tragic—it's pesky," Sam said. "I promised Rosanna Titsworth I'd make a speech Friday to that big affair they have every summer when they combine all the ladies' clubs in town for a big tea party—Unity Day, they call it. Somewhere along the line I'd like to spend a few minutes in the Quality Furniture Store, but I don't know why. I can't get hold of anything to sell, and the jobbers get real smart with me when I try to put in an order. They act like I committed a crime if I ask for a dinette set or a couple of platform rockers. People used to be nice and considerate of each other, but they're getting short-tempered now and find things to complain about. They go around worrying about what other people have if they don't have it themselves. I wish I was young enough to carry a rifle."

"It's not all that bad, Sam," Henry said kindly. "It's just that everybody's tired of the war like you are, but they know they're not supposed to complain, not with all the boys doing the fighting and risking their necks and getting shot up and killed. Everybody knows that, but they've got to blow off steam, and they blow it off in little ways that don't really mean anything. Sometimes Millie and I get to snapping at each other about nothing, and it's just because we're worried about the terrible shape things are in. It'll come to an end one of these days, but until it does, I guess we'll just have to keep doing all these uninteresting things we have to do."

John Reynolds had not been listening to Henry. His mind had lingered on Sam Pickett's invitation to speak at the ladies' Unity Day meeting. "What are you going to talk about at the meeting, Sam?" he asked.

"Rosanna wants me to speak on Bentley's role in World War II, and I haven't had a chance to figure out a speech. Haven't you got some speeches or articles down at the *Enterprise* I could use?"

"Probably I could dig out something from the files, but you don't need it. Tell them what we've been doing in Bentley since Pearl Harbor, and that's it."

"But they all know that as well as I do!"

"True. But to hear it summed up might be more interesting and impressive than they realize. It can even be inspiring. That's the kind of speech Rosanna wants you to make. Something motivational."

"I don't know how to start off. Give me an idea how to start off, and I can fill in the rest."

"Lots of ways," John said thoughtfully. Clearly, he was fascinated by the prospects. "In the first place, keep in mind that you're not giving them any new information. It's stuff they already know—like you said. So it's going to hinge on how you lead into it. That's the important thing."

He leaned back in his chair, threw his feet up on the table and looked up at the ceiling. He was silent for a bit while the others watched him curiously. "I'm not sure about this," he said. "This is only a possibility, you understand. But you might say, for example, that Bentley's just a little place nobody ever heard of. It's not famous for anything. Nobody famous ever grew up in it. People pass through it on the train or on the bus without noticing it. Some of them drive through Bentley on Highway 11 and can't even tell you the name of it or what it looks like the next day or a week later. Even among those who've been coming here all their lives and know the town, it's not a place that comes to mind when they're talking about the war.

"It doesn't have any big plants to turn out tanks, bombers, M-1 carbines or any shipyards that build landing craft, escort vessels or destroyers. It doesn't have an Army or Navy base or hospital or recruiting station or a Red Cross chapter, not even a USO. It does have a cotton mill that makes material for the Navy, and we're proud of that, even though it's not very large compared to most. But even with the cotton mill the Japs and Germans would never waste a bomb on Bentley—and one is all it would take to wipe it out—because it's not important enough militarily or strategically to be worthwhile as a target.

"Yet Bentley gives something to the war that's more

important than all those things put together, and without which all those things wouldn't be worth a pewter nickel. It gives its heart, and not even Chicago, Los Angeles or New York City's got a heart any bigger to give. When you give your heart to something or somebody, you're giving all there is, because everything else follows as naturally as morning follows the night—people, time, energy, money, concerns, wishes, spirits, prayers, the shirt off your back and the gold out of your teeth if that's what it takes. Don't worry about comparing what we do to what other towns have done. Little towns all over America can equal Bentley's record. Still, when you give everything you've got, you can't give any more. That's what Bentley gives to the war, and we've even surprised ourselves by what it adds up to.

"Specifically, Bentley and the immediate surroundings have sent two hundred and three men to the armed forces, and I would have sworn beforehand we didn't have that many men of military age to send. And we didn't—not at first. But during the war so far, many of those men's little brothers grew up into military age and went off to war, too. They're still growing up and they're still going off, and they'll keep on doing it, too, for as long as the war goes on and boys continue to grow into men.

"We didn't think we raised any more livestock around here than we needed, or that our crops were any more than enough for our regular markets, or that we had any extra butter, milk, eggs, poultry. We didn't know any of that until the United States Government began needing more, more and more for the armed forces. Then we discovered we had more than we ever dreamed of, and with only a minimum of effort we could increase that. So we—right here, Sam, get yourself some exact figures and amounts and put them in. You ought to check the figures about the servicemen, too. They're not exact. You might want to mention the casualties—in fact, you should. You see what I'm driving at?"

His three colleagues had been listening in rapt silence.

"Don't stop, John," Charlie Downs said in scarcely more than a whisper. "Go on and finish."

John took his feet from the table and sat up straight. "I was just talking off the top of my head, Charlie," he said. "I don't even know what was coming next. I was trying to give Sam a hand to get him started, that's all."

"I wish I could remember it," Sam said with admiration. "How about writing it down for me?"

John was embarrassed but pleasantly so. "I don't even remember what I said. Just take the general idea and put it into your own words. You don't need me to write it down for you. Get yourself a list of the different wartime boards and committees, the amount of blood we've donated, how much we subscribed in the war bond campaigns, what we gave to various scrap drives, and a few shipping statistics—rail, trucking and busing. Lots of people don't realize how important Bentley is as a rail transfer point for north-south freight and the east-west Georgia Railroad. Things like that. You can make a good speech. The material's all there—it's built in."

"How about making the speech for me, John? You can do it better than I can," he suggested eagerly. "Rosanna wouldn't mind. She'd be tickled pink."

"No. You're the mayor—not me. I'm the editor of the newspaper. Rosanna wants the mayor."

"You sure make us all sound interesting and more active than we really are, John," Henry Carter said appreciatively.

"Maybe it's all in the telling," John said. "I don't think it's exaggerated, though. Sometimes I feel like the most good-for-nothing man on the face of the earth. Do you know what's the matter with all of us and why we're tired and out of sorts about the war? War's a young man's business, and we're not young any more. We got left out. The boat sailed without us. We don't like to admit that there are crises in the world that nobody but the generation

327

behind us can handle. We spend our lives teaching our kids what's right and what's wrong, what to do and what not to do, but when the time comes for them to take over and do the very thing we've been getting them ready for, we get disgruntled because we can't do it ourselves. We're all trying to justify our existence maybe. But what if we are? I guess even the kids want a store where they can buy furniture, a place where they can get their oil checked, a newspaper where they can read about the folks at home, and even a bootlegger like Tooker Jordan where they can buy all the rotgut they want. So in the final analysis, if there wasn't anybody at home, there wouldn't be any reason for anybody being away from home fighting the war, would there?"

No one replied. The four of them sat in silence for a few moments. Suddenly, Henry Carter stood up and reached for his hat. "If I could talk like you do, John, I'd make that speech for Sam myself." He started for the door. "I'll see ya'll later," he said over his shoulder.

"Hold it, Henry!" Sam called after him. "We haven't had the Council meeting yet."

"You can have it without me," he said. "All those inspiring things John said are enough to last me the rest of the week." He left the room shaking his head in wonderment. "He should have been a preacher."

Alex Holly was tired of the war, too. It was too climactic. He leapt from peak to peak in the succession of Allied victories. The war was moving too swiftly for him to catch his breath, and he was drained. He was tired of high emotion, of the bad news which made the good news possible, and the anxiety that was built into all of it. No news from Ellison Hampton was bad news. Any news at all, if he wrote it with his own hand, was good news. From all indications he must have been nearing Germany itself. Paul was still in Calabria, but they opened his letters with apprehension lest he tell them he was rejoining his battalion in action.

Alex thought it would be nice to spend an hour or two with his mind idling in neutral, thinking at random about whatever should pop into his head, so long as it was unimportant. His mind was not equipped for a constant diet of significance, and it was wearing him down. He tried to recall what he used to think about when his mind was relaxed and at ease, but his recollections seemed to be those of another person entirely. He mentioned it to Mamie.

She had been having similar thoughts. "Bessie Melton told me she goes to the picture show in Monroe every chance she gets just so she can think about something besides the war for two hours. She saw June Allyson and José Iturbi last week and doesn't even know the name of the picture. It didn't matter. It was a musical and nothing serious. Maybe we ought to go to the picture show sometimes."

"It might be nice," Alex said wistfully. "I'd sure like to rest my mind a few minutes sometimes."

"Somebody's always saying some good will come out of all this, and, of course, that's got to be true or we wouldn't be having a war at all. Then Mr. Clapper was saying in his sermon a few weeks ago that as terrible as the war is for everybody, we can find some good things in it if we'll only look, but I'll declare! I can't find them to save me!"

"There are some good things, probably," Alex said. "At least this whole country is headed in the same direction at the same time. In spite of all the squabbling and disputes among the people, they've all set their minds on the same goal and are working toward that. I don't believe that's ever happened in this country before—not to this extent. Because of it, people have discovered each other. The war is the great leveler. Everybody's in the same boat. When I see a man in uniform, I see Paul and Ellison. When I see their families telling them hello or good-bye, I see us.

329

When they look sad or happy, anxious or scared, I know exactly how they feel, because I've felt that way myself—and for the same reasons. Maybe that's the kind of good Charlie Clapper was talking about."

"Maybe that's it," Mamie said. "I was in the post office before Christmas mailing those fruitcakes to Paul and Ellison, and this pitiful-looking woman was ahead of me in the line. She didn't look as if she could afford a three-cent stamp, much less the cost of mailing a package overseas—I could see it had an APO on it. The box was a mess. Tinker Ashley put some extra string on it and taped up the ends and readdressed it with heavy black crayon and fixed it up for her. She watched him like a hawk. From the way she looked at her package and what Tinker was doing to it, I could see that her heart was inside that box. Before she had finished counting out her money and left, so was mine."

The Georgia autumn moved in on them and tinted the countryside with burnished colors that deepened and grew richer under the mellowing sun. On mornings here and there after Alex had gone to the depot and Mamie was doing her housework, she paused on the back porch and gloried in the sun that had climbed only inches above the Etheridges' giant magnolia and found it impossible to believe that the entire world was not as beautiful as it was right there in Bentley.

Ferebe brought the children for the day or an occasional overnight visit, sometimes on impulse when they began to feel they were one another's jailers. Mamie watched Maggie and Ellie romping through the yard trying to climb Wylie Spencer's fence or playing in the old tire swing under the walnut tree, and the war was a million miles away. For brief moments, it did not exist at all.

Perry came infrequently and never stayed long, overnight or perhaps all day on a Sunday. He brought Lydia Regan with him once, and his parents found her charming. He had taken a Civil Defense course and was instructing the other deaf people at the Maxwells' in fire-fighting and emergency evacuation procedures. The Georgia Association for the Deaf was interested in what he was doing and had made overtures to him about giving similar instruction to other deaf people in other parts of the city.

Susie was happy at the Dixie Metal Works and was constantly intrigued by the never-ending procession of new girls who replaced one another with unbelievable rapidity. She was teaching two First Aid classes now, working at the blood bank one night each week and at the USO on Saturdays or Sundays. She came home to Bentley when she could, which was at irregular intervals.

"They don't need us like they used to, Mamie," Alex said.

"Certainly they don't! They're not supposed to. They're adults living their own lives. And we've adjusted our own lives without them, too. Don't forget that."

In October General MacArthur returned to the Philippines as he had promised he would. Holland, Luxembourg, Yugoslavia, Rumania, Greece and parts of Belgium had been returned to Allied control. The following month Franklin D. Roosevelt was reelected to a fourth term in the White House. The war in Europe was ending. Nothing short of the Allies laying down their arms could save Germany from defeat—and soon.

The Germans, however, were not ready to accept that. They threw twenty divisions at the Americans in Belgium and pushed them back to form a bulge in a line that had been pushing west like a moving wall and trapped them in the pocket. No matter how swiftly the war was moving elsewhere, until the Battle of the Bulge was won the hearts and minds and the hopes of the people at home stayed back there in Bastogne with all those GIs who were surrounded by the enemy.

# 32

MANY PEOPLE HAVE A FANCIFUL VISION of Georgia. They
think that it is steamy and hot with never a wind to rustle
the leaves on the slash pine and live oak and that the Span-
ish moss droops in long gray beards, immobile as pillars.
They see the thick haze of morning clinging to the swamps
and floating eerily in and out among the cypress and pal-
metto. It is always summer. The sun boils. The rain drips.
The nights echo. Time stops. Nothing moves.

They might be surprised to learn that winter comes to
most of Georgia, with killing frosts as early as November
and as late as March. For at least forty days of the year the
mercury drops below the freezing point in Atlanta. Indeed,
around the turn of the century the temperatures fell to
eight degrees below zero in the Atlanta region, and more
than a dozen Georgians died of exposure. In certain com-
munities schools were closed, livestock was imperiled, food
and fuel were rationed until the icy winter moderated itself. Happily, cold weather does not hang on consistently
for extended periods. It comes and it goes, and it comes
back again with surprising abruptness. In the intervals the
weather can be delightfully mild and friendly, almost as
sleepy and spellbinding as the romantics would have it.

Perry Holly loved cold weather. He enjoyed the icy
sting of the wind on his cheeks and the long drafts of

cold air in his lungs. It made him feel clean inside. In cold weather he used energy he did not realize he had stored up. When temperatures dropped, his friends thought he was a little crazy for putting on heavy clothes and tramping around outside when he could stay inside with them, huddling in front of the fire where it was warm and cozy. He suspected that Mr. Knox at the warehouse shared their opinions. On a day in February during a cold snap that had lasted longer than most, Perry decided to eat his lunch outside, and Mr. Knox told him he should have been an Eskimo.

"I like the cold," Perry said. "Anyway, Mrs. Maxwell put hot tea in my thermos bottle to warm me up, and I bought myself a new jacket last night at Davison's. It's heavy and warm."

"I noticed that when you came in this morning. You looked like a lumberjack up in Oregon with all that red, blue and yellow."

It was a winter day, true enough, but a clear and bright one with a fresh look about it. He could find himself a spot in the sunshine, sheltered from the wind, where it would still be cold but not too cold for comfort. He looked forward to it, and most of all he looked forward to enjoying it alone.

The warehouse had looked too noisy all morning. Workmen hurried too much in and out among the towers of packing cases. Tugs crossed the center aisle too fast. Too many trucks pulled up to the platform at the Receiving Station at the other end of the building. On his own end at the Checkout Station, tugs with two and three pallets in tow were lined up awaiting their turns. Their drivers wandered alongside them out onto the loading platform to smoke cigarettes, then back inside rubbing their hands and shivering. Too many people and things were in motion. Mr. Knox said the increased activity was because the war was "getting hotter" and the troops needed more supplies. At any rate, the warehouse had lost its peacefulness. He and Mr. Knox had worked without a break since they arrived in the morning. His head buzzed from the numbers and labels and look-alike words. He wanted a half hour or so of stillness. He longed for silence.

Mr. Knox glanced at the big clock over the wide doors. Noon was approaching. He stepped over to the desk and picked up a printed sign and hung it on the rear of a pallet train waiting to be checked. "LAST CHECKOUT UNTIL 1300—LUNCH." He winked at Perry as he returned to work. Perry grinned, lifted a thumb and continued his part of the checkout procedures.

The lifted thumb was a sign that had no meaning out of context. Generally, it was a signal of assent with shades of meaning: yes, okay, ready, finished, fine, I agree. It was a small part of their entire system of communication, which was a conglomeration of normal signing, manual alphabet, lipreading, contorted facial expressions and flagrant hand motions that would be incomprehensible to anyone else. Perry had long been accustomed to people talking with their lips and gesturing pointlessly with their hands. Fortunately, his association with them was usually in passing, and he tolerated them more often than he understood them.

His relationship with Mr. Knox, however, was far from casual. He was a friend as well as his supervisor, and for eight hours each workday he enjoyed his company. In many ways he reminded him of his own father, perhaps because they were near the same age and both had about them the same gentle air of kindness and good humor. Mr. Knox lived down at Jonesboro, south of the Depot, where he had been a partner in a small hardware store until the war got under way and his business had ceased to be profitable in the face of overwhelming merchandise shortages, whereupon he sold his interest to his partner and came to work for the Army. "With two daughters and four granddaugh-

334

ters, I'm the only one in the family they could send off to the Army," he once told Perry.

Their rapport had been solid from the beginning, and the means by which they could articulate it had evolved itself quite naturally. Early in their association Mr. Knox's random gestures began to take on a strange consistency that probably even he himself could not explain. In time each of them adopted some of the other's signs, and it was doubtful that Mr. Knox was aware when he was using his own gestures or Perry's signs. The result was a hybrid code that neither Perry's deaf friends nor Mr. Knox's hearing friends could understand.

"If business doesn't let up we might have to work overtime tonight," he told Perry after the last pallet before lunch had been checked. He thumbed through the stack of completed checkout sheets that had not been reconciled with the master sheets. "We can't hold these over until tomorrow, because we might have another day like this one; then we'll be two days behind, and the Major won't like that. What have you got to do tonight? Have you got another date with your girl friend?"

Perry nodded. "But I can stay if you'll call Mr. or Mrs. Maxwell for me so they can tell her."

Lunch hours at the Army Quartermaster Depot were staggered. Between eleven and one o'clock a steady line of workers flowed in and out of the warehouses and along the sidewalks, going to and from the several cafeterias and snack bars scattered throughout the complex. Some were hurrying. Others were whiling away the remains of their lunch hour in the sunshine and air. Perry stood on the loading platform with his lunch bag in one hand, his thermos bottle in the other and watched them for a few moments. Then he jumped down to the ground and walked across the grass around to the rear of the warehouse, away from the sight of moving people. In their numbers and continuing motion they seemed to be making more noise than the workmen inside. The cars and trucks on the street added to the din.

Once he had turned the corner behind the big building, he stopped and drew in a deep breath of relief. Not a person was in view. The sweet calm of solitude enveloped him. Acres of winter grass stretched before his eyes, bordered by the long row of warehouses on one side and the railroad tracks on the other. The back sides of the warehouses were windowless and resembled huge monoliths rising out of the ground and sitting end to end in silence. On the railroad tracks opposite, several flatcars loaded with steel girders and long lengths of round metal pipes sat unattended.

He strolled for a few yards along the open area and stopped to take in his surroundings. The wind was little more than a faint breeze. The shadows lining the warehouses were not deep, but he knew without moving into them that they were too cold for comfort. He walked over to the railroad tracks, where the sun flashed on the metal and gave an illusion of brightening the day. He studied one of the cars stacked high with layer upon layer of metal pipes. They formed a rectangular block, neat, symmetrical and orderly, held in position by a series of upright posts spaced at intervals around the edge of the car.

Unexpectedly, he was swept over by nostalgia. His mind went back to the depot and the Georgia Railroad tracks in Bentley when he was a child. He and Paul used to crisscross nails on the tracks, then retrieve them after the wheels of a passing train had run over them. If the train had not knocked them off the rails, they would be flattened and joined together to resemble a pair of scissors. One time they lay flat on their stomachs on the ground near the tracks, trying to catch the exact moment of impact when the train wheels flattened the nails. They were distracted, though, by the stretched-out form of a man on the rods under the train, darting past like an arrow, dangerously close to the crossties below. He thumbed his nose at them as the train moved past.

He smiled, remembering all that, and dropped to the ground for an almost forgotten greasy-smelling view of the couplings, valves, tie-rods, wheels, tracks and crossties under the flatcar. He could never understand why people flinched, made faces and jumped back when a train passed by. Susie and Ferebe had always been afraid to venture any closer than the door of the depot. Many times Paul had grabbed his arm and pulled him back from the tracks, even though he had not been close enough for danger. He had concluded years ago that it was the awkward bulk of a train that frightened them.

While he was remembering, he opened his lunch sack and took out a sandwich. He poured some hot tea into the lid of his thermos bottle. During the years he was in school at Cave Springs, his experience with trains had been restricted to summers. Even then, their father had not permitted them to play around the depot except when they were waiting for a train or sometimes when their mother sent him and Paul to take dinner to their father if Emory Haynes was sick and he was filling in for him. But he had a special feeling about trains. For many years he thought all of them were his father's personal property, for the entire Holly family had always ridden them free of charge whereas all the other passengers paid money for their tickets.

He did not realize how long he had been sitting, looking and reminiscing until he reached into the paper sack and discovered he had eaten all his lunch. He folded the bag and tried to smooth out the wrinkles. Mrs. Maxwell required him to bring the sacks home for reuse until they became unserviceable or disreputable. Then he remembered Paul's letter in his pocket. He had brought it with him so he could try again to decipher some of his scribblings. He turned to face the warehouses and, without getting to his feet, moved a little farther out from the tracks to a more comfortable spot on the grass. He took the letter from his pocket and began to puzzle over it.

Paul's letters were more interesting than they had been in combat, and they were not as heavily censored. He liked to read about the Italian people and the city of Calabria, the bars that frequently had nothing to drink, the cafés with no food to serve, the luxuries that could be purchased with a piece of chocolate candy or a package of American cigarettes. He wrote little about the details of his job except that the MP band on his arm was a magic door opener anywhere in the city. He did mention stretches of duty in the mountains, which he seemed to enjoy, apparently because they lasted only a few days at a time. In this particular letter he had written about "a girl . . . Messina . . . knockout . . . father" and something about a "curfew," a word Perry did not know. He had looked it up in the dictionary, but the definition contained more strange words than familiar ones.

He debated whether or not to ask Lydia to read Paul's letter for him. She was a much better reader than he was and read novels and magazines for pleasure. He was reluctant to ask her to read one of Paul's letters, though. They had been written for his eyes and no one else's. They were private, and he was jealous of his privacy. Still, he was curious about what Paul had done in Messina.

Lydia had changed jobs and was now working at the Bell bomber plant up in Marietta. He had gone with her to see it one Sunday and had been staggered by its immensity. He had never seen a building so large. Large enough, it seemed, to fit several Quartermaster warehouses inside and have space left over. It looked as if the entire countryside had been paved to make the parking lots. Thousands of people were pouring out of the building as they changed shifts, while vast numbers were hurrying inside. Although he was aware that war production occupied millions of

Americans, that particular concentration of workers gave him an insight into the total effort that awed him.

He decided he would not ask Lydia to read the letter. For all he knew, the part about Messina could be the most personal and private part of the entire letter. He drank the rest of his tea and was replacing the lid on the thermos bottle when two men appeared around the corner of a building and walked in his direction.

He watched them long enough to determine they did not work in his warehouse. By the leisurely way they were walking and the relaxed manner in which they were talking, he could tell they were a pair of workers using up their lunch hour with a stroll, this time away from the others. As they drew near he turned away. They were sweeping into the periphery of his vision when he was caught by an unusual movement. He looked back. They were running toward him and waving their hands.

He waved back and smiled. The smile froze on his face.

They were not greeting him. They were warning him. They were excited. One man's mouth was open wide, with his hands cupped around it. Apparently he was shouting. The other was gesticulating wildly with both hands and pointing. Perry looked about the ground where he was sitting, then back at the men in bewilderment. They came closer and stopped, but they were not standing still. They were jabbing the air with their hands in near hysteria, leaning forward, shouting and pointing to the sky above his head and beckoning him to come toward them. Come! Quickly! Hurry! With no understanding, he picked up his thermos bottle and prepared to get to his feet.

The end of a metal pipe hit the ground beside him. He jerked his head around.

Behind and above him a wall of round, hard metal was in motion. Convulsive and turbulent, it was crawling down and toward him, above him, on all sides of him, covering him. He felt a hard blow across the back of his neck, then he was conscious of falling forward on his face . . . hard . . . it was heavy on his back . . . breath . . . hurt . . . hurt . . .

The two men stood transfixed in horror.

"THEY'RE MASHING HIM FLAT—"

"RIGHT ON TOP OF—NO!"

"GET UP! GET UP! RUN!"

They could not hear their own voices. The long, round metal pipes rolled off the flatcar, thundering and roaring, clanging and rumbling, striking the ground haphazardly, end on end, crisscross, careening, ricocheting in one direction, rolling peacefully across the grass in the other, piling up in jumbled confusion. The clang of metal on metal was deafening.

One of the men ran off in the direction of the street, shouting for help. The clangor had already attracted a few people who were coming around the end of a warehouse looking curiously for the source of the uproar. Others followed. They stood at a distance and watched until the pipes stopped falling and rolling.

All was silent except for a metallic echo which dissipated itself into the cold February air.

"There's a man under there!"

"Under where?"

"On the bottom. We saw it happen—"

"Come on! Let's see if we can find him!"

They moved in on the chaotic heap and set to work trying to lift the pipes.

"Did anybody call the ambulance?"

"—and the Rescue Squad or whoever's got the lifting equipment?"

"Maybe the Fire Department—we're not doing much good this way."

The workers stopped and moved back when the ambulance and fire trucks appeared with sirens blowing. The Military Police arrived from the opposite direction and pushed the crowd back to a safe distance while the firemen and Rescue Squad got their equipment ready. Red lights flashed. Instructions, questions and answers crackled on two-way radios. Two trucks with hoists, cranes and winches arrived from the Civil Engineers Department, and their operators began lifting the pipes from the heap and laying them aside on the grass. They worked steadily, but, by its nature, the operation was slow and tedious.

Eventually they uncovered him.

"Does anybody know who he is?"

"How can anybody tell?"

"How about his I.D. badge?"

"Let's get him into the ambulance—the docs will identify him at the hospital."

"There's not much left to go on."

"Easy now. You can't never tell about these cases—he might still be alive. . . . easy now . . . easy . . ."

"He can't be alive—he can't possibly be."

"Not too high . . . keep his head level . . . easy . . ."

With sirens sounding and lights flashing, the ambulance turned out across the grass and disappeared between two warehouses.

"Did anybody see it happen?"

"I did. Me and that guy over there in the gray coat— worst thing I ever saw in my life! He kept trying to cover his head with his hands. He was sitting on the grass by the tracks screwing the lid on a thermos bottle. He must have been eating lunch. We yelled at him and tried to warn—"

"Lunch? Did you say he was eating lunch?"

"Yeah. Can you imagine eating lunch outside on a cold day like this?"

"What did he have on?"

"I couldn't tell exactly—some bright-colored jacket. Red and blue, I think. I can't remember now. Maybe yellow and red—"

"Are you sure? *Positive?*"

341

"What's the matter, mister? You know him?"

"What color was his hair?"

"Dark—that's all I could tell. Black or brown, maybe. He wasn't a blond. I know that much."

"Let me through, please!"

"What's the matter? Somebody you know?"

"I hope not, but I think it is. It's bound to be him. He worked for me. Let me by! *Please!* I've got to go to the hospital and find out—"

"We saw the posts give way and the pipes start to roll off the car, and we yelled at him to get out of the way. He waved back at us and smiled! How do you figure that? He *smiled.* Imagine that! Like he couldn't hear what we were yelling."

"He couldn't. He was deaf."

"*Deaf?* Good Lord of Mercy! That poor guy! All that noise, and he couldn't hear a thing."

# 33

ARMY REGULATIONS REQUIRED that all requests for emergency leave from overseas be investigated by the American Red Cross and the nature of the emergency verified before the request could be considered. To save time and paperwork, the United States Army urged servicemen's families to contact their local Red Cross chapters first rather than the serviceman directly. In turn, the Red Cross would notify the individual through military channels that the emergency existed and furnish him the documented information he would need to apply for leave.

Paul's request for leave had been denied. The Red Cross Field Representative from Monroe was sitting in the Hollys' living room with Alex and Mamie explaining why.

"The Army has a policy of not returning a man to the States when there's a death in the family except under extremely rare circumstances. We thought this one might qualify," she said. "It sounds cruel and cold blooded, I know, but with so many men overseas they can't honor all requests to come home. Our Regional Director in Atlanta says the Army has to turn down thousands of them every month. They have to give priority to their jobs. It's the only way they can fight the war. For every man who leaves his job, even for a week or ten days, somebody has to fill in for him, and there aren't enough men to do it. That's especially true in a combat zone, where manpower is always critical. Then, to make the problem all but impossible, the Army has to provide transportation back and forth across the ocean for the men, and transportation is as critical as manpower. It's heartbreaking for all concerned, but it's one of the many sadnesses brought on by the war. I hope you understand. I wish I could bring you a better report."

"We do understand, Mrs. Rutledge," Alex said. "We have to. We weren't expecting special treatment for Paul, even though we couldn't help but hope the Army would let him come."

"It makes you weep to know that when the boys' families need them most, they can't be with them," she went on. "Just within our own District, which is small compared to some, it would tear your heart out to see how many bona fide emergency situations we verify, and practically none of the leaves are approved. Sometimes in the case of a terminal illness of a wife or a child, the serviceman is granted leave. About the only leave approved in case of a death, though, is when the presence of the serviceman is essential to the well-being of survivors—a wife dies, say, and leaves several small children, and the father's presence is imperative. The Army considers all requests carefully. There's no rubber-stamp procedure involved in their processing of these requests."

"We're more worried about Paul than about ourselves," Alex said. "Perry was his twin brother, and not even his mother and I can ever know exactly how close they were. One of the jokes they used to get tired of was people asking how they could tell themselves apart. I'm not sure they really could."

Mamie walked to the door with Mrs. Rutledge. "You're mighty sweet to drive down here and tell us," she said, extending her hand. "Please thank all the Red Cross people for us. We appreciate your kindness and assistance. And you did it all so quickly!"

"We wish we could have done more," she said.

Bentley is lovely any time, even on a winter day in February when the centipede grass is asleep, the brown leaves of the tall oak, hickory and walnut hang in silent tatters from their branches, and the land is gray and subdued. The town has a peaceful charm that only generations and time itself can bring about. It is elegant and it is wretched, well kept and shabby, graceful and clumsy, beautiful and ugly, but it is alive, and it is lived in. When it is touched with a special happiness or sadness, mellow tradition seems to abound, and Bentley is somehow lovelier than ever. It was that way at the time of Perry Holly's funeral.

The sun was out of focus, and a cold, gentle haze had moved in. It clung to the ground in patches and floated in wisps through the town and out past the Clegg Line toward the Alcovy River and Stone Mountain beyond. Inside the First Baptist Church the daylight filtered through the many colors of the stained glass windows, bright but not brilliant, and brought out in relief the ancient and intricate hand carvings in the old polished mahogany of the choir railing and the pastor's pulpit.

Emily Lanier, who had come on the noon bus from Atlanta, was entranced. Mr. Knox was aboard the same bus, but they did not become acquainted until one heard the other asking the Bus Agent for directions to the residence of Alexander Holly. They walked in on South Chiles Street together. Ellison Hampton's parents came from Griffin. Polly Timmons drove out from Atlanta with three friends. Two ladies from Susie's Red Cross headquarters came together. Lydia Regan arrived with Mr. and Mrs. Maxwell barely in time for the service. All those people and the Hollys' family friends and relatives filled the pews. No young men came. Perry had no close friends of his own in Bentley. He had never attended school there, and, except for the two years he worked at the cotton mill, he had never stayed at home longer than three months at a time. His friends had been Paul's friends actually, and none of them were at home now. They were scattered around the world.

Two blocks south of Madison Road and two blocks west of Chiles Street lies the Bentley Memorial Cemetery. The earliest grave inside its stone walls dates back to 1783. Its old stone slab has been worn smooth by time and the weather, and only the date, long since etched in black by grime, wind and rain, is faintly readable. Because it is so near the center of town, the cemetery is a daily and familiar sight to most people, and they do not regard it with holy awe and crippling reverence. They take shortcuts through it, wander about in it, sit on its walls, meet their friends at its arched gate on the east. The Holly family plot lies somewhere near the center behind the faded slabs and elaborate monuments of long ago. It had never been used.

After Mr. Clapper had pronounced the benediction at the graveside and the people were drifting away in all directions, Alex stood alongside Mamie, Ferebe and Susie and looked across the high mound of flowers at his feet, across the cemetery and through the trees. He could see a patch of Wylie Spencer's garden, now strewn with jumbles of dried stalks. Immediately over the top of his fence he could see a corner of his own garage and his own house. The lump in his throat was as heavy as his heart. Home was two minutes away. He could see it. It would never be the same again. Time had already taken care of that. Time moves swiftly even when it seems to be crawling at a snail's pace. Twenty-three years had gone by within the hour just past.

Several days passed before Mamie could complete a letter to Paul. It was the most difficult task she had ever undertaken. She made one false start after another and half filled the kitchen wastebasket with crumpled and wadded-up paper. She wanted to tell him everything she knew of the accident and give him a step-by-step account of subsequent events.

346

She saw a kind of justice in Paul's not coming home. He and Perry had been born together and, though often separated for long periods, they had lived together in a special way that only they themselves understood. They were endowed with a lovely quality of oneness that enabled them to be together even when they were miles apart. But they had not died together, and perhaps it was an act of mercy that one did not watch the other being lowered into the ground forever.

As insurance against anything she might overlook, Mamie asked Ferebe and Susie to write to Paul. They did. Before enough time had elapsed for him to have received her letter or theirs, Mamie and Alex received one from him.

> APO 249, New York
> 17 February 1945

Dear Mother and Dad:

I've been dreading to write this letter, because I don't know what to say. I don't know what to think. I don't even know how I feel. But I know you're expecting to hear from me. The cable from the Red Cross was just a bunch of words I couldn't believe. A chaplain from Hqs brought it to me, and I couldn't think of anything to say to him.

I feel like I should have been at home with the rest of you, and not just for my own sake. I know what you've been going through, and I feel like I should have been there to help out. I know everybody in Bentley has been good to you, because you have always been good to them all your lives. You were good to Perry, too, and that's the main thing. I knew more of his deaf friends than you did, and none of them had it as good at home as he did. You'll have some stars in your crown because of how good you were to him.

My C.O. called me in and told me to take a three-day pass. He didn't ask me if I wanted it. He just told me to take it. It didn't do any good, though. I might as well have stayed at work where I know all the guys. I went over to Messina to a Rest Area the Army opened up there recently. An old Sicilian man took me out in his fishing boat to a little island that wasn't anything but a pile of rocks. I climbed around on it for half a day while he was busy with his boat. That's about all I did in Messina except wander around the streets. I looked at everything in town and didn't see anything.

I know you're expecting me to say lots of things about Perry, and maybe I will when it all gets real to me. One of my buddies from Oklahoma got his left arm shot off right after we landed in Sicily. I went to see him in the Field Hospital before they shipped him home, and he told me he didn't feel a thing until a long time later. When he did begin to feel, he said it was the worst pain he ever had. He said he hadn't had time to miss his left arm yet because he was lying flat on his back where he didn't have anything to use it for. He said he knew he would miss it a lot later on. Maybe that's what's happening to me now.

I'm all right. Don't worry about me. Just take care of yourselves. When the war is over and I get back home, we'll put ourselves all back together again, and we'll get along all right. Maybe not as good as we used to, but we'll make it. Give my love to Susie and Ferebe and the kids, and all my love to both of you especially. I know you're busy and upset about things, but please write when you have time and feel like it.

Love,

Paul

P.S. I mailed a letter to Perry the day before I got the cable. It will probably be sent to you with his other effects. When you get it, tear it up or send it back to me. It was kind of private between us.

# 34

Susie and Ferebe drove out to the Maxwells' the day after they returned to Atlanta and packed Perry's things in his trunk and suitcases. Their task was lengthy and difficult, for they interrupted themselves frequently with weeping and reminiscing.

"It's not that these clothes are so familiar-looking," Ferebe said at one point. "I don't even remember his wearing some of them. It's just that I keep thinking about why we are doing this. It's like Ell says: 'Why does it always have to happen to the good guys?' "

Mrs. Maxwell told them they should not have come so soon and offered to pack for them.

"No, but you're sweet to offer it," Susie said. "It's our job, and we'll just have to do it. Poor Mother and Daddy will have the hardest job of all. They've got to put it all away or dispose of it somehow."

Mr. Maxwell came in before they had finished. "I've got Perry's binoculars here," he said. "He let me borrow them last week. He bought them in a pawnshop down on Decatur Street. Sometimes on Saturdays he went down there and scratched around to see what he could find. I think he got a real good bargain in these."

He raised the binoculars to his eyes and turned them toward the window. "They sure bring everything up close,"

349

he said. His delight was that of a child. "That schoolhouse is two blocks away, and it looks like it's in my own yard."

He handed them to Ferebe.

"Would you like to keep them, Mr. Maxwell?" she asked.

"Oh, no, Mrs. Hampton, I couldn't do that!" he said hastily. "You take these to your mother and daddy. That's who they belong to. I couldn't take them. It wouldn't be right at all."

"They'd like for you to have them. Susie and I would, too. Perry was very fond of you and Mrs. Maxwell, and you were both marvelous to him. Please take them—they're from Perry."

He eyed the binoculars fondly and with indecision.

"I think it'll be all right, Willard," his wife spoke up timidly. "Mrs. Hampton wouldn't offer them to you if her and her sister didn't want you to have them."

"She's right," Susie said. "They're yours. They'll help you remember Perry."

"Oh, I couldn't ever forget him anyway," he said, taking the binoculars and holding them tenderly. "We raised a deaf boy, you know, and we've had the house full of deaf people nearly ever since he grew up and left. They don't have any problems as long as they're with each other. It's when they get with hearing people that their problems begin. They work their hearts out just trying to fit themselves in with hearing people, and a lot of them don't ever make it. It's too frustrating. They hit a blank wall, so they give up and sort of shrink into a shell, and you can't blame them one whit. But your brother, Perry, wasn't that way. He learned to fit both sides. Of course, lots of them do that too. He was a fine boy, and when we went to Bentley to his funeral and met your mother and daddy and saw where you lived and how you lived, I could see why. I'm just real sorry we didn't know his twin brother."

He looked down at the binoculars. "I thank you both

and your mother and daddy for these," he said. "I'll take good care of them."

He turned quickly and left the room.

Two weeks later Ferebe and Susie took Perry's things to Bentley and moved them into his room upstairs. Another week passed before Mamie could force herself to sort them and decide on their disposition.

"I'd like to leave them packed away just as they are, but I can't," she told Alex. "Ferebe and Susie didn't have time to examine anything. They simply packed it all away. I need to go through his pockets and all the odds and ends. He might have some unpaid bills or something borrowed and things like that. All his clothes are Paul's exact size. He might want some of them. Anyway, I'll put them away properly and let him decide when he comes home. I'm sure some of them need cleaning, and I know he must have some dirty laundry in there, so—I guess I'll just have to do it."

Alone upstairs, she refolded his shirts, underwear, sox and pajamas and put them into his chest of drawers as though he were at home and planning on wearing them. Carefully she arranged his suits, trousers, jackets and neckties on hangers in the closet and lined his shoes on the floor below. After everything was in place, she hung a sack of mothballs from a hook and closed the door.

Among the miscellany of his possessions was a shoe box filled with letters. They were in their envelopes and generally uniform in size. They stood on their edges as if in a file cabinet. Two blocks of unfinished white pine, sanded smooth and rubbed to a dull gloss that brought out the grain of the wood, were wedged inside to fill the extra space between the letters and the sides of the box. The interior of the shoe box was neat, precise and orderly, as if it might have been tended daily with care, pride and love.

Mamie lifted out one of the envelopes and recognized Paul's handwriting. She thumbed through the others. All of them were from Paul, and Perry had filed them chronologically. Some of the envelopes were thin and others thick. She counted them: one hundred and ten. She made some quick calculations. Paul had been in the Army twenty-nine months—one hundred and sixteen weeks. Perry's accident had been four weeks ago. She subtracted those. A letter from Paul had come later, and she had returned it unopened. She added that one. She sat in wonder.

Paul had written to Perry once each week since he was inducted into the Army three days after Pearl Harbor.

She was amazed. She was also moved. She was aware that Paul had written to his brother more often than to anyone else in the family, but she had never imagined with what faithfulness and regularity. She stared at the letters while the lives of both boys—or was it one?—flashed in quick review. Those letters to Perry were the complete explanation for Paul's negligence in writing to his mother and father. With little taste for writing letters in the first place, he had exhausted all his efforts in writing to Perry.

With a kind of reverence she put the lid back on the box. She felt that she had pried, that she should not be aware of the letters' existence. Yet she wanted to read them. Hers and Alex's knowledge of Paul's life in the Army was pitifully sketchy. She wanted desperately to fill in the gaps. Those letters would make that possible.

She opened the box again. Lined up before her eyes was the chronological account of the news for which she and Alex yearned but had not received. They had been forced to settle for widely separated and disjointed letters, many of them hastily scrawled and carelessly thought out. To read Paul's letters to Perry would be to spy, to eavesdrop. She replaced the lid, put the box on the shelf in Perry's closet and closed the door.

While she sorted his remaining paraphernalia, the letters continued to occupy her thoughts. Perry had never offered to let them read one, and they had never asked for the privilege. Paul had told them to destroy his last one or return it to him, but he had not invited them to read it. Those letters were not for her and Alex, and as much as she would like to, she could not honestly justify reading them herself.

In her lap was a stationery box half filled with pencils, keys, rubber bands, paper clips, chewing gum, thumbtacks, scraps of paper, receipts, ticket stubs, a small calendar, lengths of string, and, on the bottom, several sheets of paper folded together. She unfolded them to see what they contained. It was a letter from Paul that apparently Perry had overlooked and forgot to file with the others. It had been written from Sicily a few days after the invasion.

She was reading it before she had time to debate the propriety of it, and once begun, she could not stop.

Dear Perry:

As I was telling you in my last letter and ran out of paper, I found out something since I've been over here. War will make you better or worse, but it won't leave you the same. Sometimes I feel religious and righteous, and the next day I feel like an atheist. I never did feel either way until I got mixed up in this war. You're lucky, because God never did worry you much, and somebody's been trying to explain Him to you ever since I can remember. It almost makes me wish I was deaf myself. Well, the people doing the explaining don't know a whole lot about Him, either. When all the world starts blowing up around here I get some real close calls in a day's work, and every time I come out of one okay, I say, "God was right there beside me that time." But when one of my buddies gets his head blown off six feet away from where I'm standing, I say, "Where were you that time, God?"

I haven't figured it out yet. I mentioned it to a good buddy who knows about these matters, and he said the fact that I'm even thinking about it is a good sign, but he didn't say what it's a good sign of. Did he mean that one answer is as good as the other? If he did, then it wouldn't make much difference, would it? But I know it does. It's pretty important or I wouldn't think about it so much. I never used to waste my time thinking about things I didn't understand. I hope you see what I mean about war not leaving you the same.

I wish you wouldn't worry so much about not being in the Army or Navy. Lots of things are just as important. Like what you're doing, for example. If everybody was in the service, nobody would be around to send us clothes and ammunition and all those delicious (ha!) K rations. (Can't you think up something else to put in all those cans and boxes? If you're going to run the Quartermaster Corps, you ought to run it *right!*) Seriously, with me in the Army, I feel lots better knowing you're looking after Mother, Dad and Susie. You'll never have a more important job than that, because that's the most important job there is.

You know that trip we're going on together after the war? What do you think about adding Oregon and Washington and Canada? After we see the Grand Canyon and Yellowstone and California, we might as well go up north and come home across Canada, then head south down through New England maybe. Go to the library and look at the maps and figure out a route. Hang on to your money until then. Remember, we agreed to go first class—Pullman compartment, best hotels, best restaurants, best nightclubs, best steaks, and that will be expensive.

If you can't read all this, save it and I'll read it to you when I get home. Don't forget, if you let anybody read all these letters, I'll fix your plow to where you'll be as crippled as you are deaf (ha! ha!). And I'll also change my G.I insurance so you won't be the beneficiary any longer! Take good care of yourself, and, as always,

Love,
Paul

By the time Mamie reached the end of the letter, she was weeping aloud. She flung herself across the bed, buried her face in her arms and cried until she could cry no more. Then she read the letter again.

She knew she should never have read it the first time,

but she could not force herself to regret having done so. She loved it. She loved it with her whole heart and soul, her entire being. She took the shoe box down from the closet shelf, carefully slid the letter into its proper place among the others and returned it to the shelf once more. A calmness descended over her as she closed the door and went back to sorting Perry's things.

As she finished her work, she heard Alex come in the front door. She closed the empty trunk and went downstairs to meet him. He had gone through the hall and out the back door. She found him at the back fence by the garage facing Wylie Spencer's garden.

"What are you doing out here, honey?" she called to him, going down the steps and into the yard. "This is the third or fourth time you've come out here recently when you got home. What are you looking at—Wylie's beehives? You've seen them a thousand times."

He turned back and kissed her. "No, it's not that," he said. He smiled sadly and walked with her back to the house. "From Perry's grave on the day of the funeral I happened to look this way and I could see the corner of our house and garage. I was wondering if I could see his grave from here. At first I could—with all the flowers. But since they died, I can't tell which is which now."

"When we get the marker up, maybe you can," she said. She stopped with her hand on the screen door and looked back. "I'm so used to seeing that slice of the cemetery that I never stopped to figure out that I've been looking at our own plot all this time. I've got to go over there tomorrow and clean up all the dried stalks and leaves and some of those wire holders that must still be there. I just haven't had the heart to go yet, but it's all right now."

She opened the door and stepped onto the back porch. "A marvelous thing happened to me today," she said. "Come on in, and I'll tell you about it while I fix supper."

# 35

Susie Holly stood amid the silent crowd and gazed upward at the ornate towers of the Terminal Station. It was the only direction in which she had an unobstructed view. The windows and roofs of nearby buildings, and some not so near, were lined with men and women looking down over the plaza to the tracks and train sheds hoping for a glimpse of Franklin D. Roosevelt's funeral train. It had left Warm Springs a few minutes before noon. She had heard on the radio that people had been waiting for hours at street crossings along the railroad tracks from one end of Atlanta to the other. A few small airplanes circled overhead and dipped low for a closer look.

The afternoon was warm, and Susie held a newspaper overhead to shield her eyes against the glare of the April sun. She stood on one foot, then the other, determined not to be impatient. No sooner had she joined the swelling crowd on Terminal Plaza than she realized she would never get close enough to see the train. She was disappointed. Yet, not to wait for it to pass through town seemed disrespectful. To walk away would have put her in the category of a disgruntled curiosity seeker who had been denied a view of what he had come to see. Being there meant more to her than that. She waited.

When word swept back through the crowd that the

train was in the yards and approaching the station, she grew tense. Above the heads and shoulders of those who waited, she watched the billowing white smoke of the two locomotives until it was sucked under the train shed and trapped. She saw it emerge again at the other end and billow up again. She was choked with emotion as she saw the last of it floating up into the sky from a canyon of grimy buildings and distant smokestacks. Somewhere in the Atlanta railroad yards the two locomotives had been replaced, but she did not know exactly where or when. The white smoke had been her only view of the eleven-car funeral train.

Susie was fourteen years old when Franklin D. Roosevelt had first been elected to office, and it seemed that he had always been President of the United States. Despite his much publicized ill health and the constant speculations about how much longer he could endure the strain of office, she had not seriously faced up to how it would be for him not to live forever. The photographs of him at the Yalta Conference had been ghastly, like illustrations of a dying man's medical chart. Yet his quiet death at Warm Springs of cerebral hemorrhage the day before had stunned her. She felt she had lost a good and personal friend. She wept quietly on the streetcar going home.

She was not certain that it was only for President Roosevelt that she wept. Perry's death had been less than six weeks earlier, and she had not yet learned to keep her emotions under control when his image floated into view at awkward times without warning. He had been so gentle and lovable that she often thought that, given a voice, it would have been as soft and kind as his dark brown eyes. She remembered when they were small and she wished she could be deaf long enough to talk to him in his strange, beautiful, silent language, she stuffed cotton in her ears and held her hands tightly over them, but she could not shut out the sounds of being alive.

Two weeks after Perry's death one of the girls at the

357

office received notice from the War Department that her husband had been killed in action on Okinawa. The girl had said nothing until Susie noticed her bent over her desk sobbing and went over to see why. She knew the girl no better than she knew the others in the office, but she was alone and helpless in her shock and grief, and Susie's heart went out to her. She left the office that morning, and no one had heard from her since. They assumed she had gone back to her parents' home in Nebraska. Susie could see her coming out of Mr. Pittman's office, small and pale, eyes red from weeping. She remembered her, too, while waiting in the plaza.

The obituary pages of the Atlanta newspapers were filled with photographs of boys in uniform, many of whom looked as though they should be back at home with a bicycle and a paper route, and none of whom had died of natural causes. Death seemed to be everywhere, and she imagined she could see the fear of it in people's faces. On the streets, in the stores, on the buses, they seemed sad. They were quiet and pensive. They were preoccupied. They were worried. They had faraway, troubled looks in their eyes. She wondered if her prerogative to walk down the streets of Atlanta, to board any trolley that suited her fancy to take her anywhere that satisfied her whim was worth what it was doing to people. Was it worth killing her contemporaries—friend or foe—to make it possible? You couldn't kill a man crossing a bridge on the Rhine River or fighting his way up Suribachi on Iwo Jima without killing a part of somebody else who was harvesting wheat in Kansas or bringing in his lobster traps in Maine or chopping cotton in Mississippi or washing the breakfast dishes in New Mexico. None of that was to mention the love that would never flourish, the families that would never be created, the children who would never be born, the generations that would never begin. What kind of world could justify its own existence with that on its conscience?

It was too late to go back to the office, and she did not

want to go home. For the moment, however, she could think of nowhere else to go. In her apartment she looked at the amusement pages of the newspaper searching for a picture show—or anything—that might take up the rest of the late afternoon and early evening. She found nothing she felt she could enjoy alone. She did not want to be alone. She picked up the telephone to call Ferebe, then put it down before she had finished dialing her number. Tomorrow was Saturday, and a weekend at Ferebe's house was not what she wanted either. With Ellison gone and Perry's presence still felt, she feared she would sink even deeper into the very mood she wanted to escape. Neither did she want to go home to Bentley, and for essentially the same reason.

She prowled around in the cabinets and the refrigerator to see what she might cook for supper, but nothing appealed to her. Maybe a leisurely stroll through the supermarket would whet her appetite and give her something to do at the same time. She switched on the radio. The familiar voice of President Roosevelt came at her in one of his fireside chats. She twirled the dial, and on every station she heard beautiful, but mournful, music or another replay of another FDR speech or a tribute to the dead President or a description of the funeral train as it passed through Atlanta. She turned off the radio and picked up the book that lay on top of it. She had decided she must be the only person in the country who had not read *Forever Amber*, but now that she had it from the Public Library she was not interested in it. Especially not today. She considered calling Emily Lanier, but finding her with a free weekend was next to impossible. Yet stranger things had happened, so she dialed her number.

"Lawsy me, chile! I don't have a single, solitary thing to do!" Emily exclaimed. "I've been thinking about calling you."

"You mean Buddy isn't coming this weekend?"

"That's one of the things I've been intending to call

you about," she said with happy excitement. "He got transferred. Isn't that newsy? To March Field out in California. Maybe they'll send him overseas even yet. I sure hope so. He deserves it. He's been talking about moving to Greenville after the war, and why not? After all these years at the Air Base he thinks it's his hometown. He wants me to come out to California to see him this summer. I wouldn't dream of it. Did you go down to the train this afternoon?"

"Yes, but I couldn't get close enough to see anything. Still, I'm glad I went. It was like going to a funeral, which is about the only thing you can do when somebody dies."

"I listened on the radio, and I sat here bawling my eyes out. I had no idea I would get so sad over the death of the President of the United States. After all, I didn't know him personally. What I was going to call you about was to see if you're not busy this weekend and if maybe you could come over tonight and stay until Sunday night or Monday morning."

"That's exactly what I called to ask you," Susie said. She was delighted. "I'm tired of so much gloom. It seems like I haven't laughed or seen anything funny in ages."

"Then it's all settled," Emily said. "We'll do something reckless to celebrate Buddy's transfer—like washing our hair and fixing our fingernails and cooking something according to a recipe. *Exactly*."

"You make it sound like fun."

"It's that wild streak showing up in me. Tomorrow we'll sleep late and go down to Rich's and Davison's and ruin our credit rating and eat somewhere we can't afford and go see a picture show. There's a Robert Taylor picture at Loew's. He disturbs the savage side of my nature. By then if we're not too dissipated from the debauchery we can go down to the USO and do our duty to God and country by giving our fighting men a chance to pick us up and carry us away to some wicked place."

"But Emily! The country's in mourning for President Roosevelt! Are you sure all this would be proper? I mean, I want to come over and all, but I'm not sure we should be so happy-go-lucky. You make it sound too carefree!"

"Listen, honey, I know how it sounds," Emily said. Her tone had changed. She was serious now. "But you need cheering up. The last few times we've talked you sounded as if the weight of the world is on your shoulders. Well, it's not. It's on mine too. FDR was my President too, you know. And my mother's and my daddy's and my brothers' and everybody else's you see walking down Peachtree Street. The same thing goes for the whole war. None of us like it. We think it's the most tragic thing that ever happened to anybody. Perry's dreadful accident ripped you to shreds, and I can understand that. But you can't just keep heaping it on. If you don't brighten up a little, you'll end up in a convent and spend the rest of your life walking around in a garden wearing a spooky black shroud, mumbling to yourself and counting little beads on a chain. And what good will that do anybody or anything? Now how about it?"

"Emily, you're wonderful," Susie said. "Absolutely wonderful, and I accept. I'll think about your lecture on the way. Do you want me to bring anything? I've got some odds and ends in the refrigerator."

"Don't you have any old T-bone steaks lying around the house?"

"No, I'm sorry."

"Well, hurry before the stores close and work your wiles on the neighborhood butcher. Who knows? You might talk him out of one."

The country went crazy at exactly nine o'clock on Tuesday morning, 8 May 1945. President Truman's flat, slightly nasal voice on the radio flicked the switch that set the people loose. They had been listening for him since the death of Adolf Hitler and the fall of Berlin a week earlier. Now here he was: "The Allied Armies, through sacrifice and devotion and with God's help . . ."

Precisely what he said beyond that was lost in the pandemonium that broke loose and shook the country. *The war in Europe was over!* Words could not have added one iota of meaning to that glorious fact. Newscasters babbled descriptions of dancing in the streets from Puget Sound to Times Square. Bells rang and whistles blew, the same bells and whistles that had roused people from their beds at the beginning of that awesome D day a year earlier, but this time they were more riotous and crazier, and they rang and blew longer and louder than before.

In Bentley people did not gather at The Well. They could not stand still or be quiet long enough for a serious gathering anywhere on that morning. They walked, ran, danced along Chiles Street shaking hands, kissing, embracing, clapping one another on the back, shouting, laughing, talking, babbling while no one listened. They darted back and forth across the street or stopped obliviously in the middle of it. A Trailways bus coming in from Monroe moved cautiously past The Well, then wheezed to a halt in the middle of the block. The big door swung open, and the passengers, led by the driver, poured out onto the pavement and joined the celebration. Merchants locked their stores. The bank and most of the offices did not open their doors at all. While Miss Mattie Cofield Randolph deliberated over the appropriate time to dismiss school, school dismissed itself, and happy children fanned out all over town. The fact that more of their happiness stemmed from their sudden freedom than from V-E Day itself was of no consequence.

"Too much happened too fast," Mamie Holly said to Ethel Robinson and Flora Etheridge. They were standing in the Etheridges' front yard. "The war got away from us when we lost Perry. Of course, we kept up with Ellison the best we could. Then the President died, and well— there was just too much happened all at once. But isn't it marvelous? All I can think about is that we've got two boys coming home now."

"We've been trying to call our children, but the circuits have been busy for an hour," Flora said. "Macy Weatherford told me she's swamped with long-distance calls. I guess everybody's happy and wants to call somebody and tell them about it."

"I wish this was the end of *both* wars," Ethel said. "Maybe it won't take long to finish the other one now. Vernon says they'll divert everything from Europe to the Pacific now and clean up fast."

"Oh, my goodness! I hope they let all those boys come home from Europe before they send them off to another war, especially after all they've been through."

"Maybe they'll just divert the equipment, and not the men," Ethel suggested helpfully. "They tell me we have lots of men already trained who haven't been in action yet. Maybe they won't need the boys from Europe out in the Pacific."

While the excitement on Chiles Street was settling down from its peak, Alex Holly ran into Emory Haynes in front of Bill Beasley's Plumbing Company. They returned to work together.

"I wonder how we'll feel when the other war ends too," Alex said. They were turning the corner into Depot Street. "I don't see how anybody can get more excited than they are today."

"The war won't be over for me until my boy comes home," Emory said. "They can sign all the surrenders they want to, but until he walks in that front door and kisses his mother and shakes my hand, the war won't really be over. Do you think they've changed much, Alex?"

They walked a few paces down the hill before he replied. "They're bound to," he said. "They've been gone from home a long time for one thing. And they've been over there killing people for another. You can't be the same after that. You know that young bombardier I was talking to in the waiting room the other day? He says as long as he doesn't see their faces, he doesn't feel like he's killed anybody, and he's probably killed thousands, because he's been flying B-17s over Germany. He says if he worried about that, he'd never get anything done. You know he didn't think like that before the war. So there you are. He's different from how he used to be. What I'm afraid of is that life at home's going to be too tame for them now."

"No, it won't. It's what they want. That's why they get so homesick. It's not just being away that makes it hard on them. It's what they're doing that makes them want to come home."

They cut across past Selman's Cotton Warehouse. "Well—we've got one down and one to go," Alex said brightly. Then his mood sobered again. "Suppose Hitler had done what he started out to do and conquered the world. That would put him in charge of the entire world. Can you imagine being in charge of the whole world and all the people and all the things in it? Would you like that for yourself?"

"You kidding?" Emory replied. "I can't even keep up with what I've already got, and it's not much—a house with a leaky roof, a yard that's always overgrown, a few peach trees with the blight, and a Chevrolet that spends more time in Cy Darby's garage than in mine. Lordy! What would I do with the whole world?"

"That's what I mean. Who but a crazy man would want the entire world? And what would he do with it after he got it? He'd have to fight everybody in it to keep it. Then he wouldn't be any better off than he was while fighting to get it." He shook his head. "I still can't believe it all happened. One crazy man—just *one*, mind you—started all this and drove the world crazy right along with him."

"Yeah, I guess he did," Emory said. "But it's not over yet. It won't be long, though. Hirohito has lost his partner in crime. He's got it all to himself now. We've about cleaned out the Japs on Okinawa now, and there's nowhere left to go but Tokyo. I sure hope they don't try an invasion, though. Personally, I don't think the people of this country will stand for another invasion like we had in Europe. One of those is enough."

Alex chuckled. "The people of this country won't have anything to say about it. If that's what MacArthur and Nimitz want to do, they'll go ahead and do it." They stepped onto the station platform. "I've got to call Mamie," he added. "I sure thought I'd see her uptown. She's about the only person in Bentley I didn't see."

Ferebe told her mother on the telephone later in the day that she did not have complete confidence in Ellison's early return.

"He hasn't been in the Army even as long as Paul has been overseas," she reminded her. "They'll probably send the men home in some kind of reverse order. But I can wait now. He's safe. He's not in combat. I only hope they don't send him to the Pacific."

"There's always something else to worry about, isn't there?" Mamie said. "Maybe they won't send him out there. We can always hope. But if they do, we'll just have to put up with it like we've put up with everything else. I'm going to do my best to be patient until Ellison and Paul both come home, and I want you to do the same thing. Maybe we won't have to wait much longer."

But they did. Longer than they had anticipated, despite President Truman's warning against impatience. Many American troops must remain in Europe, he told the wives, parents and families of servicemen. Much remained to be done. A conquered nation must rebuild itself, learn to stand on its own feet again, this time in brotherhood within the community of free and decent people everywhere, else the job will not have been completed. Military administrations had been established throughout Europe to make this possible. Starving people must be fed, the homeless must be sheltered, the sick and wounded must be cared for.

The War Department issued public explanations of

the administrative and logistical problems involved in the return home of American troops. The largest military structure ever designed must not be allowed to crumble and disintegrate in a pell-mell exodus from Europe. In their exuberance, families should not lose sight of the fact that the United States was still at war and that thousands of returning troops were still bona fide members of the armed forces on active duty to be reassigned into new jobs where they could continue to serve the country best. The mechanics of shipping, receiving and reassigning them on such a massive scale would require more time than they might realize. Patience would be required. Lots of it.

Ellison wrote to Ferebe from Berlin. "You can't imagine in your wildest nightmare what the city looks like," he wrote. "It's rubble. Nothing but rubble. I hear that Hamburg looks worse than this, but I don't see how it could. The German people are standoffish and don't know what to make of us yet, but that works both ways. I don't understand the first thing about them either. Your guess is as good as mine about when I'll come home. All I hear are rumors. I do know for a fact, however, that my name is so far down on the rotation list that it hasn't even been typed yet. Nearly everyone I know has been over here two and three years. That makes me a junior member. Don't get your hopes up."

Paul's letter to his mother and father was different and infinitely more unsettling. He had been transferred to Rome and made the senior member of a twelve-man Military Police unit.

I know you won't understand this, and I'm not sure I do either. I was at the top of the rotation list, which meant I would probably be on the first boat headed your way. Or I could sign up for this job in Rome, which meant an extra six months over here and a pretty sure promotion to Tech Sergeant. I took it.

All this has something to do with Perry, but I can't put it in words. All I know is that as long as I'm over here,

Perry is over there. If I come home, he's not anywhere. I don't know if I know how to deal with that yet. When it looks like I know how, I'll come home.

Don't worry about me. I feel fine. Rome is the prettiest place I ever saw. We've got good quarters in a hotel right in the middle of town. I met a deaf Italian last week and was surprised at how good I could talk to him until I remembered that deaf people don't use language to talk— English, Italian or any other kind.

I hope your feelings don't get hurt because I'm staying here, but it's the only thing I know how to do right now. Give my love to Susie, Ferebe and the kids. I hope Ellison is on his way home by now. I never did write him a letter. I intended to ever since he got over here.

All my love,<br>Paul

Mamie watched Alex read the letter. After he had finished she said, "Paul's having a harder time than any of us, isn't he?"

"He sure is," Alex said quietly.

He took off his glasses and laid them on the table. He picked them up and put them on again. He read the letter once more. Then he sat in silence gazing through the window at the walnut tree by the garage. It was healthy, green and strong. When he spoke, it was as if he were talking to himself.

"Any time it doesn't seem real to me I can go out in the back yard and look across the top of Wylie's beehives toward the cemetery and see the headstone, and there he is. And if that's not enough, I can walk two blocks and read the words, and there he is again. Paul didn't see us put him there. So he doesn't have any way to know where Perry really is except what we tell him. That's not the same as seeing with your own eyes."

With men returning from the European and Mediterranean theaters by the thousands, Ferebe's patience was under constant pressure. It threatened to explode into bits when seven ships packed with 31,000 soldiers arrived in New York on the same day. She stayed close to the telephone just in case the rules had been changed and Ellison was among them. Then in July the Army Air Corps flew 125,000 men and women to the United States within a three-day period. Captain Ellison Hampton was among them. He had done his part in swelling the number of cheering, shouting, delirious returnees since V-E Day to a grand total of 532,258.

"Increasing that total was my single greatest contribution to World War II," he announced happily to Ferebe, Maggie and Ellie, Mr. and Mrs. Hampton, Alex, Mamie and Susie Holly, all of whom had gathered in Atlanta to welcome him home.

# 36

CLAY TINSLEY STOOD ON THE SIDEWALK in front of his grocery store. The sun had dropped behind the building and threw a shadow out to the curb. Alva Thomas had come out from the Thomas Mercantile Company next door to join him. The day was hot and humid, and the air inside their stores had become stagnant. It was nearly closing time. Not that it mattered, for not many people were uptown anyway. Most of them had come in the morning while it was still cool and had gone back home to stay out of the heat.

"I'll be real frank with you," Clay was saying. "I don't pretend to understand all I know about that atomic bomb. It's got something mysterious in it that's stronger than dynamite. I didn't know they made such a thing, but it looks like they do. I think they ought to plaster Japan with every one they've got and be done with it."

"Well, you see, Clay, they're hoping Japan will give in after only two of them. Then they won't have to drop any more," Alva said. "One of those bombs kills an awful lot of people. That first one killed over sixty thousand."

"What difference does that make? They're all Japs, aren't they? I say get rid of them while we're at it."

"We can't do that. Personally, I think they're about ready to give up. They can't stand up against many bombs like that. It's on the radio all the time about the Japs having cabinet meetings and trying to decide what to do. They're finished, and they know it. All they're doing is looking for the best way to surrender. I wouldn't be surprised if— Is that your telephone ringing?"

"Could be," Clay said without moving. "It's probably somebody wanting to ask me about something I haven't had in stock since the war started. They can do without it for all I care. I'm tired of their griping. A lady out at the cotton mill called me yesterday raising the roof because I won't sell her all the coffee she wants now that the war's practically over. She said her sister in Macon doesn't have any trouble getting it, and I told her she'd better go to Macon and let her sister get her some. What was it you were saying when my telephone rang?"

"I was saying I wouldn't be surprised if Truman comes on the radio any time to announce the Japs have surrendered and the war's over."

"That's what everybody's waiting for and expecting to happen. They've been like that ever since they dropped those two atomic bombs. It's kind of peculiar for the war to be over and not be over either. People have been wanting to celebrate for a week, but they're afraid to until they get the final word."

"I don't know what kind of celebrating there'll be left for everybody to do after all that carrying on on V-E Day."

Clay Tinsley probably typified the American citizen in his inability to grasp the nature and significance of the bombs dropped on Hiroshima and Nagasaki. Sixteen hours after the first one was dropped, President Truman had come on the air and announced that an American plane had dropped one bomb on Hiroshima. "That bomb had more power than twenty thousand tons of TNT. It is an atomic bomb. It is a harnessing of the basic power of the universe. The force from which the sun draws its power has been loosed against those who brought the war to the Far East. . . ."

That was impressive, even awesome, but for a nation that had been conditioned to reckon bombs by the thousands of tons, 20,000 was a finite quantity. It could be weighed. It could be visualized. In two minutes sixty thousand Japanese citizens had been killed, four square miles of a city had been obliterated. That, too, was comprehensible. After all, more than 250,000 Japanese in Tokyo alone had been killed from B-29 raids, and more than fifty-three square miles of the city had been destroyed. Their imaginations needed stretching.

They were aware that the new bomb was the most powerful ever built and that a few could do the work of many. But most people had never seen a real bomb with their own eyes except in pictures, and fewer had actually seen the detonation of one on impact. All of them had seen airplanes, though, and when they began to compare one airplane with two thousand and realized that one airplane could cause as much destruction as two thousand, they began to get a glimmer of the fearful weapon their country had created and now held in its possession.

The word "atom" was not strange to them, but neither was it a familiar household word. It nudged at them uncomfortably from little remembered and scarcely digested textbooks—was it chemistry or physics?—but they had thought of an atom as a thing that *existed*. They were not aware that it also *acted*. They took a quick cram course via magazines, newspapers and radio in how a peaceful atom, too small to see, could be turned into a destructive monster, too large to contemplate. While they were learning—or not learning, as was often the case—Atomic Bomb became fixed in their everyday vocabulary whether they understood what they were saying or not. It rolled off their tongues easily and with no self-consciousness, for they knew it was the weapon that would end the war. In the face of that, understanding was secondary and could wait.

Pet Wilkerson came out of the Bentley Beauty Salon and opened her blue flowered sun parasol. She was wearing her summer voile, also blue with white roses climbing up from her uneven hemline. Her auburn hair was precise and stiff from a new finger wave. The talcum powder on her neck had not been spread evenly. Clay and Alva watched her approach.

"Good evening, Mr. Tinsley . . . Mr. Thomas," she said, nodding politely. "I'm surprised you're not at home with your radio. The President is coming on the air at seven o'clock." She looked at her lapel watch. "That's only forty minutes away. I hope it's the announcement all of us are waiting for. I'm on my way home to hear it now."

"I hope you're right, Pet," Clay said. "We've been waiting a long time for it, haven't we?"

They watched her cross the street and walk toward home.

"Let's lock up and get on home, Clay. I feel like I was born in this store. Don't you get tired of it?"

"Tired? I wish one of those atomic bombs would land right in the middle of my meat counter. It doesn't have anything in it, anyway."

At seven o'clock President Truman told the expectant nation that Japan had accepted the terms of the Potsdam Declaration, and World War II had ended. It was still daylight on the East Coast, but when darkness fell Atlanta was ablaze with lights. They glowed from the top windows of the tallest buildings to the head beams of the cars parked at the curbs. The city was a miracle of brightness. The long-dimmed streetlights burst into brilliance. Neon signs flashed on. Thousands of tiny lights raced busily around the edges of theater, hotel and nightclub marquees. The gold dome of the State Capitol was splendid and luminous in the summer night. Glimmering white water sprayed up happily from the fountains in the parks. Atop water towers, along the edges of buildings, up and down the spidery frameworks of construction projects, cranes and derricks, strings of lights twinkled. Out on Paces Ferry Road multicolored Christmas lights sparkled merrily in and out of the landscaped gardens of one of the city's most handsome estates.

In Washington the dome of the Capitol building, the Lincoln Memorial, the White House and the Washington Monument were chalky with white lights again. In New York Harbor the Statue of Liberty held a lighted torch above her head. From Maine to Miami, from Seattle to San Diego, blackout curtains were torn from the windows, and the seacoasts of the United States beamed friendly lights out across the dark waters.

Mamie and Alex Holly were sitting in their living room. Alex had decided the kitchen was not the proper setting for the important news they were preparing to hear, so he moved the radio into the living room. He sat in the big overstuffed chair by the fireplace. Mamie sat across the room on the end of the sofa.

She heard only the first few words of President Truman's announcement. She began to cry, and before he had finished his message she fell over onto the sofa and wept uncontrollably. Her body shook, and she made no effort to calm herself. Alex listened to the radio a few minutes after the President had finished speaking; then he got out of his chair, turned off the radio and stood looking across the room at his wife.

"Mamie?"

"Leave me alone," she gasped. "This is what I've been wanting to do for years, and—but—it was never the right time, and I just want—" She started crying anew.

"Don't you want to go to the church?" Alex asked. "Mr. Clapper told us he'd have the church open ten minutes after the announcement whenever it came."

Mamie sat up. "Certainly I want to go to church," she said. She blew her nose and dabbed at her eyes. "I'm so happy I could die. Then I think about those thousands and thousands of boys—theirs as well as ours—who died fighting, and I just *can't stand it!* And for every one of those who got killed, there's somebody somewhere else who had to do the killing, and I cry for them, too. Then I think about the millions of innocent people who died while sitting at home just like we are. I hope it was all worth it, and I have to make myself believe it was, but it takes a lot of understanding to see how it could be, and— Oh, Alex! I don't know how I feel!"

"Who does?" he said softly.

She lost herself in another fit of weeping.

Alex sat down beside her on the sofa and waited for her to stop crying. She sat up, and he put his arm around her.

"Not all of those millions of people were innocent, Mamie," he said. "Somebody was the cause of all this. Somebody had to make it possible for Hitler and Hirohito to exist, and I don't know who it could have been unless it was people sitting at home like we are. Somebody had to approve the whole war, somebody besides the men firing the guns and dropping the bombs. I'm not sure who's innocent and who's guilty. Maybe all of it was a mistake. I'm not sure about that anymore either. It's too much and too big for me to handle. We'll have to take it by pieces—a little bit at a time. Right now we've got to be happy that there won't be any more casualty lists and no more families blasted into nowhere and no more people trying to kill as many other people as they can. Whether it's been right or wrong, we've got to be thankful it's over. That's about all I can handle for right now." He stood up and held his hand out to her. "Come on and put your face back together or we'll miss the church service. Charlie Clapper said it wouldn't last long."

The church was already filled when they arrived. They stood behind the last pew at the rear.

". . . Our hearts are not big enough to contain all our emotions tonight, and our tongues are not eloquent

374

enough to articulate them," Mr. Clapper said. "But we can say, 'It's over now' and glory in that. We've waited a long time to say those words, and sometimes we wondered if we'd ever get to say them at all. It was a long and dreadful war. To us it seemed interminable. To God it was but a brief darkness in His scheme of everlasting light. During that darkness the world got sick—real sick—and it will be a long time recovering. But with God's help we'll see it healed and on its feet again, strong, healthy, standing straight and walking with its head held high. That's our job now, and unless we see to it properly, the war will have been for no reason; our hopes will have had no foundation; our victory will have been empty. Let us go on from this day with compassion and love in our hearts and make the world a good place for all human beings everywhere and for all time. Many good men fought and died to make that possible. Let us dedicate ourselves to the task of rebuilding man's spirit as well as his home and his country. . . ."

When Mamie and Alex arrived uptown, every light in every window, upstairs and downstairs, on Chiles Street had been turned on. The block had been roped off. A loud-speaker atop The Well was blaring out a steady swing beat:

> Hut sut rawlson
> On the Rilla-raw
> And the brawla brawla suett . . .*

"Alex! A street dance like on Bentley Day!" Mamie exclaimed. "You've got to dance with me!"

"Mamie! You're crazy! We haven't danced in years!"

"All the more reason why we should dance now," she gushed excitedly. She caught his hand and tugged at him. "It's a celebration. This is V-J Day. Everybody's supposed to do things they haven't done in a long time. Now come on!"

"That piece is too fast," he said, pulling back. "I'd look like a fool."

"You won't look any worse than Inez and Miller Goolsby. Look at them!"

Alex was inspecting the scene about them. The block was thronged, and the crowd was festive, this time with no reservations or qualifications. Little boys threw lighted firecrackers at the feet of dancers. They climbed lampposts, chased one another, teased little girls and pestered their parents. Everybody was eating and drinking. Sim Holder had moved his snow cone and popcorn machine down to the middle of the block. He was handing out red and green ice as fast as he could fill the cups. Six feet away Elizabeth Holder was sacking popcorn and distributing it. Glen and Olivia Coker were dipping ice cream into cones in front of their Downtown Drug Store. Giles Cutler and his wife were serving coffee and doughnuts from a table on the sidewalk. Clay Tinsley's sleeves were rolled up to his elbows, but he got them wet anyway as he fished Coca Cola and Orange Crush out of his long cooler. Everything was free, the compliments of the people who were serving them.

The only commercial transactions within sight were taking place from the rear end of Tooker Jordan's old pickup truck, which he had parked around the corner on Madison Road by the bank. He was selling firecrackers for five cents a package, for which he was somehow paid in folding money, and most of which he handed to his customers in paper sacks large enough to contain pint and quart Mason jars. His business was booming.

"Hurry it up—I haven't got all night," he grumbled to his patrons. "I've got to get back down on Tin Can Alley. They're having a celebration out in front of Cuby Jackson's Café that makes this one look like a prayer meeting, and they'll be running out of firecrackers."

Mamie and Alex made no attempt to stay together. She went in one direction and he the other. An hour later they met by chance in front of Ellen Presley's Ladies-Ready-to-Wear.

"You've *got* to dance with me now," she insisted. "Listen to what they're playing. It's Glenn Miller's orchestra. You like them. And it's not a fast tune."

> Kiss me once
> And kiss me twice
> And kiss me once again. . . .

She coaxed him out into the street, where he put his arms around her self-consciously and they danced.

"I always did say you were the best dancer in the state of Georgia," he told her as they moved awkwardly away from the curb.

"I'm glad you remembered," she replied, smiling at him. "It should be easy, though, because I know for a fact that I'm the only person you've ever danced with in your entire life."

He held her tighter. "I didn't know there *was* anybody else," he said.

He stepped on her toes. She winced. He did not notice.

"Do you know what I think I'll do?" he asked.

"No. What?"

"Kiss you."

He did. Then he danced her across the street, where they got two red snow cones from Sim Holder to eat on the way home.

# 37

Dr. Jesse Randolph died on Friday, 17 August 1945, three days after V-J Day. Death came from a massive stroke followed by a coronary occlusion, neither of which his worn-out body and exhausted mind could withstand. The town put aside its rejoicing over the ending of World War II to pay its respects. He was eighty-one years old.

Remembering the throng that jammed the church for their wedding four years earlier, Miss Mattie reasoned—quite correctly, as it turned out—that her husband's funeral service should be conducted at a place large enough to accommodate a similar sized, if not larger, crowd. The churches were too small. Not even the churchyards, sectored by hedges, shrubbery, flower beds and trees, offered enough open expanse for a formal religious ceremony that surely would be attended by many. The high school auditorium was being replastered and repainted and could not be restored soon enough for the funeral on Sunday. Someone suggested the athletic field back of the high school building, but the ground was soft and mushy from the summer rains and not yet serviceable.

On Saturday morning Mayor Sam Pickett called the Town Council into special session, and with a unanimous voice it voted to rope off uptown Chiles Street and offer the space to Miss Mattie for Dr. Jesse's funeral. She accepted with gratitude.

"It's a lovely tribute," she said, "and there's something right about it. He belonged to the people of Bentley, and this will give everyone, white and colored, an opportunity to tell him good-bye."

On Sunday morning a group of men moved a stack of lumber onto Chiles Street and set to work with hammers and saws. Using the south side of The Well as a backdrop, they built a low wooden platform with railings at each end and erected a canvas canopy above it. A man from Greer's Funeral Home in Monroe came before noon and laid green carpeting on the platform and wrapped the railings in green felt. Two State Troopers arrived in town at one o'clock and erected barriers to detour the highway traffic around uptown Chiles Street.

Sunday was hot and humid. When the service began, the thermometer in front of the Security National Bank stood at an even ninety-one degrees. Many said the heat was even more oppressive than on the Sunday Dr. Jesse and Miss Mattie got married, although that hardly seemed possible. That had been the stickiest and most uncomfortable day within their memory. The sweltering people crushed together, white and colored, and filled the sidewalks and the street for the length of the block. Those who arrived early enough found shelter from the sun under the awnings that fronted most of the buildings. The others stood in the sun, some with parasols and some with newspapers held above their heads, slanted against the glare. They strained to hear the First Baptist Choir sing "I Won't Have to Cross Jordan Alone." They fidgeted, mopped their faces, fanned themselves with their hats and newspapers while Mr. Clapper paid tribute to Dr. Jesse in a eulogy that only those standing close to The Well could hear.

Then Sissy Carpenter emerged from the crowd and stood on the platform before Dr. Jesse's casket and the wall of flowers that blanketed The Well and flanked it from curb to curb. Clasping her hands together below her big bosom, and with her brown face glistening from sweat, she closed her eyes, opened her mouth and began to sing.

She sang with a richness and a depth of which no one was aware she was capable. Before she had reached the end of the first stanza, a strange and reverent stillness descended on those at the front. It swept past and behind them in widening billows to those standing in front of Holder's Five and Ten Cent Store at Depot Street. Even from that distance people claimed to have heard and understood every word that came from her mouth. She sang without accompaniment, and the song she sang was as wondrous as it was simple:

> . . . Lead me on to the light
> Through the storm
> Through the night.
> Take my hand, precious Lord
> And lead me home. . . .*

Not even by the most charitable of judgments could Sissy Carpenter be termed an accomplished singer. A number of people in Bentley could sing better but, of course, not with as much volume. Yet Bentley had never heard singing like this. They never knew if it was the melody or the words, Sissy's presence or her voice, the occasion or the memories it evoked that awed them into stillness. But no one moved, and when the last note had fallen and faded into the day, Mr. Clapper stepped forward, cleared his throat and said a simple "Amen." Then he nodded to Mr. Greer and his attendants, who took charge of the service and the procession to the cemetery. As he explained later, "I hadn't intended to end the service then and that way, but after Sissy's song, there wasn't anything left to say. Not even a prayer."

The florist in Monroe had received more orders for flowers than she could supply and had diverted some of them to her counterparts in Covington and Madison, who shuttled them into Bentley until the funeral service began. The Randolph home had been filled with cut flowers and potted plants since Saturday morning. On Chiles Street the florist had arranged as many flowers at The Well as she thought would be tasteful. All the others had been delivered directly to the cemetery. Immediately after the benediction at the graveside Mr. Clapper announced that Miss Mattie wanted Dr. Jesse's friends to take the flowers and distribute them among the graves of their own loved ones, leaving only the roses she herself had selected and placed atop the grave.

Toward sundown the flowers had been spread throughout the cemetery and the people had dispersed to their own homes and their own thoughts.

Neither Alex nor Mamie knew how long they had been standing gazing at the white carnations nestled against Perry's headstone.

"I just picked up the spray closest to me," she said. "I wouldn't have felt right to pick and choose."

"These are fine," Alex replied softly. He stood beside Mamie, holding the brim of his hat with both hands.

Mamie looked around at him. The gray around his temples had whitened and spread. The wrinkles around his eyes and at the corner of his mouth had deepened. He looked older than his fifty-eight years, but he had gained a dignity and an assurance that set well on his thickening figure.

"What are you thinking about?" she asked him.

"I was just trying to understand," he said. "Paul was in the business of killing or getting killed. He had an even chance. He knew it. It was a risk he had been trained to take and live with. It guided his every step. Perry wasn't in that kind of business. His was a live-and-let-live kind of business. He didn't have any enemies. No one wanted to kill him. Not even that carload of metal pipes. Yet—"

"It's as if we lost both of them," Mamie said.

"Paul will be back. He's just getting used to the end

of the war over there instead of over here. But he'll come back. He'll never get it straightened out until he does."

They stood in silence for a few minutes more.

"I'm ready to go whenever you are," Mamie said. "Let's go out the side gate and cut through Wylie's garden. He won't mind."

They wandered slowly among the graves, stopping every now and then to admire the fresh flowers, to read the inscription on a headstone or to speak to someone who still lingered. The sun was losing strength and touching the top of the Clegg Line. Their home across the way was streaked with long shadows. Their back porch was sinking into a blur. At the wall of the cemetery Mamie stopped to look back.

"Alex, look!" she breathed. "Just look at all the flowers."

He turned back. Stretched before them was a carpet of brilliant colors, the reds, yellows, greens, oranges, pinks and whites blending one into the other as though a weaver had selected his skeins and woven them together in careful design, all blending with the amber of the late day.

"Have you ever seen anything more gorgeous in your whole life?" she murmured.

He stood and marveled with her until he felt her hand slip into his. He grasped it tightly and went with her through the gate.

Later they sat on the front porch. The sun had disappeared now, and a faint breeze was coming from the northeast. Bentley was slipping into night. It was stilled with a hushed reverence. Mamie rocked back and forth gently. Alex was not moving.

"Are you hungry?" she asked.

"No, not really."

"There's some roast left, and I can heat it with the gravy. Or it might taste good if I slice it cold."

"I'll find something if I get hungry enough," he said.

At the end of the street a car drove into the yard of

the Macedonia Baptist Church. A Negro man and woman got out to join a cluster of people talking at the entrance.

"I didn't realize it was so late," Mamie said.

"It must be," Alex said, looking in the opposite direction toward Chiles Street. "Here comes Miss Emma, and she's always on time."

They watched the black, gaunt figure of Emma Horn hobbling along the sidewalk toward them.

"The poor thing's getting to where she can hardly walk," Mamie said. "Somebody ought to go get her on Sundays and drive her to church."

She came abreast of their house.

"How're you, Miss Emma?" Mamie called out to her.

She turned her head slowly in their direction and smiled. "I'm all right, I reckon," she replied. Her voice was tired. She stopped. "How you been feelin', Miss Mamie?"

"Just fine. That's a lovely dress you're wearing. Is it a new one?"

She chuckled. "No'm, it ain't new," she said. "I been havin' this dress a mighty long time. I jes' wear it to special occasions, and Dr. Jesse's funeral look like it was special, sure 'nuff. I jes' never did get 'round to changin' it 'fore church time."

She looked at Alex.

"How you feelin', Mr. Alex?" she asked.

"I'm all right, Miss Emma. I guess all of us are kind of sad and blue today, though, aren't we?"

"I know I sure is," she said, shaking her head. "I ain't never cried so much at nobody's funeral since Asa and Elvin done died. It was mighty sad today." She paused. "You both is lookin' fine," she added. "Real fine."

"Stop by and visit me, Miss Emma," Mamie said. "You haven't done that in a long, long time. I've been missing you."

"I been gonna do that, Miss Mamie, but it seem like I don't get down this street early enough no mo' 'cept jes' to git to church."

"Well, you'll just have to leave earlier some day and give yourself time to stop."

"Maybe I'll do that," she said, "and if you is out on the porch like you is now, I'll stop and we'll have a nice little visit like we use to have."

The night moved in. They sat in darkness and watched the lights come on in the Robinsons' living room across the street, in an upstairs window in the Lassiter house down the block and over the door of a garage through the trees. A car turned off Chiles Street and proceeded cautiously along Madison Road and turned in at the church.

"Somebody's late," Alex observed.

Mamie did not hear him. She was listening to the singing from the church. It came through the open windows out onto the stillness. It was slow, drawn out and plaintive:

> Don't you hear the bells now ringing?
> Don't you hear the angels singing?
> It's a glory Hallelujah Ju-bi-leeee!
> In that far off sweet forever
> Just beyond the shining river
> When they ring them golden bells
> For you and me.

"They make it sound like a sad song even when it's not, don't they?" Mamie said.

Alex had fallen asleep and did not hear her.

She did not disturb him for a time. Then she reached across and touched his arm.

"Alex, wake up, honey," she whispered. "It's time to go to bed."

He stirred. "Oh—I wasn't asleep."

"I know you weren't. But come on and let's go in, or you won't want to get up in the morning."

He got up from his chair and followed her into the house.